RAGTAG BATS

BOOKS 1 - 3

FURRY UNITED COALITION NEWBIE ACADEMY

A. GREGORY

BAT AND THE BONE

RAGTAG BATS BOOK 1

1

MILA

"I'm really sorry for everything you've been through. I swear I will get you the justice you deserve. That's a Mila Starling guarantee."

I look down at the pile of bones on my glittering metal worktable and give the remains a comforting smile.

It appeases me to talk to my work like this.

Not that I ever expect a response from a cadaver. Not in the conventional way. Whatever I hear from the osseous matter comes strictly from the things I can decipher. Age, sex, any signs of trauma. That kind of thing.

It would probably make my life a hell of a lot easier if the bones did start talking to me. Alas, I have to rely on science.

That's better, anyway. People lie. Science doesn't.

The remains currently on my table have seen better days. Judging by the fractured disks, the neck was snapped. I search my brain for the obvious joke there, but nothing comes to mind. There are gouges and grooves along the humerus. It must have been anything *but* humorous to have those wounds inflicted.

That's the thing about working with dead bodies all day long. I love my work, but things tend to get a little dark in my brain. Making jokes, no matter how inappropriate they are, helps to lighten my mood. Not that I would *ever* share these quips out loud. I'm not a *monster.*

I'm a forensic anthropologist.

Some might say that's kind of the same thing, but they would be wrong.

I make all the necessary annotations about the state of the bones, documenting every unnatural indent in them. This is meticulous work, and it's easy to get completely engrossed in what I'm doing. I let the thundering booms of the music soothe me, and I bring the volume up a couple of notches. I'm not even concerned about disturbing anybody. The entire wing of this sub-basement floor is mine.

From my lab to my archives to the classroom across the hall and the airlock tombs where we keep the bones of unsolved murders, this kingdom is mine. At least, it is while I teach at the Furry United Coalition Newbie Academy.

I flip up the lens of my magnifying glasses to look at the clock. It's not even midnight. *Good.*

That means I have plenty of time to finish my work for FUC and the Academy. If I get it all settled in the next sixty minutes, then I'll have a few hours to work on *Project Broken Mama* before my students start streaming in for their forensic anthropology class at five.

The cadets absolutely hate the fact that the class is so early, but I appreciate the hell out of the Academy's director, Alyce Cooper, for scheduling it then. It works out perfectly for nocturnals like me, and the cadets who are non-nocturnals get the benefit of having their brains jostled early in the morning. It's a good experience for life as a FUC agent.

"I'm going to put you away for now," I tell the bones, "but that doesn't mean I'll forget you. I'll find your identity and give it back to you." With gentle hands, I start putting the remains away.

"Agent Starling." My name spoken in a loud, deep baritone voice makes me squeak in surprise.

Echoing bloodbag!

I whip around to see who has invaded my lab. It's too late in the evening to be one of my students stopping by. My office hours ended a while ago. I flip up my magnifying glasses, settling them on the top of my head. They slide into my hair, pining the long red streaks back.

Oh, sweet mother of Thor. Who is that?

"Do you think you could put a stop to that racket?" The stranger gestures to the air, no doubt meaning the song currently blaring from the lab's speakers. But that's only because I'm completely distracted by the huge blond god standing in my lab. My skin feels hot and flushed as I dig around through the pile of cases. Do they have to make remotes so small? Sure, I can find a hairline fracture in a bone, but remotes? Forget it.

"Ha!" I shout in victory, finding the damn thing and pressing pause on one of my favorite songs.

My instant attraction to the stranger takes me by surprise because *Tall, Gold, and Muscular* is nothing like my usual type. Even though he's wearing a black thermal long-sleeved shirt and a pair of beige cargo pants, his muscles seem to be rippling like some kind of insane optical illusion. I even start to wonder what it would be like to run my fingers through his short, cropped beard. It looks soft, and my fingers itch to confirm my *very* scientific hypothesis.

"Thanks." His voice is a sexy rumble that reminds me of rumpled up sheets and long, steamy showers.

"Not a fan of Cradle of Rot?" I bat my eyelashes, playing innocent. He sure doesn't look like someone who would even know that Cradle of Rot is only one of the best death metal bands in the world. This man might be a walking sex dream, but he is as straight-edged as a scalpel blade. It's written on every molecule of his insane body.

"No, I can't say I am," he answers, eying me in what can only be described as pure shock. It's okay. I'm used to that look. I come by it honestly. "How can you think when that is on?" he asks, furrowing his brow in complete consternation.

"It helps me clear my head for one," I reply. "And secondly, this is my lab, so no one dares to question my tastes in music. Especially not random dudes."

I'm taunting him again for his dig at my favorite band. *And* because he is making my heart pitter-patter.

Unacceptable.

Truth is, if he has found himself in my lab, he was given clearance by Director Cooper to be in here. A special pass is needed to get through the three different security doors that lead down to the sub-basement.

"Right." He pulls out a badge from his back pocket, making his biceps bulge.

I can't help the way my eyes track the veins running along the corded muscles. There's a lot of healthy, delicious blood running through him, and I can't stop myself from noticing.

"I'm Agent Thrussell with the Royal Canadian Mounted Police. I'm the point agent between FUC and the RCMP. But that's not really why I'm here right now. We require your expertise on Sveta Markov. She's escaped from prison."

The tray of instruments I'm holding clatters to the floor in the loudest, most unpleasant *clang.* The sound rattles in my head as I blink at him, trying to make sense of his words.

Impossible. She couldn't *have escaped.*

Judging by the frown on his handsome face and the tension in his beautifully wide shoulders, Agent Thrussell is telling the truth.

My mother, the most prolific serial killer of the century, has flown the roost.

2

MILA

My mother escaped.

I repeat the words over and over again, willing sense into them.

"Agent Starling, are you all right?" Agent Thrussell asks, his brows drawn together in concern.

"Yeah." It comes out in a squeak. "Yup." I try again and fail to sound unfazed. I flip my hair forward, twirling the edges around my fingers. "Yes, I'm fine."

There.

I sounded extremely convincing.

I step around the fallen tools and reach for my phone, which was lying on a pile of files a few moments ago. "Have you warned Edward?" I ask the attractive harbinger of doom.

"Who?" Agent Thrussell questions, his worry turning to surprise. How could he *not* know who Edward is? Agent Delicious's ignorance can mean only one thing.

My dad has no idea she's escaped.

Earthquakes of dread go off along my spine as I search for my phone.

Where is the damn thing? The device might be smart, but it sure makes me feel dumb when I can't find it. I flip the documents over, moving around my work area, searching for the fucking piece of plastic that holds all of my precious information. It needs a pager or something so I can spot it easier in times of crisis.

"What are you doing?" Agent Thrussell asks. "Did you hear me? I'm here to get your expertise on Markov. No one knows her better than you do."

"Bah," I snort, shaking my head. "If only that were true," I grumble, still digging through all of my paperwork.

"I don't know what you're looking for, but perhaps if you were better organized, you could easily find your belongings."

Before I could threaten to pass equal judgment over him in his most personal space with a clever, snarky response, I spot my phone's skull case on a box of teeth I've been meaning to document.

"Ha! No need." I shrug, my hands still shaking. "It's exactly where I left it."

One of his eyebrows does the curvy thing again, his hazel eyes caught between annoyance and amusement. He opens his mouth to say something, but I silence him with a raised finger, full teacher mode activated.

I scroll through my contacts until I find my dad's number and click on it.

"What did I do to deserve such an unexpected call from my favorite daughter?" my dad asks by way of greeting. He might not be a nocturnal creature like me, but he adjusted his entire life to the nighttime when I was a kid. He's good like that.

And now I have to break insanely disturbing news to him.

"Dad, are you sitting down?"

"I don't like the sound of that, Spooky. What's happened?" His voice, usually sweet and gentle, takes on an edge.

"Mom escaped prison." I ignore Agent Thrussell's sharp inhale. I can deal with him as soon as my dad is safe. "I don't have any more details than that, but you need to follow the protocol I set up in case this happened. Do you remember what we talked about?"

"Oh." My dad's voice shakes. "She escaped?" he asks as if he isn't sure he heard me right the first time around.

Yup, I get it, Dad. This is about as fucked up as using a rusty blade to start an autopsy.

"Apparently." My eyes go to the agent who is now standing with his arms crossed, suspicion and fire in his eyes. *What's his damage?* "You need to pack a bag and go."

I wave my hand over to Agent Thrussell, who is now openly glaring at me. "When did she escape?" I ask the Norse-god lookalike. He shakes his head and nods toward my phone.

"Right," I snap at him. "Look, I know you guys dropped the ball by not calling Edward, but he needs to go someplace safe."

"If you could please hang up the phone and explain to me what is happening, that would be great."

"I have to make sure my dad is safe. She could go after him."

"Am I understanding this properly? You're Sveta Markov's daughter? You are the child of this generation's Elizabeth Bathory?"

I bristle at the description the media created for my mother based on the notorious woman of the sixteenth century, but with a deep inhale, I calm myself enough to glare at Agent Thrussell.

"I'd prefer it if you addressed me as Mila or Agent Starling." Agent Thrussell gives me a curt headshake, apparently as an apology. "When did she escape?" I make sure to enunciate every word clearly, hoping to sound as badass and annoyed as I feel. It's my instructor voice. Equal part bitch and boss. I like to think that I'm channeling Professor McGonagall.

"She vanished about thirty minutes ago. We have uniforms going to your father's house as we speak. I didn't realize his name was Edward. I apologize for the confusion."

"That's nice, but I've got this under control." I turn my attention back to my father. "Dad, the protocol. Follow it. Contact me when you're safe."

"What are you going to do to protect yourself?" my father asks. "Like I've told you a million times before, you'd be her target. Not me. I'm too old."

I ignore his words. They hurt too much. For all we know, Dad is right.

"I'm a FUC agent, Dad. I'm fine."

"Okay, Spooky." He breathes unsteadily. "I love you."

"Love you, Dad. Be safe."

I don't even have time to push down on the *End* button before Agent Thrussell is on me like a vampire bat on a juicy calf. He closes the distance between us, his eyes digging into me as if I were a suspect, not a colleague.

"Is there a problem?" I bite, crossing my arms.

Holy bloodbag. I get why he is mad. It's not every day that you learn that an agent is the direct descendant of the century's most infamous slaughterer. But still, he doesn't have to look at me like *I* committed the murders.

Also, if he could stand a bit farther away from me, I'd appreciate it. He smells too good, like sandalwood and freshly cut grass. I don't know whether to shove him away or maul his handsome face.

From this close, I can see the gold flecks in his hazel eyes, making me a bit loopy. Did I use chloroform today? That has to be it. There's no way I'm all woozy because of a dude.

Definitely not a man who makes the Hemsworth brothers look like silly little boys. The Viking look is *so* not my type.

Especially not one who invaded my lab with only the worst news ever.

"You're Markov's daughter?" Agent Thrussell's eyes take me in, no doubt looking for any outward sign that I am like my mother. That's a look I get a lot when people figure out whom I'm related to. "How is that even possible?" He sounds about as incredulous as if I'd just announced to him that the moon is made of Styrofoam.

"Well..." I sigh with a deep eye-roll. "When a mommy and a daddy love each other very much..." I begin.

"I get *that*, Agent Starling." He doesn't snap, exactly, but it's clear I'm pushing his buttons.

Deciding to play nice for *now*, I shrug. I have to tuck away my sass and focus on getting Mom back behind bars. If this delicious mancake is the one who has the information I need, I have to keep him on my side.

"I have my father's name. My mother kept her own because it was the name on her doctorate. It would have been too much of a hassle to change all of her practice documents when she got married. She's a Markov; I'm a Starling."

"Fine, but how are you the expert on her crimes?"

That's a fair question. From what I'm told, most people wouldn't have submerged themselves in every detail of every murder their mother committed.

Nope.

They would have been in denial or been too distraught to delve into the dark mind of a killer.

Me? I might have been only sixteen when she was caught, but I immediately needed to understand. Why, how, the woman who tucked me into bed and read me bedtime stories turned out to be such a monster.

"When I did my masters and Ph.D. in forensic anthropology and criminal psychopathology, I used my mother as my case study. I visited her in prison and played on the mother and daughter bond to get information out of her. She had no idea, of course, that I was using her."

It hurts to think of the deception I applied to get her to talk to me, but hey, the woman was lying to me most of my life. You know, sneaking around to kill people instead of going to PTA meetings.

Ugh.

If only that were true. She never missed one single teacher conference. And she was at every single science fair I ever entered, cheering me on as I beat out the other kids for first place.

She was a good mother. *That's* why it was so shocking when her secret life exploded. It was the last thing I expected.

After I found out who my mother really was, I had to do *something* to make right what she had done. I threw myself into my studies to offer some kind of peace to the families that mine had destroyed.

"That..." Agent Thrussell clears his throat and runs a hand through his hair, ruining his beautiful pompadour-stylized hair.

"Yeah, that's... Well, let's just say I'm impressed. Now I need you to help me find her."

His tough-guy veneer slips very slightly, and there is a pleading in his eyes.

I get the fear.

We *have* to get her back behind bars. With hundreds of confirmed kills, my mother is way too dangerous to be out in the world.

3

T-BONE

I pause and take stock of what I've learned about this woman in the past fifteen minutes.

First, when I walked in, she was *definitely* talking to the bones on her worktable while the most disturbing music played in the background. How Mila can enjoy music that is head pounding with no way to understand the lyrics is beyond me. This doesn't exactly make her odd, just... peculiar. Perhaps that is a kinder word to describe her. Second, she is *not* what I expected.

Agent Starling's reputation and her work in forensic anthropology is very much at odds with what I'd expected. She is one of the most respected people in the field, but she looks entirely too young to have garnered so much experience in the field. I've read some of her papers. She's smart as hell, and I always appreciated how she seemed to understand the psychology of killers.

Now I know why.

She was raised by one.

I shake my head, running a hand across my beard.

I was expecting a clinician. Perhaps an older woman wearing scrubs or a power suit. Definitely not a tiny woman blessed with curves for days, sharp blue eyes, and waist-length hair dyed fire engine red. It can't be a natural color, but it works with her very pale skin and her black attire.

Not that I want to judge her for the way she's dressed, but her tastes definitely mesh well with her history. She's the daughter of the most monstrous person in recent history. A *female* serial killer.

And here Mila is, wearing a shirt that reads *I'd be more interested in you if you were dead.* The humor is shocking, but I suppose forensic anthropologists need their dark humor to survive, just like police officers.

"What can I do to help you find my mother?" She crosses her arms and watches me closely. She is definitely sizing me up like I was just doing to her.

I like feeling her eyes roam over me. That's inconvenient. We have a killer to find. *Her mother,* for fuck's sake. It's not the time to notice that she has the most alluring beauty mark at the corner of her right eye.

I take a deep breath, ignoring her sweet smell of orange blossoms. It does nothing to help me center my thoughts on the task at hand. I hate feeling destabilized. It irks me, like an itch I can't quite scratch.

"I need to know where she would most likely hide." I finally manage to answer her question.

It's difficult to look away from her. Her deep crimson lipstick is a little bit distracting. I'm here on a mission, goddamn it. I have to track Markov down before she kills again. I won't have any bodies on my conscience. Not when I'm the incident coordinator chosen to apprehend Markov before the public is made aware of her escape. I can't let the pretty woman standing there, attitude rolling off of her, distract me.

"You know Markov better than anyone," I explain, getting back some of my composure as I step away from her. "I didn't realize how true that was until just now. We need to find her."

"I completely agree. But before we figure out how to track her down, I also need to think about the announcements you're putting out in the media, which of course you have to do because people are in danger. But I also have to mitigate the attention it shines on me."

I try to interrupt her, but she seems to be on a roll.

"When she was arrested, my life became a circus. I had to hide for months to keep my identity secret. I'd rather not have to go into hiding again."

"No media." Her shoulders tighten at my words. It's not the reaction I was expecting. I had anticipated that she would be relieved that the vultures wouldn't be notified, so I go on. "We can't have mass hysteria. We're trying to keep this contained. Besides, if we were to release this to the media, we'd be inundated with thousands upon thousands of bad tips. We don't have time to deal with that."

"That seems risky." Mila shakes her head, releasing a deep sigh. "People should be on the lookout for her. She has a very clear MO. She goes for people between the ages of eighteen and twenty-five. We should put all of the university campuses in the region on alert."

"Agent Starling." I put a hand up to get her attention. "Stop, please. You're talking extremely fast, and I'm scared you're not breathing. Let me explain what we've done to contain the threat. We are canvassing the towns surrounding the prison. She was seen leaving in a white truck, so every similar vehicle is being stopped. There are roadblocks in and out of the city."

There's no way in hell this stopped Sveta Markov. She was killing people, undetected, for nearly thirty years. Before she was arrested, she was the most respected hematologist in the world; she is a genius. I'd bet anything she's been planning this escape for a while. There's been no word on who her accomplice could even be. One thing is for sure; there was definitely a getaway driver.

"She's already long gone, and you know it." There's an edge of panic in Mila's voice.

"I do." She's right. I can't deny it. "So help me find her."

"We *have* to find her," Mila clarifies. "She can't be allowed to kill again. I'm still trying to clean up her first mess. Good thing I have an idea as to where we can look."

The determined set of her shoulders and her clear voice are pretty admirable. At least she doesn't seem to be rooting for her mother.

That's a huge comfort.

Mila walks to one of the multiple workstations on which a large box named *Project Broken Mamma* sits.

"What's in the box?" I ask, frowning in curiosity.

Ignoring me, she pulls out a large map and unfurls it onto the table. "The first step should be to go to her old safe houses."

"That's too obvious," I argue, surprised she would even suggest that.

Mila shakes her head and rolls her eyes. "Not the ones we know about and raided. Others. Ones that we never discovered."

Looking down at the map, I'm hit with a profound sense of sympathy for Mila. She's clearly spent a lot of time thinking about her mother's crimes, and I can't even begin to imagine would that would be like.

The map is an organized mess of color. Some cities are circled in red with a wider black circle traced around. Others are marked in orange or yellow.

"So," Mila begins, "while she was an active serial killer, my parents rented a few lake houses for the summer holidays. I looked up each little town, and I traced back the number of missing people. The yellow is for towns with zero to five missing people during the time we visited. The orange is between six to ten, and red is eleven to twenty." As she speaks, she points to different areas of the map. "Taking into consideration the national average of missing people, I've pinpointed the ones that seem likelier to be an epicenter of her victims. I've cross-referenced each concentration of missing people with places we visited during my childhood or where my mother lived or worked."

Mila seems so detached from the fact that we are talking about her mother that I have to wonder how it must have been for her to discover that her mother was a serial killer. And at such a young age.

"We can check a few of these, but I'd start there." She drops a delicate finger on the map over a small town by a lake. "When I was a kid, we had a cabin there for a few summers. I'd bet this is the first place she'd go. She put go-bags everywhere. Like the one that was found at the Maple Ridge property." Mila's mention of one of the country's most notorious mass graves makes me shiver. "She had fake IDs, passports, and enough cash to disappear without a trace at each location. A total of four different go-bags were discovered. So *that's* why we have to check these. She's going to be looking for cash and identification. If we don't find her at Willowbend, then it'll be at Lake Murray." She points to another town by a lake.

"Why do you suspect Willowbend above the others?"

Realistically speaking, she could be on her way to any of her old haunts to find a go-bag.

"It's either one of these two." Her conviction is strong. "These seemed to be some of her favorite locations. Not to mention, the go-bags at those cabins were *really* well hidden. Even if my mother suspects that her stuff was found, she'd head to one of those two."

"Right. I remember." The recollection of Mila's own books pop into my mind. "She buried them far away from the bodies instead of *with them*."

"Precisely. *And* those two cabins are so far back in our family history that she might think they're safer than the rest."

"You've thought about this." There's no stopping the wonder in my tone.

"I was hoping that this would never happen. I really wanted my research to be used to find more hidden bodies, not to find her."

Mila sighs and flips her long hair over her shoulder, taking the ends to twirl them around her fingers.

"How much time have you spent on all of this?"

I reach into the box and pull out case file after case file of notes Mila has taken.

"A lot." She sighs. "I've dedicated my entire adult life to finding all of her victims. I want to give those families peace. Closure. I know it can't bring their loved one back to life, but..."

She turns around and begins typing away on her computer. Sensing that she needs a few moments to compose herself, I take in the lab.

Her workspace is confusing. The office part of the area is pure chaos, a mess of papers and files. On the other side, a few metal examination tables are kept in pristine condition. Even the glass partition between the two areas is spotless.

One thing is obvious: Mila takes pride in her work.

The outer perimeter of the lab is framed by glass boards. A few of the names listed in various different colors catches my eye. As I get closer to the neat and tidy list of names and pictures, the bottom falls out of my stomach.

It's a list of all identified Markov victims, as well as dozens of more names like *Mid-twenties Martha* and *Short Pete*. Mila has given them temporary names. I understand the need for the descriptors, but the fact that she has humanized them breaks my heart.

She clearly thinks about her mother's crimes often. A flash of doubt presses against my conscience. Perhaps now that I know Mila is Markov's daughter, I should leave. Though her knowledge of her mother's thought process is impressive and would be a great asset, I don't want to put too much on Mila. She clearly does that all by herself.

She doesn't deserve to be made to feel like she has to stop her mother. She has definitely taken on enough.

"FUC gave me permission to keep working on some unsolved cases to see if they're connected to my mother." Mila comes to stand beside me. Seeing this extensive work makes me feel like a creep. Like somehow, I've crawled into her head to see all of the skeletons hiding there. "These are the eleven that I think she is responsible for. I haven't been able to identify them yet. It's not easy, going over all of the missing people reports and trying to identify each one. But..."

She cuts herself off. Mila doesn't have to go on. I understand what she isn't saying. This is her way of coping with what her mother did. By giving the families closure, she is hoping to obtain her own. A wave of uncomfortable sadness rises in the pit of my stomach.

I'm used to dealing with the bereaved families. Not with the guilty person's loved ones. It's new, and I don't know what to do with the sympathy I feel.

Clearing my throat, I look around the room, looking to distract myself. Mila is frantically pulling papers together and filling her bag.

"When did you start working for FUCNA?" I ask, gesturing toward the framed Ph.D. diploma that's leaning up against the wall as if no second thought had been given to it.

"Oh, that." She bites down on her lower lip, her white tooth digging into the deep red flesh. I don't know why, but the gesture makes my skin hot. I roll up the sleeves of my thermal shirt, trying to cool down.

"My dad insisted," Mila answers, digging through a drawer. I can see the light tremor in her hands as she rushes around her workspace. "He had it framed, and he wanted me to put it up in my office. I just haven't gotten around to it in the last..." She pauses, scrunching her face in thought in the most adorable way. "Two years?"

"Is that a question?" I arch my eyebrow, punctuating my question.

"How long I've been here and why that isn't up yet aren't as important as the work I do."

"Is that why you talk to the bones?"

Nice, T. You're teasing her like a creep. Not. The. Time.

"Well, it's only fair. They talk to me."

I feel the color drain from my face. "What?" For a few seconds, I start to doubt her sanity. Someone so hot *would* have a flaw.

"Not *actually*. I might look like the perfect candidate to be a female Hannibal Lecter down here, but let me assure you that the bones don't physically talk to me. They tell me their story merely by the state they're in."

Mila shoots me a wicked grin, and my heart stops for a whole different reason that time.

4

T-BONE

Mila walks back toward the map and points at the red circle, indicating a high concentration of missing people.

"We need to go to Willowbend first," she instructs again.

Quelling the various feelings warring in my head, I grab my phone and quickly send off a text to my superiors and the team leaders working under me to let them know we might have a possible lead.

"It's only about a three-hour drive from here," Mila goes on. "We can go now, but there's something you need to know about me before we head out on the road together." Mila takes a deep breath and releases it as she speaks, making the end of her words squeaky. "I'm a vampire bat. That means that I have a very severe allergy to the sun. We'll need to take one of the Academy's armored cars, which have insanely good tinted windows."

"You have an allergy to the sun." I repeat the words, letting my eyes roam over her body. That definitely explains the perfect creamy tone of her skin. She's never felt the pain of a sunburn or the joy of lying in the grass on a cool spring day. Seems like a shame.

"That's right. And I need to grab some food before we go. I doubt my dietary restrictions can be met where we're going, and I need to eat something specific once a day... or..." Mila looks away, her cheeks nearly matching her lipstick.

"Or?" I prompt.

"I get a bit sick." She says it quickly, avoiding my gaze.

I narrow my eyes, not quite understanding the undertones of her comment.

"Let's just get to the cafeteria. The sooner I eat, the quicker we can get out of here."

Mila rolls up the map and slides it into a cardboard cylinder, which she stuffs into a large messenger bag. I watch her move around the lab with agility and efficiency.

The energy in the elevator is electric. Clean stainless steel walls glimmer, and no matter where I look, I see Mila. She's nervous, I can tell. Though her back is straight and her shoulders squared off, she is chewing on the inside of her lower lip. There's a dip in her skin where she is working the sensitive flesh. What I wouldn't give to work off some of our mutual tension right about now.

I have to bite down on the inside of my own cheek to keep from asking her if she's really okay with coming on this retrieval mission. I have a feeling she wouldn't be too pleased with that question, however. This is a clearly capable woman. More than that, she seems determined. She wouldn't have all of that research if she weren't. She wants to do this, and I won't be the one to stand in her way.

But that's not to say that I won't worry about her wellbeing. I vow to keep an eye on her and pull her at the first sign that she is taking on too much. I get the distinct impression that Mila is quick to blame herself for other people's shortcomings and wrongdoings. Not many people would choose to dedicate their lives like Mila has.

It's admirable, and I don't know her enough to fuck with that.

The elevator's clear *ding* echoes through the enclosed room before the doors slide open.

Just as I'm about to walk out, a familiar face stops me. It's like worlds colliding, and it rattles me.

"T-Bone? Is that you?" Ben is just as surprised to see me here as I am to see him.

Although I really wish he hadn't used that painful nickname to greet me. I was hoping Mila would never learn of it. It's too late, though. Her perfect eyebrows are already arched into a question. She'll be asking me about *that* later.

Ben Beaufort is an old family friend. Our parents got together a few times, taking all of us kids camping to find a few good grazing spots. Cattle shifters always find a way to graze in groups. Eating in large social groups is good for the digestion.

"Ben, hey. I heard you had joined the Academy." We do a quick hug and back pat by way of greeting. I can feel Mila's eyes roaming over me with curiosity.

"What are you doing here?" Ben asks, still fairly shocked to see me at FUCNA. After all, I work for a human police force, and it's not common knowledge that I am the liaison between FUCNA and the RCMP.

"Here on a case," I answer, gesturing to Mila.

"You get to work with Mila?" He smiles at me like I'm in for it.

I already know that. She will definitely be an interesting partner to work with.

"That's right." I shoot her a smile.

"Well, good luck with that," Ben says before retreating into the elevator.

Mila leads me down the hall toward the cafeteria. For a few precious seconds, I think that I'm home free, that she won't ask me about the *T-Bone* thing.

"So...*T-Bone*? Why the *hell* is your nickname T-Bone?" She doesn't even try to contain her smile.

"Because my last name starts with a *T* and because I'm a Hairy Coo."

"A what now?"

"Highland Cattle, you know those great red-haired bulls from Scotland? I have wicked horns," I add, giving her a sly smile.

"Wait." Her eyes open wide in panic. "Aren't those bred for *meat*?"

"Yes," I confirm.

Laughter explodes out of her. "That is both hilarious and kind of fucked up. How is *T-Bone* better than your actual name?"

I clamp my mouth shut, avoiding her gaze.

"Agent Thrussell, let me see your badge." Mila's entire face is lit up like she's about to solve a great big mystery.

"No, that's okay."

Without warning, Mila's hand shoots out, going for my back pocket where I'm storing my badge. Her fingers graze my ass, and my skin breaks out in goosebumps. I close my hand around hers, trying to stop her process, but it's no use. She's already opened the badge.

"Courtney Thrussell III?" She reads it again before looking up to me. "Your parents called you Courtney?"

"They did," I confirm. "It's my grandfather's name and my father's as well. It's a well-known name in the RCMP. Besides, my father says that it was good for me to have a name like Courtney growing up."

"Your dad Johnny Cashed you." Her laugh is musical, even the little snort that surprises the hell out of her. She covers her mouth as she starts humming *A Boy Named Sue.*

"Historically speaking, Courtney was a masculine name," I try to defend. The fact is true, but it does nothing to staunch her giggles. I won't say that I like the sound of her laugh. Nope. Not even a little bit. Especially not the way it tickles down my back, warming my heart.

"Sure, T-Bone. That's what I'm calling you from now on, by the way."

We walk into the cafeteria, and Mila immediately goes to the cash register. I watch with interest as she interacts with the staff while I grab a few things because I am *always* hungry. Contrary to popular beliefs, cattle do *not* have four stomachs. We do, however, have a very complex digestive system, which does leave us feeling peckish more often than not.

One of the staff members scurries off into the back and soon returns with an opened to-go container on which a patty of raw meat sits. I don't miss the way Mila's eyes grow wide in anticipation.

"What is *that*?" I point to her repulsive-looking meal as we make our way out of the cafeteria on the way to Director Cooper's office.

"Steak tartare," she answers, taking a reverent bite.

Really, that is the only way to describe it. Her eyes roll back before she closes them, her lips sliding along the fork.

Mila is eating raw cow.

I'm bovine.

Very much unlike me, I have a dirty thought as I wonder if there is another type of beef cut she would like to taste. Particularly something in my southern region.

I shake the thought from my head, choosing to focus on the dish instead.

"That is very disgusting," I state. "Is it supposed to be that...juicy?" Really, it's blood that is pooled at the bottom of the Styrofoam container. I try not to be grossed out, but it's difficult.

"Have you *ever* had steak tartare?" she asks.

"That would be a firm *no*."

"Well, then you can't say anything. The staff keeps it on hand, especially for me and cadets like me. I am definitely not the only one who enjoys it. Try it. It's guaranteed not to be a shifter."

She stops walking, and with her fork, she digs into the raw ground beef and reaches over to me, letting it hover near my lips. It doesn't smell all that bad, but it's the look in her eyes that makes me pause.

Mila's blue eyes seem to be on fire as she watches for my reaction. I lean forward, close my lips around the prongs, and take the bite into my mouth. Savory sourness bursts on my tongue.

"Hmm." I swallow slowly, my gaze still glued to Mila's. "It's actually pretty good."

She tosses her long red hair over her shoulder with a triumphant smile. "Technically, I just watched cannibalism."

My face falls for all of two seconds until her laugh bubbles out of her. "I'm joking, but your expression was well worth it. FUC would never use non-certified dealers, so all the food here is guaranteed to be non-shifter."

She scoops more of the tartare onto the fork and cocks an

eyebrow, daring me to take another bite. I do, but this time, I reach out for her fingers, stabilizing her shaking hand.

"Does this curb the vampire bat's craving for blood?"

Mila rolls her eyes and starts walking, munching as she goes. "It depends. Sometimes, as soon as I shift, I'm flying off to the nearest mammal to get a fix. I have to do it, though. We die if we don't ingest blood at least once a night. It's barely a teaspoon of blood, so the animal doesn't even feel it."

"I guess it makes sense that your mother would have a fascination with blood."

Nice one, jackass.

Did I really have to go there?

"Sorry," I mumble. I do find the information interesting. Markov is a hematologist who is also a vampire bat. That's just a fancy way of saying that she is a *blood doctor* who actually needs to ingest blood to survive.

Mila's eyes catch my own, and she shrugs. "Totally fine," she says. "You're not wrong."

In short, Mila is fascinating. She is equal parts chaos and control.

She keeps surprising me. Coming here, I knew I was getting an expert in all things Sveta Markov. I didn't expect to be working with Markov's daughter. And I sure as hell didn't anticipate that she would have a war room dedicated to her mother's crimes.

To *solve* them. To give the families some closure. It takes a special kind of person to do that, and I admire Mila.

It takes strength of character to do that.

Mila isn't conventional in the least, which is usually my type. But there's something about her that calls to me. Typically, the women I am attracted to are predictable. It's what I prefer.

I never know what might come out of Mila's mouth next, and I've known her only a few hours.

If anything, working with her should prove to be interesting and a test of my composure.

5

MILA

I don't even have to knock on Director Cooper's office door.

It swings open to reveal my boss in all her tall, powerful glory. She's dressed in a killer red power suit, and her face is pulled into an unimpressed look.

"Took you long enough. I was just heading out to make sure you found our resident Dracula." Her words are aimed at T-Bone, who is standing right beside me.

I barely contain my eye roll. Director Cooper is a badass, and I definitely don't want to piss her off. I deal with all of her vampire jokes because I am extremely grateful to work for her.

As a bat, I'm in an odd position. Though I *am* a mammal, I fly. My body might by furry, but my wings aren't. The Avian Soaring Society has been trying to get me on their team since I applied for FUC. They firmly believe that my expertise should be theirs, and theirs alone. But ASS is a stuffy place. I'm much more comfortable working here for Alyce. She has fought to keep me, and I don't want to let her down, giving her faith in my abilities.

Really, it's too bad it's not the Mammal United Coalition instead of the Furry United Coalition. I'd never be asked to join ASS if the name was different.

"We were discussing Markov and our strategy," T-Bone cuts in before I can say anything.

"Good. That's good. We just sent out two of our teams to join the RCMP's manhunt. Are we still sure that we shouldn't alert the media?"

"I have the same concern," I say, earning me a nod from Director Cooper.

"Yes, I think it's best." His voice is clear. "I know you don't agree."

"I see it as your organization trying to save their own hide from public outcry. This is exactly why we wanted Markov kept in a FUC facility in the first place."

"Well, seeing as her victims, all hundreds of them, were human, we had to put her in a human prison. There was no other way to work around it. Or so I was told, because, let's be completely honest, that decision was made fifteen years ago when FUC was relatively new. Did the organization even have the resources to hold shifter prisoners then?" He gives Director Copper a small smile, but she doesn't go for it. "Besides, it was way above my pay grade. I wasn't even a cadet yet. I'm sure we will agree that she needs to be relocated to a FUC jail once she is captured."

"I agree." Director Copper settles behind her desk, and she gestures for us to come in. "But I didn't get the impression that your superiors agreed. Before you go, we need to go over our strategy for getting Markov into FUC custody with minimal efforts. I need you to spare me a minute."

Unlike my office, which would require me to clear off room for someone to sit, her office is meticulously clean, free of any clutter. T-Bone and I perch in the chairs across from her without any need to make space for us.

"My superiors definitely don't agree that Markov should be placed in FUC custody," T-Bone says, shaking his head in regret.

"I heard you're up for a big promotion. Superintendent. You'd be quite young to achieve that." The fact that Director Cooper looks impressed makes me look at T-Bone in a whole new way.

Not just as this very hot, very strait-laced man but also one who is competent enough to climb the ranks quickly.

"That's two full years older than my dad was when he got the title."

There's a sort of odd bitterness to his words. It's more regretful than nasty. It's not the time to delve into that, but Director Cooper doesn't miss the emotion, either. She fully leans into it, as only she would do.

"And you'd put that promotion on the line, go against your superiors, and demand Markov be placed in our custody. Break from family tradition to boot."

T-Bone nods. "No personal advancement is worth going against what is right for the greater good. My own ambitions come second."

Director Cooper breaks out in a smile that is half victorious and half impressed. "That's very noble," she says.

And she's right.

It is noble. Most agents I know would definitely defer to their bosses if any sort of prestige were on the line. Not because they're bad people or bad agents. It's just human nature to look out after yourself before thinking of the impact on your fellow man.

The fact that T-Bone is challenging this long-held belief of mine makes me happy and uncomfortable all at once. It definitely doesn't help that he is so hot.

"Not noble at all," he argues. "It's what's right." He punctuates that last thought with a shrug.

I can tell that it's a sore spot for him that his father was superintendent already at his age. I wonder if that's a point of discussion during family gatherings.

The only thing Dad and I talk about during our family time is what movies we've seen as we pass each other the chicken fried rice and egg rolls. Usually, he repeats about ten times per hour how proud he is of me. Though it's nice, I know that my dad works hard to counteract how things turned out with my mother.

I guess every family has their hang-ups. Ours is that one of our third is a killer. T-Bone's is because he is a lazy layabout who didn't make superintendent quickly enough to beat out the family average.

"And so now that we've decided that Markov is to be imprisoned in a FUC jail, what is the next step?"

How Director Cooper just assumes she will get her way is one of the reasons why I absolutely fucking love her. She's a hardass, and she will most definitely get her way on this. She's as hardheaded as any other llama shifter.

"Well, we already have a lead." T-Bone shoots me a nod and a crooked grin.

How Mr. Conservative can make my heart beat fast and my core clench while I'm sitting in my boss's office, I will never be able to understand. The attraction is inconvenient as hell.

If he were a tall, lanky dude rocking a band shirt with a few tattoos marring his skin, then maybe I'd get it. He's the polar opposite to what usually gets my juices going.

"I just showed him the map," I clarify.

"Ah, yes. The map. Agent Thrussell, as I told you earlier, I'm very much concerned about this escape. Agent Starling will go with you. That is not negotiable."

T-Bone turns to me, his eyes going to mine. "Though I agree you would be a great asset to have while I search for her, if you would rather stay here, that's fine."

His concern is tangible. It was pretty clear to both of us in my lab that I was going with him. I try to find the motive behind his action of saying this in front of Director Cooper.

The only thing I can think of is that he wants to make sure I feel like I have a choice. An option.

A way out, if I should choose to have one.

It feels nice.

I don't actually remember the last time I've felt like I had a choice. All of my actions, from the time I was a teen to this very moment, have been reactive.

A reaction to the fact that my mother has killed a bunch of people.

A reaction to the fact that I am the only thing my dad has left.

A reaction to the fact that I'm scared to be a monster. Like her.

Director Cooper's eyes are trained on me, slightly narrowed. "Well, Mila? You're up for this." It's not a question. Her long neck is a force to be reckoned with. She twists it toward me. She knows me enough to know that, come hell or high water, there is no way I am backing down from this. Even if it was nice of T-Bone to give me a choice.

"I'm going with him," I answer. "I'm ready to go." I gesture to the messenger bag.

"Have you had your daily *bite*?" she asks. Another bad vampire joke.

"Yes, Director Cooper. Thank you."

"Fine. Let's recap, shall we? As soon as she is found, Markov will be brought to a shifter prison. The fact that she was able to escape is unacceptable."

"I agree." T-Bone sighs. "We're looking into the how. We already know she had an accomplice. It'll be a matter of figuring out who this person is and how he plays into all of this."

"Hmm," Director Cooper says. "And you have a solid lead to follow on her location?"

"I do," I answer. She *knows* I do, but like any good boss, she needs to make sure we've got this under control. The fates of my mother's future victims hang in the balance.

It's not enough that half of the police force is out looking for her. We need to track her down using logic and strategy.

"I won't press the importance of this," Director Cooper says, echoing my thoughts. "I'll have your morning class canceled, and I'll warn Eliza that she might have to step in for a few lessons."

"All the material has already been shared with her."

Eliza is a lab tech who is currently completing her Ph.D. in my field. She's a great assistant, and I have no qualms leaving her in charge. In fact, it might actually be good for her to step in front of the class and take charge.

"Excellent. You'll be wanting one of the SUVs."

Director Cooper opens one of the drawers and produces a set of keys to one of the vehicles with UV-blocking windows, protection I definitely need due to my sun allergy. Thankfully, Alyce always keeps a set in there. She's like that, always prepared, always one step ahead of the rest of us.

"Let's go find Markov." T-Bone closes his hands around the keys and motions for me to lead the way.

And that's exactly what I'm doing. Leading the arm of the law straight to my mother.

6

MILA

When we get to the garage, I don't even argue with T-Bone when he takes the driver's seat of the armored car. Any other time, I would have taken the keys out of his hands, and I would have insisted I be the one to drive. But I can't. I'm too distracted. Driving right now would be very irresponsible.

My thoughts keep racing, never latching onto a memory long enough for me to find any sort of peace. It's silly, because I knew what I was doing on this mission.

But where we're going I won't find any solace.

What I will, no doubt, find are more lies.

The very few positive memories I have of my childhood will disappear, vanish in a cloud of grief. I *feel* it. I almost want to roll my window down and fly away, never to be seen again.

The time my family and I spent at the lake house in Willowbend was kind of idyllic.

It was serene and a lot of fun. I even remember my mother playing board games with me by the large bay window on rainy nights when it was too cold to swim. When she was around, when she wasn't distracted by whatever was going on in her head, she was actually a good mother.

If I'm right and we find something at the lake house, all of those good memories of us during those summers will be lost.

"Hey..." T-Bone pulls me from the darkness in my head. "You okay there? You've gone quiet."

"I'm fine," I lie.

I'm *not* all right. How can I be? This feels like my mother has been caught and arrested all over again. I feel sixteen again.

I thought these wounds were slightly more healed. I really did believe that helping those families get closure would help me move on, but wave after wave of sadness and anger crash into me, leaving my insides feeling hollowed out like a piece of driftwood.

"You know I don't believe you. I can't even imagine what you must be going through. I took your word in Director Cooper's office, but if you change your mind, you tell me. Are you sure you want to be here for this?"

"Yes," I say immediately before T-Bone can entertain any more doubt. "This is where I need to be. I never felt like I could do enough for the victims. Now I have a real tangible way to make a difference."

I won't let myself sabotage this chance.

No matter how much it hurts.

"If that changes, you need to tell me."

I just nod

"Would it make you feel better if I let you choose the music? You can put on that god-awful stuff you were listening to earlier."

I shake my head, a thin laugh escaping me. It's a small gesture, but it's very sweet. I fiddle around with controls, connecting my smartphone. The speakers fill with the not-so-subtle *boom boom* of my favorite album.

I try not to think too much about the fact that these were the songs that played on a loop during my mother's trial. There is comfort in the aggressive strum of the guitars and the guttural singing. It reminds the sixteen-year-old part of me that if I survived the last time, then I can surely survive this as an adult.

"Can I guess what *you* like to listen to?"

T-Bone laughs, and the sound surprises me. It's a beautiful rich sound that reminds me of an acoustic guitar being strummed over a campfire.

"Think you got me pegged, do you?"

"I'm a fairly good judge of musical tastes," I respond, knowing that it's a weird thing to brag about. "I'm going to say, based on your choice of pants and your haircut, that you're a top forties guy. You don't like it necessarily, but it's there, and it beats silence. It's predictable, and the same things get played over and over again."

T-Bone's laughter fills the car this time around. He shoots me a quick look before letting his eyes focus back on the road.

"How the hell did you do that? Based on my pants—" He stops, scrunches his face, and shakes his head. "What's wrong with my pants?"

"They're *cargo* pants, and the ugly, clunky things need to be burned. I hate the bulging pockets filled with all of the stuff you feel the need to carry."

What I don't tell him is how the loaded pockets aren't fair to my eyes. He has powerful, muscular thighs, defined calves, and the most bubbled ass I've ever seen on a man, and he hides it all.

"Your choice in clothing means that you choose functionality over style. But you pay close enough attention to popular culture to choose the pompadour haircut. So even though you're not vain—we're back to the pants on that one—you do like to look nice."

He shakes his head. "My barber picked this haircut. And seriously, what's wrong with my pants?"

"Nothing. But I bet you *love* to be prepared for any eventuality."

"Absolutely," he agrees. "That was really cool, by the way. Any other superpowers I should know about?"

I tap my chin, biting down on my lower lip. "I don't *think* so. The music thing is the only one. It's probably because of my bat hearing. I bet you anything music sounds different to me because of my echolocation hearing."

I don't add that my bat hearing is also so that I can hunt my pray by their breath. That's creepy information he doesn't need to know just yet. If ever.

"That makes a lot of sense," he says.

Needing to move the topic away from vampire bats and how we like to hunt, I decide that questioning him about his own life is a much safer topic of conversation.

"How about you? Any cattle superpowers you'd like to share?"

"Hmm." T-Bone inhales deeply and shakes his head. "I'm built like a bull, and that's about it. I do take orders well, but that's about it."

"Then I guess you picked the right profession. You said it was a family thing, right?"

"I did. My grandfather joined when he was eighteen. Same with my dad. I didn't join straight out of high school. I decided to enroll into university first."

"No! You rebel, you," I tease.

"Laugh all you want," he says, a smile on his face, "but that's exactly how it was seen by both my father and my grandfather." He adds a shrug. "When I turned thirty-one, and I wasn't the head of my own division, they both sat me down and asked me what I was doing with my life."

"Yikes. That's rough."

"It took me three years to get my degree in political science. Then I joined the RCMP. Apparently, it was lost time. But I'm happy I did it. When I was going through my training, I knew myself. I knew I'd made the right choice by joining the force."

"That's very sensible of you," I say, because it is. It also makes a lot of sense. The fact that the men in his family become police officers shouldn't automatically mean that should be his path.

Just like my mother being a killer doesn't mean I'll turn into one.

"I suppose it is reasonable. I had to be sure."

Silence falls in the car, and for a few miles, we ride in without any more interactions. The SUV slides through the night as we head toward Willowbend.

"I just want to add a second superpower that you have," T-Bone says.

I crane my head to look at him.

"You read people. Their behavior, their motives. I bet that would have made you a very good field agent."

I swallow hard, nearly gulping as my throat gets dry.

He's not wrong.

I trained myself to observe people, to garner who they are with as little information as possible. It's made relationships and friendships slightly difficult. I tend to see monsters everywhere.

Not like anyone can blame me. I was raised by one without realizing it for nearly two decades.

.

7

MILA

The narrow winding streets are replaced by the unpaved dirt roads leading deeper into the forested area surrounding Willowbend.

Being back here now, after all these years, is a little bit surreal.

Ghosts of laughter and good times echo through the wind, making me shiver in the warm vehicle. T-Bone doesn't miss my shudder, and he gives me a side-glance, his eyebrows knitted together with concern.

"Did you come here often?"

"We only rented this cabin for three summers when I was really little. My dad wanted some quality family time away from the city. He thought Mom was putting in too many hours in the lab. He was scared she was losing herself to her work. I remember that she was here with us most of the time. But I also have this weird memory. It was the middle of the day, so that's the middle of the night for you non-nocturnal types, and she was sneaking back into the house. She smelled like blood. When I asked her why, she said she'd had a nosebleed. I replay that moment again and again in my head. It wasn't a nosebleed. She was most likely coming back from one of her experiments. One of her victims.

"I'm really sorry, Mila. If you want, you can stay in the car."

"If she's at the cabin, there is no way in hell that I'm going to sit in here. And if she's not, I need to look around. I need to make sure that there are no more bodies."

I add that last part, trying to sound cavalier and unaffected.

T-Bone doesn't buy it. He nods and inhales deeply. "If you think that's best."

For the last thirty minutes, we ride in silence. I don't know if T-Bone senses that I need to disassociate and retreat back deep inside of myself, but he doesn't say anything. Not even when he pulls into the drive for the lake house.

There are no cars, but that doesn't mean that she hasn't been around since her escape. Not if she was looking for cash and identification papers. I slide out of the SUV, thankful that I still have a few moments of moonlight before the sun comes up and I have to hide behind the SUV's tinted windows.

"She was here." I point to the shed at the back of the property.

The fresh tire tracks lead straight to it. T-Bone squats down, his flashlight illuminating the fresh grooves in the soft dirt.

"These weren't made by a truck. She must have switched vehicles."

"So we know she came here and found her go-bag gone."

I walk through the back half of the property, and cold snaps through my spine. There is a large swath of land that has been disturbed. Away from the original gravesite. I make my way to it on shaking feet.

I can hear T-Bone close behind me.

"What is it, Mila?" he asks me.

"Look." I point to the base of the line of trees.

Some of the soil has been disturbed recently. Whoever dug tried to cover it back up, but it's a rushed job. With the help of my eyes, made to see in the dark, I see the odd indentations. I can't be sure until the ground is dug up, but the cold sitting in the pit of my stomach tells me that there is at least one other victim buried here.

"You might want to call over a team and a coroner." I'm unable to suppress my shiver. "I bet you there's a body"—my voice breaks—"or *bodies* buried on this property. I'd start by this strip of land right here."

T-Bone furrows his brow.

"New ones? Because this property was seriously excavated during the initial investigation."

All I can do is nod. I take deep breaths, letting the night air fill my lungs as the realization that, in her short time out of prison, my mother has already found a new victim.

"New ones," I croak. "I'm positive. This has been freshly dug. No rain has tamped down the shovel marks."

T-Bone looks down, taking note of the indentations in the ground. He swears under his breath, taking his phone out of his infernal cargo pants. He quickly makes a call to his team, demanding a coroner at our location immediately. His next calls are to both of our superiors, letting them know of this new development.

"Are you okay, Mila?" he asks me.

If anyone else were to ask me that question as many times as T-Bone has, I think I would pick a fight. Maybe scream and say some very hurtful things. But there is something about the way he asks. Like he legitimately wants to know. It's not a sick sort of worry, like *oh, how you doing with yourself, daughter of a murderer?*

It's real, and it doesn't feel forced or disingenuous like it usually does.

With a deep breath, I give him a small headshake. "I knew this was a possibility the second she escaped. Somehow, getting the confirmation that I was right isn't making me feel any better about all of this."

"That's normal, you know. Entirely valid. The fact that you expected this doesn't make you in any way responsible."

I nod but turn my back to him nonetheless.

Somehow, being in my lab, working with the bones, looking over maps, and going over theories in my head is entirely different than being here, possibly discovering more victims.

It's hitting me hard.

The sting isn't as painful as it was when I learned that my mother was a killer. But it hurts nonetheless.

How can the woman who gave me life be the harbinger of death for so many families?

I make my way back to the car and sit on the edge of the seat, my eyes focused on a small pebble on the ground as I force my lungs to expand and deflate with deep puffs of air.

T-Bone is on the phone, sometimes pausing his conversation to tap out a message. He is clearly a master at multitasking. It's no wonder he was chosen to be the incident coordinator for this particular escape. The way he sees the world and compartmentalizes everything in its appropriate box makes him the best person for it.

Somehow, the small rock at my feet loses my attention, and I fixate on the wide set of T-Bone's shoulders and the way he rolls his shoulder in between tasks as if to ground himself and reset.

"Mila," he calls out. If I could reassure myself right now that there is anything good left in the world, then the goddess herself is delivering me proof in the form of T-Bone's ass. "We need to go to the prison. They just figured out how she escaped. There's also some stuff in her cell that we absolutely need to see."

"How far is it? We need to get to Lake Murray. If I'm right, we're only just a few hours behind her."

"Mila, you don't get it. We have to go. I'll dispatch teams to all of her known dumpsites and make sure a few others are out looking for her. You need to see this."

T-Bone takes a few long strides toward me and hands me his phone, a picture filling the screen.

"Holy shit..." Dread crashes into my gut, making the acid rise to the back of my throat.

The walls of her cell are covered in drawings, some papers looking worse for wear. They look maniacal, dipped in evil. I use my thumb and forefinger to zoom on the picture. Some are the renderings of DNA strands while others are scrawled out writing I can't quite read.

"We need to get over there," I whisper. "This..." My voice breaks, and I shiver. "This isn't her usual clean, methodical note-keeping. Something has changed. These drawings are disorganized. And look…" I point to a few dates scribbled on the walls in the picture. "Those are recent. This is how she kept track of her victims. This doesn't make sense. Why would she be tracking dates from prison?"

T-Bone furrows his brow and shakes his head.

"I don't know, but I'm going to log this." With his phone, he takes a picture of the dates. "I'll have someone check these to see if they line up with any missing people."

If the things in my mother's cell are any indication, things are about to get much worse before they get better.

8

T-BONE

The sun is just about rising on the horizon when Mila and I pull onto the prison grounds. After we were done making some calls to dispatch teams to every location Mila had named, the drive was quiet and uncomfortable. I wanted to reach inside of Mila's head and shake her out and away from the dark thoughts.

Her sharp teeth kept working on the soft flesh of her lower lip or biting down on the inside of her cheek. For the first half of the drive, I kept myself in check and kept my hands to myself. But slowly, as we drove closer to the jail, Mila's breathing pattern changed. It was erratic and almost choppy.

My composure broke.

I reached over the center console and took her hand in mine.

Her fingers interlaced with mine, and she gave me a squeeze. I was scared she would push my hand away, but instead, she tucked it onto her lap. Her breath eased, in turn making it easier for me to focus on the road, not just the brave woman sitting beside me.

"Are you ready?" I ask her once I've parked the SUV in the prison's parking lot.

She blinks rapidly, each movement making her eyes clearer. "Yup," is all she says as she hops out of the car, pulling her messenger bag behind her.

My hand finds the small of her back as we walk toward the administrative office. Again, I'm surprised when Mila doesn't push me away. She leans into the touch again. No doubt seeking whatever comfort she can.

It's hard not letting my mind run away with itself. Even under these messed-up circumstances. I shouldn't want to have my hands all over her. I shouldn't be looking to catch her eye.

Mila isn't mine to worry about.

She's a colleague. One who is going through something pretty intense at the moment.

I can lie to myself and say that I'm simply trying to do the right thing and be there for her, but I know there is something else going on deep inside of me.

My entire being responds to her. I try to tuck away the glow of my attraction to her as we're led into Carlyle Winthrop's office. The warden of the human jail is a mole shifter, and at the time of Markov's sentencing, it was decided that having a shifter jailer would be enough to tend to Markov's need for specialized incarceration.

Carlyle's workspace is sparsely decorated, and only a few framed diplomas line the walls. He's been the warden for nearly twenty years, but it's clear he has spent very little time making his office feel like his own.

I can't help but wonder if it's because he is too busy or if it's because he spends very little time at work. It's an unfair judgment. One I'm making based solely on the fact that Sveta escaped.

"Agent Thrussell, Miss Starling," the large man says by way of greeting.

I want to correct him and tell him that he should address Mila as *agent* or *doctor*, but think better of it when she doesn't intervene. It dawns on me then that Carlyle knows her because he knows Mila as Miss Starling. As Sveta's daughter. Not a respected forensic anthropologist. Not a FUC agent.

"Where should we start?" Carlyle asks.

"Let's get to Markov's cell," I say. "Maybe we'll get lucky and find the next step of their plan."

The long walk to Sveta's cell takes entirely too long.

It doesn't help that we already know what we will find there. The pictures one of my team leaders sent me were enough to have the hair on the back of my neck raised in apprehension. I let my hand go to Mila's back again, hoping she doesn't mind that I offer her comfort in front of Carlyle. Her shoulders do slump a tiny bit. And I can only hope it's because she knows that she isn't alone in this. That I'm right here with her, ready to offer whatever support she needs from me.

"Here we are," Carlyle says, pointing to one of the cells. "This is where she bunks when she isn't in solitary."

"Whoa," is all I can think to say when we walk into the cell.

There isn't an inch of the walls that isn't plastered with drawings of DNA strands, mathematical calculations, and pages upon pages of notes that don't seem to have a beginning or an end.

Instinctively, my eyes go to Mila to see how she is faring with the scene before us. Her arms are crossed, and she is staring daggers at Carlyle.

"Your mother has been quite ill recently," Carlyle says by way of explanation for the state of the cell. "It's been going on for weeks now," he adds, taking care to look saddened by his own words.

"She was fine when I came two months ago," Mila responds, narrowing her blue eyes slightly.

"Yes, well, around that time, she started being more erratic. She spent quite a bit of time in solitary. More so than usual."

"How often does she get sent to solitary?" I hear myself asking.

"More than the others. She makes the other prisoners uncomfortable. There's also the fact that they love to poke fun at her. They know just what to do to get a rise out of her. They call her the *Bloody Doctor*, and a fight breaks out. Every time, without fail. It's easier for everyone if she's kept from the general population sometimes. Especially when she is agitated. And as I said, she's been ill. She was hallucinating a few days before she escaped."

"What?" Mila, who is pale to begin with, goes even paler. Her face goes ashen, her hands trembling. "Hallucinating?" she repeats, her voice barely above a whisper. "She was seeing things?"

"I'm afraid so," the warden confirms.

It's on the tip of my tongue to say something, but the look in Mila's eyes stops me. I could swear that her blue eyes go black as she squares her shoulders.

"Why wasn't a psychiatrist called to look her over?" It's a demand for a real answer, one that makes a hell of a lot of sense. "Between hallucinations and the state of this room, it's pretty clear she needed help."

Carlyle shakes his head. "This cell is nothing compared to those of some of our more... creative inmates. And as you know, your mother was thoroughly evaluated by multiple psychiatrists when she was on trial."

"It's been over a decade. She should have been reevaluated."

"Oh?" Snark drips from Carlyle's tone. "You don't think I wanted that? The system is flooded with psychiatric requests. Your mother was put on a waiting list, just like any other inmate."

"You're telling me that when the *Bloody Doctor*, a woman responsible for hundreds of murders, started hallucinating, you weren't able to put a rush on things?"

I haven't known Mila for very long, but I can tell that there is wrath in her eyes. It's not quite fury that plays in her gaze, but something wilder, something that is both beautiful and impressive. More intelligent than simply raw anger. She faces Carlyle, her face set in a serious mask.

She is formidable. Though I'm quickly becoming addicted to Mila's blue eyes, that is not a look I would ever want to see directed at me.

"You have to understand. Despite her notoriety, she doesn't rank above anyone else in the prison. They're all humans, all get the same treatment."

"But she isn't human, is she?" There is no question in Mila's tone. "Those bodies we found at the cabin, they fall on you for not being more careful. It falls on me for not providing care. Do you understand that?" Carlyle shakes his head. "We found a fresh dumpsite earlier. She's killed again. We have blood on our hands."

I don't agree with her, but the force of her conviction keeps me quiet. It's shaken Carlyle to his core. This is Mila's battle, and I'm man enough to let her be the general in this fight.

Mila shouldn't feel like she is responsible for her mother's actions. It's clear that she has felt guilty for Sveta's crimes her whole life. I don't know how to appease her, to tell her that it's not her fault. That no matter what she believes, there is nothing she could have done to stop any of it.

It's not my place.

Maybe if Mila was mine, I could take her in my arms, hold her close, and whisper in her ears, over and over again, that she doesn't need to be absolved... Maybe then she would believe me.

The thought strikes me deep in the chest, and I have to shake my head to clear it from thoughts of tucking Mila into my side to protect her from the world, from her own beliefs.

She crosses her arms, her eyes still narrowed at Carlyle.

"Had this been brought to my attention, I would have paid for an evaluation out of my own pocket. Hell, I could have gotten FUC involved. They would have sent someone over if they thought the Bloody Doctor was a rising threat."

"Be that as it may, there is a long process to get a private evaluation completed. It involves lawyers and about a mile's worth of red tape. We had no way of knowing that her situation would go into a tailspin. We sure couldn't predict an escape."

"And now my typically deranged mother is on the loose and in an unknown mental state." Mila inhales sharply. "We should have warned the public."

It's Carlyle's turn to blanch this time around.

"No, absolutely not. That would be nothing but a huge mess."

"Sure. For the system that let her go. For the jail that, *perhaps*, has faulty security systems." There's an underlying threat in Mila's words. Carlyle doesn't miss it.

"I assure you, Miss Starling, that we have every security in place, just like any other prison."

"If that were true, she would still be behind bars. And please address me as *Agent* Starling." When those last few words leave her mouth, I want to fist-bump the air in victory.

Carlyle's demeanor slips and changes slightly. "I didn't realize you worked for an agency."

9

T-BONE

Standing in the horribly upsetting cell that housed her mother, Mila crosses her arms, staring down Carlyle.

"I do work for FUC. I'm not here as a daughter. I'm mostly here as a professional who has to find her before Sveta adds another victim to her long list. Now, we would like to see the visitors' log." She points to a stack of letters on the floor by the bed. "I didn't write her those. I want to know if her pen pals paid her any visits."

There's a dare in Mila's blazing eyes. With a sigh and a head-shake, Carlyle turns on the tablet he brought with him. After a few keystrokes, he turns the screen toward us.

"She very rarely has visitors. Besides, she spends too much time in solitary to be available for visits."

My eyes scan the list of people who visited her. Mila's name is the only one there, but then, out of nowhere, a man by the name of Oscar Trow appears. He's come by to see her a handful of times in the past six months.

"Who the hell is this Oscar Trow person?" I ask, taking out my phone to run his name through a search engine.

"That sounds sort of familiar," Mila says, scrunching up her face, deep in thought. "Oh." Her blue eyes go wide. "I know where I've seen it before."

Mila takes out her phone and starts scrolling through it. "I have media alerts for Sveta Markov to keep an eye on things. A little while ago, I ran by this sick, twisted fan page operated by this guy." She flips the phone over to me. "It's anonymous, but I had Jessie, the FPU's super hacker, look into the IP address. It was Oscar Trow. I check the website every now and again to keep an eye on him."

As I scroll through the site's blog posts, I get a deeper sense of just how twisted this man is. He has a website dedicated to the research and study of Dr. Sveta Markov's work. It's all praise and filled with hypotheses on where her exploration of blood, eradication of diseases, and the quest for immortality went wrong. He offers up what the next avenues of analysis should be.

None sounds very plausible. Or sane.

"The last blog post is a long, drawn-out description of his visit with Sveta," I say, my eyes scanning the entry. "He gushes about her bright intelligence and the scintillating conversation they shared."

"So he's visited her a few times. The last was a couple of weeks ago," Mila says, her eyes still trained on the visitors' log.

As she does, something catches her attention, and she takes a step toward the wall.

"The body at Willowbend..." Her voice is pensive. "I don't think it was my mother. I think it was Trow. He might have become a copycat killer. Maybe that's what's in those letters. That could even be what they talked about during their visits. Look at these dates. My mother was still in jail during these. Could she be tracking Trow's kills as part of her own work?"

If I've learned anything in the last few hours, it's that anything is possible when dealing with Sveta Markov.

"Shit. That's not just participating in a jailbreak. He's a person of interest in a murder." I send texts to a few of my team leaders for both the RCMP and FUC, letting them know they need to be on alert for a man of Trow's description.

Armed, dangerous, and definitely to be arrested on sight.

"I still need to understand *how* she was able to escape," Mila asks while I'm penning the last note to our field teams. "It's one thing to be in contact with a crazed fan, but it's another thing to bail out of prison."

"Well"—Carlyle sighs—"she disappeared from the hospital wing. She flew out of an infirmary window using her bat shape. This can only mean that she found a way to stop taking the anti-shifting serum."

"Or it wasn't administered properly." My tone is clipped because I seriously doubt this man's capabilities. There is no way I'm letting Markov get put back here. It's a FUC prison for her.

Carlyle sputters, but I ignore him.

"In the security footage, she can be seen getting into a truck." I direct my words to Mila. "It would only make sense that Trow was the driver. We won't know for sure until we apprehend them, but it's a valid guess."

"It tracks," Mila agrees. "Any way of knowing if he's a shifter? I didn't think to ask Jessie to check. I should have paid more attention to this website."

"No, don't do that," I say, reading through the barrage of messages flooding my phone since putting out an APB on Trow but a few moments ago.

"He doesn't seem to have a record, so there's no way of knowing for sure," I answer. "There's an all-points bulletin out for Trow now. Director Cooper has someone checking into his background to see if he *is* a shifter."

Carlyle's tablet *dings* with a notification. "Oh. I need to see to this. I'll leave you to it and go back to my office. There's a lot to deal with because of this escape." He gestures to his device as if that explained it all.

Mila shoots him a warning glare, and he clamps his mouth shut.

"If you have any questions, please let me know," the warden adds before turning on his heels.

His footsteps echo down the hall before Mila lets out the breath she's been holding. Her tough exterior cracks a bit, and her hands go to her mouth. She shakes her head in complete disbelief.

"This is... I can't quite believe what I'm seeing. This doesn't look like her space. She was always such a clean freak. If I didn't recognize her handwriting, I would say that this isn't her cell," she whispers.

She isn't wrong. From what I've learned of Markov from reading Mila's book, she kept very clinical notes, and she was known to be methodical. There seems to be no method to this particular brand of madness.

"There is clearly something even more deranged about her," Mila whispers. "And that's saying something.

"She isn't well. She might actually be worse off than she was before," Mila goes on, taking a sheet down from the wall.

As she continues to pluck notes off the wall, I go to the metal locker at the foot of the bed. Thankfully, Carlyle has already had his men unlock the compartment.

I flip the lid up and immediately cover my mouth as a foul stench assaults my nostrils.

"What is it?" Mila asks, taking a step toward me in the small cell.

"You don't want to see this, Mila."

She narrows her eyes at me, stepping around me to look in the locker.

"Those are vials of blood." Her voice breaks on the words as she begins to comprehend just how badly her mother's state has worsened. "Those are *a lot* of vials of blood."

Using a latex glove she produces from her messenger bag, Mila wraps a few vials into tissues and slides them carefully into her bag. Some have cracked and spilled, explaining the vile odor.

"I'm going to tests these," she says. "We need to know if she is taking blood from herself, other inmates, or both."

"That hardly sounds sanitary or clinically sound."

Mila points to the writing on the walls. "I don't think she's too concerned about being clinically sound anymore. Something is clearly wrong with her. Look at her handwriting. It's barely legible. That isn't her. And this?" Mila points to red ink splotches on some of the notes. "That's blood. I can *smell* it." Mila gasps. "Steaming blood-bag!" She rushes to the wall, barely touching it with the tips of her fingers. "I think I know what it is."

"What could be compounding her past afflictions?" Because, really, how much worse can things get?

"I think she has the Foamies." Her tone is serious and her face grave, but the word she's just used doesn't track.

"I hate to ask...What the fuck are the Foamies? Sounds like a bath product for children."

"It's not good," Mila answers, shivering as she backs away from the wall. "It's the vampire bat shifter version of rabies, and it's a very dangerous affliction. It's pretty rare but more common in older bats who don't digest enough blood. It basically attacks the brain, breaking down the protective mucus around the organ. As it gets worse, hallucinations and delusions get increasingly worse until the person dies from a dried-up brain. Can you imagine the kinds of delusion a person like my mother is having right now? Out there in the world?"

Mila grabs her phone and quickly flips through her contacts. It's on the tip of my tongue to ask her what she's doing.

"Nolan." She sighs in relief. "I'm so glad you answered my call. I'm in my mother's cell. She escaped." Loud gasps and fast talking blares out through the phone. "Yes, yes. I know. Look, I have every reason to suspect that she has the Foamies. We need to be prepared for treatment when she gets to the FUC prison."

I miss the end of the conversation, but Mila signs off and shakes her head.

"I'm guessing that was the FUC doctor?"

"Yeah, Nolan the lion. He'll have all the necessary treatment for her when we bring her in."

"So there's a cure," I assume.

"Yes, it's different than or rabies. She needs iron-fortified blood and to be given a few antibiotics. And sooner, rather than later. She won't be getting any better. In fact, it's only going to get worse."

"The Foamies sound atrocious. They really should have picked a more threatening name for it," I grumble as the gravity of the already intense situation sinks in.

Mila takes a deep breath, closing her eyes against the heaviness hanging in the cell.

"Are you okay?" I wonder if Mila will get sick of me checking in on her. But I can't help the concern. This is some heavy stuff. I have to commend her for being a force of absolute composure. But again, I fully reserve the right to worry about her. I can't help it.

The color of her eyes is softened, the corners of her mouth downturned.

"I'm okay," she whispers. "I hate to admit it, but I truly appreciate how you keep checking in on me. Really. But I'm only going to be fine when we get out of here and get her back."

"That's fair. So what can we do? Logically, we should head to Lake Murray. But perhaps we should look into Oscar Trow and see if he has any properties."

As I speak, I pull out my phone and start typing away furiously as Mila packs away the series of journals kept by Markov and the stacks of letters.

"I have my best guys digging into Trow. Let's just head to Lake Murray."

Taking one last look around the small cell, Mila sighs heavily.

"When I was a kid, she baked the absolute worst sugar cookies. They were always a tiny bit burned, and the icing was always too clumpy. But she would hand me one, beaming with pride. I'd eat it because she was my mom and I loved her. It's hard to reconcile the two people she is."

As we walk back to the car, I don't say anything.

I don't know the words that could possibly make this better for Mila.

10

T-BONE

The sun is fully rising by the time we get back to the SUV. I drive the car as close to the entrance door as possible so that Mila only needs to put on sunglasses and tuck her head under her hoodie to avoid the sun's damaging rays.

In the safety of the dark vehicle, she takes a deep breath and leans her head back on the seat. Tears line her eyes, and her entire body begins to tremble. Mila shakes her head, and I get the distinct impression that she is trying to dislodge whatever emotion she's having about her mother and the state of her cell.

Seeing strong, energetic Mila so affected by this is hard. I feel bad for involving her in this mission. If I had known from the get-go that she was Sveta Markov's daughter, I like to think I wouldn't have approached her for her help.

But that's a lie.

I would have, for the good of the case. The only reason why I'm reacting so strongly to Mila's distress is because I want to protect her from the turmoil she is living

"Mila, it's okay." I pitch my voice low.

"No." Her voice is so small, so hurt that I just let my instincts take over.

I tug her toward me, over the center console, settling her on my lap. I wrap her up in my arms and squeeze her small, curvy form to mine.

"It makes sense to feel a whole mess of things right now," I whisper against the crown of her head. "It's all right to be torn between caring for a woman who raised you, who is sick, and the woman who did horrible things."

Mila stays very quiet, her hands pressed up against my chest. She inhales deeply, eyes closed, and a shiver runs across her body.

"After all this time, I still try to make sense of the things that she has done, you know? Some days, I hate her. Flat-out hate her for ruining our lives, for hurting people. And other days, I think that she wanted to do good but let her hubris get the better of her. On those days, it's not her that I hate." Her body begins to shake in earnest, as she has stopped breathing. A few tears escape her, making the blue of her eyes go gray. "It's me. For even thinking of sympathizing with her, even just a fraction. If she had just gone through the proper channels. Getting grants and permissions, using blood donors..."

"Mila, look at me." I hate to interrupt her, especially since it seems like she is in desperate need of talking to someone about all of this. But her breath is impossibly erratic, and I'm scared she'll have a panic attack. Her eyes settle on mine. "None of this is your fault. That includes her escape. Even if she had been evaluated by a psychiatrist, if she wanted out, she was getting out. Sveta is a very smart woman. *None of this is on you*," I repeat, trying to make her understand.

I let my hands roam up and down her back in a soothing motion. "There's no way for me to even begin to comprehend the kind of guilt you feel, but I think I can understand on some level. Mind if I tell you a story?" She nods against my chest. "When I was young, maybe ten, my father was posted in a fly-in-only town. It was a scary place to be." The winters were insanely long, and there was only one small grocery store. It was a dark place where assistance and resources were limited. I didn't feel the effects of that, but I saw it in those around me, and it made me ache that I couldn't do *something* to help those who needed it. "There were barely any other kids, and we were cattle among wolf shifters. Tensions ran high. But there was this one family that lived on the edge of town. They had a boy about my age and my little sister, and I played with him."

Even now, I regret not noticing the signs more clearly. I was so naïve, and I let my need for a friend cloud my understanding of what my friend was going through.

"He was quiet and kind, but I knew something wasn't right. It turns out he was being neglected at home. I found out years later, but I always felt like I could have done more for him. Because I had known something was off. I regret not stepping in to help him more. But the fact of the matter is, I was a kid. I didn't understand just *what* was off about his home life. I didn't have the words of the life experience. It's the same thing for you. You were sixteen when all this happened. You were old enough to understand, but you were too young to have the words and the maturity to fully process what it all meant. You also had to cope with the fact that, for a full decade and a half, your mother was good to you. You couldn't have spoken up, Mila. You didn't know what was going on. And now, as an adult, you can't step in and be the one taking the hits for the things she does. That would be like blaming a victim for getting killed. You can't live with the pressure of this. It will destroy you. I made the assumption that you *should* be on this mission with me before I knew you were her daughter. Now, I know that you're the expert on Sveta, but if this is too hard for you to witness, that's okay. You can still be helpful at a distance. If you want, I'll bring you back to FUCNA. There's absolutely no shame in that. No one will judge you."

"But I will. I was completely powerless the last time. This time, I have the power and the knowledge to make a difference. I get what you're trying to say, but I have to fix it, T. I have to. I don't know how to exist, how to keep going if I don't. I'm not saying it'll be easy or that I won't need another amazing hug again, but I want to do this. *I need to do this.*"

I study her beautiful face, searching for something, anything that would change her mind.

There's nothing.

Mila is determined to see this through, and nothing I could say is going to change that. If this were any other agent, I would pull them. She's too close to it, but I understand her need for closure.

"Okay, so then let's get her back," I say, running my fingers through her long red strands. "Let's put her back where she belongs. But you need to know that, once this is all said and done, there is no way that I'm letting you carry this on your own. If you need a hug, to vent, something to punch, just ask. We're in this together."

Mila is a strong, capable, intelligent woman. She wouldn't be a FUC agent and a FUCNA instructor if she weren't. Maybe that's why she calls to something deep inside me.

I know that being this attracted to her, too invested in her well-being, is the last thing I should be doing, but I can't help myself.

11

MILA

The drive to Lake Murray doesn't take very long. T-Bone is flooring it. Or, at least, what is probably his version of putting the pedal to the metal. He is going all of ten kilometers over the speed limit.

I have to admit that being in his arms was one of the most comforting places I have ever been. It's not just that he smells fantastic or that his huge muscular arms made me feel safe. It's that he has so much empathy. It's kind of the last thing I expected from a big hulking dude. He's nothing like a bull; he's more like a gentle giant.

My hand is tucked in his on the center console, his thumb drawing circles across mine. I don't want to think about just how right it feels to get any sort of affection for T-Bone.

Not because he isn't my type at all.

Not even because he is an agent from another agency.

But because I shouldn't be entertaining any sort of happy thoughts. I don't deserve them, for one. But mostly, it's not the time to be having soft, gushy feelings about a man.

Not while I'm on a mission.

I'm probably getting confused because it's the first time I've let myself be vulnerable in a very long time. If ever. There is no way I am falling for T-Bone in these insane circumstances.

I keep my eyes on the changing scenery, trying to focus my attention there. The small dirt paths of Lake Murray have been paved, no doubt a sign that this area has become more popular as a vacation spot. My parents loved it so much here; they almost bought this particular property in my first year of high school. It was only a year before my mother was caught.

In the mid-morning sunlight, the lake house looms above us. Most people feel safer during the day when the monsters are hidden away in the shadows, but this is terrifying.

The house's white exterior looks pristine and well maintained. It makes sense. It wouldn't have been in the house that the horrors happened but rather on the property itself. While my dad and I slept peacefully in our beds.

There is a small blue car parked by the cabin, doors and trunk wide open. There are a few dirt-covered boxes piled beside it. That can mean only one thing.

T-Bone is already pushing the speed dial button on his phone and requesting all available backup at our location, including an ambulance to help us deal with my mother's case of the Foamies.

"She's here," I whisper as soon as the car rolls to a stop. My hand is going for the handle while I brace myself from the sun's rays.

"Mila, hold on, we can't just barge in. Let me call this in." T-Bone puts a hand on my shoulder to stop me while his other hand goes to his phone, his fingers flying over the screen. "We need a plan."

"A plan? She's there, and we grab her and bring her back. There's your plan."

I rush out of the car, making my way toward the car, covering my face with my hood. The sun burns my skin, makes my eyes water, but I push through.

"Mila?" My mom walks around the corner of the house. Her clothes, which cover most of her body, are covered in dirt. Her graying hair is trying to escape the baseball cap she has on her head to shield her from the harsh sun. Her face is ashen, and there's a thin layer of sweat across her skin. She looks emaciated, white residue stuck to the corner of her mouth. She is definitely sick. It's definitely the Foamies, but there's something else, too. If I had to put money on it, I'd say she was injecting that blood we found in her cell into her body. She probably gave herself blood poisoning.

My mother blinks rapidly, her brow furrowed as if she isn't too sure if she's seeing me. She drops the very dirty, very small box from her hands and takes a few steps forward. "You should be in bed, Spooky. It's way past your bedtime."

"Mom?" Her words aren't making sense. I shouldn't be surprised, but the tone of her voice is one I've heard so many times I can't help but feel pulled in by it.

"Go find your father and ask him to read you another bedtime story to get you to sleep. I have to go to work." She kneels down to pick up the box, but when I don't move, she narrows her eyes. "Are you really my Mila?" Her eyes are lined in red, another clear sign that she has the Foamies.

"She's hallucinating, " T-Bone warns, treading carefully toward me. "Take a step back."

I shake my head at him and gesture for him to go. Reluctantly, T-Bone backs away, heading toward the back of the property. Oscar Trow could very well be around.

A random memory pops into my head as I watch my mother struggling to look at me. It was my sixth birthday, and no one from school came to my birthday party because it was at night. I was devastated, but Mom brought me to a drive-in, and we watched two old horror movies. She had held me all through the double feature, not because I was scared, rather because she knew I needed to be held. Comforted. *That's* who my mother was.

Not this sickly raving lunatic standing in front of me. Not the woman who had been described during the lengthy trials.

"Mom." I can't even keep the pleading out of my voice. "You need to come with me. You're in danger."

She looks around, looking for a threat, her eyes so like mine darting around.

"No, no. Oscar is my friend. He won't hurt me."

"Mom, the danger is inside of you. You're sick. You have the Foamies."

"That's not possible." Her hand goes to her forehead, checking her temperature. "I don't have a fever."

The glassiness of her eyes and the trembling of her hands betray her. She is definitely running high.

"Mom, I think that you might have given yourself blood poisoning. Did you experiment on yourself while you were in prison?"

"It had to be done," she answers haughtily, giving me a glimpse of the woman she was before.

"You need iron-fortified blood. Come with me, and I'll give you the medicine you need to get better."

My heart feels heavy as I speak, dragging me way down. Because I can give her all of the iron-fortified blood, and I can give her all of the antibiotics in the world, but there is no fixing her homicidal streak.

"Mila, you don't understand. We are so close to a breakthrough. We'll be able to fix all of the diseases in the world. People won't have to age. The answer is in the blood."

"Okay. That's fine. You can keep doing your work if you just come with me."

It's a lie, but I'm banking on her being gone enough to not clue in. I've heard all of her reasoning before. It didn't make sense to me then and sure won't now.

"No." She screams like a small child in the throes of a temper tantrum. "I can't stop. I'm so close. I just need a few more samples. A few more test subjects."

"Mom, you hurt people because you're sick. You need to follow me so we can give you help."

Her eyes darken, and she narrows them in a way that has me taking a step back.

"There are always sacrifices to be made in the name of science," she growls at me, flipping on a dime.

I flinch, inhaling sharply at her cold, senseless words. Standing before me for the first time is Sveta Markov, notorious serial killer. In all her sociopathic glory. She no longer bears any resemblance to the woman who raised me. I don't know her at all. I *knew* that the second she was arrested, but seeing her like this is an entirely different thing.

Even when I was speaking with her, researching my master's thesis, she wasn't this cold. At least then, she was apologetic. There is no trace of that now. I don't know if it's the fever talking or if she was putting on a show all those years ago.

It's not like she doesn't know *how* to act. To pretend. To manipulate. She did it for years while she was playing wife and mother.

"I think the time for civility is over." T-Bone's voice is pitched low, only for my benefit.

"One second," I beg. I take a step toward my mother, willing her to listen to me. There is nothing of my mother in her eyes, but still, I can't give up. I have to believe that I can get to her. "Mom, please come with me."

And just like that, her eyes go impossibly colder again.

"You know what they called me?" Mom's voice is high pitched, so high it makes my teeth chatter. "The Bloody Doctor, a nod to Elizabeth Bathory, the Bloody Countess. *That's* what they called me. Like I was some kind of crazed lunatic who killed all these young virgins to bathe in their blood. That's not even historically accurate."

I open my mouth to argue with her, but a shadow comes up from behind my mother.

And that's when I see it.

A gun pointed directly to my chest.

12

MILA

It doesn't take me very long to figure out who the armed man is. It's Oscar Trow. I put my hands up defensively and look straight into his eyes as he comes into the light.

He's in his early forties, with a bit of a gut, a wide red nose, and a balding head of pale yellow hair. There's an ashen quality to his skin, and I'd bet anything he has also taken to injecting foreign blood into his veins.

"You're the daughter." His voice is raspy with surprise, the gun still aimed at me. His eyes move to T-Bone, and his face breaks out in a disturbing smile. "Do you know that story? The one about Elizabeth Bathory?"

I swallow loudly, my heart racing in my chest. Having a weapon pointed at you is never the right time for a history lesson.

With my hands up, I can't reach the gun I have strapped to my hip. And it's not like I want to whip out my weapon at this precise moment. I don't intend to shoot anyone. I also have very little field training. After I was done with the basic six months training at FUCNA, I went directly to the lab. It's not like my aim would be true, and I don't actually remember how to deal with this situation. No one is *trained* to come face to face with my mother.

It doesn't help that Mom takes a step toward Oscar. She's on *his* side. The man pointing a weapon at her only child.

T-Bone looks as cool as a cucumber, his face calm, though his shoulders are set wide and at the ready as he rounds the corner, right beside me. I really hope he has a weapon hiding in those ugly cargo shorts of his.

"The Bloody Countess." T nods, engaging Oscar. "Isn't she that countess who killed over six hundred people, all her female servants? Wasn't she one of Bram Stoker's inspirations for *Dracula*?"

"Do you actually think that it happened that way?" my mother asks, the hysterical edge back to her voice. She hates the comparison between her and Elizabeth Bathory.

In fact, the entire time she was on trial, she kept interjecting into the court proceedings, raving that both she and the countess were being vilified. She was held in contempt of court and then eventually flat-out removed from the room during her own trial.

"Honestly?" T-Bone answers. "I've never spent much time thinking about the validity of it."

"Turns out," Oscar said, "she was a very rich, very powerful countess in Hungary. She was also a widow in the early 1600s with all of this land and money. Her accuser was none other than her cousin, a political enemy. It was all a lie. She didn't kill six hundred people, and she *didn't* bathe in their blood. It was all done to vilify her."

"Has Sveta been maligned?" T asks, still completely collected.

"Of course." Oscar's hands are shaking slightly, no doubt a symptom of blood poisoning. He's been injecting himself too. "Sveta is a genius. She's found the answer to aging and disease in the blood of the young. If we can harness it, pull it from healthy donors, then we can eradicate all illnesses. We could all live forever."

"So, she didn't kill hundreds of people?"

I can't help my sharp gasp at T-Bone's question. It's a dangerous thing to ask a deranged man who is pointing a gun at me.

Although now the gun is aimed between T-Bone and me. I don't know if it's because Oscar has lost focus or if it's because he doesn't know which one of us to shoot first.

"She did. But that's the price to pay for brilliance. She shouldn't be locked up. She should be celebrated."

"Interesting," T-Bone volleys back. "And so were these test subjects willing participants?"

"No, but—"

"There wasn't enough blood from the volunteers," my mother interrupts. "I needed it all. I needed to drain them dry to get all of the life force in the blood. The formula wouldn't work without it."

Apparently, when she was in the very beginning of her mission to cure all diseases, she did get a few volunteers to donate blood. A couple of them testified at the trial. But it soon wasn't enough. It didn't take long for science and magic to get confused in my brilliant mother's head.

"Do you know how they killed her?" Mom asks. "The Countess was bricked into a single room of her castle, where she died. That's what they were doing to me... Locking me away in a single room, just like the Countess. The walls were closing in on me, Mila. I was going to suffocate."

Oscar shuffles closer to Mom and whispers something into her ear. His eyes go from me to T-Bone and back again. Mom's face falls, and she shakes her head.

"Mila," she says, "is it true that you want to put me back in jail?"

"I want to give you the help you need, Mom. You need medicine."

"So it's true then..." she whispers.

Oscar hands her the gun. "You have to do it, Sveta," he says to her. "Think of the blood we could collect. *Shifter blood*. From a young bat. I bet this is exactly what we need to finish the formula."

If I thought it hurt when my mother was arrested, that was nothing compared to this.

She takes the gun and points it directly at me.

My mother's hands aren't even shaking as she aims a weapon at her only child.

I let out a breath, accepting this realization. I always wondered if I would have grown up to be one of her victims. I guess I have my answer.

I might be a shifter who can easily heal from a bullet wound, but she is pointing it directly at my heart. There is no recovering from that.

"Mom." I say the word, hoping that she remembers that she carried me for nine months. That she held me as a baby. That she kissed my skinned knees and read me bedtime stories. She lowers the gun one single millimeter.

"Do it, Sveta," Oscar eggs on. "We can use her blood to fix you. To find the missing link to immortality."

Her eyes slide over to Oscar. He is caught between pleading and faked bravado.

"Sure." I shrug. "You could kill me, Mom." I make sure to enunciate that last work, really hammering it home. "But would you be ready to face Dad at that trial? Look into Edward's face and tell him what you've done? Mom?"

The gun slides another millimeter down. If she were to shoot now, it would maybe nick an artery, but my chances of surviving have significantly increased.

"Sveta," Oscar growls. "We have worked too hard to stop now. What are you thinking? Do it. I can fix you."

"Mom, look at me. It's me, Spooky. Remember? You called me that because I was the only little girl who wanted to dress like a monster instead of the princess at Halloween."

She bites down on her lip, a mannerism that is so like me that it makes my heart ache. Mom lowers the gun, but Oscar anticipates her move. He grabs for it, and the two begin to scuffle for the weapon.

"Mila." T-Bone pushes me behind him and backs us up a few feet. I step back around him, trying to find a way to break between Oscar and my mom.

"Why are you doing this, Sveta?" Oscar shouts. "We had a deal. We said we would find a cure to death, to aging. You're ruining it."

"I can't hurt her." Mom weeps, clawing at her accomplice. "She's my own. My Spooky. I can't."

I can only watch in horror as the two very sick people battle it out for the weapon. It would be comical if it weren't so goddamn sad.

She's too frail from battling the blood poisoning *and* the Foamies, and she loses the gun to Oscar.

T-Bone surely notices the turn of the tide as he dives in front of me.

I vaguely hear the sound of the gun going off, and I can only wait for the pain.

It doesn't come.

But T-Bone's leg buckles, and blood gushes from his thigh.

Mom launches herself at Oscar, screeching at him that he could have killed me. Her pale face is a mask of fury as she claws at his face.

I kneel by T-Bone and press my hand to his leg. A lot of blood is spouting out of him, and he's unconscious.

"You're going to be okay," I say. But there is a lot of blood. Enough for me to know that he has indeed been shot in his femoral artery.

A few feet away, Oscar and my mother have stopped fighting. She's the one holding the gun. This time, it's pointed straight to Oscar.

"You could have killed my daughter, you idiot," she shrieks.

"It was for us, Sveta. You know you've grown old, and I only wanted to fix you. With her blood, we could have made you younger." He takes a step toward her, his hands outstretched for the gun. "We can still find the cure. We can make all of this better. You said, remember, that we could be heroes if we found the secret of life that lies in blood. We just have to kill her." He inclines his head in my direction.

I have no idea why he has fixated on killing me, but I don't particularly enjoy being his target. My hands are applying pressure to T-Bone's wound, trying to find a way to get a handle on the situation.

"You know that legend, that daughters steal their mother's beauty and youth? That's what she did to you."

Oh, that mother fucker. If T-Bone's leg weren't bleeding so profusely, I'd beat Oscar's ass for believing—and perpetuating—that asinine tale.

If T-Bone's shifter healing could kick in, he would regain

consciousness to hold his own wound while I tried to untangle the mess between my mother and Oscar.

Mom narrows her eyes at him. "I've been fighting against the image of Elizabeth Bathory put on me, and here you are, spouting another misogynistic bullshit story. I should have known that you were just like the rest of them."

In the distance, the sound of sirens can be heard.

Her eyes slip for a second, and then with a sigh, she shakes her head.

"What's a few more years added to my sentence?" she says, emptying the rest of the clip into Oscar's chest.

I can't help the gasp that tears out of me.

My knees go weak, and if I weren't already sitting on the cold ground, I would have collapsed. I've completely forgotten how to breathe. My vision blurs, and I can't seem to get a handle on my reeling mind. Thoughts speed by, and I can't latch onto any.

Mom just killed someone.

Reality stops making sense as she walks toward me, drops the gun at my feet, and then sits on the porch. As if nothing has just happened.

"What are you doing?" I ask her, finding my voice, but only just barely.

"Well, you all hear them coming. He's injured, so you'll be the only thing between me and my freedom. I won't hurt you, Mila."

I blink at her, and I try with all of my might to keep quiet. But I can't. "It's too late for that."

She nods sadly and looks away. "I know, Spooky. I know."

13

T-BONE

The world comes back into focus, slowly and painfully. The sun is hurting my eyes, and I want to stand to get Mila out of its harmful rays, but my body won't answer me.

I watch through half-opened eyes as Mila and Markov exchange a few words. Even injured, I can see the sadness on both women's faces. I'm surprised to hear Markov admit that she'd hurt her daughter.

The words feel heavy on the air. She leans her head back on the cabin wall and closes her eyes. It's surrender.

All because Sveta refuses to hurt her daughter.

It's kind of fascinating. She was holding a gun to her head not five minutes ago.

The sound of the sirens is now accompanied by the flash of red and blue lights against the white building. A dozen agents spill out of the various vehicles, weapons drawn on what can only be described as the oddest scene.

The escaped convict is sitting quietly, not making a single move to run, while her accomplice bleeds out beside her.

"Agent Thrussell." One of my team leaders, Meg, comes to stand above me. "That's a nasty wound. It'll take a bit of time to heal up. You'll need to get that checked out."

She's not wrong. I'm suddenly very grateful that I called for medics as well as a few teams to meet us at the Lake Murray location once we spotted the car parked out front.

Not that I need the medical attention, per se, now that the blood flowing from my leg has progressed from a mild deluge to a slowly decreasing flow. But my team leaders are all RCMP agents who have no idea that I'm a Hairy Coo shifter who can literally take a bullet and walk away without becoming ground beef. Injured, to be sure. But I definitely won't be steak tartare anytime soon.

"Thanks, Meg. But I just need a minute. Cuff her." I gesture to a still very demure Sveta.

My shifter blood is already healing the hell out of my wound, and it's not as bad as it was a few minutes ago. It'll be tender for a day or so, since an artery was definitely nicked, but I've definitely survived worse in my time.

"Here," Mila says, helping me up with her slender shoulders. "You're kind of kooky, you know that?" she adds, shaking her head. "You're not as straight-edged as I originally thought. Diving for bullets and all."

"What's going to happen to me?" Sveta asks as her hands are cuffed behind her back.

"Well, I'm guessing more time will be added to your sentence. For the escape and maybe for the death of your accomplice."

"What's a few more years to a thousand-year sentence?" She shrugs.

She's not wrong. She was given over a thousand years behind bars. It was a gesture the judge posed for the victims' families.

"Mila," she says, "my head is a little bit confused. I think... Wait, are you still in school?"

"No," Mila answers sadly. "I graduated a little while ago. I became a professor. Remember?"

"Oh." Sveta nods. "Oh, yes. That's right."

But it's written all over her face that she isn't sure what year it is or even where she is. Mila leads her mother to one of the police cruisers and tucks her inside.

"I'll be right behind you," Mila swears. "This time you're headed to a FUC prison. They'll know how to help you. Just... be good, okay? Listen to the officers."

"Mila..." Sveta shakes her head. "I have work to do. I need more test subjects."

"Okay, Mom," Mila answers. She closes the door and turns back, her shoulders slumping way down.

I limp toward Mila, ignoring Meg, who is clamoring for me to get checked by the medics.

"Hey." I drape an arm around her. "You'll be okay."

"Yeah," she whispers. "Better than you. You took a bullet for me." Mila's voice is nothing but a whisper, and I know she's being brave. My wound is healing, but it might take a while to get past this for her. I took the bullet for her, but I would take the emotional hits if I could.

"It was pure instinct," I tell her. We both look down to the wound that has mostly stopped bleeding. "I wasn't going to let you get it."

"I'm a shifter, too." She furrows her brow. "I would heal just as fast as you."

"Impossible woman." I laugh. "Can't you just thank me for being noble?"

Mila rolls her eyes. "Oh, sure. You're noble as fuck for jumping in front of a bullet." She leans up, one of her small hands running against my furry cheek. Her soft lips brush against mine in an impossibly sweet kiss. "Thanks, T," she whispers against my lips.

It's not enough.

Cupping the back of her head, I press her closer to me and bring my own mouth to hers. This time, when our lips meet, there is no sweetness, only an uncontrolled burn.

I can pretend that I'm kissing her because I'm happy to be alive. I can lie and say that kissing her is a lapse in judgment because I was afraid I'd die.

But I'm not a liar.

I'm kissing her because I *need* to. It feels like this has been destined to happen since the second I walked into her lab as Mila chatted up a pile of bones.

I run my tongue along the seam of her mouth, and on a sigh, Mila lets me explore her mouth.

It's like sipping fire.

It goes straight to my cock, deep in my heart. I should have known that Mila would be the most potent force in the world.

"What is happening?" Mila asks, pulling away from me.

"Well, I was giving you some of my best work," I tease, needing to bring some levity into the lust-filled atmosphere.

"Huh." She shrugs. "Good try."

Is she serious? There is no way she didn't feel the intensity of that kiss.

The glint in her impossibly blue eyes and the deep blush of her cheeks tell me that she is just as affected as I am.

Mila is such an intense livewire, smart as hell, strong as alloy steel, and she's without a doubt the most beautiful woman I've ever seen. I should be so lucky as to get her affection.

"I'm sorry if I just mauled you." My voice comes out raspy and low, belying my words. I'm not sorry. I'm tucking the memory of that kiss deep into my heart, and I'll replay it over and over again.

"Don't be sorry, T."

Mila runs her lips against mine, drops a quick peck, and hugs me close.

"Thanks," she whispers. "I don't think I could have gotten through the last twenty-four hours without you."

I hold her close to me. "I'm the one who should be thanking you. If it weren't for you, we wouldn't have found her so quickly. She didn't put anyone else in danger."

Her eyes go to Oscar, her cheeks blanching.

"He made his choice when he decided to help her escape from prison. You can't feel guilty about that."

I tuck her long hair behind her shoulder before placing my hand there.

"I have to pretend to go to the ambulance and get checked out before my team leaders figure out something is off about me. Hang tight, and we can go see your mom. Make sure she's getting the right meds."

Mila nods her head. "I should call my dad and let him know that he's safe. That he can go back to his place." She bites down on her lip, and before I can even react, her lips find mine. She wastes no time demanding entrance into my mouth. Our tongues tangle and rub in a passionate embrace. Mila moves her hands through the hair at the back of my neck, across my shoulders, down my chest, her fingers trailing little paths along my skin.

I wish we weren't in the middle of a crime scene, surrounded by agents. I wish that we had met under better circumstances.

What I want is to lay Mila on the softest, most luxurious bed and make her come until the only thing she can say is my name. Over and over again.

Those are hardly the kinds of thoughts I should be having right now.

"T," she whispers, "you need to go tend to your wound, but just so you know, if you were to ask me out, I'd say yes."

"Fair," I respond before diving back for her lips, because I can't help myself. "Mila," I say between more searing kisses, "let me take you out to dinner."

"I didn't mean right now." She smirks.

"I have *no* game when it comes to this kind of thing. I like you. Let me take you out."

"Only if you take me someplace where we can share steak tartare."

My eyes go wide, and she giggles. "I'm just teasing, T-Bone. Go." She pushes me toward the ambulance. "Pretend you're a hurt human."

She watches me as I sit in the back of the rescue vehicle, being tended to by a very confused paramedic. Once I'm properly cared for, Mila retreats to the SUV to call her father.

The last day plays over in my mind. I can't believe I've only known Mila for such a short time.

Maybe it was the intensity of our mission, or maybe it's the way we balance each other out, but all I know is that if she is offering to spend time with me, I'll take it.

I'll always choose Mila if she lets me.

14

T-BONE

The glass walls of the sub-basement lab aren't really undulating with the thumping of Mila's music, but I swear the god-awful noise is so loud it makes my teeth rattle.

The woman responsible for said racket is leaning over a shiny metal worktable, a pile of bones in front of her and a pair of magnifying glasses hiding half of her beautiful face.

I knock on the door, hoping to catch her attention, but of course she doesn't hear me.

"Oh, that must have hurt," she tells the remains. "Sorry about that."

I barely hear her words as I search for the remote. It's fascinating that her workspace is a mixture of cleanliness and organization while her desk is a pile of stuff taken directly taken from my nightmares. I almost wish I could organize all of it for her. But Mila would have my ass for even trying that.

I spot the remote on the corner of the precarious pile of papers and hit *Pause.*

Mila jumps at the sound of silence and turns to face me.

"Hey, if it isn't my favorite crime-solving partner." I can't help but smile at her.

Her shirt reads *Forensic Anthropologists - Will Date Anything* with a
large smiling skeleton under the writing. The tee is black, of course,
as are her leather pants. They could be painted on, showcasing all of
her curves.

I've missed her, and I want to hold her body close to mine and
kiss her painted red lips. We haven't actually seen each other since
Sveta was brought to the FUC prison. It's been a crazy two days,
between filling reports and getting my superiors to agree that Sveta
had her place in the shifter prison.

I was lucky to get Carlyle, the warden of the prison Sveta's
escaped from, on my side. He was kind enough to state that he didn't
feel his facility was equipped to deal with a person of Sveta's capabilities.

The last kiss Mila and shared was in the FUCNA parking lot
when I dropped her off. She's been prancing in my mind since then.

Everything Mila does is either cute or sexy as hell. Even now, she
looks adorable, with her magnifying glasses sliding on her nose as
she looks at me. Her lab coat drops off her shoulders as she places the
spectacles down.

"Please do *not* tell me you're here to ask my help with another
case. My mother better be solidly behind bars."

She cocks an eyebrow with a smirk on her beautiful face.

I would say that I don't know how Mila ended up being so sweet
and caring when she has Markov for a mother, but the truth is she
came by those attributes all on her own. Sure, she had a good dad
who was there to support her and help her navigate her new world
when Sveta was arrested. Mila could have gone in a million other
directions, but she chose forensic anthropology to seek answers, not
just for herself but also for the families of all of Sveta's victims.

"I got that promotion I was after. I wanted to thank you. Without
your expertise, I never would have caught Markov." I purposefully
distance her from the deranged serial killer.

"You know I was just doing what needed to be done. There's no
need to thank me. Besides, if it weren't for the escape, I wouldn't have
met this really cool guy."

I arch an eyebrow. "A cool guy?" I echo, but she doesn't bite.

"Wait, a promotion? Does this mean that you've finally achieved the ultimate Thrussell family goal of making superintendent?"

"Oh, no. I was offered something different. I realized I wasn't ready to give up the field. Besides, I don't think that the titles are as important to me as they are to my father and grandfather."

"What job were you offered?"

"Furry United Coalition agent," I say with a sly smile.

Mila's jaw drops, but only for a few seconds. The smile she flashes me is resplendent.

"Look at you, breaking from family tradition. You really *are* a rebel."

She laughs, and I join in. She's entirely too far from me. I take a few more steps toward her. Her smell, the sweet scent of orange blossoms, fills my head with all kinds of ideas.

"Does this new job have anything to do with why you're here?" she asks. Mila flips her hair back, but as she has the habit of doing, she flicks a section through her fingers, twirling the length nervously.

"No, I'm not actually here on business."

"Oh?" One of her eyebrows rises with interest. "Social call? This better be about the date you promised."

I take a few steps toward her, closing the distance between us. "I promised you a date?" I furrow my brow in mock concentration. "As I recall, you told me that if I were to ask you, you'd say yes."

"Yup, then you asked. Remember? Two days is a hell of a long time to keep me waiting. Not even a call."

Standing close to her, I place my hands on her hips, and her hands go up around my neck.

"That's true. Especially since I've been dying to do this."

I lean down and capture her mouth in a kiss. Her soft, full lips move against mine, a small moan escaping her as she melts into me. I dip my tongue into her mouth, running it along hers. Her fingers run up my neck, tangling into my hair as she angles herself for better access to my mouth.

"I want to do things with you, Mila. But the setting is a bit disconcerting to me."

"The things you say." Her mouth is upturned in a smirk. I kiss it. "So very romantic."

"Yeah, I know." I give her a wink. "Let's get out of here."

"I'm at *work*, T. I can't just leave." She lets go of me, but I reach out and keep one of her hands in mine.

"Sure you can. You're not on the clock right now. Stop being a workaholic for a night and let me take you out properly."

"Hmm. That's a nice suggestion." She closes her arms around my neck, rising up on the tips of her toes to be able to reach me. "I thought maybe we could stay in."

"Really, now."

Thank fuck. Though I do want to bring Mila out on a proper date, there are a bunch of very dirty things I've meant to do to her. With her.

"Your place or mine?" Her whisper sends of awareness across my body.

"Mine," I manage to say, because my house is about ten minutes from the academy. "But just so things are clear, Mila, this isn't just about sex for me. You're an amazing woman, and I'll take whatever time you give me. Tonight, we can stay in, but I want to take you out. Take you to the movies and hold your hand during the previews."

"Why, Agent Thrussell, you're positively blushing. That's very sweet."

"How long do you need to get out of here?"

"Maybe thirty minutes?" she ventures. "I have to put the bones back in their crypts."

"Okay, I can wait that long." Unable to stop myself, I kiss her again. "I'll order us some dinner. That way, at least I can still feel like a gentleman."

Mila giggles and slides her magnifying glasses back onto her head.

"If that makes you feel better, T."

And it does.

It's not like I have much experience in the hookup game. Oh, sure. I've had long-term girlfriends.

But not one single ex even compares to Mila and the way she has my insides all knotted up.

I all but skip to my car, feeling pretty good with myself for stopping by FUCNA to see Mila. She wasn't wrong that I should have called her earlier. But I'll make it up to her.

All night.

15

MILA

I won't say I drove like a bat out of hell to get to T-Bone's place, but I'd be lying.

It took me way too long to put all of the bones away. It's not like it's a process that can be rushed. If it were any other man I was going to meet, I would have gone home to primp and change. But the truth is I don't feel like I have to do that with T-Bone.

He's already seen me crying hysterically. In fact, I'm pretty sure he had some of my snot on his shirt, and he didn't even say anything. I have never met anyone as steadfast as him before. He's not just this brawny man, but he's also strong inside. He's got solid values, and I respect that.

Maybe my outward appearance doesn't exactly scream *I'm a conventional chick who wants the dude and the 2.5 kids and the nice house.* But I do want those things. I just never really gave much thought to getting it.

Who wants to tell a potential boyfriend that their mother is a notorious serial killer?

Not me. It's attracted some weirdos in the past. T isn't like that. Hell, he already knows all about my mom, and he didn't go running for the hills when he found out.

In fact, he ran straight for her and took a shot for me. That's the kind of man I want to have in my life. One who won't be scared away and chased off by the skeletons in my closet.

I park my car in front of T-Bone's house, a quaint little white house on a quiet street. Somehow, it's exactly where I would have imagined T-Bone living. The lawn is perfectly cut, and the front door and garage are freshly painted. I'm having a vision of T cutting the grass, wearing his cargo pants with a pair of noise-canceling ear-protectors.

I can't help but shake my head and giggle at the thought. He *would* protect his ears while operating machinery. He's cautious like that. I'm still smiling when I knock on the door.

It doesn't take long for the door to swing open.

"Hey." T-Bone greets me with a huge smile, his hair wet from a shower.

Just seeing him makes my whole body zing with awareness.

They say that couples who go on first dates with high adrenaline activities are bonded quicker and deeper than couples who just go to the movies. And honestly? I believe it.

T-Bone and I might not have met because we were dating, but the twenty-four hours we spent together definitely bonded us to each other in a very deep, very real way.

He stands there, in his entrance, a smile on his face as he gestures me into his home.

He's wearing his usual cargo pants and his classic black tee. Even though I hate those fucking pants, T-Bone looks so comfortable, so at ease, that I can't help myself. I launch myself at him, hands around his neck, mouth on his. Thankfully, T-Bone is fast and strong. He catches me and palms my ass, lifting me up into his arms.

I kiss him, delving into his mouth with my tongue. I even nip on his lower lip.

"Mila, if you keep kissing me like that, dinner will get cold."

"I don't care," I whisper, running my lips along his scruffy cheeks. "Take me to the bedroom. We can eat after."

"So long as you don't mind cold Chinese food."

"Bedroom, T-Bone."

"Yes, ma'am," he groans as I start to grind up against him.

With impressive agility, T-Bone walks us up the stairs and down a hallway.

The pale blue walls of his bedroom are comforting, and the soft gray comforter looks inviting. T-Bone lays me down gently on the bed, and before he can move away, I grab at the hem of his shirt and pull it over his head.

I've only ever had sex with tall, lanky dudes. So my reaction when T pulls his shirt off his head is entirely pure and absolutely embarrassing.

I moan.

I moan because I have never wanted to lick an entire body from head to toe in my life. Every inch of T is gold skin and rippling muscles. The definition of his abs is insane, and they just keep testing the bounds of my wits by ending in a deep V leading down, dipping into the waistband of his cargo pants.

I have never hated those fucking pants more than I do right now. Because they're keeping me away from something I definitely want. I tug at the button, the starchy material hindering my movements.

"I want to burn your pants," I grunt in the least sexiest way possible, tugging at the plastic disk.

"You don't have to burn them, Mila. Just got to get them off of me."

He tugs my tee off and throws it to the ground.

"I'm trying, but these things are an evil contraption."

His entire body shakes with laughter as he swats my hands away. "I gotta say your impatience is about as sexy as your bra."

I look down to the black lace and mentally high-five myself for having a pretty serious obsession with black lacy things.

T-Bone cups my breasts and runs his thumbs across my nipples. I arch up, offering more of myself to him.

Typically in bed, I am the leader. I have to take charge to make things good. Or at least mildly enjoyable. I don't even have time to do that with T-Bone. He's large and *definitely* in charge.

With a quick motion, he peels my pants off of me.

"Fuck, Mila. Do you always wear lingerie at work?" He groans when he gets a good look at the panties that match my bra.

"Life is too short to drape my naughty bits in ugly garments."

"I agree with you," T growls. "You should always be wrapped in something this delicious looking."

He leans down and places a kiss against my sex through the lace. The softness of his lips against the material has me arching off the bed. He drops another kiss before gently sliding them down my legs.

"The only reason why I'm not tearing these off of you right now is because I definitely want to see you in these again."

T pins my legs down onto the bed, an untamed look in his eyes. His pompadour hairstyle is sticking out every which way, only adding to the image of the lust-wild. His gaze locks on mine as he lowers his mouth. His tongue takes a long swipe up my slit, and I don't know what is sexier.

The way he is looking at me or the way he is touching me.

His next lick is slow, and he moves his tongue from side to side as he settles in on my clit. It's a teasing gesture designed to make me insane. He laps at me, twirling his tongue, suckling the hardened nub into his mouth like he knows exactly where to touch me, how to touch me.

One of his thick fingers traces the edges of my entrance, and he slowly eases the digit in, quickly adding a second finger. T pumps in and out of me, his tongue never losing stride. Small little earthquakes of pleasure start quivering inside of me, and I pant desperately, shamelessly grinding my hips into his face, chasing my release.

When the explosion happens, T-Bone doesn't stop. He continues licking me until I beg him to stop, my core fluttering continuously on powerful aftershocks.

I lay in a pile of satiated goo for all of ten seconds. I pull T down for a kiss, letting my hands roam down to cup his cock. He helps me by kicking off his underwear and kneels between my legs.

His erection is impressive, nothing short of a feast for my eyes.

The smooth, silky skin seems to be aching, begging for a release of his own. I close my fingers around the girth and move my hand up in a few motions.

"Shit," I groan, "do you have any condoms?"

A huge grin breaks out on T-Bone's face.

"I'm prepared for any eventuality."

"Are you telling me that you have a condom in those atrocious pants of yours?"

"Wallet, which is in my pants, so, yes."

"I take back *every* bad thing I have ever said about your pants. Wear them all the time. They are my savior."

T laughs and kisses me sweetly, a smile still playing on his lips. He grabs said condom from the now revered cargo pants. I watch in fascination as he rolls the condom onto his impressive erection. I can't help but lick my lips. He catches me taking him in, and he pumps his hand up the length, his eyes trained on me.

"I want you so fucking much." He hums, kneeling between my legs again.

He runs the tip of his cock along my slit, pulling a shiver of need out of me.

"Mila." My name on his lips is a rumble of pure lust.

"Yes," I say, somehow knowing he was asking for permission.

He sinks into my core in one powerful thrust. He inches back out and moves back in slowly. T draws out every single movement, relishing every single moment. It's written in the fire in his eyes, in the kisses he peppers across my chest.

I let my fingers rove over his muscular back. Every single ridge is a delicious exploration.

I can't help myself. I let my teeth bite down on the corded muscles of his neck. Not enough to break the skin, but enough to leave a mark. T roars above me.

"Mila, fuck. You bit me."

"I did," I purr, leaving tiny kisses over the skin.

"You can do that any time you want." He moans, increasing his rhythm.

I wouldn't need to be told twice. Smiling and feeling every little bit the vixen, I nibble on his tender flesh.

"You feel so good, Mila. I just want to stay right here, doing this over and over again."

"We're not even done yet." I moan, arching off the bed when T closes his lips around one of my nipples.

"Don't think we'll ever be." He kisses his away across my chest and laves my other breast with tender attention.

Arching my back, I push my hips off the bed, meeting T thrust for thrust. The tingles start deep inside of me, leaving me more breathless by the second.

It feels so good. It feels so right.

"Mila," he whispers against my neck, sweat beading on his forehead.

I moan my answer, unable to formulate a single coherent thought as he keeps sinking into me over and over again. My fingers dig into his shoulders as my orgasm coils in my core. It starts as a gentle flutter of pure pleasure, builds into a small flame, and slowly it burns brighter, heating my skin with an intoxicating buzz.

The flames grow hotter, and my walls clench around T's cock as I come and mewl his name.

T follows closely, his grasp on my thighs tightening, his thrusts becoming erratic, losing some of his finesse. Above me, T closes his eyes, his shoulders strained as he loses himself to me. My name is on his lips as he roars his release. It's a beautiful, powerful sight to watch a man as formidable as T go over the edge of pleasure because of me.

T collapses next to me, taking care not to crush me, which I appreciate. What I love even more is that he rolls me into his side, nonetheless. He kisses the top of my head softly, and I don't miss the way he inhales deeply. I do the same, committing every single touch and smell to memory.

This wasn't just sex.

This changed something between us, even if we've known each other only a short time. I hug him close, already knowing, deep inside of myself, that T-Bone is mine.

"Well, that will work up an appetite," I tease.

"I'll say," T says, his breathing still labored.

Our first night together is spent making love and feeding each other cold sesame noodles and egg rolls. In the morning, when we finally get to sleep, T-Bone spoons my back to his front and murmurs in my ear, "Go steady with me."

"Are you asking me to be your girlfriend, T-Bone?"

"Yeah," he answers, kissing my shoulder.

"It's very innocent. I like it. It's very *you*."

"Is that a yes, Mila?"

I turn and kiss him until he knows my answer.

16

MILA

It's weird being here. The white and gray walls are weathered by time and passing inmates. Really, the FUC prison isn't much different than any other prison. It's a line of jail cells with inmates in each. The difference is that the cells are fortified for shifters, and it's not always a human body that you'll see watching you through the bars.

There are lions, tigers, bears. You name it, they can be found here.

I make my way to the visitors' room. A metal table, on which a pair of shackles have been soldered, sits in the middle of the square space.

My mother is sitting in her prison orange, hands cuffed to the table in front of her. It's not necessary, in my opinion. She had the chance to hurt me, and she didn't. But it's policy, so there is nothing I can do. It also helps to know that she is back on the anti-shifter serum. She can't shift out of her shackles or fly out of here. This prison is where she is to stay.

"Mila, you're back so soon to visit me."

Her smile seems genuine, and she looks a lot better now that she's being treated for the Foamies and she's stopped experimenting on herself. She's pale, just like me, but at least her skin has lost the sickly purple tinge to it.

Sitting there, she looks composed and sure of herself. *This* is the version of my mother I've always had to contend with when looking over her crimes. The side of her I couldn't reconcile with the murderer. It's hard to look at her right now and think that she has done such unspeakable things.

I suppose the one small comfort I can have is that she has *some* lines she won't cross. Sure, that line is only me, but that means more than I could ever say out loud.

"Hey," I say, sitting in front of her.

"Does this mean that you have my answer? Can I have access to a lab?" She blinks at me pleadingly, like it was all up to me. "I *know* I'm close to a breakthrough. I could feel it."

"Do you really think that's a wise choice, Mom?"

"But..." I shoot her a look, and she stops herself.

"Let's think back, shall we. You escaped with the man who was completely copycatting versions of your murders. Then you killed said accomplice."

"To save you," she interjects as if that could ever be enough to make up for all the bad she has done.

"There's no way I can argue that for you. Not for a long while." *Not ever*, but I don't say that. I don't really feel like getting into a fight about this particular topic.

"So why are you here, then?"

"I came to see how you were doing with the meds. It's just a nice visit, Mom."

She laughs. It's a dry, humorless thing. "A nice visit. Mila, you shouldn't be here." She sighs heavily. "I should not have allowed you to study forensic anthropology. I should have..."

"Wait, no. You didn't get a *say* in that choice. I had to do that. For me. So I could understand what became of my life when you were arrested. I would have gone down that path with or without your help. It sure made my master's thesis and my Ph.D. work more interesting."

"I didn't know that's why you were asking me all of those questions, you know. I thought that you were just visiting me. I didn't even think that I was becoming your subject. And I..." She looks down and swallows hard. "I didn't think about my actions and how they would completely affect you. But now that I know that you built your entire life around what I did... I feel terrible."

"You do realize that you should feel dreadful for all the people you killed, right? Not just for seriously messing up my life and Dad's life."

"Well, that's a lot to ask of me, Mila. I can't spend too much time thinking about it. It would make me crazy. Can I just apologize to you and have that be enough?"

"Not even remotely, Mom. Seriously. You've hurt so many people."

"What can I do? It's too late to make amends." Her shoulders slump, and I have to remember who she is and what she has done. I can't just look at her with my daughter eyes.

"If you mean that, then help me bring closure to the families you've hurt."

"How?" She furrows her brow in confusion.

"Give me a list of all your victims. Tell me where you hid all of the bodies. I know you. You must have a log of some kind."

She looks away, crossing her arms, the shackles clanking loudly against the metal table. "Mila."

That's it. That's all she says.

She rises and sighs. "Guard," she calls, avoiding my eyes. "I'm ready to go back to my cell."

Well. At least I tried. I should have known it would be asking too much of her. It's not because she didn't kill me that she would do this for me.

"I'll do it, Mila."

I jump up and rush to her.

"Say again, I don't think I heard you."

There's no way she just agreed to help me.

"You'll be doing it yourself. With my help or not. I want you to move on and have a life apart from the things I've done. If helping you is the only way to get you to stop being completely immersed in my..." She stumbles on the words and looks away. "My crimes. I'll do it."

Her motives are purely selfish.

She isn't helping me because she feels any sort of remorse for the things she has done. She's doing it because she doesn't want to feel guilty every time she thinks about me.

It's not much, but I'll take it.

I can't force her to feel guilty for the things she has done. You can't crawl into someone's mind and make them have the emotions that would be appropriate.

It's clear that Sveta Markov is a psychopath. But at least she'll help me.

"Thanks, Mom."

"I have a few logs. You'll have to do some digging to find them." She rattles off an address. "It's a cemetery. I buried them by the cluster of graves at the back, by the statue. They all died from tuberculosis." She turns back. "Come back in a week or so. I need time, Mila."

She doesn't look back, but it's still a win. I'll take it.

Like I told my mother, this won't bring her victims back, but they can be given proper burials.

My footsteps feel lighter as I walk out of the visiting room. T-Bone is waiting for me by the prison entrance, pacing. He wasn't too keen on letting me see my mother alone. He was concerned that it would upset me.

"How did it go?" T-Bone snakes an arm around my waist, tucking me into his side. He drops a kiss on the top of my head. "Do I need to go in there and kick her ass?"

"No." I laugh. "Your protective side can be put to rest. She's agreed to help me close out all of her murders."

"Shit, Mila. Are you absolutely sure that you want to put yourself through that?" His brow is furrowed in concentration, and I smooth it out with my index finger.

"I most definitely need to do this. All of those families deserve it."

He inhales, nodding his head.

"You're incredible, you know that?" He reaches out a hand and cups my cheek. "I mean it, Mila. There is so much strength in everything you've done and everything you're willing to take on. I know you feel like you've got to do it alone. That you think that's the only way you can be redeemed. But I want to help you. *Let me* help you. You don't have to go at this by yourself. I'm right here to give you whatever support you want or need."

I bite down on the inside of my cheek, and T-Bone strokes the dip in my skin. The gesture echoes the moment perfectly. I want to punish myself quietly, where no one can see. But T does. He sees me, and instead of cowering in fear, he's there. Willing to help me. Seeing me through the darkness of my history.

"If you promise to be around with all of the steak tartare I could ever want, then sure. You can help me."

"Thank you, Mila."

"What?" I don't quite understand why he would thank me.

"I know how hard it is for you to let people in. And I'm very grateful, very happy that I get to be that man."

I inhale and close my arms around his neck, holding him close to me like a solid grounding force in the world of the living. He's proving once again that he is the best.

"You know I should be the one saying that."

"How about this," he says, tucking me into his side as we walk to the car. "We can always be grateful to have the other there to help us deal with our baggage."

"Like actual skeletons in the closet?" I tease.

"Yup. That."

"How about the ghost of evil beige pants?"

T-Bone raises an eyebrow at me. "My pants?"

"I can't see your ass in these, T. It's a crime. And as an agent, you should be very concerned about that."

I dip my hand into the back pocket and give his left cheek a good squeeze. T laughs before kissing the crown of my head.

"The pants stay, Mila."

"Fine," I pretend to grumble, giving his butt another tap.

T-Bone takes my hand, kissing my knuckles, keeping our fingers locked as we drive back to his house.

The night sky stretches out before us. It's not exactly driving off into the sunset, but the moon is shining and the stars are winking at me, and for me, that's kind of the same thing.

EPILOGUE

SIX MONTHS LATER

In a quick scan of the main floor of the house, I spot T-Bone sitting at the kitchen island, poring over case files. That cute little pucker is drawing his eyes together, and he is running his hand through his hair. Twice forward, once backward. Always in the same sequence. His thick blond hair sticks out every which way.

I have the biggest urge to go stand beside him, let my own hands dance through, and kneed those strong shoulders of his I love to nibble on.

But I have a mission.

It's an important one.

Cargo Pants Annihilation Mission.

It's not my first try, but this is it. I can feel it. This will be a victorious operation.

On the very tips of my toes, I make my way up the stairs and into the master bedroom.

The pile of offending cargo pants is *right* there on the very top shelf. T likes to keep them way up high so that I can't mess with them. I always find a way to hide them.

I might have only moved into his place a week ago, but even

before then, I was plotting against his very ugly pants. A man who looks as good as him shouldn't be wrapped up in a beige tent.

I pull a pair down, and they all come tumbling down with a *thunk*. It echoes through the closet out into the bedroom. I stay very still for a few seconds, listening for the telltale sign of a chair scraping against the kitchen tiles.

Nothing. T-Bone must not have heard me.

"Victory is mine," I grunt, bundling all of the pants into my arms.

"Mila, what are you doing?" T-Bone asks, leaning against the bedroom door.

I jump, completely caught. I try to shove the mound of clothes behind my back and fail miserably.

"Nothing," I squeak. "How can a bull be so quiet?"

T ignores my question. "Are you trying to get rid of another pair of my cargo pants?"

"No." I shake my head emphatically, blinking rapidly, trying to play the innocent.

He holds out his hands, a smile on his handsome face. I lean up and kiss the scruff of his face, trying to distract him.

"That won't work, Mila. Give 'em."

"But hear me out. Jeans are just as versatile."

"I like having all my pockets. I like knowing I have everything within arm's reach.

"Your ass is hidden in these." I pout.

"Well, my ass is only for your viewing pleasure, so that's a good thing."

T-Bone pulls the garments out of my hands and piles them on the bed and starts folding them up *just so*.

"You know, it's almost eerie how you are with your cargo pants and black tee uniform."

He arches an eyebrow up at me. "You can't mess with these anymore. There's important stuff I hide in these. I can't have you throwing anything out."

"What do you keep in these?" I ask, reaching out for a pair, my hands digging into the cavernous pockets. I narrow my eyes at him.

"You wash these before putting them away. Why the hell would you *store* stuff in clean pants?"

"You're an impatient woman." He chuckles. He digs inside a pocket and pulls out a black velvet box.

My eyes pop out of my head, and my heart thunders in my chest.

"What is that?" I whisper, taking a step back. "What, T?"

He kneels down in front of me and takes my left hand in his.

"Mila Starling." His deep baritone tone isn't as smooth as it usually is, the thickness of it coated with emotion. "I've loved you for about as long as I've known you. You're wicked smart, you keep me on my toes, and I never know what to expect from you. You surprise me every day, and I'll love nothing more than to keep being surprised by you for the rest of my life. Do me the honor of marrying me?"

My legs give out, and I bury my face in his chest, inhaling his scent. For a few long seconds, I just stay very still, memorizing the thumping of his heart, the smell of his shirt, the feel of his scruff against my forehead. I want to stay in the moment for as long as possible.

"Hey, Mila. Is that a yes?"

"Of course it is." I weep.

"Those better be happy tears," he teases, tucking my hair behind my shoulders.

"They are," I swear. "I didn't expect this. We just moved in together."

"Well, in full disclosure, I was going to wait a few more months to ask you. But since you're intent on getting rid of my favorite hiding spot, it was best to do it now before you toss the ring into the trash."

T slides the ring onto my finger, the shiny stones glimmering in the closet light. It's a white gold band with a black diamond flanked by two rubies.

"This is so on-brand for me." I laugh.

"Yup, I figured you'd say that." He beams with pride, dipping down to kiss me softly.

"You did good, T," I whisper against his lips.

"I agree. I did. Because, somehow, I was led to you."

"Aw." I close my arms around his neck, and he lifts me clear off the floor, his hands cupping my ass as I wrap my legs around him. "You're such a softy for such a big Hairy Coo."

T-Bone kisses me again, squeezing me close to him.

In the animal world, I would be a vampire bat who would feast on his bull blood for thirty minutes a night.

In the human world, I'm his spooky woman, and he's my straight-laced guy. I make him wild, and he keeps me grounded. It works, somehow, that we are such opposites.

"What do you want to do to celebrate our new engagement?" he asks, leading us down the hall and back downstairs.

"Can we watch the new horror flick that just came out?" I ask, running my lips against his.

"How did I know you were going to ask that?" He chuckles.

"We can order a shit-ton of Chinese food, get in our PJs, and watch a movie."

"You've got yourself a deal if we get lemon chicken instead of spicy beef."

I feign a gasp. "We can just get both. That way, you don't have to be a cannibal."

"Why, thanks, future wife, for thinking of me."

"Always," I say before kissing him.

And that one little word sums up T and me perfectly.

Always.

The End.

BAT AND THE JACK

RAGTAG BATS BOOK 2

For Mr. Fire,

1

VERA

This is it.

This is my big moment.

In a few seconds, I won't just have a diploma but a *badge*. I will no longer be Vera Slaski, failed attorney. I'll be *Agent Slaski*.

My palms are a sweaty mess, marring the smooth line of my petal pink skirt every time I flatten it, but I don't care. For once, I don't mind a less-than-perfect attire.

Agent Slaski doesn't care if she's flawless.

She cares about law, justice, and locking up bad guys.

I am a bat. Hear me echolocate.

The small room isn't exactly packed, but there are enough people here to witness my triumph. My parents, who flew in from Toronto, beam at me with pride. They are physically incapable of *not* being proud of me. That's sweet, really. But it also has a price: soul-crushing pressure to make sure that I deserve their praise.

I could quit everything, join a circus, and I'm pretty sure Mom and Dad would still cheer me on.

Beside me, my little sister, Raya, drums her fingers on her distressed jeans. Thin white veins of material, unweaving themselves in protest, stretch against her bent knee. It's seconds away from tearing from an almost-hole to a full one.

Not that Raya would mind if her holey denim broke out with more tears. She doesn't care about anything much. Pissing me off? Now, there is something she excels at with very little effort. Were it an Olympic sport, she'd be the undisputed champ.

When I invited Raya to the ceremony, I specifically requested that she wear something appropriate for the occasion's gravitas.

Raya rolled her eyes and scoffed when I chided her for her attire earlier. A pair of pale blue jeans one chromosome away from being a rag, a white ribbed tank, and combat boots don't scream *Congratulations, graduate.*

People *say* we look alike, but it's a sisterly optical illusion. Where my brown hair is always coiffed into an immaculate elongated bob, Raya lets her waves run wild. Even in the dead of a Canadian winter, she could pass for Queen Beach Bum—nonchalant and unruffled. I'm all about order, while Raya will disorganize her life simply to stress me out.

Sort of like how she dropped out of university to join up with FUCN'A—the Furry United Coalition Newbie Academy—a few weeks after me.

I was *livid*, but today isn't about her or the leather jacket I begged her to ditch before the ceremony began.

This is about me *finally* attaining my goal. I will *finally* be able to make a difference in this world.

My cousin and a FUC forensic anthropologist, Mila Starling, gives me a thumbs-up from across the aisle. Her husband, FUC agent T-Bone Thrussel, gives me an encouraging head nod. They understand what this means to me. Their presence here is heartwarming and emboldening.

Alyce Cooper, director of FUCN'A and all-around badass, rattles off the names of a few other newly minted agents before she calls *my* name.

My heart climbs into my throat as I leap to my feet.

This is it.

I'm getting my FUC badge.

This moment is made all the more amazing because my personal hero, Chase Brownsmith, is here with his wife, Miranda. Mila pulled about a thousand strings to get him here so I could meet him. It's awesome and terrifying all at once. Chase Brownsmith is a legend, and I've based my future on his path. He might be a bear, but I'm positive that I can follow in his paw prints—even if I have to fly overhead.

Chase used to be a lawyer, but the bear joined the ranks of FUC after a series of events that included becoming the target of an evil scientist's scheme, getting kidnapped, being rescued by FUC's sabre tooth bunny, and falling in love with said bunny. He's an inspiration to me. I really thought I could change the world when I became a lawyer. *Wrong.* So damn wrong. I couldn't exactly pick and choose my clients, even if I wanted to.

Let's be real.

There's only a certain amount of mental gymnastics I can do to convince myself that the big, burly man with the rap sheet as long as my two arms combined is *innocent.*

Lawyers don't only protect the innocent.

Sometimes, we have to defend the bad guys.

I didn't like it. At all.

I wanted to be the kind of lawyer who helped people, but I managed to defend crooks and villains in my short career. How was I supposed to live with myself?

I couldn't.

When my older cousin Mila joined FUC, she told me all about Chase Brownsmith. That led me right here. Standing in front of my family and peers and Director Cooper. My life will definitely change forever.

"Come on, Vera." Director Cooper waves me forward like this isn't the most significant few seconds of my life.

Do not fall flat on your face, Vera.

She holds out her hand for me to shake while grabbing a rolled-up sheet of paper. She passes it to me, and my trembling fingers stretch out to take it. It's significant. Monumental. It's not just reaching out for my diploma; it's starting a whole new life.

In my excitement, I zealously grab the diploma and tug.

The sickening *swish* of paper slicing through skin rattles in my brain. Director Cooper winces as a string of blood pebbles along her finger. She wiggles her hand before bringing her injured digit to her mouth to staunch the bleeding.

The most amazing moment of my life is ruined.

I *know* it. I *feel* it.

Do. Not. Pass. Out.

I look away, my stomach rolling with acid. The floor lurches under me, and I reach out to steady myself on the wooden podium. And that's when I see it. The drop of blood on my pale pink skirt.

Flapping membrane.

I grip the pulpit and force deep gulps of air into my lungs. The edge of my vision blurs.

I should've had some blood last night.

On shaky legs, I turn away from Director Cooper. Mom and Dad watch me, expectant and worried. Raya, cocky and annoying, crosses her arms. She *knows* why I'm fighting to stay conscious.

Then there's Chase Brownsmith, lawyer turned agent, standing there looking as perplexed as a vampire bat trying to drink from an iron bull. He frowns, no doubt confused by the sudden stop to the ceremony.

I really should've drank some blood last night.

That's my last conscious thought before my eyes roll back and I fall into the dark.

"Oh, no-no-no. Did she pass out?"

"Sure looks like it."

"Is she okay?"

"This happens sometimes," Mom sighs.

Wait.

Why is my mother here? Where is *here*? Why does my head hurt?

Slowly, I crack one eye open. Above me, the ceiling shimmies and undulates. A few people stand, gawking down; frowns and smiles melt together in the perfect puddle of embarrassment.

"You okay?" Chase asks.

"I've got some carrot cake here." Miranda shoves an overfull container crammed with a piece of cake about the size of a small child toward me.

"It's hardly the time," Chase explains to his wife, grabbing the dish. "She's lost consciousness." He flips the lid open, grabs the cake, and bites into it, leaving merely crumbs behind. If I wasn't about to hurl, I'd be impressed with his eating skill.

Miranda clicks her tongue. "Hence the cake, Chase. It'll level off her blood sugar. Or it would have before you ate it all."

"I really don't think that blood *sugar* is the problem here," Raya taunts.

How my own sister—my flesh and blood—can look so pleased right now is proof alone that I've messed up.

"What in the name of FUC happened?" Director Cooper pipes up, tapping her foot. "Why is one of my future agents in a dead swoon? What is this? A salon for temperamental ladies? Up, Vera. On your feet."

"Yes, Director."

Only problem is, my knees have stopped being knees. Oh, they're still there. My kneecaps are intact, and by rights, I should be able to stand on my own two feet—if my legs weren't suddenly made of jiggling gelatin. The floor *needs* to stop moving before I even *try* to stand.

The smell of blood lingers in the air, the sharp metallic scent prickling my nose with the promise of more fainting.

Pull yourself together, Vera.

"Well?" my future boss snaps. She's not merely tapping her foot; she's ready to break out into a full jig.

Chase takes hold of my hands and hoists me up. I am nothing but a collapsed rag doll in my hero's arms.

Kill. Me. Now.

It took me all of two seconds to fail at being an agent.

"Here we are." The bear shifter helps me into one of the chairs and pats my shoulder like a clumsy uncle who doesn't know how to console his niece. "You okay?"

I nod because what the hell else am I going to do? Admit to a room full of people that I am a vampire bat who passes out at the sight of blood?

I can't.

That would be the fastest way of losing my position as a FUC agent before I even get my hands on my badge.

"Someone really needs to explain to me what's happened," Director Cooper grumbles. "Nolan is on his way to check you out, Vera."

"That's not necessary," I say. Rather, I plead. "I'm fine."

Director Cooper wags her still-bleeding finger at me. "Don't tell lies, Vera. I can sniff 'em out from a mile away."

My ass melts into the chair, and I really long to disappear. Actually, if I'm wishing for things, it would be the ability to not faint every time I see blood. That's what I really need.

"My office," Director Cooper commands before turning on her heels and leaving the room.

Mom sits beside me and drapes her arms around my shoulder. "Are you okay, Moppet?"

I wince at the nickname I've hated since the day it was bestowed on me on my fourth birthday when the clown got a nosebleed. Other kids pass out because clowns are scary as hell and have no business being at a kid's party.

Me? I nosedived into my cake because the man bled.

Dad sighs. I can *feel* his shame and disappointment. "I thought you were over all that."

"She's over it all right," Raya quips. "Looks like I'll lap you." She grins, shrugs, and saunters out.

Not a chance in hell am I going to let Raya get her badge before me.

2

NORBERT

Every time I hear *whistleblower*, my mind fills with the image of a crossing guard. A living, breathing statue stuck in the middle of a busy intersection, wearing an ugly reflective orange vest, hands out to stop traffic and blowing like mad into a bright yellow kazoo.

Cars and trucks perpetually rush by with no concern for the rules or basic human decency.

There the guard stands, honking his kazoo, knowing that, at any second, he could be killed.

That he *will* be killed.

That's me right now.

I'm not using a whistle but my mouth, and I have to admit some pretty horrible things.

The cars are rich and powerful shifters, and the only thing standing between me and certain death is my contact with the Cryptozoian Council.

I miss the simplicity of my farm life.

This is my own damn fault. I got myself into this mess because—just like Icarus—I wanted to fly too close to the sun.

Shoulda stuck to your plants, dude. People suck.

A faded green ball cap is smashed down on my head to hide my easily recognizable tight black curls. The visor knocks against my glasses every time I look around the room. I'm two seconds away from being discovered. I can almost *feel* the walls closing in around me.

I thought meeting in a busy coffee shop would be a good idea. I even picked a town away from my farm. No one *should* be capable of following me back to my place, but that's a problem for Future Me.

First, I have to survive this meeting—*if* my contact actually shows up.

She better be here soon because one of the teenagers buying overly sweet iced drinks is seconds away from taking one gander at me and screaming *Unabomber.*

That'll be the end of that.

I tug on my hat, cross my arms, and scan the coffee shop once again. The pack of teens gathered at the counter shriek and shrill like ordering a coffee is the new mating call.

I miss the quiet of my gardens.

Plants don't talk. Not exactly anyway. Their language is way more subtle, something I appreciate.

It would be way easier if I knew *who* I was expecting.

Val Downer, the agent I'm meeting, gave me no description of herself. All I know is that I was to come into this café, order two coffees, and wait until she made her appearance.

Did I watch one too many spy movies in preparation for this? Maybe.

Not that it helped. My paranoia is ratcheted up to a million. If she isn't here in the next two minutes, I'll leave.

Pfft. Who am I kidding?

I can't go. I'm stuck here, and I'm stuck in my own damn life.

The door swings open, and a petite woman with long black hair braided back from her face walks in with a laptop bag and one serious glower. Without warning or preamble, she grabs the chair at my small round table and plops into it.

"I'm saving that seat," I grumble. "Waiting on someone."

"You don't say," she snaps back, producing a compact computer from her black bag. It sings its way into life before she begins typing furiously at it.

It's on the tip of my tongue to ask her if she is Agent Downer, but it's not like I'm used to this.

Hell, the last time I left my house was six months ago. I hated every second of my time away from my cabin and farm. When I got back, more than a few of my precious crops were dead. No doubt, it was their protest at my absence.

The same would happen again.

If my fennel and Brussels sprout kick the bucket while I'm here, I'll be *seriously* pissed off. I wasn't leaving again for a decade. That was a damn promise.

"Look..." I inject all of my macho manliness into my tone, pitching my voice low. "I really am waiting on someone. If you'd kindly—"

"Don't get excited, Norbert." She rolls her eyes and spins the laptop toward me. The webpage for Vitality stares back at me.

"Oh," I mumble. "So it's you. You're Val Dormer."

She nods. "Did you bring the files?"

It's my turn to give a surreptitious bow of the head, only *slightly* panicked that I might have given myself away to my enemies. "How do I know you're who you say you are?"

She arches a brow, seconds away from scowling. "I don't have time for this."

"And I don't have time to die." Not my best line, but it does the trick.

Downer produces a badge, and on the sly, she flips it toward me. "I'm a koala shifter. Satisfied?"

I slide a small flash drive onto the table. Agent Dormer scoffs at the bright butternut squash-shaped memory stick.

What was she expecting? I'm a botanist. A subsistence farmer to boot. Obviously, I've got a passion for veg.

"It's all here?" She slides the squash into her computer and begins typing away furiously.

"Everything I could get," I correct.

Her brow furrows. "Norbert, if we don't have everything we need in this, our deal is off."

My hands fist on the tabletop. "No way. They'll kill me if they find out I have these files. You *swore* you'd give me protection."

She has the nerve to wave me off. "If the Cryptozoian Council and our FUCN'A go-between, Erhart Knop, don't have enough, neither organization can continue the investigation. And without a proper case, we can't put the company on trial."

"Everything you need is in there," I promise. "Now, you guaranteed that your people could keep me safe. That you'd stop the toxic waste dumping. I've held up my end of the bargain."

Downer makes a noncommittal sound, and I wonder what kind of disposition koala shifters have. Could she dispatch me in two seconds flat with a well-aimed blow, or would she have to be a bit more creative about it?

"We're good?" I repeat, ready to leave and move on with my simple life.

I'm never, ever getting involved with a human again.

Val narrows her keen eyes, a small pucker drawing her brows together. "You're hiding something."

Somethings. S. Plural.

My shoulders tense, but I try to wave her off. "What?" I cough. "No." I fake-sneeze. "Not in the least." I grab my cup of coffee, toying with the sleeve. *What a waste of natural resources.*

"Norbert," she warns. "What aren't you telling me?"

"Why would you ask that?"

She doesn't know. She can't. It's impossible. Be cool, Norbert. Be cool as dirt in the spring.

"You're twitchy." Val crosses her arms, continuing her staredown. "If we can't rely on you, you'll be removed to a secret and undisclosed location."

"I'm not hiding anything," I lie. Might as well be a cucumber growing in the garden for all the lying around I'm doing *right* to Val Downer's face.

"Fine. If you say so. We'll figure it out if you are, you know. We're sending a FUC agent to keep watch over you. They're going to stay here with you until you testify for the Cryptozoian Council. Keep you safe."

I snort. "Sure. Keep me safe from Lisbeth Bannon."

"She's not all-powerful."

"She's trying to be," I shoot back.

Downer nods. "Hopefully, this will be the first step to stopping her."

And just like that, as fast as she arrived, Agent Downer is gone. She leaves no more information about my protection or the next step. My gut churns with panic. This might've been a grievous mistake.

But it's too late now.

I can't put the knowledge back into its hiding spot like I can't undo the experiments.

All I *can* do is go back to my farm and hope I'm around for harvest.

3

VERA

I'm a broken bat.

Not a piece of wood dudes use to hurl balls at each other. Nope. A flying, blood-sucking vampire bat. Itty bitty with a biological need to drink a bit of blood every single day to survive.

I'm broken because I am *terrified* of blood.

The mere sight of it makes me queasy. I can't stomach it. It's a damn miracle that I can live with so very little of it. It's even more of a wonder that I managed to complete my training at the Furry United Coalition Newbie Academy without falling in a dead faint.

Every time someone got hurt, I teetered on the edge of discovery.

Maybe it would've been better if someone had called me out on it before yesterday.

I didn't get my badge.

I got *grounded*.

Director Cooper might as well have stamped *Cadet* on my forehead in permanent marker. I am not allowed to graduate or go on missions until I can prove to her that I can be around vast quantities of blood without passing out.

Vast quantities.

Those were the exact words she used once Nolan was done checking me over.

Every single person I walked past today gave me the side-eye. I could *hear* their pity and scorn.

I wanted to spend the day in my dorm room, feeling sorry for myself, but Mila and T-Bone stopped by and basically forced me to have lunch with them.

At least they keep nocturnal hours like me, which means that the cafeteria wasn't packed. I settled at one of the tables, too emotional to eat anything. My cousin and her dashing husband grabbed food, bickering like an old married couple despite the fact they haven't been paired up for all that long.

They met on a mission, fell in love, got engaged after six months, and before Mila could walk down the aisle in a black tutu like she wanted to, she was pregnant.

And to think their love story never would have happened if Sveta Markov hadn't escaped from prison. The notorious mass murderer known as the Bloody Doctor is my aunt and Mila's mom. The former hematologist is obsessed with blood. It turned into full-blown mania that led her down some dark and seriously twisted paths.

The Bloody Doctor is *all* about the blood.

Apparently, I'm the only vampire bat who can't cope with blood.

It's not one of those ironic situations.

I had an aversion to blood *way* before Aunt Sveta was caught. The long—disgusting—list of her crimes didn't exactly turn me on to blood. She loves it too much, and I love it none. A balance, life is not.

"Stop moping," Mila instructs with her teacher's voice. My hugely pregnant cousin is clad all in black, her T-shirt, which reads, *I grow bones* with a baby skeleton, stretched over her baby bump. She rubs at it with a wince of pain. She's about to pop but refuses to go on maternity leave. There is every chance she'll go into labor in her creepy basement office, surrounded by bones.

"This is for you, Vera," She shoves a plateful of steak tartar right under my nose. "Compliments of our dear director."

My stomach rolls with bile. My hand flies to my mouth as I screw my eyes shut. "Nope." The mound of raw ground beef oozes blood onto the white plate. The tuft of green garnish is downright comical. As if *that* makes the dish palatable.

"Come *on*," Mila scolds. "It's not that bad. It's actually delicious. You need it to survive."

"I don't see how." I turn my head away, thankful for my lip gloss. The happy aroma of cotton candy wafting up from my lips saves me from passing out. *Again*.

Mila clicks her tongue and digs into the tartar with gusto. "You know Alyce won't let you go on your first assignment until you get some blood down your gullet." She points a bloody fork at me. "No hurling."

"Leave the poor woman alone, Mila." T-Bone settles into the seat beside her, his hand instinctively going to her stomach. She slaps it away.

"Hands to yourself, beefcakes, or I'll make a meal out of you."

T-Bone beams at her with cow eyes, full of love and adoration. "You're so motherly. It gives me so much joy to know how caring you'll be for our little one."

Mila scowls at him. "I better be growing a bat. If I gotta push out an enormous Hairy Coo, I'm never speaking to you again."

He kisses her cheek before tearing into his massive sandwich.

Undeterred by her potential calving, Mila nudges the rest of the steak tartar toward me. "T's had some before, and he enjoys it. Give it a try."

Until that second, I didn't know it was possible to feel like a color, but I am definitely the color green. Not envy. Nope. Green like cartoons before they blow chunks.

This week has turned into a nightmare. I peek down at my clothes to make sure I'm not naked. I'm not entirely convinced I'm clothed with the way things keep going from bad to worse.

I'm fully dressed, and this isn't a night terror.

It's real life.

Damn.

I *almost* had my diploma in hand. My whole destiny hinged on a papercut, and *voila*. Just like that, all my plans vanished.

You don't know what shame is until you pass out in front of your peers and own personal hero.

Now *everyone* knows I'm the vampire bat with an aversion to blood. The shame!

Oh. And Director Cooper is keeping me grounded and as a cadet until I manage to drink some blood. I don't think it's fair to add a condition to my training this late in the game, but Alyce Cooper can do whatever she wants. She's the boss.

"Maybe I'll just go back to practicing law." I don't mean it, but I've got no clue how to get past this. I am forever doomed as a cadet. Raya will lap me and wave her badge in my face every chance she gets.

Mila shakes her head in response, her firetruck red hair flying everywhere. "Not a chance. This is way too important." She pushes the plate closer to me. "First step tartar, second step blood."

"Stop," I plead.

"You're giving us a bad name," Mila quips.

I snort out a laugh. As the resident forensic anthropologist with a penchant for listening to death metal while talking to the bones of murder victims, Mila isn't exactly the picture of a well-adjusted adult. She is married to a cattle shifter: the very same animal vampire bats are known to prey on. Not to mention her addiction to inappropriate shirts. I love my cousin, but last week, she taught a class while wearing a tee that read, *Will Work For A Bone.*

That makes us eccentric. Not my aversion to blood.

It doesn't *really* give us a bad name. On the contrary, the cadets actually adore her, even when she has full-on conversations with bones. Mila is unusual, that's it.

"Yum," Raya exclaims, plopping down in the chair beside me. Her fork dives right for the tartar. A huge jiggly bite goes right into her mouth, sending a fresh wave of nausea bubbling in my gut. "So good." She licks the fork with the evilness only a sibling could muster.

She relishes the thought of getting her badge before me. Not that I can let that happen.

The shame of being lapped by my little sister has me reaching for the fork.

Almost.

I'm saved by the appearance of Director Cooper. She points a finger at me before hooking her thumb over her shoulder.

"You're coming with me." She has all the seriousness of a woman on a mission.

I mumble goodbyes to my family members, wondering how worse things are about to get.

Alyce doesn't speak a word to me until we are in her office with the door closed behind us. She leans against her desk and crosses her arms. She's formidable. She drips authority and power as she stands there, assessing me.

"I'm furious with you."

"Yes, ma'am."

"I don't like being lied to, and your omission was basically a lie."

"I'm sorry, ma'am."

"Oh, you will be."

My heart sinks. Maybe since our conversation yesterday, she's changed her mind, and now she wants to kick me out of the Academy for real.

"Sit." She nudges her chin toward one of the chairs. I sink into it, grateful to give my trembling legs a break. "I have your first assignment."

I straighten my back and plaster on an unaffected mask, but inside I'm doing a series of cartwheels. "Thank you, Director Cooper. I won't let you down."

"Did I say first assignment?" She clicks her tongue. "My bad. What I meant was, I'm sending you out on a test. Basically a babysitting mission. There shouldn't be any bloodshed."

Her large eyes watch me, studying my face for a reaction. I brought this on myself, I know that, but it doesn't make it any less painful. I don't know how to respond, so I merely nod.

"We'll talk about your status as an agent as soon as you return."

"So I'm not an agent?"

Her glowering look is all of the answer I need.

"Right."

"Take comfort in the fact that because of you, from now on, we are checking cadets for reactions to blood."

I wring my fingers together. *Yikes.* I can't defend my actions. Not in the least. Director Cooper is right to be worried. What would've happened to me if I passed out during a call? I could've gotten myself or my partner seriously hurt if I passed out at the wrong moment.

"You'll be spending the next little while with an important witness. He isn't necessarily in *that* much danger, but he needs to be kept alive at all costs. Do you understand me?"

"Yes, Director Cooper."

"Good. While you're babysitting this whistleblower, maybe you can train yourself to be around blood. Just make sure it's not Dr. Norbert Palomer's blood. We definitely need him alive."

With a wave of her hand, she dismisses me without giving me further details.

Not that any of it matters. Director Cooper is giving me a chance to redeem myself, and I won't squander it. Whatever she asked of me, I will gladly do it if it leads to a badge at the end of the assignment.

I'm back in business!

4

NORBERT

My log cabin, a small little structure I built with my own two hands, stands in the middle of a forest right by a spring. There's a natural break in the trees where I planted loads of fruits, vegetables, flowers, and basically anything I need to survive.

It's my haven.

No one knows where this place is. It doesn't have an address in the conventional sense, and it's off-grid.

I've got electricity, but it's all powered by sustainable energy. Sun, elbow grease, that kind of stuff. The internet is spotty, only accessible at a specific time of night when the earth's orbit passes over a specific satellite. I was lucky to be willed down this spot, one of the perks of being the son of two environmentalists with an eye on land and resource preservation.

Not that my parents would be proud of me if they were alive.

I'm in a right pickle.

Everything they taught me went out of the window. And for what? All because my ego got the best of me.

That and my dick.

Point out a man who doesn't get overly excited when his boss taps him for a special and *super*-secret project, and I will show you a damn liar. But, of course, seven months ago, I didn't know *why* the research was special and secret.

Now I know.

Replace special with *maniacal* and secret with *illegal*.

Quick tip: if something sounds too good to be true, it most definitely is.

Lisbeth Bannon made it all sound so damn simple. All I had to do was tweak my research from beauty products to medicine.

Well, medicine adjacent.

Just unlock the secret of immortality.

Lisbeth Bannon and her rich cronies want to live forever.

If we hadn't been sleeping together, Lisbeth *never* would have learned about my parents—how they died from some mysterious illness that had no name and definitely no cure. She dangled some pretty powerful and motivating stuff over my old wound.

You could save other people from diseases, Norbert. All kinds of illnesses could be cured and completely eradicated from existence because of you.

I fell for her bullshit hook, line, and sinker.

That's what I get for interacting with *people* again.

I get roped into a scheme so nefarious I'm now a prisoner in my own home. I have to let an agent live with me.

I hope whoever this dude is, he keeps to himself. Hell, maybe he'll be okay with throwing up a tent and hunkering down in the great outdoors. Protective custody doesn't have to mean that I've got to share my territory. It's not like my cabin has space for another soul, anyway.

There's one bedroom. One bed. One tiny bathroom. Everything is powered by my personal army of solar panels.

I've got acres of beautiful forest to explore. Thankfully, it's also my security system. My little house and farm are so deep in the woods that no one can find me unless they have my direct GPS coordinates.

The only person who has them now is Agent Val Downer.

I'm out on a ledge with this, and if whistleblowing kills me, it'll be because I trusted the wrong person.

Again.

With a series of grumbles, I slide on my boots and plaid shirt. My crops and gardens need some tender loving care. It's not their fault I've gone and fucked up my life.

I follow the path from my front porch to the back of the house. The small barn—a red shed, really—holds all of the equipment, but I bypass it, heading straight for my gardens. I'm pleased to see that everything is growing just fine. There are slugs wreaking havoc on my lettuce, but that's to be expected. I mostly plant it for them, anyway.

As a vegetarian, I've got to eat something more substantial than salads. That's why I've got an actual pumpkin patch. It's more of a *gourd* patch. All manners of squashes grow there. They're a great source of protein, and they're easy enough to grow.

Their outer protective shells are precisely why I picked *them* for my experiments. As much as I love all plants, I don't trust those that grow bare and vulnerable.

Strawberries are delicious, and they're rampant. Plant one bush of them, and you're sure to be overrun with the weed.

Biologically, it makes sense. It's such a fragile fruit; it has to be a persistent grower lest it is completely destroyed.

Plants with protective layers just make more sense to me. They're just as easy to grow, but I don't have to worry about them.

Sort of like how I don't have to worry about myself out here in the wilderness.

I might be a pumpkin, my skin is thick.

That's a whole other problem I need to fix.

If I have to be a pumpkin, I'd rather be sentient instead of morphing into a literal defenseless *thing*.

As I inspect my crops, I let my mind wander. This is where I do some of my best thinking. A nice long walk through my field usually sparks some kind of idea. I'm in serious need of some inspiration.

"Oh, you are parched, my darlings," I coo to a row of corn. I remove my finger from the dry soil and tut. If it doesn't rain soon, I'll have to use my rain barrels to water my harvest if I want to eat in the next few months.

For another little while, I roam and inspect, still clinging to the hope that something will pop into my mind.

There's nothing.

I'm way too distracted by my meeting with Val Downer. Giving her all of the information and files I have on Vitality Holdings was the right thing to do, but it also put me in hot water.

Not the pleasant kind found in the warm spring.

Nope.

The kind that will flay my hide raw.

My satellite phone is tucked in my back pocket, not a usual thing, but I'm eager to hear back from Agent Downer. She dropped *protective custody* like it was nothing.

It's not.

It's terrifying.

I've got to be careful now when I'm nervous. It's dangerous for my health—and my secret.

As if the koala shifter senses my thoughts, the phone goes off.

"There's an agent on the way," Agent Downer says by way of greeting. "Should be there sometime today. FUC will be sending some supplies later, too. I'll check in on you every now and again, but please keep a low profile."

I snort because Agent Downer has never seen my home, and it shows. There is no one around for miles and miles. "I'll make sure to hide from the family of squirrels that's taken residence in my shed."

"This isn't a joke, Norbert. If Bannon finds you..."

"I know." *Fuck, do I.* A shudder works its way up my spine.

You know what feels great? Being a fully grown man who has to hide because his ex is a psycho killer with *actual* plans for world domination.

I sure know how to pick 'em.

After disconnecting the call, I head back to my cabin and plop onto my sofa and look down at my crotch. "You're not to get us into trouble again, do you hear me? It's Mistress Palm for the rest of our lives now. Hope that makes you happy."

I throw my head back and focus on the wood grain of the overhead wood beams. The latticework makes me ache.

Everything in this world is connected by life's tendrils. Every single *thing* is linked to everything else.

I have to sever myself even more from that. As lonely and as alone as I've been for most of my life, I've learned my lessons now.

Those ties and bonds only lead to trouble and bullshit heartache.

It's not like I loved Lisbeth. That's not why my chest hurts. What makes my inside want to jump ship is the betrayal. It boils in the marrow of my bones.

There is an easy solution.

I am *never* going to trust another human. Ever.

Fuck loneliness.

I'll just expand my garden. Plants don't let you down.

5

VERA

When Director Cooper gave me coordinates—not an address—I got a little excited. My heart fluttered with hope because she trusted me with a mission, but now that I'm looking at a dirt path suffocated by overgrown shrubs and arching tree branches, I'm not entirely sure she isn't playing a prank on me or something.

That's not exactly her style, but I'm not too keen on turning down a road that isn't actually a road that leads to potentially nowhere.

The GPS is *adamant* that I turn right.

I am *adamant* that I am about to die by driving off the ledge of a steep cliff.

What would Chase Brownsmith do?

He'd go.

Of course he would because he is a professional and a trained FUC agent who believes in his capabilities. I might not be an agent *yet*, and I definitely have no faith in my abilities, but I can fake it.

No one is around to see that my hands tremble on the steering wheel. I can just turn the wheel a few degrees to the right. I can do that. I can turn the armored car toward the direction of the GPS and go babysit a witness.

Flaming guano.

I don't know why I'm so nervous as the SUV hops and stumbles on the rough road. Every time I'm jarred, my gut reminds me that it's there, full of acid and an impressive projectile capacity.

The moon, nothing but a fingernail clipping in the dark, cloudy sky, is no help at all. The farther I drive, the more I hunch over the wheel as the shadows draw me in. I'm not scared of the nighttime— I'm nocturnal.

I *am* terrified of buffing this up. *That* equals never getting my badge. Failure is simply not an option for me.

Panic settles like a best friend in my sternum. The aching flutters pull up a seat in my brain, kick back, and relax like they own the place.

I am a bat. Hear me echolocate.

Say it three times fast and hope you believe the lie.

Finally, after three-hundred-and-two hours, I spot it.

A small log cabin pops out from the line of trees. There are no lights on inside, which isn't exactly surprising, given the late hour. Dr. Norbert Palomer is probably asleep at nearly eleven p.m.

I didn't get many details about him, but I'm expecting an older man. Maybe a hippie in his seventies, a throwback to another generation. I only hope that my arrival doesn't give the man a heart attack. Scaring my charge to death doesn't exactly scream *I'm a wonderful agent*.

With hands doing their best impressions of a paint shaker, I park the vehicle and grab my duffel bag, swinging it over my shoulder. A quick glance at the obscure house and its surroundings reveals very little about Dr. Palomer.

Director Cooper didn't exactly tell me *why* he is to be in our protection. All I know is that I must protect the fragile human.

I roll my shoulders back and rap my knuckles on the wooden door three times. The taps reverberate in the night, but there is no sign of life within. Then, with more gusto than necessary, I knock again.

Nothing.

A shaky breath stutters out of me. "Dr. Palomer, I've been sent by the Cryptozoian Council and FUC. I'm Agent Slaski." Okay, so that's a lie, but he doesn't need to know that.

Still nothing.

What if the old man is dead? What if someone already got to him?

I drop my duffel on the porch swing and crack my knuckles before grabbing the door handle. A wiggle and a jiggle tell me it's unlocked.

Not a good sign.

I push my way in, letting my eyes do the work. There don't appear to be any light switches, which isn't a surprise. I didn't expect this place to have electricity. Not that I *need* a light source.

My night vision is pretty great as a nocturnal creature, but that's not my real secret weapon. I click my tongue against my teeth and wait silently as the echo builds an image in my mind.

That's all it takes for me to know the layout of the cabin. There's a small living room to my right. One plaid couch, one massive coffee table with books and papers piled precariously high. To the left are a bedroom and bathroom. I'm shocked that both are empty.

Another click of my teeth as I walk on toward the kitchen uncovers a door that leads down.

Huh.

I didn't expect a basement in a secluded log cabin.

"Dr. Palomer?" I call down the stairs as I step into the thick obscurity. "I'm here to protect you." A snort bubbles out of me. What a weird thing to say. "I've been sent by your contact, Val Downer."

The stairs end in a narrow hallway with a single direction: a steel door. The hairs on the back of my neck stand, making me shiver.

A door in a subterranean corridor doesn't exactly announce *this is safe*.

It actually reminds me of serial killers and cannibals.

"Hello?" I ask for the thousandth time, pushing my way through the heavy door.

There is no answer.

I run my hands along the wall, my fingers hitting against a nob. I turn it a quarter turn, and somewhere off in the distance, the whir of a generator kicks into life.

Overhead, a few bulbs blink into life, slowly unveiling a sizable room that's half lab, half greenhouse. The walls, gray concrete, match the stainless-steel countertops. The back of the space is overrun with huge plants, long and vibrant green shrubs, which I could never name.

"What is this guy *into*?" I mumble, continuing my exploration.

The lab is deserted save for an enormous pumpkin in the middle of the room. I kneel down and poke at it, the bright orange hue way too vivacious to be natural.

The large gourd squeaks a human and living sound.

I stumble back, my hand going to my chest in shock.

What the guano?

The squash shimmies and vibrates as it lets loose another squeal.

Demonic pumpkin!

This is how I die. Killed by a possessed gourd.

Taking a step back, I nearly fall flat on my ass. I steady myself, gripping the stainless-steel counter.

"I'm Agent Vera Slaski from FUC. I'm looking for Dr. Norbert Palomer."

I've lost my mind. I am talking to a pumpkin. If Chase Brownsmith could see me now...

Any good agent would have been scanning the lab for signs of intrusion or for the good doctor, but I'm riveted—and okay, a lot terrified.

The giant veg isn't behaving like any other plant I've ever seen.

Vegetation doesn't *have* behavior.

Yet there the pumpkin goes, vibrating like it's filled with cell phones and bees and vibrators.

"Hell—" My greeting dies when the explosion happens.

A loud *splat* sends wet and cold pumpkin guts scattering every-where in the lab. My horrified gasp strangles itself when I finally manage to wipe pumpkin goo from my eyes.

Standing in the orange carcass is a very tall, very *naked* man.

6

VERA

The naked Pumpkin Man stands there, in all his buff glory, blinking at me in shock.

"Dude!" I turn, slapping my hands over my eyes.

It's too late, though. I've seen *it*.

Oh, sweet heavenly gourd.

"Who are you, and how did you get in here?" His baritone voice sparks tiny shivers up my spine.

"I'm Agent Vera Slaski." My voice trembles because there is a nude man behind me. A very *au naturel* and very attractive man.

Did he just climb out of a pumpkin?

Do. Not. Panic. If you can turn into a two-ounce bat, there's going to be a logical, scientific explanation for this.

"I've been sent by FUC," I continue, my tone as wobbly as my legs. "I came in through the front door, which wasn't locked. I was concerned for Dr. Palomer. Would you happen to know if he's around?"

"I'm doct—" He sighs. "I'm Norbert."

Hell to the no.

There's not a chance in this wild world that the person I was sent to protect is Pumpkin Man. "Think you could put some clothes on?"

He mumbles something under his breath, but I don't quite catch it.

"I'm decent."

He most certainly is *not* decent.

Dr. Norbert Palomer has wrapped a small towel—the *smallest towel known to man*—around his trim waist. Above it is a deep V, planes and valleys of abdominal muscles that have no place on a Norbert. Soft black hair pulls my focus back down to his towel-covered area.

Nope. Eyes up, Agent.

Only, that isn't helpful.

His pecs are as toned and defined as his abs, and his shoulders are so wide and strong I have the urge to *bite* into the corded muscle.

Me. Broken bat that I am, I want to nibble on him like my favorite snack.

Flaming guano bomb, but this isn't good.

He runs a hand through thick, lush black curls, brushing the hair away from his deep and fiery hazel eyes. He grabs a pair of glasses from the counter and slides them up his patrician nose, blinking frantically at me.

Look, I am not the kind of woman who swoons or loses her mind over a dude. I reserve that for blood.

I haven't had a boyfriend in nearly three years, nor have I felt any compulsion to tie myself to the opposite sex.

But.

I've never exactly seen a man like Dr. Norbert Palomer—especially not *nude.*

It is exceedingly hot down here. It *has* to be a hothouse or something. I wish I could fan my face for a bit of relief.

"What are you doing here?" he asks, opening a cupboard.

"FUC sent me."

He turns toward me, and his bespeckled gaze takes me all in. I gulp because—*sweet, suffering mammal*—he is one intense man.

"They sent *you?*" he snorts and, with a twirling finger, demands that I turn. "Do they even understand the danger I'm in?" he says to my back.

"Meaning what, exactly?" My temper flares, twinging my retort with sass. "I assure you, Doctor. I am more than capable of protecting you from whatever threat you face. Even exploding pumpkins."

"Vera, you said?"

"Yes." *Ouf.* He draws out the *a*, turning it into an *ah* that evokes dirty, naughty, sweaty flutters in my nether region.

"Do you know why I need protective custody?"

"Yes."

He chuckles. "I really doubt they told you everything."

"Well." This guy. Arrogant, much? "I have to keep you alive long enough so that you can testify in a trial. I don't know why exploding pumpkins are part of this, but there you have it."

"I'm not an exploding pumpkin. You can face me, by the way."

I turn, ready to reply, but my mind is as lost as a bat in a tanning bed.

Norbert has covered his dangler and other enticing bits with a pair of black jeans so faded they might as well be gray, a white tee, and a red plaid shirt, unbuttoned with the sleeves rolled up to his elbows.

Note to self: forearms can be erotically charged.

"Do you often garden in your underground lab in the dark while nude?" The words blurt out of me, and I go twenty shades of red.

"I wasn't gardening." He runs a hand back through his hair, but the stubborn curl that loops over his forehead takes position again. He huffs out a breath to remove it, but it's no use. "You're sworn to secrecy while you're here, right?"

"Basically, but if you murder someone, I'll have to arrest you."

Norbert—I really need to find him a better name—purses full lips at me. How a pair of lips can be so damn captivating framed by a short black beard, I've got no clue. The good doctor has this whole '90s grunge vibe going. It would have made teenage Vera loopy for the bad boy.

Only he's not a bad boy.

He's a fully grown man under my charge. Maybe I should stop ogling.

"I wasn't gardening. The lights are on a timer. They go out when there's no movement for ten minutes."

Something prickles at the base of my neck. "*Steaming blood bag*," I gasp. "You were the pumpkin?" I shake my head, clearing the webs of insanity weaving my thoughts together. "*You* were *in* the *pumpkin*?"

He bristles and crosses those sexy, muscular, veiny arms. "I wasn't in the pumpkin. I *am* the pumpkin."

I blink at him. "I'm sorry. You shift into *vegetation*?" I shake my head once again. "No. That's impossible. There's no way."

"I don't have the time or desire to explain, but yes. I shift into a pumpkin when under threat."

"You turn into a pumpkin when you're scared?" What in the damn hell has Director Cooper gotten me into?

"No." His hazel eyes narrow into angry slits. "Not when I'm *scared*. When I'm *threatened*."

"Isn't that the same thing?"

"Absolutely not." He puffs out his chest. "Scared if when I feel *fear*. Threatened is different. More like a threat is *right* in front of me, or I'm in danger."

"Sounds like the same thing to me."

"Well, it's not."

"So if I were to threaten you right now, you'd turn into a jack-o'-lantern?" I grab a scalpel from the counter and point it at him. "Get on with it, Cinderella."

"Don't," he growls. "It's no laughing matter."

I want to make a joke about pumpkin spice. Something like, *Rub your spice all over me, Jack*, but I decide against it.

Suddenly, being a non-agent, a broken bat who can't ingest blood, all of that vanishes. I'm not the only fucked-up person in the world.

It's comforting.

It's also a little bit attractive.

There is some cosmic thing, some impossible-to-decipher pull, binding us together.

"Explain to me how a grown man can morph into a gourd."

"No. I can't, and I won't. It can't be common knowledge, so forget that you even saw that."

I take in the pumpkin guts still scattered across the lab. "Unlikely to happen. I need to know how to deal with this in case we come under attack."

"Agent Vera, my predicament is none of your concern." He continues, spewing all kinds of scientific terms that go way above my head. Maybe if Mila was here, she'd understand.

I lift a hand. "Okay, Jack. Enough with the blabbering. If you don't tell me what the hell happened here, I'll grind you up for my next latte." *You'll be delicious; I just* know *it.*

I think my comment is hilarious. He does *not.*

Jack pushes his glasses up his long, slender nose, the brightness of his gaze burning through the thick lens. "I'd prefer if you called me by my name."

"Which is?" I already forgot it. I dub him Jack, and he will forever be known as nothing else in my mind.

Jack, the Nude King in the Pumpkin Patch.

"Norbert," he reminds me uselessly.

"Right, well, don't get your plaid in a twist. Explain the pumpkin thing."

"It's late. We should get to bed."

"I'm nocturnal," I snicker. "It's basically early morning for me. I've got all night to chat." I smile at him sweetly.

His scowl isn't sexy *at all*. Not even when that stubborn forehead tendril quivers from his annoyance.

"Come on, Jack," I tease, hopping onto the counter. "Tell me how you became the Pumpkin King."

7

NORBERT

Agent Vera Slaski hops onto the stainless-steel counter, crosses one leg over the other, and props up her head by cupping her cheek. Her perfect Cupid's bow, painted pink and glossy, turns up into a smile.

Do not be pulled in.

Her eyes are a shade of hazel that flirts with amber and emerald. Every time she blinks her long inky lashes, I get a new color show that makes me want to lean in and study her.

She's an agent. A shifter.

I. Do. Not. Trust. People.

Her brown hair is short, barely brushing against her shoulders, but it's thick and a shade so rich it reminds me of melted chocolate. I want to bury my face in it and take a whiff. I bet it smells better than any damn thing in this world.

Stand the fuck down, Norbert, you absolute perv.

After everything that's happened with Lisbeth Bannon and Vitality Holdings, I am definitely *not* ready to trust another human.

Or another shifter, as this case may be.

I'm not about to spill all of my secrets to an agent that will have to report everything I say to her superiors.

There's every chance that I'll be charged and jailed if FUC and the Cryptozoian Council ever figure out just how involved I was with all of the testing and research.

As noble as I was raised to be, I don't have a burning need to be locked behind bars because of an experiment gone wrong.

It's not like I hurt anyone. Only myself—and a few pumpkins.

"You really won't tell me how you came to be a pumpkin?"

"No."

"But what if it's information I need to protect you?"

"It won't be," I assure her.

"Well, at the very least, tell me what I need to do if you do turn into a great big veg again."

"Pumpkins are fruit, actually," I mutter. "It's a seed-bearing fruit. Not a vegetable. To the point, it's a gourd, which in tu—" I stop blathering when I spot the grin on Vera's face.

By rakes and hoes, she's lovely.

That's a dangerous thought.

I can't stand there, melting and going all gooey for the FUC agent here to defend me should Vitality Holdings send a hit man or six. Not when I have to keep so many things secret.

But she already knows one of them. What's another?

Nope. Not happening.

Vera Slaski, with the pretty lips, lush hair, and shining eyes, is definitely the last person I will—can—trust.

"I have quite the imagination, you know," she says. "I'll just make up something." She taps her chin, scrunching up her button nose in a cute way that has my male equipment perking up. "When a mommy pumpkin and a daddy pumpkin grow in the same patch—"

"I beg of you, stop." I rip my glasses off to pinch the bridge of my nose.

"Once upon a time, there was a botanist. He grew all kinds of gourds. One day, he noticed that—"

"It was an accident," I grumble, and Vera finally lapses into a beat of silence.

"You accidentally turned yourself into a gourd?"

"Well, yes and no. I was doing some minor experiments, and things got out of hand."

"So you don't have a full family growing in that garden then? You're a real boy, Pinocchio?"

"I'm a real man," I amend because let's be real. Vera saw me in the nude. If she thinks my hardware isn't all man, maybe she didn't get a good enough look.

Maybe I need to remedy that.

Fascinated, I watch as an adorable blush creeps up Vera's cheeks. She tucks her brown hair behind her ears, her hand landing at the base of her throat.

"I can't give you any more details than that." My voice is gravel and sand. I can't stop staring at the pink hue of her lovely face.

"And so you explode every time you shift back into a human?"

I tense. "Not quite."

"I get the sense that you don't trust me. I understand, I do. You don't know me, and obviously, if you need protective custody, it means that you might have some paranoia."

"I'm not paranoid."

"Right. Well, I was a lawyer before I became an agent. How about we operate under the pretense that we have attorney-client privileges? Whatever you share stays between the two of us."

"Unless I murder someone," I shoot back, throwing her earlier words back at her.

"Exactly. Though, if there is a threat, please let me deal with that. I've got a license to kill." She winks, and I swear, all the oxygen whooshes out of me.

No. Nope, Norbert. Avert your eyes. This siren is not for you.

"What kind of shifter are *you*?" I ask in hopes of turning the attention away from myself.

"Vampire bat," she answers with a shrug. "Mini but mighty, I assure you."

"A vampire bat?" I repeat.

"Yep."

"So you're about this big when you shift?" I cup my hands where a baby bird could easily nestle.

Vera nods. "Like I said, mini but mighty."

"And what if my enemies send a rhino or a bear? You'll duke it out with a huge, hulking predator?"

She leaps off the counter and stalks toward me. Vera isn't short, but I'm tall. Her head reaches just above my chin, but that doesn't stop her from trying to be intimidating. She jabs a finger into the center of my chest before pointing it at me.

"Listen here, Jack. *I'm* a predator. I have to drink blood every day to survive. I've got the sharpest incisors in the mammal world. My saliva has some anticoagulant particles. If I wanted to, I could bleed a one-ton bear dry in a matter of minutes."

For the first time in my life, anger and attraction get confused. Vera pokes my chest again. This time she keeps her finger pressed into me. The touch, reprimanding as it is, has no right being so damn sexy.

It is.

My dick notices all kinds of things about the batty lady.

There are gold and amber flecks in her eyes, and her brown hair shimmers like strands of cooper. Her lips are full and pink with the sweet scent of cotton candy. If I crushed Vera into my arms, all our good parts would line up and touch in a perfect greeting.

"Anything else you wanna say, *pumpkin*?"

"I'm going to bed," I announce.

Vera's gaze flashes, and her breath hitches. Or maybe that's my imagination. There's a tiny possibility that I'm attracted to the FUC agent.

That means I need to be a dick, set up some solid boundaries, and make sure Vera keeps her distance.

Should be easy enough for me to manage, given that I very rarely interact with other humans. They don't call me the Reclusive Botanist for nothing.

"We can have this whole night and day thing down. You do your guard duty thing while I sleep, and then I'll take the daytime hours. There's no need for us to interact at all."

I don't miss the hurt and disappointment that plays across Vera's features.

Okay, so maybe I'm not that comfortable being an ass with Vera Slaski, but that is exactly *why* I have to do it.

The last time I was pulled in by attraction, things didn't end so well for me. Or for the environment. Or for the entire human race.

"I'm gonna clean this up and hit the hay."

Vera makes her way out of the lab without looking back. If the basement wasn't soundproof, I would most likely hear her pacing the floor above me as I wipe down the floor, counter, and cupboards of pumpkin. Hell, some even found its way up to the ceiling. I probably spend too much time cleaning up my shifter mess, but better that than another charged exchange with my keeper.

It's nearly midnight by the time I climb up the stairs. Vera is nowhere to be seen, and I assume she's gone to take a lap around the property.

Good.

It's better that way.

I complete my nighttime ablutions playing a new game: thought ping pong.

Every two seconds, an image of Vera pops into my brain, forcing me to lop at it. But it bounces back, gathering speed and clarity while I brush my teeth and change into a pair of pajama bottoms. I close the bedroom door behind me before Vera can return from whatever agent business she's taking care of.

Even if she *is* an agent, I don't feel right making her sleep on the couch. It's not exactly the most comfortable surface. Maybe we can share the bed.

At the thought, my dick stirs and starts to thicken, but I knock the thought far away.

Ping.

It whips round right back at me, whipping my brain as if I were playing against a pro.

Not share-share, I explain to myself like a true squash-brained dude. *We won't be in bed at the same time.*

Since I've already established that Vera can keep her nocturnal hours, we can both use the bed. At different times. Not together.

Not even if she finds a way into my dreams. I'll ping pong that to the depths of hell before I dream of Vera Slaski.

8

VERA

As it turns out, babysitting a grown man is boring.

Even if said grown man is a complete *dish*.

Even if the complete dish turns into an enormous pumpkin.

Of all the damn things to shift into, a large orange gourd is the last thing anyone should want to morph into. Jack indicated that it happened by accident, but I'm not clear how that can even happen.

Granted, I'm no science buff, but it seems to me that I've walked into Frankenstein's lab. Only instead of creating a dude out of decomposing bodies, Jack has turned himself into a Halloween cartoon character.

I want to ask more questions, but he has managed to dodge me like an expert in the last twenty-four hours. As soon as I woke up, he went to bed.

He wouldn't use my nocturnal hours to avoid me.

I made sure to get to bed early when the sun was still up, so I would have a few hours with my charge.

No such luck.

I shifted on the super uncomfortable couch, and Jack rushed to the bathroom. The shower kicked on, and before I even got a chance to imagine what it would look like to see Jack under the spray of hot water, he hurried by in nothing but plaid pajamas, slunk down on his hips.

He did that on purpose.

Or that's what I'm going with.

He *has* to know that the material stretches over his bubble butt.

He's *got* to know that the V disappearing into the waistband is *made* to scramble lady bits and brains.

Jack won't be able to hide from me for much longer. My severe sun allergy makes it difficult for me to change up my hours, but dusk isn't *too* painful. The man can't go to bed at seven and expect me to believe that he's in there catching Z's already.

Since our tense conversation in the basement lab, he hasn't said much to me.

"If you keep your nocturnal hours, you can have the bedroom while I'm up and about."

That was it

It was also clear as day the man *wanted* to avoid me.

It couldn't be easy, sharing his small cabin with a stranger, but we didn't have to keep on walking on eggshells around each other. Who knew how long it would take for FUC to complete their investigation into whatever Jack was mixed up in? Who knew how long it would be for his testimony to be needed?

I could be here for weeks. Months.

The man had to get over himself and get used to it.

To me.

The sun is still pretty high in the sky when I force myself awake. My head is woozy from lack of blood. I haven't had a sip of the stuff in days. I can only stomach it in my bat shape, and even then, it's hard to hunt. Harder to stomach the thick, life-giving liquid. Harder still to take back my human form without needing an hour-long shower, a gallon of antacids, and a liter of mouthwash.

There's nothing for it, though. I'll have to hunt some poor creature down tonight to get at least a teaspoon of blood.

The last thing I need is to be off my game because of my aversion to blood. That would hardly endear me to Director Cooper. Especially if we come under attack.

Psyching myself out for the gross meal, I get dressed, slipping on a pair of fuchsia leggings and a pale pink tee. Tucking my elongated bob into a half-pony is a challenge, but I don't waste precious time coiffing myself.

I am no longer a lawyer who needs to dress for success.

I am an agent. The rules are very different but *so* liberating.

I *almost* understand Raya's unaffected attitude. *Almost.*

"Good evening," I keep my tone chipper and friendly when Jack enters the cabin a few minutes later.

His graying black jeans are dusted with dirt, as are his white tee and green plaid shirt. His glasses, perched on the tip of his nose, are just as filthy. A streak of mud along his cheek matches a few others down his sinewy arms. I force air into my lungs, demanding that my brain settle.

Don't get your wings in a twist, V. He's only a dude. An everyday kind of dude with super sexy black curls and an ass that I could use as a chew toy.

Whoa.

The last thought is startling, making me squeak.

Weird. So weird. I definitely need to ingest some blood before I become a danger to Dr. Norbert *Jack* Palomer.

"You're up," he grumbles, walking straight for the kitchen. He turns the tap on and scrubs his hands and forearms in the huge white sink. The soapy water glides over his muscular arms as he turns back to give me a once-over.

I lean against the wall and watch him wash his skin raw. "I'm up. I think it's ridiculous that we're avoiding each other like the plague. This is a very small cabin, and who knows how long I'll be here?"

Why did I frame that like a question?

I take a deep breath and try again. "We should try to be civil."

"Civil." He repeats the world like it's a completely foreign concept to him.

"Yup. You know, talk, maybe share a few meals. Maybe even get to know each other."

"No, thank you."

My jaw drops. "What's *with* you? I get that you have this whole quiet, broody farmer thing down, but I'm gonna go insane if I don't have some kind of human connection in the next few weeks."

Jack grabs a towel and dries his hands before balling it up and throwing it onto the small kitchen table. "I'm not used to having someone underfoot."

"No. Ya don't say."

He purses his lips. "I'm also not accustomed to long-winded conversations."

"Or conversations at all," I volley back.

His eyebrow hooks this time, and there's the suggestion of a smile on his lips.

"I get that you're a secretive dude. You're gonna testify against a big evil corporation. I understand that. Only, I don't, because my superiors didn't exactly give me a lot of details and you haven't been forthcoming."

"You already know enough to seriously screw me over."

I frown, confused. "I won't tell anyone you're a pumpkin, Cinderella." I draw a cross over my heart before pretending to zip my lips. "I'm guessing you're sketchy about it because if FUC or the Cryptozoian Council found out, you'd face some serious repercussions."

He nods, his entire body tensing.

"If we both want to get out of this with our reputations intact, we need to work together. I call for a truce." I hold out my hand, but Jack looks at it like it's a pesticide bottle. I move my fingers expectantly, but he continues to stare.

"You'll stop calling me Cinderella?"

I scrunch up my nose. "If I must."

"And you'll drop the Jack thing?"

"I can try," I lie.

Am I going to tell this man I can't call him Norbert because I have a hard time imagining myself moaning out *Norbert*?

No.

Absolutely not.

I'm here on assignment. Not just any kind of assignment, but one that is meant to save my career before it can even start.

"If I tell you something *super* embarrassing about myself, will you explain to me how you turned yourself into a walkin'-talkin' Jack-o'-lantern?"

Jack inhales deeply and crosses his arms. "It'll have to be one hell of a good story."

"Why don't we sit down, have some breakfast or whatever meal you're at in your day, and chat. It's a normal thing to do, Jack. Sit and converse with whomever you're sharing lodgings."

"I'll park it, but only because you used *whomever* in a sentence and that's sexy."

My eyes pop out of my head. They're probably rolling on the ground somewhere along with my jaw. There is no air to be had for my poor, suffering lungs.

Jack called me sexy.

Sort of.

Judging by the crimson tint of his scruffy cheeks, he had *no* intention of making the comment. It popped out of his mouth before he could even stop it.

I grin at him, arching a brow in what I hope is a flirty, teasing way. I pass by him en route to the solar-panel-powered refrigerator, its loud hum the only sound in the cabin. It takes a decent amount of self-control not to brush up against him on purpose.

I grab milk, berries, and a box of cereal before settling at the table. I'm already scarfing down my meal when Jack decides to sit in front of me with his own bowl.

"Breakfast for dinner?" I ask.

He grunts his reply.

"So Norbert is an interesting name. Your parents pick it for any particular reason?"

"Not that I know of, no."

"Do *they* know how you turned yourself into a pumpkin?"

Jack shakes his head. "No. They're no longer with us."

"Oh. Shit. Sorry."

He shrugs, slurping a huge spoonful of cereal. "Before I get into any of that, you owe me *your* embarrassing tale. If I deem it worthy, I might share."

"It's worth it, all right." I push my bowl away and tap my fingers on the table. Sure, I don't *really* mind telling Jack that I can't ingest blood without needing smelling salts. Everyone knows now, so it's hardly this dark secret.

It's the embarrassment that stalls me.

Hey, hot farmer dude I barely know. Guess what? I'm broken, and I was only sent here to prove that I can be an agent without putting anyone's life in danger.

That wouldn't go over well, methinks.

With a deep sigh, I launch into the tale of the blood-hating vampire.

Jack listens intently, his eyes settling on me like I'm the most fascinating person in the world. That won't last long. As soon as he learns I need to ingest blood to survive, any possible attraction he has for me will evaporate.

It's probably for the best. Agents shouldn't want to strip their charges naked and ride them till the moon comes out.

Jack, King of the Pumpkin Patch, is way off-limits.

9

NORBERT

Vera is lovely.

She sits at my kitchen table—a place no woman has ever occupied before her—and she tells me her greatest shame. She is a vampire bat with an aversion to blood. Her flushed cheeks and misty eyes throat punch me. Her sadness is palpable. I reach over the table and squeeze her hand.

Why?

No idea.

My brain is probably turning into spaghetti squash.

"I'm sure you're not the only vampire bat that has reservations about blood." I grin at her with all of the comforting energy I can muster.

She purses her lips. That damn lip gloss of hers shimmies, catching the very low light in the kitchen. She smells like cotton candy. It shouldn't be an erotic aroma, but on her?

Well, it's a good thing there's a table between us and that we're not standing around the lab with me in my birthday suit. Vera would get a whole other view of me in *that* situation.

"You're sweet to say that, but there's no real proof."

"Proof," I scoff. "What's *your* pool of intel?"

"My whole family." She winces. "That includes Sveta Markov. She's my mom's sister."

I whistle low.

Shit, shit, double shit sandwich.

What are the chances that the Bloody Doctor's niece would end up being the agent charged with my safety? Is this some kind of cosmic joke? I'd love to know the punchline before it nuts me.

"Yikes. Seems to me that you don't like blood because your aunt kept more than her fair share of those genes."

"Huh. I never thought of it like that, but I do like that idea." Her smile is sweet and tentative.

"So why is this such a big deal, then?"

"It's embarrassing. I've passed out loads of times, including in front of my personal hero. Not to mention the pressure I feel to *get over it*. You know, I don't actually think I should get over it. I mean, I *have* to, but only because I feel like a broken bat."

"Hey, now. None of that."

Vera shakes her head, clearing her thoughts. Her movements scent the air with cotton candy, and my mouth waters. Would she taste like sugar if I kissed her? The thought has a vise grip on my balls.

"It's your turn, now. Come on, Jack. Tell me how this happened."

I lean back in my chair, crossing my arms. "I should make you sign an NDA or something."

"I was a lawyer. I assure you I can keep a secret."

"So long as no one gets killed," I finish for her.

She nods.

"I feel like we should pinky swear." *Or kiss on it.*

Damn it, Norbert. Keep your zucchini to yourself.

Vera leans over the table, pinky out and grinning wide. I crook my finger with hers and squeeze. Our gazes collide. They hook together like thunderclouds, electric and so *natural*. It steals the breath right out of my lungs.

"You gonna let me go, Jack?"

It'll be fucking hard, V.

I drop her finger to run my fingers through my hair. "This isn't a good story."

"You heard me say that my aunt is the Bloody Doctor, right?"

I wince. "Yeah..." *Shit. I wonder how she's going to react when she hears* that *part of my tale.* "I guess I have to start way back at the beginning."

"You mean when your parents decided to name you Norbert?"

"Something like that," I chuckle. Her eyes spark with humor. "So my parents, both brilliant botanists focused on resource protection and environmental changes, name me Norbert. I wasn't actually born here. I lived the first ten years of my life in the Amazonian rainforest. I didn't go to school, not conventionally, anyway. My parents taught me everything they knew. Everything I know."

"That must have been a lot of fun. Traipsing through all that wildlife."

I smile at her genuine enthusiasm. "It was a lot of fun, yeah. At least until my parents contracted a rare disease. To this day, no one knows what hit them. The best guess is that they played with genomes they weren't supposed to toy with."

She gasps. "Genomes?"

"Genes, yeah. They were botanists, but something of mad scientists, too."

"Hmm," she sighs, getting to her feet to clear away my dinner and her breakfast. "Now I see where you get it from."

"Right. I should have probably learned my lesson from their deaths, but I can't help myself. You give me a string of plant DNA and I wanna uncover all of its mysteries."

Vera's giggle is adorable. She settles back at the table, choosing the seat beside me instead of facing me. The heat of her leg caresses mine, and I should definitely move away. I don't. It's nice to be close to another person. To *her.*

"Go on, please." She draws her elbow onto the table and cups her cheeks, ready to listen some more.

"I followed in their path," I continue. "I became a botanist. I did my Ph.D. on the study of..." I stop myself short. "Well, that's boring. Basically, I was playing with plant genome."

"Sounds *fascinating*."

"It is. I was fine making a living here, researching and publishing some scientific papers every now and again. Last year, I was approached by a company. A major corporation. Top of the beauty industry, actually. They wanted to hire me to use my research to develop completely organic and plant-based products."

"Oh, that must have gotten your botanist zucchini *real* hard."

A deep laugh rolls out of me. "It sure did, though I wouldn't put it quite like that."

"I did it for you." She punctuates her thought with a wink that zings me right in my *actual* zucchini. Not the botanist one, the very real, very fleshy one.

I clear my throat and rub a hand over my mouth in hopes of covering my blush. "It all started fine. I was doing my work here by correspondence. Sending my research in. I had some good ideas, so I wasn't *too* surprised when the CEO, Lisbeth Bannon, basically demanded that I make a visit to headquarters."

"Wait. Are you telling me you were working for Vitality?"

"Yeah." I'm not surprised she knows who they are. It's probably one of the biggest beauty companies in the world.

Now I know why, too. Those crooked bastards.

"What did she want?"

"She wanted to pull me from the project. The company was working on something else. Something secret but life-changing. They took my research and gave it to another employee. They didn't want me to muck about with plants anymore, but with DNA."

"A different kind of genome."

"Exactly."

"Human?" she guesses.

"*Shifter*," I correct.

Vera gasps and covers her mouth. "Jack, please tell me you did *not* mix shifter DNA with plant DNA and inject yourself with it."

"I mean, I don't have to *say* it if you don't want me to."

"But that's what you did."

I nod. "That's what I did."

"Of all the dumb things to do. You could've killed yourself."

"I reached the end of the work. I could do nothing more without testing theories. Science is all about taking chances and going for the big risk. I knew I couldn't die, exactly. But Vitality demanded results. They were insistent, and I could tell there was a rush on things. That if I didn't do what they needed me to do, they'd get someone else. It felt too significant to give up, though. And in the wrong hands, it could be bad. Very bad."

Vera narrows her eyes. "Why do I feel like you're keeping something big from me?"

Here was the rub: how much did I tell her?

Did I admit that Lisbeth and I got a little too friendly? Did I tell Vera that her aunt's research was involved? How far could I go before it was all too much for her? I already shared most of this with Agent Downer. My reservations are strictly because Vera is...

Truth be told, I don't understand why I give two tosses about what Vera thinks of me.

Lie. Such a lie. Good thing fibbing doesn't make an exploding pumpkin out of me.

"'Cause I am. Vitality was dumping toxic waste in a few spots. One not too far from here, actually. I was livid. I went right back to Lisbeth Bannon and told her about it. She promised they would stop. She insisted she had *no* idea it was even happening but that she would get to the bottom of it. A month went by, and it happened again. That's when I called the Cryptozoian Council. I knew they would be the only ones who could help me because Bannon and the rest of the Vitality bigwigs are shifters." *Sort of.*

"All this is about toxic waste? Not about you messing around with shifter DNA?"

This is it. The moment that decides how much I tell her.

There's so much hopeful expectation in her eyes. Not to mention that I feel like a damn fool for falling into such a basic trap.

"That's it," I lie.

It rolls off my tongue like it's nothing, but it's not.

Vera's right to call me Cinderella. Eventually, the clock *will* strike midnight, the pumpkin will blow, and it won't be pretty.

10

NORBERT

A truce.

That's the only thing that can ever be between Vera and me.

A temporary agreement between a FUC agent and a witness in protective custody is where the buck stops for us.

By rights, the second she told me she needs blood to survive—that she is the Bloody Doctor's niece—I should have asked her to leave. I should've pretended to be grossed out and scared that I'd wake up in the middle of the night with Vera sucking on my neck.

But of course, the thought of her climbing into my bed, straddling me, pinning me down into the bed elicits other kinds of reactions—specifically below the belt.

That's probably the only reason why I rush through my daily chores around the crops. Usually, I drag it out, taking my own sweet time.

Sometimes I even stay and chat with the plants. Not because I'm a psycho but because I like to explain why I sheer them every now and again.

I don't do any of that today.

Not only did I get a later start after changing my hours to overlap a bit with Vera's, but there's an excited energy thrumming inside of me as I imagine spending a few hours chatting with her. I've always been solitary, but Vera turned the lights on in my cabin. Not the real, solar-powered lights.

Metaphorical ones that illuminated the lonely shadows that have always been my companions.

She's been here just over forty-eight hours and she's already changed my life in small but irrevocable ways.

When all of this business with Vitality Holdings ends, Vera will have to leave. Something will be left behind, though. Knowledge that as much as I claim to enjoy my life as a reclusive subsistence farmer, having someone around is okay.

If that person is Vera? Even better.

I wipe my filthy hands down the front of my jeans, but they're a dirty mess. It's not like I can make myself presentable in the small barn by the pumpkin patch. I shouldn't even be *thinking* like this.

A truce.

That's all we have.

I keep her secret, and she'll keep the one I shared.

I kick off my boots by the door and shrug out of my plaid shirt. My white tee sticks to my dewy skin; I've nearly sweat through the thing. I must smell horrible, but maybe we need that buffer between us.

Vera stands in the kitchen, her curves wrapped in bright blue leggings and a neon pink tee. Her hair, shorter in the back and longer in the front, is all smooth and silky. My fingers itch to run along the strands, but I'm filthy.

Not to mention I *lied* to her last night. The omission is one massive weight around my neck. I push it out of my mind.

So what if I'm attracted to Vera? She's only here because it's her job. I don't *owe* her anything. Besides, I'm a grubby, reclusive subsistence farmer. If I were to be all, *Hey, so my sort-of ex also manipulated me into doing research into immortality*, Vera would bolt faster than a clock could strike twelve.

"Morning," I say to her from the sink.

She doesn't respond but continues scowling at the kitchen table.

A small metallic cylinder sits in the very center, but why she's staring at it like it's about to sprout legs and walk away, I don't know.

"What the hell is *that*?"

"Blood." Her shoulders tremble at the mere thought of it.

"It's not a bomb, V."

Her sneer turns teasing as she looks in my direction. "Oh, but it sure feels like it. Director Cooper sent over some supplies while you were out working. She included *this* to prove a point."

"Blood is a point to make?" I ask, already knowing the answer.

"Most definitely. The canister thingy is ingenious, don't you know. It keeps the blood at precisely the right heat to mimic the average blood temperature of a mammal."

Gross. So gross.

I'm hardly going to tell Vera that her basic functional needs are a tad repulsive. She knows. It's also not her fault, and I'm the very last person to judge.

"Is there anything I can do to help you with this?"

She shakes her head. "Nope. Either I drink it or toss it and have to find some source of blood soon."

"What do you mean?"

Vera purposefully avoids my gaze. "Because I haven't ingested any in a while, and that's sort of dangerous for bats like me."

I thump my way over to the table and grab the receptacle. It's surprisingly warm to the touch. "What if we mix it in spaghetti sauce or something?"

Her mouth drops into a perfect O when she gasps. "And ruin spaghetti forever? You're out of your gourd. No way, Jack. I'll just have to hunt tonight." She clutches her stomach and goes green in the face at the mere thought of it.

It sparks an idea in the back of my mind. "You won't drink this?"

As pale as an unripened ash gourd, she mumbles, "I have to toss it."

"I'm gonna go work in the lab for a bit while you figure out how you'll track down prey large enough to survive without a teaspoon of blood. Let me know when you're back."

Vera nods and retreats to the bathroom while I make my way to the lab.

If I can find the answer to immortality in human blood, I'm sure I can find a way to make *something* that will fulfill Vera's needs without making her queasy.

"And?" I ask Vera a few hours later.

It's almost midnight, and she's brushing her teeth for the second time since I emerged from the lab. She shakes her head, holding out a finger before vanishing into the bathroom.

"I hate, hate, *hate* it. I will never get used to it."

"Your parents must've had a fine time getting you to take your blood."

She nods emphatically. "You've got no idea. It's was bad, too, 'cause my little sister Raya would pipe up. *I drank my blood*. It was her point of pride. She was the good daughter. The *better* daughter because she didn't fight them every day. She drove me nutso bananas all the time about it."

"Your aversion to blood doesn't mean you're a bad daughter."

Vera settles onto the couch, curling her legs under her. "I had to fly pretty far to find something decent." She completely ignores my comforting line. Maybe it wasn't enough, or maybe I'm clumsy with my words. "Poor moose," she goes on. "At least he didn't even feel it. How was the lab? Did you turn yourself into a pumpkin?" I want to kiss her smirk.

Wait. What? I do?

Oh, I definitely fucking do.

"Nope." I take a seat beside Vera. There's a good two feet between us, but I long to be closer. Her pink lips are *right* there. Not that I'll actually kiss her. Ever. "Doing a bit of research on another project. Unrelated to my situation."

"Can you reverse your gourd problem?"

"Unlikely. The formula rewrote my genetic code."

"So any time you're threatened, you're gonna go all orange and defenseless?"

I wince. "Unless I can figure out what to add to my DNA, yes."

"Add?" she gasps. "Is this a *joke*? You can't *add*. You've already turned yourself into vegetation. What's next?"

"You don't wanna know."

Her eyes go wide. "But I really do. I'm kinda terrified that I'll walk into the lab one day and find a pumpkin with legs and arms."

"If I get things my way, that's exactly what will happen."

"What a nightmare. A scarecrow with a pumpkin head."

"Huh. Now there's an idea. That could be how to make my gourd sentient. I wonder if there is something…"

Vera smacks my leg. "Do not even go there."

I grip her fingers. The playful touch is anything but innocent to the southern parts of me. "Jack Scarecrow could be my shifter alter ego."

She giggles. "Hey, now. That's not so bad. It would also go with your whole vibe." She motions toward my body—or maybe my clothes.

Please let it be my body.

"Yeah," she goes on. "The grungy bad boy farmer thing you've got going on."

"Bad boy, huh?" I can't help it. I lean into her. Two feet becomes one. "You ever into the bad boys?" One foot becomes an inch.

She grins, sly and cute and way too close. Her hand draws up my thigh. "Nope. I like the studious types. You know, always in the library with glasses on the tip of their nose." She punctuates her breathy line by poking my nose.

My anatomy is suddenly very interested in the tip of my nose. It's not an erogenous zone, but damn it all to hell if her fingertip on me doesn't feel like the most erotic sensation.

I swallow hard as my dick stirs happily.

Mistress Palm? More like Mistress Bat.

I try to shrug the thought away, but it's too late. Vera is *right* there, simmering my blood with her hazel eyes and tempting lips. I want to say something clever, flirt back.

I've got nothing.

It's probably for the best. So what if she's gorgeous and sweet? She's an agent sent to keep watch over me. I can't get myself into any more trouble. Vera is nothing like Lisbeth, but that doesn't mean I should lean into the trust.

"Jack?" Vera's voice is raspy, evoking all kinds of naughty things. "Can I have my hand back?"

Stunned, I look down to see that I'm holding onto her hand, our fingers woven together. I let go and jump to my feet. "Gotta go check on the gourds."

I slam the front door behind me in hopes of shaking loose the desire pulsing inside me. I lumber to the pumpkin patch with the stars blinking above me in the dark blue sky.

Have I really not learned my lesson?

Note to self: don't sit close to Vera.

Don't touch her. Don't even look at her.

Or else, she'll fly away with my heart...

11

VERA

Jack.

Tall, wide-shouldered, grungy hunk with curly black hair and brown eyes that peek out from his glasses.

Jack, who has more definition than a 4k Ultra TV.

The man who shifts into a pumpkin and has a deep voice that fans all kinds of naughty forbidden flames inside of me.

That's the man currently lying on top of me, nibbling at my neck, kissing my shoulder like he needs me more than his next breath. His erection presses into my side, and I arch up to get that oh-so-delicious friction against my lady bits.

If he doesn't peel me out of my clothes soon, I'm going to explode. I *need* him. I need his lips on mine, his hands exploring my heated flesh, his hips thrusting deep inside me.

I moan his name, gripping his tight curls with a plea. He chuckles and pulls my nipple into his mouth. I didn't even realize we were naked, but *thank plasma,* we are. His skin is hot and taut under my questing fingertips. I reach between us to grip his erection, desperate to feel him inside of me.

A startled scream rips out of me when I grip his dick.

It's not made of flesh but a cold, bumpy surface. I pull my hand away, horrified.

I'm holding a zucchini.

Jack isn't above me.

Nope.

There's a massive pumpkin sitting on my chest, its jack-o'-lantern face cackling at me.

What the actual punking pumpkin?

With a jolt, I wake and sit up.

It takes me a few seconds to realize that I'm lying on the couch in the cabin's living room.

I had a sex dream about Jack.

The realization heats my cheeks with embarrassment. Especially since it quickly turned into an absolute nightmare.

Serves me right for lusting after the Pumpkin King who is under my protection.

I seriously doubt Chase Brownsmith would've fuck someone he was meant to protect. More than that, if Director Cooper found out that her broken bat non-agent was going around having almost-dirty dreams about important witnesses, she'd boot me from FUC.

Ousted from FUC because of a fuck is hardly how I want my career in law enforcement to end.

Honestly, I blame Jack for this.

Yesterday, we sat on this very couch and flirted. I put my hand on his *thigh*, inches away from his very human zucchini. When he leaped from the couch and disappeared for the rest of the night, that should've been my clue that he *wasn't* thinking about kissing me.

I almost did.

I was seconds away from kissing Jack before he got out of here like a bat out of hell.

Way to ruin your already precarious career, Vera.

I've got to do something to completely ruin my silly attraction to Jack. Maybe I should start by calling him Norbert. That should do it.

For his part, he better stop wearing those faded jeans that make his ass look more delicious than a juicy steak. And if he doesn't keep his forearms to himself, hidden under his plaid shirt, I'll just have to remind him that this is his home.

Not a strip show.

"Morning, sleepyhead." Jack leans against one of the thick support beams, steaming cup of coffee in hand. His grin is made of sex.

I burrow deeper under the quilt, my face flushing from shame. Does he know? Did I accidentally moan his name out loud while I was dreaming? How am I going to explain *that*?

"Hey, Norbert."

He frowns, his glasses sliding down that sexy nose.

Stop, V. Noses are not sexy. They're functional organs. Nothing more.

"Norbert?" he repeats. "What happened to Jack?" He winks as he hands me the mug of coffee.

Our fingers brush as I accept his kind offering. My already keyed-up organs do a happy flutter, and it takes all of my professionalism to gulp the too-hot coffee.

"I was rude for giving you a nickname. I'll stick to Norbert."

"Why?" he chuckles, settling into the armchair with his own cup of hot bean juice. "I like it. Besides, I *am* a jack-o'-lantern, so the name works."

"Are you asking me to keep calling you Jack?"

His smirk isn't made of sex anymore. Oh, no.

Now it promises orgasms and perfectly dirty kisses.

He takes a swig of his drink and licks his lips to catch a stray drop.

I am a puddle of bat on his couch.

I am a responsible FUC agent. I am not *attracted to my charge.*

"Did you sleep all right? You look a little pale." His concern is very real and all too sweet. "You should take the bed."

"Not a chance. This is your home. I'm not a guest but an agent on a mission to keep you safe. I can hardly take your bed."

Now maybe if we shared it...

Oh, for the love of echolocation. *Stop.*

"Besides," I quickly add, "I don't want to disrupt your life. It's bad enough you've got to sneak out of here and stay in the lab or in your crops all day."

He chuckles. "I do that whether you're here or not, V. At least now I've got company. I woke up much later today and won't go to bed until sunrise. That way, we can keep the same hours."

I blink at him. "That's hardly a good idea."

Because if we spend more time together, my badge will be on the line.

"It's a great idea," he argues, smiling. "That way, you can take the bed."

"We can alternate," I mumble. "Compromise."

"Great. Love a good compromise. Get dressed. I wanna show you something in the lab."

"Please tell me you didn't scarecrow yourself."

"Nope. This is something for you. I'll be waiting for you downstairs." Jack winks before making his way to the lab.

Do I watch him walk away? Of course I do. There's no way that I can ignore his butt. Or the way his black curls tease the nape of his neck. Everything about the man is delicious.

I really wish I hadn't seen his equipment my first day here. It's one thing to find a man *hot*. It's another to be attracted to him in an *I-have-sex-dreams* way. It's a disaster to know exactly what he's packing.

The dude could do some serious damage with that thing.

Like ruin my career.

I took a quick shower, and after much deliberation and a little slip of sanity, I coif my hair. I could lie to myself and say that I only did it because it's easier to go about my day with my elongated bob styled just so.

But the second I slide on my black leggings with mesh material weaving its way around my legs, I know I'm playing a dangerous game. Why I even packed my sexy leggings, I don't know.

I certainly don't have to wear them.

I also don't have to match it with a white crop top.

I'm full of bad choices today, but hopefully, they're all out of my system before I join Jack in the lab.

Ha-ha-fucking-ha.

When I make my way down, back straight and with a solid resolve to be professional, it takes two seconds for that to go right out the window.

Jack is bent over a microscope, and his plaid sleeves are rolled up to his elbows, putting his sinewy muscles on display as he turns the nob on his device. It would be easy enough not to get all aflutter, but *of course* his curls fall over his forehead. He *has* to pucker his lips in concentration. If I didn't know any better, I would think the man is doing this on purpose.

He is trying to make me nutso bananas with lust.

"You're here." He grins and pushes his hair back.

I swallow my tongue. Or maybe it only feels like that because the floor shifts under my feet as his eyes catch mine.

"Come here." He waves me forward and steps away from the microscope. "I wanna show you this. I think you'll really like it."

I am one thirsty bat.

My limbs are glued together with randy goo.

I make my way across the lab, taking breaths that don't quite make it to my brain. Thankfully, I can lean on the countertop as I look down into the scope. It can support me while I watch as two burgundy rings mold together on the thin glass slab.

"What am I seeing?"

"Blood particles."

My stomach lurches, and I jump back. "What?"

Jack's hand settles on my lower back, his fingers grazing the very top of my ass. "Sorry. I should have warned you. I sort of got excited there for a second. I'm trying to break down the nutritional value of blood."

"Why?" My voice is as queasy as my tummy.

"Well, I figure I can try to make something that has all the benefits of blood without actually *being* blood."

Be still my batty heart.

My mouth opens and closes. I'm in shock but also melting because *aw-oh-my-guano-but-this-is-the-sweetest-thing-ever.*

"Wh-what? Why? Why are you doing that?"

"Well, no one should be in physical and emotional distress once a day to survive. Doesn't seem right to me." He shrugs like it's nothing.

But it's not.

It's... well, it's kind of *everything.*

Jack isn't from a shifter family, and that might be why, for him, my blood aversion isn't some kind of flaw.

It's not something I have to work through or *fix* in myself.

For the first time in a long time—if not *ever*—I don't feel broken. The solution isn't that I need to *get over it* or *toughen* up. Nope. Jack gives me hope that the answer could come from the outside.

And he's willing to fiddle in his lab.

For me.

"Thank you," I whisper. "You really don't have to do that."

"Trust me, V. I really do."

His nickname for me, a simple letter, is so personal, so intimate. No one has ever called me that before. In his deep baritone, the single syllable is an ode to me. It's almost as endearing as his latest experiment.

"I've got a lot of bad shit to make up for while I still can. This is gonna be good for you. Besides, I'm sure there are other bats out there who'd be happy not to drink blood anymore."

He was wrong. Most vampire bats *adored* blood. They thrived on it and on the connection to the old ways, the vampiric ways of the old country. I was the odd bat out, but I wouldn't ruin this moment. It was too special.

I throw my arms around Jack and hug him tight. He's as surprised as I am by the physical contact, but he quickly recovers and wraps his strong arms around my waist, drawing me impossibly closer to him.

"Thank you, Jack," I murmur in his ear before kissing his cheek.

It's a whim. A dangerous one. He stiffens but only for a second. He pulls away slightly, keeping us tied together. One of his hands tips my chin up, and our gazes lock. I can't breathe, but I don't need to when I'm this close to Jack.

"Anything for the batty lady keeping me safe."

For one delicious heartbeat, I believe he'll lean in and kiss me. I lick my lips, tasting my cotton candy lip gloss. I'm so ready for this kiss. I'm pretty sure I've been waiting for it my whole life.

So, of course, it doesn't happen.

Jack's pocket begins to ring, the sound ripping us apart.

12

NORBERT

Saved by the fucking phone.

Did I even *want* to be saved from this moment?

I'm *seconds* away from kissing Vera. My lips tingle in protest as I step away from her and reach for my back pocket.

"Hello, Agent Downer," I say into the device. She's the only person to have this number. It stands to reason she would be the one to call at *the* least convenient time.

It's lucky she did, though, much as it pains me to admit.

"Norbert. How's my favorite whistleblower?"

I wince. "Fine."

"Anything to report?"

I've got blue balls, I'm falling for the agent you sent, and I'm pretty sure I'm one day away from losing my damn mind.

"Nope," I respond. "Everything's good here."

"Nice. That's what we like to hear."

"How about on your side? Did the files help? Are you almost done putting together the charges?"

Downer lives up to her name. "No, Norbert. Sorry. There's lots of great stuff in what you gave us, but we can't tie any of it to Lisbeth Bannon."

"It's her company," I growl.

"It sort of is, but not on paper. She might give the orders, but she's not the top of the pyramid."

"What does that even mean?"

"You caught a decent fish, but it wasn't the big fish."

My stomach churns. "She's the one who told me to look into the..." My eyes cut to Vera, who is watching me intently, listening to every word. *Shit.* I've got to mince my words. "Lisbeth is in charge," I insist, refusing to bring up the Bloody Doctor's research. "She's the one who's questing hard for this." *There.* Speaking without saying a damn word.

"We have Vitality dead to rights on the toxic waste dump, but it's not gonna do anything. It's too big of a company. They've already paid the fine and agreed to fund part of the cleanup."

My heart sinks. "But they destroyed a full ecosystem."

"Yeah, and we live in a consumer's world where no one gives a fuck if we destroy the planet."

I snort out a dry, sarcastic laugh.

You'd think that the people searching for immortality would give a shit about the state of the environment, that they would treat the *planet* like she's immortal instead of their own personal dumping site.

Where do they think they're going to live if they ever do unlock the secret of eternal life? On the moon? It sure won't be on Earth if they keep treating her like shit.

"So what does this mean? For me? I gave you so much evidence, Downer. Not only with the toxic dumping but with the other experiments, too. It should be enough."

"You're right. It should be. It's not, though. Can't tell you why. The answers are way above my paygrade, and all my superiors have told me is that they need another few weeks to figure out how to deal with this mess."

"A few weeks?" I swallow hard.

Is Downer *really* telling me that Vera will be living with me for months? I can deal with my attraction to her for a few more days—

probably. If she has to stay much longer? I don't know how I'll keep away.

Not when she turns those bright hazel eyes on me, smiling with hope and encouragement.

I run a hand across my mouth. "Look, Downer, that's not good enough for me. I can't live with a threat looming over my head for months."

"Maybe you'll think about that next time you decide to play hide-the-pickle with a multi-billion-dollar corporation CEO who wants to live forever."

I can't even argue. Downer is right.

"FUC has agreed to extend your protective custody. If you want, we can alternate the agent. Switch 'em out or whatever."

"Yes." *Wait. That means no more Vera.* "No." *But that means resisting her for months.* "Yeah-no."

"Norbert," Downer warns. "Make up your mind.

"We're good for now."

"Fine. Meanwhile, if you can dig through your files for anything that links Lisbeth Bannon to VH, that'd be great."

I don't bother telling her that I've already given the Cryptozoian Council and FUC everything I have. Downer *knows* that. It's her not-so-subtle way of telling me I am well and truly fucked.

"They won't protect me forever," I grumble.

"You're right. They won't. You might want to start thinking about a change of identity. New home, new name, new career. I'll call you soon to check on things. In the meantime, if you need anything, don't hesitate to call." She ends the connection.

"Well?" Vera nearly hops, waiting for me to reply as I slide the phone into my back pocket. "What's happened? Will the trial be happening any time soon?"

I shake my head before giving her a brief—and abridged—rundown of the news. Vera listens intently, her cute nose scrunching up as I go along.

"None of this makes sense. I'm missing a piece of the puzzle. If

Vitality paid the fine and won't get into any more trouble, why do you still need protective custody? It's done, isn't it?"

I don't imagine the sadness rooted in her tone. The corner of Vera's mouth droops down, and I hate it. I want to make her smile again, but I can't. This is the second time she's flat-out asked me for the truth. All of it. If I keep it from her again, there's every chance she'll never forgive me.

For some dumb reason, that's more dangerous than Lisbeth Bannon and everything the shifter could send my way. I weave my fingers with Vera's and lead her to the small garden at the back of the lab. We sit together on the edge of the wooden plant box.

"Okay, so let the record show that I'm slightly freaked out by your silence."

I wince but try to cover it with an uneasy grin. "I've been keeping something from you." My throat bobs like an apple in a barrel.

"Yeah, I kinda figured."

With a sigh that could power my home for a decade, I launch into the whole sordid tale. I leave nothing out. I tell her how Lisbeth seduced me, how my hubris was my undoing. I tell her about the Bloody Doctor and how I've been using her research to find the key to immortality.

To her credit—and to my horror—Vera is quiet as I continue to spew out all of my dark secrets. I've known this woman for four days. Her opinion of me shouldn't matter as much as it does, but there you have it.

I care what Vera Slaski thinks of me.

I want her to think I'm a good man even though I took the work of Sveta Markov, a mass murderer with hundreds of deaths on her hands, and tried to make sense of it. I want Vera to look at me and see *Jack*, the subsistence farmer, and botanist who accidentally turned himself into a pumpkin.

Not the idiot who thought he could fix the world by making the rich and powerful immortal.

"It was about finding a cure for diseases," I repeat for the thousandth time in a minute, hoping against hope that Vera believes me. It's the truth.

But really, why should she take my word for it? We're basically strangers, and I don't have much to recommend me.

"I really wanted to find solutions, but all I did was create a problem. One big fucking problem."

"Did you give Vitality Holdings immortality?"

I shake my head. "No. I don't actually think it's possible. I looked at perennial plants and broke their genome down to the very barest of genes. Even at that, it's not a perfect system. It would mean immortal beings would need to change vessels. Bodies. Cell reconstruction or regeneration is very hard to recreate. They won't get it from plants, anyway. I reached the natural conclusion of my research because... you know, everything has a conclusion. Nothing should be eternal."

Vera stands and begins to pace the length of the lab. She doesn't look my way, keeping her eyes fixed on the floor. A few times, she stops, breathes in deeply with the beginning of a thought, but then deflates and continues pacing.

It's torture, waiting for her reaction.

"Lisbeth Bannon is the CEO of Vitality, right?"

"Yeah, and Vitality Holdings, too. But apparently, she isn't really the top of that company."

"She wouldn't be. It's got to be a front."

"How do you figure?"

"Well, Bannon is hardly the only person chasing immortality. My aunt was all up in that, but she had a bunch of followers. There were blogs dedicated to studying her research. Even when she went nutso bananas and busted out of jail, people praised her work as world-changing. Bannon is probably the mouthpiece for a lot of people who want to live forever."

"Rich, famous, powerful people who don't necessarily want to be associated with a scientist who went mad and killed a bunch of people," I continued for Vera, catching on to her thought process.

"Exactly," Vera agrees. "Downer mentioned they can't bring this up any higher or charge Vitality with anything more serious than the toxic waste, right? What if she's being blocked by someone or some*ones*?"

My eyes pop wide. "You really can't be saying there is a mole in the Cryptozoian Council or FUC."

Vera throws her hands up in the air, defeated. "Well, why not? You're positive you gave them enough evidence against Lisbeth Bannon that they should be able to charge her?"

"I'm not a lawyer. I don't know the law that well."

"I do." She is so invigorated she begins to bounce on her feet. "You need to show me everything you gave Downer."

"Including my research notes?"

"Yup."

"I don't want you to hate me for the shit that I've done."

"Well, I guess we'll cross that bridge if we get to it."

Well, at least that will solve one problem. Vera will despise me, and my attraction to her will be moot.

It takes hours for Vera to read through everything I shared with the Cryptozoian Council.

It's near sunrise by the time she pushes away from the old computer. She arches her back before bending at the waist, letting her fingertips brush the floor. I try not to look at the curve of her lush ass. I fail. Vera's hips flare out like a perfect hourglass that makes my mouth water. Here we are, in a tense and uncertain junction, and I'm ogling her.

You're an ass, Jack.

"And? What's the verdict, counselor?"

Vera continues to stretch, throwing an arm over her shoulder, arching into the movement as if she were presenting her breasts to me. The thin material of her shirt stretches over her chest while her crop top inches dangerously high, giving me a quick peek at her bra.

Trouser zucchinis are in season, apparently.

"Well, I honestly have to agree with Downer on this one. Lisbeth Bannon is listed as the CEO in absentia. She isn't the one pulling strings. She's a puppet. Probably a fancy puppet like a possessed ventriloquist doll, but there's someone with their hand up her ass." She cringes. "Sorry for the bad analogy. My brain is a little bit fried from all that reading. I haven't read that much since law school."

"It was quite the visual." But what did that make *me*? I was the string puppet to a ventriloquist doll?

Double damn with a side of fuck.

"Unless we got access to all kinds of financial information, it would be impossible to figure out who Bannon is working for. Even at that, if she really is the mouthpiece for the rich and powerful, they'll have all of that intel buried in offshore accounts and all kinds of shady shit."

Wrecked like a carriage after midnight, I slouch down onto the wooden plant box. "What does this mean? What do we do?"

Vera slides down beside me. "Honestly? I've got no idea. Full disclosure? I'm not a full agent yet."

It's my turn to jump to my feet.

"Director Cooper is keeping my badge until I can ingest blood like a normal vampire bat. I'm not as connected as a *real* agent would be. I don't think Alyce expected this to be so complicated. On the surface, this really was just some glorified babysitting job."

"Sorry."

"Don't be. You were played, and then you tried to make it right. Now we need to evaluate our next course of action. We also need to figure out why Director Cooper didn't have all of this information from Downer. I know she and Erhart Know, the rep for the Cryptozoian Council don't exactly get along, but this is weird. What's Downer's plan for us?"

"Downer wants us to stay here for weeks. Months maybe, while they figure their shit out."

"Right. Maybe we can help them along with that. Can you do more digging from here?"

"Not really," I answer. Her shoulders deflate slightly. "I only have internet for a few hours every night, and it's not super reliable."

"Damn. If we could do more digging here, at least we could have hope of finding *something*. We can't trust anyone right now. I would reach out to Jessie Cyngclair at FUC. She's the tech pro and swan shifter. I *know* she's one of the good guys, but it's something I'd want to discuss in person. I don't know that I trust any phone lines right now. Not to mention, we're stuck here. It's not a secure location. Not anymore, anyway. If we don't know who to trust, we have to assume this place is compromised. Downer would have told her superiors. Director Cooper knows, which means others might as well. Hell, maybe I was followed."

"We can't be naive and think Bannon didn't figure out my location, either."

"Then there's that, yeah."

I push the heels of my palms into my eyes, taking deep breaths. "I fucked this up royally."

"If it wasn't you, it would be someone else. Maybe someone who wouldn't have blown the whistle. No use playing *what-if*. We need a game plan."

"I'm all ears."

"I have an idea. It's bad and dangerous, but it might be our only shot at rooting out any potential moles all the while figuring out who Lisbeth Bannon represents."

"Okay?"

"We have to go on the run."

I still. "On the run." I test the words on my tongue, but I don't like them. "That does sound pretty perilous."

"Well, we wouldn't be on the run or in the wilderness for long. I think we should make our way over to my cousin Mila's place."

"The Bloody Doctor's daughter?"

"Yeah. She and her husband, T-Bone, are both FUC agents, but I trust them with my life. The second Mila learns that her mother's research is being used by other people, she'll want to be involved. She'll want to stop it as much as we do."

"And you trust this cousin?"

"She's as batty as they come, but yeah. I trust her. If someone is using her mother's research *again*, she'll want to know and help us stop it. That's a guarantee."

I fill my lungs until they ache. I hate leaving the cabin and my crops. I'm not a fan of the big wide world. Not to mention the fact that I have zero defensive skills. I turn into a huge pumpkin when I'm threatened.

Visions of Vera running through the forest holding a massive gourd while being chased by Lisbeth makes me shudder.

"Give me twenty-four hours."

"Twenty-four hours," Vera agrees.

13

VERA

The preparations for our escape are going as well as can be expected.

Jack is reluctant to leave his farm behind. If he didn't give his crops constant attention, he might lose them all. He wouldn't have much—or any—food when he returns.

If he returns.

There's no way of knowing how this plays out.

Lose your crop, or lose your life.

That's not exactly the best choice. I feel for the dude. I really do. It has *nothing* to do with how he makes me feel.

As I pack up some supplies for us, the very last thing on my mind should be Jack. I can't help myself. As hard as it was to share a small one-bedroom cabin with the man, it'll be impossibly harder to share a tent with him as we hike our way back to civilization.

We considered taking the armored car that I drove here, but there's risk there. FUC has trackers in all of its vehicles. We can't take any chances and take an easily traceable car. We can't take the chance that there is a mole in FUC.

That would completely defeat the purpose of going on the lam.

When Jack requested twenty-four hours before we depart, I don't know what I expected him to do. I thought he needed time to wrap his head around leaving home.

Not so much.

He hasn't left the lab for more than ten minutes at a time. Every time he surfaces, I ask if he's okay, if he needs help. He assures me he doesn't, grabs a protein bar, and returns to his lair. I don't really know what he's doing down there, but I'm assuming it has to do with the straw he hauled in earlier this evening.

The only time I almost crept down to see how he was doing was when the scent of burning sugar hit my nostrils, but he rushed up the stairs to tell me that all was well, grabbed the fire extinguisher from under the kitchen sink, and vanished again.

That was about three hours ago.

It's late now.

Late enough that the sun will be rising soon. I'm *starving* enough to gnaw on some raw veggies as I continue to stir the stew I've made for us. Cooking vegetarian isn't as easy as throwing a bunch of vegetables into a dish and calling it a day.

The human body needs protein—loads of it—to function properly. I threw all kinds of beans and gourds into the stew, making it as hearty and filling as I can.

Not that I know what I'm doing, really. I'm following a recipe in one of Jack's cooking books, but I've tweaked it to use the ingredients the sexy subsistence farmer has on hand.

Jack's footsteps echo up the staircase, and he emerges, plaid shirt discarded, his white tee rumpled and filthy. Even his gray jeans are a right mess. "Hey," he sighs, his voice rough and tired.

"You should go take a nice long shower before you pass out on your feet. Dinner is almost ready."

"Yeah. Thanks. Good idea." He reaches back and pulls his shirt off in one smooth motion that has my nether regions fluttering.

I ogle because of *course* I do. I am mesmerized by the muscles on his back as he walks by. How does the body's musculature work? I've got no clue, but I'd love to understand how his back undulates with power and grace as he stalks away.

The sound of the shower kicking on snaps me out of my temporary hypnosis. I return to the kitchen and busy myself over pots and pans as I do my level best *not* to imagine Jack in the shower.

Why is that, every time the dude bathes, I imagine what it would be like to be a total creeper and watch? Standing there, stirring a stew over the stovetop, picturing Jack stroking his impressive hardware isn't helpful.

It's *definitely* not professional.

I like rules. I love to follow them. I *never* break them.

Yes, I sort of fibbed about the whole blood thing, but no one thought to ask, and I thought I could get over it.

This is different. I can't exactly help the way Jack makes me feel. I'm a hopeful, giddy mess because I know there's something between us. Or there could be if our circumstances weren't so messed up.

By the time the water turns off, I've overcooked dinner, drooled enough to power a dam, and made myself way too horny for a trek through the wild. I'm not here to obsess over Jack but to get one up on an evil shifter corporation seeking immortality.

I give my loins a talking-to.

Listen lady, Jack isn't for us. He is our charge, and he is in some serious trouble. Complicating things with a roll in the pumpkin patch is not a good idea.

There.

That should do it.

I roll my shoulders back and decide that my silly attraction to Jack can—and will—be totally ignored until it no longer exists.

Like my blood aversion.

I super have this under control.

That goes out the window *real fucking* fast. The bathroom door swings open, and there he stands, in all his wet and naked glory. A brown towel is wrapped around his trim waist, but it leaves very little to the imagination.

Especially an imagination that's *seen* the goods and dreamed about them every night since.

"Forgot to grab clean clothes," he explains, blushing deep red. He scurries to the bedroom, leaving wet footprints behind.

I'm not entirely sure Jack didn't do that to torture me or something. Maybe he's trying to tease me to death. Is that a thing? It has to be.

Here lies Vera Slaski, slain by her overeager and lonely loins.

"Sorry about that." Jack is fully clothed, and I swear to the good lords of birth control, my vagina weeps.

"All good." My voice is way too high-pitched and cheery. Jack would see a shade of red as-of-yet undiscovered by the human eye if he saw my face.

I load a plate down with mashed potatoes and top it with a few massive scoops of stew before placing it on the kitchen table. It smells really good if I do say so myself. Jack settles at his seat and digs in. He shovels a huge bite into his mouth and winces.

"Is it bad?" I wince.

He shakes his head, gobbling up some more. "No. So good. Really hot, but I'm too starved to wait. Thanks for this." He wipes his mouth on the back of his hand, his handsome face turning sheepish. "Sorry for the whole savage act. I didn't realize how hungry I was until I ate."

"It's fine. You've been in the lab for a while. I needed *something* to do, or I was gonna go batty. Maybe cool your jets, Jack." I giggle as he devours the rest of his plate and gets up to grab some more. "But I'm happy it's edible. Especially since it may very well be our last warm meal before we head out tomorrow."

"That reminds me..." Jack settles at the table. "We need to find a solution for your sun allergy if we aren't taking the car."

"I've mapped out our journey. We're going to be in the woods for two nights."

"That means two full days of sun you need to avoid. It seems like too big a risk. I've been thinking... What if we drive the car in the *opposite* direction? Ditch it. Buy a clunker somewhere. It seriously reduces our travel time and your risk of sun exposure."

I ponder this. "It sort of goes against all of my training."

"I kinda think that this whole situation isn't exactly your run-of-the-mill mission."

You're telling me.

I doubt other agents are out there, falling wingtips over tail for their charges. Not that I'm admitting that I've developed any sort of feelings for Jack in seven days.

That would be *ridiculous.*

As ridiculous as a grown man shifting into a pumpkin every time he's threatened.

"I'd prefer we didn't take any chances with your health. What happens if you catch some sun?"

"I explode into a pile of ash," I deadpan.

His fork stops halfway to his mouth. "You're hilarious." He rolls his eyes. "For real, V. Be honest. Our plan can't only factor in the outward danger. We also need to take our limitations into consideration. And that's not to say only your sun allergy. We need to be smart about this. If we're out in the wild, hiking up to your cousin's place, and we get attacked? I'll literally turn into a useless gourd. Your bat can't carry me, and you can't defend yourself *and* my orange ass all at once."

His tush is not orange, though I'm willing to bet it's just as firm as a ripe gourd.

"I think," Jack goes on, completely oblivious to the impact he has on me, "our best bet is taking the car."

It takes a few minutes for my brain to catch up with the conversation. I'm not sure it's a good idea, but I don't want to shoot it down without thinking about it. I grab my empty bowl and bring it to the sink as I mull it all over.

Jack's right, of course. If we were set upon and he turns into a pumpkin, the odds are stacked against us. Does it make me a bad agent—or *almost* agent—that I want to take his plan into consideration? Shouldn't I have all of the answers?

I rinse my bowl and begin clearing away the dishes.

Jack is quick to join me. "I can feel you thinking."

"Impossible."

"I think that hearing thoughts' echolocation might be my super-power." He winks.

"That's not a thing."

He shrugs. "No, but I can tell from the small pucker right here"—he brushes his fingers along my brow—"you're thinking real hard."

His skin on mine set off sparklers in my brain. The touch might be chaste, but it's intimate.

That's the only explanation for why my hands end up on his shoulders, inching up to settle at the back of his neck.

"Thanks for dinner." His voice caresses my face.

"You're welcome," is what I *think* I say.

I'm not too sure if I actually open my mouth to speak because, the next second, my lips are pressed to his in a tender kiss. Jack's arms wrap around my waist, holding me close to him. His lips are soft but demanding as he takes control of the embrace.

Right there, in the small kitchen of a one-bedroom cabin, I devour Dr. Norbert *Jack* Palomer's face like I need it more than my next breath.

One of his hands finds its way to my hair, and the other cups my ass. He presses me into him, making it pretty damn clear that this kiss is heated.

It could definitely lead to something more.

I tense as I remember who he is and, more to the point, who I am and why I'm here.

Good agents don't check out their charges. If Director Cooper could see me now, my aversion to blood would be the least of my worries.

Rules and control, Vera. Rules. And. Control.

"V," he whispers against my mouth. He doesn't say anything more but presses his lips to mine again in a sweet kiss, bookending our make-out session with something straight out of an afterschool special.

"I should continue the cleanup."

I blurt out the words as I push away from him. The second I leave his arms I miss him. I want more of him.

Hell, I want all of him.

My responsibilities as an agent and my desires as a woman clash more than lipstick on a bat.

I am in deep *guano*.

14

NORBERT

Vera nervously brushes her hair back as she pushes away from me.

Damn, damn, double damn.

I should not have kissed her, but I don't want to regret the best kiss of my life.

I understand I crossed a line, but I couldn't help myself. Seems that Vera was into it herself until her brain caught up with her.

Needing to reconnect with her and make up for mauling her after she made me such a good meal, I take her hand in mine and tug her toward the door. "Come with me. I wanna show you what I've been working on."

I bound down the steps, pulling Vera behind me. I pull out a stool for her and help her settle on it before grabbing the prototype. The small canister of blood Director Cooper sent has been washed and sanitized and emptied of the stuff that makes Vera ill.

I replaced it with my own creation.

"This is only a trial. It will need tweaking, but it was the best I could do in such a short amount of time." I open the receptacle and hand it over to her. "Go on. Take a sip."

Vera arches a brow at me. "Am I supposed to trust the man who accidentally turned himself into a pumpkin?" Her teasing smirk goes straight to my heart.

"That's a fair point. But trust me, this is gonna be wonderful."

"Are you going to tell me what this is first?"

I uncap the container with a grin and take a sniff from it before offering her the chance to do the same. "And?" I ask. "Any adverse feelings?"

She shakes her head. "Should I have a bad reaction?"

My smile widens. "That's a blood substitute. Or at least, what I *hope* can be a blood substitute. Taste it."

Vera pales, but the apples of her cheeks become bright like cherries. "What if I get sick? Or pass out?"

"Then I'll take care of you. I promise I did the very best I could to make this as palatable as possible. I've had some, and I'm still standing."

Warily, Vera takes hold of the canister and brings it to her nose. She gives it a couple of sniffs and twirls it, taking another whiff. "It doesn't *smell* like blood. I don't feel faint." Slowly, as if she were about to drink poison, Vera brings it to her lips and takes a cursory sip.

"Why does it taste like cotton candy?"

Heat burns my cheeks.

Because that's what you smell like. Because that's what your kisses taste like.

"I wanted it to have a pleasant aftertaste," I answer with a shrug.

"This definitely explains the smell of burning sugar."

"Yeah, let's not talk about that. Production was interesting. Let's leave it at that."

"You shouldn't have done this," she whispers. "Though I'm not sure I've ever had someone give me a gift so sweet and meaningful. But you should've been focusing on *your* situation, Pumpkin King."

She's not wrong, but I can't help it. Somehow, making sure Vera is safe and can survive easily became my priority.

Because that's super normal when you've known a woman for seven nights.

Only, it hasn't just been seven nights. Not really. It's not like we're meeting in the real world, going out on a couple of dates here and there. All of our time is spent together, and we're literally the only person around. That's not to say I wouldn't have wanted to impress Vera if we met under different circumstances.

I *know*—down to the very core of me—that Vera would have caught my eye and my interest no matter where or how we met.

"What am I gonna do if you turn into a gourd out there? Kiss you with my magic cotton candy lips?"

She thinks she means because of the blood.

I mean her lip gloss.

I can't help it. My hand moves of its own volition to tuck a strand of her hair behind her ear. She leans forward, her breath hitching along.

"Your kiss would definitely have some magical qualities. Fairy tale stuff, for sure." And because I'm a lot cheesy and a little into her, I brush a kiss on her smile.

I'm not prepared for the sheer magnitude of the desire that hits me. Vera sighs into my mouth, her hands pressing against my chest as she arches up to kiss me.

A real kiss.

One that has her standing from the stool to pin herself to me. Her lips on mine, moving to the same rhythm. Her hands on me, mine gripping her ass to pull her into me.

I was right. *This is a fairy tale* kind of kiss. It erases everything for my mind except Vera Slaski, bat shifter, lawyer, agent, cute as a button, hot as sin, and everything in between.

She came here to protect me from the outside world, but she's why I want to rejoin it.

I want to take her out on proper dates. I want to hold her hand as we walk down the street. I want to lay her down and show her how good it could be between us.

So much for never trusting another person ever again.

"This is really sweet, Jack." The warm brown of her eyes melts into whirlpools of chocolate, pulling me closer to her with the force of a vortex. Vera stands on the tips of her toes and kisses my cheek. "Thank you."

She's *right* there. So close to me. Vera doesn't want to let me go any more than I want to let her go.

I know Lisbeth Bannon really fucked me over. Shit, she might have very well ruined my life if it hadn't brought me to this exact moment. If Lisbeth hadn't used me for her own gain, then I never would have blown the whistle on Vitality. I never would have reached out to Val Downer.

I never would have met Vera Slaski.

A world without the batty lady seems so dull and colorless.

Now that I know this woman exists, I don't want to ever forget that her hazel gaze shines amber when the light hits it just right. I want to memorize the Cupid bow of her lips, the sweet scent of cotton candy.

If I had to get my ass handed to me by Lisbeth Bannon to meet Vera Slaski, I would do it all over again. That's saying something.

"I'll have to make more of it. Probably tweak it to maximize its nutritional value, but at least it's a good start."

"Well, when I was growing up, Raya used to talk about the powerful satiated feeling she had after drinking blood. I never had that because I was too busy feeling sick. I feel pretty satisfied right now. That's a good sign. Though, that very well could be because of the kiss."

Vera smacks a hand over her mouth, surprised by her own words.

Pleased and every bit victorious, I chuckle. "It could be. I'm pretty *satisfied* with that, too." *Though I could go for more.* A quick glance at the clock on the wall tells me it's nearly time for us to get to bed.

Separately.

Right?

I definitely *shouldn't* push my luck and try to take things further with Vera. Nope. It would be a bad idea.

"I should go back upstairs and finish packing and cleaning up the kitchen."

"I'll help. I've done enough science experiments today."

"I really can't complain about that. I really thought you were down here trying to find a solution to the pumpkin thing. Not making a blood substitute for me."

I shrug. "I've been working on the pumpkin situation since it happened. I've got a few things up my sleeve. Besides, it always helps me to work on a different project while I let things simmer in my brain. It's like taking a shower or gardening and having some brilliant ideas pop in randomly. The answer comes when your mind is busy doing something else."

"I'm very grateful, Jack. It really was the sweetest thing anyone has ever done for me."

I smirk, my heart expanding big and wide in my chest. "You're very welcome."

"Now, you stay down here and try to find a way to not explode into a pumpkin." She arches a brow at me, giving me a stern look that makes me want to throw her over my shoulder and bring her to bed. "If you succeed in your experiment, there might be more of this." Vera kisses me softly before retreating up the stairs.

There will never be a greater motivator than a kiss from Vera Slaski.

15

NORBERT

By the time I climb the stairs up to the cabin, I'm exhausted.

I made a bit of progress.

Enough to inject myself with it.

Is it safe? No.

Do I know what will happen? No.

But I *have* to try something.

The very last thing I want is for us to be attacked and Vera to be all alone. She isn't a defenseless creature. She is a capable bat. She wouldn't be an agent—sort of—if she weren't. It's bullshit that she was kept from graduating because of her blood aversion, but I don't make the rules. All I can do for her is help her however I can.

That's creating the blood alternative.

Two large backpacks are propped up against the wall by the entrance. A small, rectangular orange bag holds the wee two-person tent.

It's been difficult enough on my sanity to have the delectable Vera in my space this past week. I can't even imagine how difficult it'll be to share a tent.

Not that I want us to be attacked or anything, but it would be that much easier to resist her if we were running for our lives.

Vera sits on the couch, feet tucked under her, book clutched in her hand. Her brown hair is down and frames her face perfectly. The loose red tank droops low, giving me a teasing glimpse of all the things I shouldn't want. Her white sleep shorts are patterned over with little red hearts. One of those is mine.

"And? How did it go?"

"It went," I answer, taking a seat beside her.

"Did you find a solution?"

"Time will tell."

She frowns, her lips pulling into a pout I want to kiss. "I really wish you would have focused on yourself instead of my dumb blood thing."

"It's not a dumb blood thing," I assure her, cupping her knee to give it a comforting squeeze. I mean for the gesture to be sweet, but my dick doesn't understand the friendly touch. I ignore it as best I can. "You've been more than brave about your aversion to blood your whole life. I'm happy to help. Really. It's *not* dumb."

Vera shrugs and drops her book onto the coffee table. "It sure set me apart."

"That's not a bad thing. Besides, if you were all down with the blood, you wouldn't be here."

Her eyes catch mine, flitting from left to right as she tries to decipher my meaning. For a second, I think she'll flirt back. Help a fellow out.

She doesn't.

She folds her knees up to her chin, curling herself into a tiny ball of delicious Vera. "We'll be ready to go as soon as we wake up," she explains. "I think we should get to bed now. We'll wake up when the sun is still up, but at least we can hit the road. The sooner we get to Mila's place, the better."

"I still think we should take the car." I really don't like the idea of her out there, at the mercy of the sun. I didn't create a blood alternative only to have Vera die because of her sun allergy. "You really haven't considered it?"

She shakes her head. "If there *is* a mole in FUC or even the Cryptozoian Council, I don't want to be tracked."

"Fine. But that means we share the bed tonight." Without preamble, I scoop her into my arms.

Vera squeaks and squirms as I walk us to the bedroom. "What the hell do you think you're doing?"

"If we're going to sleep in a tent for the next two nights, if you insist on putting yourself in direct contact with the sun, well then, you need to have at least one decent night's sleep in a bed. I insist."

"Apparently," she grumbles when I lay her down on my pillow.

She sits up and crosses her arms. "You don't play fair. You can't just *manhandle* me like that." Her eyes sparkle with amber and gold. Her nostrils flare with something. Passion? Desire?

Her nipples peeking through the thin material of her tank are answer enough.

A burning need to tease the nubs with my tongue makes my already interested cock perk up with more interest.

"You really think we should share a bed tonight?"

"Yup." I take off my tee and throw it into the laundry basket. I turn to face her, and Vera's pupils dilate as she takes in my bare chest. "It's happening. We can build a wall of pillows between us if that'll make you more comfortable."

"Okay." She doesn't move, her gaze hooked onto mine.

"Okay," I repeat, standing there in nothing but a pair of jeans that put my erection on display.

She peeks down, and her breath hitches when she notices the impact she has on me. "Maybe this is a bad idea."

Vera's words don't match her actions. She pounces off the bed and leaps into my arms. Her lips find mine as she holds on to my shoulders. Stunned but oh-so-pleased, I wrap my arms around her and lift her off the ground. Her legs wrap around my waist, and I pin her to me by cupping her ass. My tongue delves into her mouth. Cotton candy, want, and need explode through my senses, leaving me dizzy and moaning into the kiss.

I lay her down onto the bed and cover her body with mine, quick to return my lips to hers. Her fingers dig into my nape as she explores my mouth, her hips clear off the bed to grind against my erection. My hand travels up her shirt, savoring the soft skin of her stomach, pebbling under my touch. I graze her nipple with my thumb before rolling it between my fingers. Vera nips at my lower lip in answer.

"Jack," she moans, arching her hips toward me.

"V," I whisper in her ear. "What are we doing here?"

"I don't know." Her eyes are pools of dark, warm honey, pulling me, gluing me to her.

I don't want to be anywhere else than right here.

"I want you," rumbles out of me, heavy with truth and lust and a longing so profound it has a vise-grip on my spine.

"Ditto."

No sooner is the word out of her mouth than I take her lips with mine, nipping at the lower one, exploring her mouth, letting our tongues melt together. Her hand fumbles with my pants while mine peel her out of her sleep shorts. Thankfully, they slide right off, giving me plenty of time to get rid of her top, leaving a very bare, very naked Vera on my bed.

There's never been a lovelier sight.

I want to relish this moment and remember it forever. Her look of sheer desire and raw passion nearly sets me aflame.

"You want this?" I ask, my voice rough.

"Yes. I want *you*."

Thank fuck. I don't know if I speak the words or think them because I'm too concerned with having a taste of Vera. Her bent knees grip my waist as I lower myself down her body.

"What are you doing? Get back here and kiss me," she huffs.

Oh, I'll kiss you all right.

My lips settle right onto the apex of her thighs with a full open-mouth kiss. Her hips lift from the bed as she chases the sensation.

Saucy bat.

I run my tongue over the tight bundle of nerves over and over again before sucking it into my mouth. Vera's pants spur me on, and soon, her legs tremble at my sides. She purrs my name, pleading for that sweet release. I slowly slip a finger inside her heat, quickly followed by another one.

That's all it takes.

Vera cries out, grinding against me to squeeze every ounce of pleasure from the moment. I continue to lap at her center, my gaze fixed on her blissed-out face.

She is, without a doubt, the loveliest woman I've ever seen.

"That... you..." She tries to speak but gives up, lying back against the pillows with a giggle. "I need a second before we go further."

"We don't have to." I make my way up and hover over her. The tip of my erection brushes against her skin, weeping for attention.

"Uh, yeah. We really do."

I chuckle. "My oral skills not enough for you?"

"Not sure it would ever be enough," she responds before surprising the hell out of me and using her toned thighs and arms to spin us around. Vera straddles me, pinning me to the bed, her soft brown hair a halo around us. "Please tell me you've got protection somewhere in this cabin."

I wince because I do. A leftover box of condoms from my time with Lisbeth, but that doesn't matter. If I can empty the box with Vera, then it'll have been worth it. I reach over to the bedside table and grab one. Vera leans over me, kissing me sweetly to grab it from my hand. I watch, riveted and fascinated, as she rips the wrapper and rolls the condom onto my erection.

It shouldn't be sexy to watch her do that, but it is. Vera looks down at me with her hazel eyes burning for me. That's heady as hell.

"You ready?" she coos, pumping my girth with a naughty smirk.

"Vera," is all I'm able to say.

She lines us up and eases me in. She takes all the time in the world to lower down onto my length, prolonging the moment in the most amazing torture. When I'm finally encased in her wet heat, she tilts her hips forward, clenches her walls around me, and rolls her hips.

By all the good gods of creation.

The pleasure surges up my spine, a vise closing around my balls. If she does that again, I'll embarrass myself.

Vera places her hands on my chest for leverage as she continues to ride me. I grip her hips, letting her drive. For now, at least. Her breasts hover over my mouth, and I tug her down to circle the nub with my tongue. She bucks against me with a gasp. I repeat the gesture before sucking hard, letting my teeth graze it. I lick a line across her chest to give the other nipple the same attention.

Vera is a mewling vixen above me, taking me for everything she wants, everything she needs.

Her back arches back as she pushes away from my chest. Her eyes hook on mine, and I see it right about the same time as I feel it. Her core grips me hard, and her pace increases. She gasps, and heat floods me. Vera cries my name as she chases her release.

I'm not far behind.

There's no chance I can last much longer after that. I buck off the bed, pistoning my hips to meet her. My hands tighten on her hips, and I hold her there as I go over the edge, bellowing her name.

It takes me a few moments to move again. When my legs start being legs again, I run to the bathroom to discard the condom and dive back into bed, nestling Vera into my side.

This might have been ill-advised.

Shit, it might even end in my heart breaking.

But if Vera would be willing, I'd give this thing between a chance.

16

VERA

Sweet flying mammal, that was amazing.

So damn good and so damn unexpected that I'm not entirely sure what to do. I don't really want to move. I want to stay right here, lying in Jack's arms, listening to his heartbeat settle after our tryst.

"I guess we ended up sharing the bed after all," Jack whispers before kissing my shoulder.

Naked and sprawled, intertwined and drunk on the afterglow, I giggle. "It seems that way, yes."

"You're not going back to the couch after that, Vera. You're staying right here."

"You better believe it," I shoot back with a snort. "This bed is so damn comfortable. I might never leave. Think we can drag it with us on our trek?"

He chuckles, the sound smooth and warm. "Anything you want, V."

Jack is being funny.

Yet, there is something else. It's heavy like he means something more. Something profound.

Get it together, V. You've known the dude a week. You've kissed a couple of times and had sex once. This is hardly the greatest love story ever told.

A small voice in the back of my mind argues softly with an *it could be.*

"Do you snore?" Jack asks. "Should I be prepared for some seriously bad sleeping habits?"

I pinch his side, and he laughs, holding me tighter. "I'm a great sleeper, but we can't stay in bed yet. We still need to prepare some last-minute stuff. We gotta be ready to go as soon as we wake up."

"One more minute," he murmurs, making me shiver. He nestles his head in my hair, sniffing me. "You smell so damn good. One more minute."

"Fine," I relent dramatically with an eye roll, but really, I don't want to go anywhere. I want to soak in this moment for as long as we possibly can. "One more, but then it's up and work time."

"Yes, Agent Slasky."

"Oh, call me that again. It was super sexy."

Jack brushes the shell of my ear with his lips. "Agent. Slaski." His breath flutters against my skin, and I swear I'm ready for round two.

"You're an evil, tempting man, Jack."

"I do my best," he chuckles, making my body zing all over again.

A loud and echoing *bang* makes the walls of the cabin shake and quiver. I jump out of bed, naked as the day I was born, in a defensive stance.

"Stay behind me," I order Jack.

He's already slipping on his boxers and stalking toward the door. "It's probably the damn squirrels. They likely made on of the rakes fall. They do it all the time."

"Jack," I hiss. "If you go Full Gourd on me, I swear..."

I don't have the time to finish my thought. Jack swings the door open, and there stand three people, dressed in black from head to toe, their faces covered by balaclavas.

Shit shit shit. Jack is about to turn veg on me.

"Who do you think you are, busting into my ho—" His sentence dies down as one of the intruders strikes out at him.

Jack dodges, and I lunge, ready to strike. It takes very little time for my human body to shrink down to my bat. I might be an itty-bitty thing, but I can do lots of damage.

As a vampire bat, I've got teeth and claws for days. I slash at one of the interlopers, slicing through his mask. The smell of blood immediately hits me, but I don't focus on it.

Nope.

I keep repeating to myself over and over again that Jack is about to be one defenseless creature. I need to get the upper hand and fast.

Protect Jack is my only rational thought.

I fly up to the ceiling, only to dive down again, incisors at the ready. My batty gut churns at the thought of tasting blood, but again, I push the thought away, thinking only of Jack.

I latch onto one of our attackers, my teeth digging deep. I'm not careful, not like when I'm forced to feed on other mammals. I rip the sensitive skin of the neck like a rabid hound. I even use my legs to gash and slice.

Hot, disgusting blood oozes.

It's a lot.

My brain and body want to revolt, but I'll do that later.

I'll need about a gallon of mouth wash and another of antacid to get over *that*.

I fly up to the ceiling, hooking my claws into the wall. From the vantage point, I spot one of the prowlers helping the one I've wounded while the third just stands there, staring down at an enormous orange gourd.

Wait. Why would a trespasser be immobile right now?

Horrified — and surprised as hell — I spot Jack.

I shout his name, but it comes out like a loud squeak. I dive down toward him, my poor, sweet, defenseless Pumpkin King. But before the goon can get the jump on him, the large gourd begins to rattle and vibrate.

I've seen this happen before.

Jack is about to blow.

I hold my breath and wait for a very naked Jack to appear.

That's not what happens.

The pumpkin wobbles to and fro as if it were sitting on hydraulic limbs. The man staggers back, equal parts confused and terrified. It's not every day you see a grown human turn into a pumpkin before said vegetation begins to move of its own accord.

The jack-o'-lantern, with an actual face carved onto its surface, *sprouts two stubby legs.* As the gourd continues to gain height, the legs grow and grow and grow some more. It takes me a minute to realize that the pumpkin has also grown arms.

Jack is no longer a pumpkin.

He's a scarecrow with a jack-o'-lantern for a head.

I. Am. Freaked. The. Fuck. Out.

He isn't too steady on his legs but staggers forward. The remaining intruder whimpers and edges back, making the shape of the cross with both of his index fingers.

I want to laugh, but I get it.

It's a downright shocking sight to see.

The two others, still trying to staunch the bleeding, notice Jack. The injured one slips to the floor, holding on to his neck, while the other grabs for a gun. He shoots directly at Jack, and I swoop down, claws at the ready. I slash at the gunman's forehead, barely managing to slice through the material of his balaclava. A quick peek at Jack to make sure he's okay has my wings sputtering mid-flight.

The gun didn't shoot bullets. Nope. Huge tranquilizer darts stick out of Jack's straw chest, leaving me no doubt that Jack hauled hay into the lab to make himself into a scarecrow.

I really hope he can change back.

At the very least, Jack doesn't seem to be the least bit affected by the tranquilizer. He keeps advancing toward our foe, swiping long hands made of straw. He looks like something right out of a nightmare or a horror movie, but I can't make myself look away.

His body—if I can call it that—makes no sense.

The straw of his limbs and torso are woven together like one giant poppet with a pumpkin sitting atop a neck like a crown.

I'd bet my left incisor that if he had spent more time on his formula than on making a blood alternative for me, he would have figured out a way to dress his scarecrow somehow.

My man is brilliant.

Only, he isn't my man, and this is certainly not the time to be thinking about what the sex meant.

I flap my wings a few times and fly by his line of vision, making sure to catch his attention. He makes a terrible groaning sound, and all I can do is hope he follows. The interlopers, stunned and scared that their weapons are not working on the massive scarecrow, scamper out of his way. The incapacitated one on the floor whimpers and rolls out of Jack's way.

I land on one of the bags I packed and flutter my wings.

Please understand me. Pick up this bag. It has some clothes for our naked asses.

"They're gonna get away," one of the men shouts.

"Yeah, well, *you* go after 'em."

"Not a chance," comes the answer. "Did you see? That's too freaky for my pay grade."

With strange and stunted movements, Jack picks up the bag, swings it over his shoulder, and it flies across the room before crashing against the wall. Without being prompted—*thank blood bags for sentient beings*—he picks up the second one and lumbers out the door and down the steps.

He goes to the passenger side of the vehicle and nearly rips the door off its hinges before throwing the bag into the backseat and plopping onto the seat. His head falls and rolls at his feet, but I don't have time to deal with that.

I need to get us *out* before the idiot goons wise up. I shift back into my human form, naked once again, and hop into the car. I scan my thumb against the small biometric pad in the dash. It's a good thing to have for shifter agents. When we take our human form, we're nude with no pockets or nook or cranny for our keys. The fingerprint key is... well, key.

The armored car roars to life, and I floor it.

17

VERA

I clutch the steering wheel with all my might to keep the panic at bay, but really, the last thirty minutes of my life have been a little bit intense.

Amazing sex with a hot farming scientist.

Cute post-coital cuddling.

Three intruders barging in.

Yup. This is definitely *not* a regular mission and *definitely not* how I planned on leaving the cabin.

On the seat next to me, the straw scarecrow slowly starts to lose shape, basically melting into a pile of hay.

"If you go and explode on me right now, Jack Palomer, I'm gonna be so pissed."

I have no idea what happens when Jack shifts back into his body. The only time I saw it happen, there was pumpkin goo everywhere in the lab.

As I try to navigate the massive SUV down the narrow and overrun dirt road, I take quick glances at the gourd. Slowly, it begins to vibrate.

"Do. Not. Splat," I warn.

But he has no real control over it. It's not like humans are *supposed* to morph into vegetation. It's enough of an oddity that I turn into a bat the size of a child's teacup. But this?

Well, it defies all nature *and* logic.

"Where do your organs even go?" I ask aloud, probably to find something to think about other than the impending pumpkin bath I'm about to take.

A quick glance at the rearview mirror, and it's clear. Whatever the goons are doing, they aren't following us.

Weird.

At least it gives me a good idea. I slam on the brake, leap out of the car, run around the front, and grab hold of Jack.

It's a really good thing this man has already seen me naked.

I lay the pumpkin down on the forest ground and wave my hand over him. "Let's go. Be human."

It shakes and vibrates, but nothing happens.

I kneel by it and give the gourd a peck. "Come on, prince charming. Be human again so we can hit the road."

The pumpkin shimmies and hops and nearly does a backflip. I have just enough time to duck for cover before a loud *splat* echoes through the crepuscule. I peek out from above the car and see Jack standing in the carcass of a squash.

Literally.

"You okay?" I ask, rushing toward him. I run my hands down his chest where the tranquilizers would have hit him. There isn't one needle prick or one single blemish.

The man is perfect, even naked in the pre-dawn, wearing nothing by pumpkin.

All hail the king of the pumpkin patch.

"I'm fine, V. Maybe stop running your hands on me, though." He grins like it's the most appropriate time to make a dick joke.

"Get your ass in the car. We gotta make like a Jack and blow."

"Not funny," he mumbles, settling back into his seat.

"A little funny," I shoot back with a snort, starting the vehicle.

"I wonder why you turn back to your human shape. Think it has to do with the threat being gone?"

"Maybe," he answers, wincing on the hay-covered seat.

I would like to report that I'm a good little non-agent and drive the speed limit and obey all of the rules of the road once we're we *finally* spat out of the forest trail. It would be a lie and not so bold-faced because time is of the essence.

"If they found us, it means either Lisbeth managed to find my coordinates or Agent Val Downer isn't exactly on the up and up."

I ponder his words for a few moments. "Who does your gut tell you is behind the attack?"

"It's gotta be Lisbeth. She has the cash to hire muscle. Downer? Not so much. Besides, if Downer is a mole, wouldn't she report to the same people as Lisbeth, if not the woman herself?"

"Hmm. Yeah. I guess that's a fair point, but there could be *two* different groups of people after you."

Jack groans. "Great. That's all I need."

"I guess there's no sense in us trying to figure out everything right now. We're naked and in a car that is currently being tracked by FUC."

"So much for our trek through the woods." Jack is wistful as he takes my hand in his.

Do I need two hands to drive? Nope. Not if it means holding hands with Jack.

"We'll have to go with your plan, then. Drive in the opposite direction that they would expect, which would be right toward FUC and Mila's house. When we spot a town, we can ditch this SUV and —" I stop myself short.

"What? What's wrong?"

"Well, depending on which bag we were able to grab, we might not have any cash." I roll my lips into my mouth and try to take a deep breath. "I can't steal a car."

"I'll steal a car."

"You can't do that," I gasp. "It's a crime. I'm an agent of the law, and I can't actually commit an offense or let you do it for us."

"I'm pretty sure your director won't be mad in this situation."

"I mean I'm making a hash of this mission. First, I fall for my charge. Then I *sleep* with him. *Then* I proceed to go on the run nude, with no method of communication and without money."

Jack squeezes my hand, and I glance at him when it's safe to do so. The last thing I need is to kill us in a crash. "What?" I ask.

"You just said a really nice thing."

"I did?" I laugh nervously. "It sounds like I listed a whole big mess."

"You fell for your charge."

Oh. Shit. I'm naked and blushing.

It's not just my cheeks that are burning and red. My whole *body* is, and Jack can see it all. I grip the wheel tighter with my free hand and scour my brain for some kind of explanation, but I draw a blank.

"That not a bad thing, you know." He interlaces our fingers. "I should probably tell you right now... I fell for you, too."

"It's weird," I sigh.

"It is," he agrees with a smirk. "Very soon. Very quick."

"Seven days."

"Alone in a cabin, though," he amends with a shrug.

"Right. That makes a difference, does it?"

"Yes, of course," he answers.

"Are there dating rules I don't know about?"

"There might be," he teases. "The rulebook I got explained things very clearly. When you meet a woman who makes you as nuts as much as she makes you laugh, then you know it's the real deal."

"I make you nuts?"

He chuckles. "And you make me laugh."

"Well, as sweet as this is, we still shouldn't have done what we did. We should have waited until this was all over. Director Cooper won't be happy with me. More than that, if we hadn't been in the bedroom together, those goons might not have been able to get the jump on us."

"Um, not sure that could have gone better, actually. I think I scared the crap out of them when I shifted into the pumpkin thing."

"About that..." I chanced another side-eye his way. "How did *that* happen?"

"Well, you gave me the idea, actually."

For the next forty-five minutes, Jack goes into detail about the science behind the transformation. I understand the first two minutes, but the rest is way over my head. I'd need a Ph.D. in genes and botany—and maybe a few other disciplines—to understand how he managed to morph his genome.

"I'm just gonna call it magic," I tease.

"Science is kinda like magic. A potion is simply another word for experiment."

"If that were true, I would have liked my science class a lot more in high school." I tap my fingers on the well. "I didn't like those classes much. The debate team was more my speed."

"I can definitely see that. You're great on your feet."

I snort my argument. "I *always* had a strategy in the courtroom. Tonight? Not so much. I didn't have much of a plan beyond *keep us alive*."

"It worked."

"For now," I argue. "We need to get to safety."

"You're right. There's a small village down this road. We'll be able to boost a car. I'll leave a note," he quickly adds as I'm about to argue with him. "We'll make it clear that we're going to bring the car back to them eventually."

"Fine," I mumble.

But really, we don't have a choice.

We're low on options, and the sun is about to come out.

18

NORBERT

I'm not going to lie. When we finally manage to find a car to *borrow*, I'm relieved.

Not because I want us to put clothes on or anything so prudish, but I'm sitting on a pile of hay, and that shit is itchy as hell.

At the time, it seemed like a good idea to morph into some kind of scarecrow figure. Now, I am seriously doubting my decision. Maybe I should have focused on tweaking the whole blasting-open part of the shift.

If I am going to be an exploding pumpkin every time I have to turn back into my human form, I will buy stock in cleaning product companies.

The bag Vera made me grab from the house had a bunch of my clothes in it. They're too big for Vera, but that works in our favor, given her allergy. The sun is beginning to rise, and the only car we managed to find *doesn't* have tinted windows. Not to the extent that Vera needs, anyway. She's in the passenger seat, bundled up in layers to protect her skin from the rays poking through the early morning sky.

Vera directs me as we drive toward her cousin's home. If calculations are correct, it'll be the middle of the day by the time we get there. That's the middle of the night for nocturnal creatures like Mila and Vera.

"It must be quite difficult to be nocturnal," I comment, hoping to relieve some of the mounting pressure. It's not like we're out on a jaunty drive. This isn't a laugh. We're on the run, and until we figure out who was behind the attack on my cabin, we can't really trust anyone. Instead of focusing on that and panicking—which could very well lead to me becoming a pumpkin again—I can make pleasant conversation. "Do you wish you didn't have a sun allergy?"

Vera shrugs. "It would make life easier if I could be out during the day. It made my career as a lawyer very difficult. It's not like the most upstanding citizens were up for meetings in the dead of night. I always had to sneak into the courthouse because they don't have night court. I got used to the strange schedule, but I missed the moon."

"Huh. You missed the moon?"

"Yeah. I suspect it would be like you not seeing the sun for days. You need it like I need the moon."

"That's interesting. I never even thought of that. You're a night-blooming flower."

Vera giggles. "Did you seriously compare me to a plant that grows by the light of the moon?"

"Yup. I sure did."

"Only a botanist and subsistence farmer would find that romantic."

"The question is, did *you* find it romantic, V?"

Her breath catches, and from the corner of my eye, I see her smirk.

"Yeah, but only because it comes from you."

"Fair enough."

"Jack, can I ask you something? I don't want to upset you..."

"Go right ahead. It's the perfect time. It's not like I can run away from you."

She laughs and toys with the sleeve of her shirt. "I wonder why you like to stay hidden in your cabin. You're obviously a brilliant scientist if you can create a blood alternative in such a short amount of time. Not to mention that you also managed to tweak your shifter genes *twice* now. What's that about?"

"You give me too much credit. I had most of the work already done for the shifter stuff. As soon as I realized what I'd done to myself, I started working on *not* being a defenseless gourd every time I'm threatened. The blood thing, well..." I run a hand over my mouth. "I did a lot of research and experiments when I was still working for Lisbeth. It wasn't too hard to do. I basically pulled the nutrients and added some water and flavoring. I know the Bloody Doctor's work inside out at this point. She broke down everything anyone would ever need to know about blood. That's why her work is so critical. She's unlocked quite a few mysteries. In the wrong hands, that knowledge is..."

"Dangerous?" Vera offers.

"Exactly. When I was working for Lisbeth, I asked her about the ethics of it all. If there were certain lines I wasn't to cross. She told me I had a free pass. Assured me that there wasn't a thing I could do that she couldn't protect me from. It might not cast me in the best of lights, but when you give a scientist *carte blanche*, things can get interesting. I didn't concern myself with the morality of what I was doing. I wanted to find the cure to all illnesses. Can you imagine what that would do for the world? No more disease? There would never be another pandemic. There would be no more endemics. No more cancer or degenerative diseases."

"That's pretty revolutionary."

"It would have been, yeah. But that's not what Lisbeth wanted from me. It was all about immortality. She wanted me to focus on how to regenerate cells so the body never ages and dies. That was too tall of an order for my skills."

"You did it because of your parents?"

I sigh and let my mind spin out before answering a shaky, "Yes."

"They died suddenly, and that made an impact on you."

"It did. Imagine it. I was a kid, living in the rainforest. The only people I ever interacted with were my parents and a few locals. I wasn't exactly socialized properly."

"So that's why you prefer living in your cabin alone."

"I choose when I want to be with people. I get tired very easily around others. Talking and all that is difficult."

"You seem fine around me."

"Well, that's because you're quite easy to be around, V."

"Oh."

"I mean it. When Downer first told me that I would have to host an agent for my own protection, I fully intended to make that person sleep in a tent outside. But then *you* showed up, and I don't know. I didn't get the usual panic I get. I don't know if it was because you didn't seem overly fazed about the pumpkin thing. After the Lisbeth debacle, I didn't think I could trust another human, but you walked in with your attitude and lip gloss... and your morals."

"My morals?"

"Yeah. You left your job as a lawyer because you couldn't uphold the law. Because you had to defend some bad people. You became an agent, and you were adamant that you'd report my ass to FUC and the Cryptozoian Council if I stepped a toe out of line."

"You like me because I follow the rules?"

"Among other things, yes." I take her hand and bring it to my lips to give it a quick kiss. "Even the fact that wouldn't steal a car even though we're on the run is refreshing. I need the physical boundary of a forest around me to feel secure. You have your principles as your boundaries. It's commendable."

"Not a very sexy quality."

"I beg to differ. Solid boundaries are definitely sexy."

She snorts. "You are not like other men, Jack Palomer."

"I know. I'm the Pumpkin King." I wink at her, grinning like a fool.

Vera snorts before laughing softly. "It's funny that you like that about me. That I like rules, I mean. I think I only developed that as a defense mechanism because of my blood thing."

"How do you mean?"

"Well, I always felt like a broken bat. I can't do a basic thing. A biological need I rely on to survive. It's basically a rule of nature. I thought if I followed all of life's other rules to the letter, then it wouldn't matter so much if I could drink blood or not." She shrugs, sighing. "I've been trying to make up for it my whole life. I try to perfect every other way that I can."

I tighten my grip on her hand. "So I'm a recluse because I don't know how to interact with people and I'm wary of all of the social norms, and you're hyperaware of them. We're a pair and a half."

"We really are."

"This was my way of asking you how this thing between us is gonna play, by the way."

"You're my charge, and I don't have my badge yet. Would you be mad if I want to put a pin in it until it's not against the rules anymore?"

"Sure thing, V." I kiss her hand again, but I sure hope it's not our last kiss.

19

VERA

The house Mila shares with her husband is... *normal*.

It has a yard, flowerbeds, and cute shutters. I can't exactly imagine Mila working in the garden and tending to the plants. T-Bone, now, there is another story.

This house *screams* T-Bone. I can only imagine that the inside resembles something that would make Dracula proud. It's probably some kind of compromise. Mila and T-Bone could *not* be any more different. They are polar opposites, but they fit so well together.

Not to go full cheese, but they really do complete each other.

I really hate bringing trouble to Mila so close to her due date, but if she ever found out that I was dealing with Bloody Doctor stuff and *didn't* involve her, I'd be in serious trouble.

Do not piss off a forensic anthropologist. They know how to get rid of bones.

"This is it?" Jack asks, pointing to the house.

"Yup."

He loops around the neighborhood and parks the car near a park. Leaving a stolen car in my pregnant cousin's laneway is hardly a good idea. We don't want to draw attention to our location.

Dressed in clothes that are way too big for me, I rush through the streets. It's only about a two-minute walk, but by the time I'm standing under the awning, I'm in a bit of pain.

The cure for a bad sun allergy reaction?

Blood.

No, thank you!

I knock on the door, banging against it like a lunatic. "Mila, it's Vera. Please open the door."

It swings open, and T-Bone stands there in a pair of boxers, his hair a mess of blond spikes. He rubs sleep from his face. "Vera? What's happening?"

"What in the name of anthropometers and Boley gauges is going on?" Mila wobbles over in a black nightgown with the words *Lazy Bones* printed across her baby bump.

"Can we come in?" I plead. "There's been some trouble."

T-Bone motions us forward, and we settle in a very neat, very tidy living room. For a few seconds, I think that there is no Mila influence on the decor, but I notice the painting. It's a massive piece that takes up nearly the entire wall. The canvas is white with a whole mess of inkblots à la Rorschach test splashed over it in shades of black and red. Either I'm harboring some pretty intense homicidal compulsions or the painting is actually meant to depict a few skeletons.

A little freaked, I look away, only to spot a series of skulls on the bookshelf.

And a set of teeth used as bookends.

And a few scalpels laid on red velvet encased in a shadowbox.

I wonder what T-Bone thinks of his home's decor, but he must not care. Every time he looks at Mila, his eyes burst out in tiny red hearts. The doting and loving husband helps Mila settle on the couch.

We go through the introductions, momentarily pretending that this is a normal social call. Sort of difficult thing to do when both hosts are in their pajamas and still fuzzy with sleep.

"How far along are you?" Jack asks, sitting in an armchair. He tries not to stare at the quilt patterned over with tiny skulls neatly folded on the coffee table.

"I'm a thousand years late," Mila answers while T-Bone says, "Our little one should be along in the next couple of days. They're talking about inducing if the baby isn't born by next Friday."

"I'm about to induce myself," Mila grumbles.

T settles next to her on the couch, his hand going to her thigh in a comforting squeeze. They're very different but so damn in love. It gives me hope for Jack and me, even though we're not supposed to even be together. Or even thinking about being together.

"Now, will you tell us why you're here in the middle of the day?" Mila winces and rubs her belly. "It's gonna be a boy. We've gotta a bull in here, I swear. He's got horns and loves to jab into my organs."

"If you're here, I take it to mean that your guardian duty isn't going too well." T-Bone is serious and stern with a twinge of concern.

"You're right," I agree before delving into the whole story.

Jack interjects and adds the information he can about Vitality Holdings and Lisbeth Bannon. When he gets to the Bloody Doctor's research, Mila blanches.

"Will I ever be free of that woman's actions?" She looks down at her belly. "I promise you I'll be a batshit mother, but not like that. Okay? I won't kill anyone, but I will embarrass you because it is my uterus-given right." She focuses her eyes back onto Jack. "Please tell me you didn't find the key to immortality."

"No, I didn't. But I think it's fair to assume I wasn't the only person Bannon and VH taped to look into the research." He continues the tale of our adventures up to this very moment.

"You're right. We need Jessie on this. Good thing it's daytime. She'll be up and at work." T grabs the phone, but my squeak of surprise stops him.

"We don't know who we can trust at FUC." My words are like a bomb.

Mila and T are two loyal and dedicated FUC agents.

"That's preposterous," Mila gasps. "Like a mole could ever operate under Alyce Cooper's nose."

"This is a secure line. Jessie set it up herself. This is as safe as need be," T-Bone promises.

Jack and I exchange an uneasy look.

"I just don't want to put you in any danger." I point toward Mila's stomach.

She waves me off. "If anything, the excitement will make this little creature come out. Besides, this is too important. If I'm gonna give birth, I'd rather do it in a world where my mother's research isn't going to be a long and overreaching shadow on my child. Make the call, beefcake."

T-Bone heads for the kitchen to have a rushed and hushed conversation.

"That's fair." Jack runs a hand back through his hair. "I'm really sorry I've brought this down on you."

She shakes her head. "If it wasn't you, it'd be someone else. There are a lot of psychos out there who are trying to find the secrets to immortality. Bannon and whoever she is working with are hardly the first people to take the Bloody Doctor's work to heart. Unfortunately, they won't be the last."

"It would be nice if they were, though," I comment.

"Jessie is on the case," T-Bone announces. "She'll stay at FUCN'A to not arouse any suspicion, but she's looking into Bannon and VH. She'll call as soon as there's news. She'll also look into Val Downer and FUCN'A's Cryptozoian Council rep, Erhart Knope, to see if there are any links between them and VH."

"And what can we do right now?" I ask. "I could bring Jack to another location. Someplace safe."

"Not a chance," Mila roars. "He stays right here where we can keep an eye on him. If this goes bad, I'd rather T be around to help you out. Last time, they came at you with tranquilizers. Your whole pumpkin-scarecrow thing scared them once, but now that they know what you can do, you've lost the element of surprise. They'll come with more effective weapons next time, and probably with more people."

"She's right," T-Bone agreed. "You're to stay here. I've got a small arsenal of weapons in the basement, anyway."

"But we can hardly shift to defend ourselves in the heart of suburbia."

"Why not? T shifted last Halloween. We had a whole demonic farm theme going."

"Hardly the same thing," I point out to my eccentric cousin.

"We really have to… wait here until something happens?" Jack isn't too pleased with this plan.

"That's exactly right," T says. "Until we have more intel from Jessie, there is nothing we can do. We can't pick a fight with an enemy we don't know."

"I feel useless," Jack grumbles. "And a right ass for bringing this to your door."

"Stop," Mila grunts as she tries to stand up. "I need something to eat. I'm ravenous. Let's take this meeting to the kitchen. Might as well graze and talk while we wait for our next step."

T-Bone and Mila retreat to the kitchen, but I hang back in the living room with Jack. "We can't do anything more right now than wait until we have more information. I know you don't like this, but there's nothing we can do. You're still an important witness in all of this. As an almost FUC agent, my job is to keep you safe and out of harm's way. It's the same for T-Bone and Mila."

"I don't like that I caused more trouble instead of making the world better."

"Well, when all of this is resolved, I'm sure you'll find a way to make amends if that's how you feel."

Jack nods, but his eyes have lost their spark.

He feels really bad. It's written all over his face.

I can only hope that he doesn't use this as an excuse to continue his reclusive ways.

I can't exactly date a man who won't leave his forest.

20

NORBERT

When I'm in the lab, waiting to see how one experiment or another works out, I keep busy. I've typically got a few things going on all at once to make sure that my time doesn't lapse into quiet and motionless moments.

Being a subsistence farmer on top of that is also helpful.

If I don't take care of my crops, I don't eat.

There's a mound of food on the kitchen table in front of me, so that's *that* need taken care of. There *really* is nothing for me to do but sit here and speculate.

And think.

Lots and lots of thinking.

I'm about ready to rip my hair out at the roots. Vera's hand hasn't left my thigh since we sat down thirty minutes ago. She can feel my impatience and the urgency burning a hole through my sanity. She gives me a whole bouquet of encouraging nudges and smiles.

Mila hovers her laptop on her baby bump as she scrolls through gossip columns and social media feeds, looking for any mention of Lisbeth Bannon. Apparently, you can't be the CEO of a large corporation without making some headlines every now and again. Mila and T-Bone aren't too concerned about having their research ping any VH security alerts because of the VPN, firewalls, and all of this other security stuff Jessie, the computer pro, set them up with.

Whoever this Jessie woman is, I need to get her help to secure the cabin, apparently.

If I can ever go back.

"Lisbeth Bannon dated Jefferson Cabot?" Mila scrunches up her face and turns the device to show us a picture of Bannon with one of Hollywood's heartthrobs. The guy is in everything, and it's not because he's got talent. "Isn't he a groundhog shifter? Rich, connected daddy?" *That's* why he's in everything.

"He is," Vera answers. "He's basically shifter royalty. His dad is a big deal in the finance world. I remember reading an article about it. Daddy Dearest was really pissed his son didn't want to follow in his footsteps and went into acting instead."

"So we have a rich and famous actor with a tie to the finance world who just happens to be a shifter." I sigh and run my hands back through my hair, hoping to renew blood flow and get a new idea or lead from thin air.

"That can't be a coincidence." Mila continues to scroll. "What if Bannon is out there, dating all these dudes she thinks can help her cause?"

"Mila," T warns before shooting me an apologetic glance.

"What?" She shrugs. "Sorry, that was hurtful, Jack."

"No need to apologize. You're not wrong. She used me. Stands to reason she would do the same thing to another dude out there."

"Oh!" Mila gasps. "Jessie is trying to video chat. Hey, lady. Did you already find something?"

Jessie clicks her tongue. "Some*thing*? Try things. Lots and lots of *things*."

"Gather round, kids." Mila lays the computer on the table where we can all see Jessie's face on the screen. We do another quick round of introductions, but it's pretty clear that Jessie is burning to tell us something.

"You lot need to be super careful. I did some digging into Vitality Holdings and lemme tell you. None of it is good. From what I can tell using *purely* legal ways"—the flush on her cheeks suggests otherwise —"there's a bunch of rich and powerful shifters out there who don't feel like our shifter nature is enough. They want immortality."

"We know this." Mila snaps her fingers. "If anyone tells me I'm being impatient, I'll ask you to refer back to the Hairy Coo growing inside me who is two days away from his or her due date."

"Right." Jessie grins. "I'll try not to take it personally. Now, these bad shifter types are *funding* VH. From what I was able to find in such a short amount of time is that Vitality is nothing but a big front. Yep. You heard me right. One of the largest beauty companies in the world is actually this massive conspiracy to take over the world."

"No one is surprised by this." Vera rolls her eyes. "I'm addicted to my cotton candy lip gloss, but I hate that I feel the need to cover my whole face in concealer to hide a single zit."

"Preach," Mila quips. "D'you know people are *already* asking me how I plan to bounce back and get my pre-baby body? Fucking ridiculous. It'll be what it'll be. I grew a human. What did those fuckers do today?"

"My hero," T-Bone says before kissing the top of her head. He means it, too.

There isn't one ounce of sarcasm in his voice. The man is completely in awe of his partner. Mila and T remind me of my parents. Both strong in their own right and in their own beliefs but so perfectly accepting of the other's strengths. It's something to see.

I long for that.

I never really let myself believe I wanted it, but now that I'm surrounded by people and a couple very much in love, I've realized something.

The reason why I always need to be busy at the cabin is that I'm lonely.

Deeply, profoundly lonely.

If I keep working and occupy every single waking hour with one dire task or another, then the solitude can't get to me. I'm above it somehow.

How will I be able to go back to it now that I've discovered the meaning behind it?

Do I even *want* to go back to it?

If I survive this whole ordeal, what do I want my life to look like? Alone in a cabin off in the wilderness?

No. That's not what I want anymore.

I'd like a house not too different from this one—okay, maybe a lot different where aesthetics are concerned. Maybe a partner to share my life with...

Perhaps a woman with a hazel gaze and pretty brown hair that always smells like cotton candy and happiness.

"Are you with us, Jack?" Mila pulls me out of my tailspin.

Every pair of eyes is on me, including Jessie's. "Sorry, what? Did I miss something?"

"We need to know where you met Lisbeth," Vera repeats. "Where you worked when you weren't in your lab. Where she lived. Her usual haunts. It'll give us a clue as to who she's working for."

"Can't you track down the off-shore accounts?" I aim my question to Jessie.

She laughs like it's the most hilarious thing in the world. "Oh, sure. Because they're not smart enough to hide behind more companies with more fronts than a Dungeons and Dragons' dice. It would take me a long time to pull at that thread. Time we might not have if they're after you."

"And let's be real," T cuts in. "If they only wanted to kidnap you or silence you *before* they knew what you could do? That'll be nothing compared to their excitement when they realize you've turned yourself into an invulnerable *pumpkin*."

"I'm not even going to ask," Jessie quips from the monitor. "On paper, VH is only the larger corporation behind all of Vitality's products and smaller companies. But no one who is on the up and up has *this* long of a trail."

"What's our next step then?" Vera wonders. "Why does it feel like we'll have to bring Director Cooper in for this?"

"Because we have to," Mila answers. "Not only is she our boss but if Erhart Knope and the Cryptozoian Council have gone rogue or have a mole, she needs to know."

"There isn't a chance in hell Erhart Knope is a bad guy. He's is more straight edge than T." Jessie quickly adds, "Sorry, T."

"You're not wrong." He shrugs.

"Are you really telling me that we have to tell our boss that I fucked up my first non-mission? Leaving the cabin? Stealing a car?" Vera puts her hand over her mouth. "I think I'm gonna pass out from the disappointed look on her face and she's not even here yet."

"Not gonna lie. Alyce will be hella pissed at you. But you also made some very good calls. Don't freak out just yet. Let's see where this all leads, okay? You'll be fine, Vera. And we're right here with you."

"See?" T-Bone says. "My wife is gonna be the best damn mom."

Mila clicks her tongue, but she's also pleased. "Easy, beefcake." She blows him a kiss before passing the landline over to Vera. "It's secure. Promise. Call Alyce."

Vera nods and heaves out a breath before calling her boss to admit she might very well have fucked up her career as an agent before it even got started.

21

VERA

Director Alyce Cooper is not the kind of woman you want to piss off.

She is a—*the*—boss for a reason.

I also admire her. A lot.

Letting her down after what happened at the graduation is a little too much for me. As soon as I end the call—after Director Cooper coolly told me she was on her way and that we *would discuss it in person*—I have to rush to the bathroom to splash cold water on my face and neck.

Rule breaking isn't something I'm exactly used to. Disappointing figures of authority I admire? That's a big bucket of mental flagellation.

The gentle sound of knocking pulls me away from my racing thoughts.

"V, it's Jack. Wanna talk?"

I slowly open the door and lean against the frame. Jack mimics my position, his head hovering inches over mine. His lips graze my temple while his hands grip my hips.

"I'd ask if you're okay, but I can tell you're freaking out."

"I broke so many rules."

"Sometimes, to do the right thing, you gotta do a couple bad things. From where I'm standing, you did nothing wrong. You kept me alive and brought me to a safe place."

"But then there's the other thing..."

"I definitely don't think that was wrong. In fact, I think that was really good. Fantastic, even. I'm looking forward to more of that." He smiles at me. "Are there really rules that prevent relationships between agent and charge?"

"I assume there have to be. It's a weird power dynamic, isn't it?"

"I gladly relinquish all of my power to you, oh my batty queen." He winks and pulls me into his arms for a hug so warm, so powerful, that even my soul feels it.

"All your power, huh?" I tease before inhaling his sweet woodsy scent. It's as comforting as it's emboldening.

"I actually have a lot of faith that this will all work out for the best."

"Oh, really? How's that?"

"Just a feeling I have, but I can't see Director Cooper being mad that you did the best you could in an impossible situation. And if she is mad? We'll deal with whatever comes. Together."

"Together," I repeat, as if the word were foreign to me. It's not, but the idea of Jack and me as a unit, a team, for an extended time is a potent thought. Almost as much as the man himself.

Holding hands—because Mila will hardly rat me out to our boss —we make our way to the living room. My cousin is in the large armchair, feet up, eyes closed, and hands rubbing her belly. She peeks at us and grins.

"So that's how it is. I told T something was going between you two. Tell me everything."

"Mila, leave them be. Rest, Spooky. You need to rest."

"I know, I know. Apparently, I'm supposed to stock up on sleep before the baby is born. As if it works that way. *Exhausted?* No, thanks. I'm good. I had a wee nap before pushing a twenty-pound coo out my —" She clicks her tongue. "I'm a tad scared about giving birth."

"You don't say," I tease. "You're literally the strongest, most stubborn woman I know. You'll be fine."

"I second that sentiment," T-Bone cuts in.

"Besides, you know I'll desperately want some baby cuddles. You two can nap during that time." I mean it, too. I hope Mila knows that. It's not like she has a doting mother around to help her with her fears about motherhood.

Aunt Sveta is in prison for hundreds of years because she killed over three hundred people. That doesn't exactly scream, *Let's go spend some time with Granny.*

The energy in the house is tense as we wait for Director Cooper, but there is every chance that it's only my own panic coloring my perception.

When the doorbell rings—interrupting a very heated debate between T-Bone and Jack about the right kind of grazing grass for cattle—I jump to my feet and rush for the door.

"Director Cooper, thanks so much for coming," I say as I let her into the house.

She walks in with all of the gravitas that is attached to her title. I want to duck tail and run like a kid that's thrown a baseball through the window. I'm not a child, though. I'm a grown woman who has to face the consequences of her actions.

"You gonna tell me what the hell is going on?" she demands, crossing her arms.

"Well..." I stumble over my tongue.

"Out with it, Vera." She snaps her fingers at me before going toward the living room. She greets the others with a curt head nod, still waiting for me to speak.

"See..." I begin as I nervously shuffle from one foot to the other. "Everything was going fine until three intruders attacked us." I go into detail, telling my boss everything that's happened in the last twenty-four hours.

Only *not* everything. I don't tell her anything about Jack and me. Not yet. Let's take things one at a time.

Mila and T-Bone jump in, filling in the director with Jessie's findings. She doesn't seem overly concerned that we went to the tech guru before going to the boss. In fact, she leans back in her seat and listens to the whole sordid tale as if she were watching her favorite soaps. It's not exactly too far off the mark.

Stranger than fiction and all that.

She doesn't even bat an eye when we tell her about Jack and his pumpkin situation.

"You should hear some of the stuff that's out there in the world. I'm pretty sure nothing can faze me anymore. I think my last shock came when this one got married." She hooks a thumb toward Mila, but there's humor in her tone. She's joking with her employee.

This gives me hope that she won't be too pissed off that I slept with a charge. After all, T and Mila met on a case. Sure, they were both agents, but Director Alyce Cooper has to know that sometimes life just happens.

Once all is said and done, Jack jumps in. "Is it possible that Val Downer is a mole? What about Erhart Knope? If it's not FUC, then it has to be one of them," Jack insists. "There's a chance it could be Lisbeth, but she never knew where I lived."

"And you didn't think it was weird that the woman you were screwing didn't care where you lived?" Director Cooper pulls no punches, but I don't really want to hear his response.

By the flushed color of his cheeks, Jack doesn't want to reply. "I made it clear that I like my privacy and that I didn't have a conventional address. She didn't question it, and I like my solitude."

"That's weird, but it's your life." Director Cooper shrugs. "Let's put Lisbeth aside for a moment. There isn't a chance in hell that Erhart Knope is crooked. He's way too sanctimonious for that. But if there is a chance one of his people is more bent than a stop sign in a hurricane, I want to be the one to tell him."

"They have a contentious relationship," Mila explains.

"That hyena shifter *loves* to lord it over me that he's the rep for the Cryptozoian Council. Like he's better than me. My *superior*. Pfft. I am the Director of the FUCN'A, for fuck's sake. All new agents pass through my doors. That means something." She purses her lips. "Did Jessie find anything about this Val Downer? Koala shifter, isn't she?"

"Yes," Jack answers. "We have no more information than that. We were waiting on you to make any sort of further decision."

"That's a good idea. Now I get to call Erhart Knope and give him this news." The woman rubs her hands together, relishing the thought of one-upping Knope. "If this turns out to be the mole, I'm gonna be so happy. I'll buy you fresh hay for your scarecrow. Now, someone give me the phone. It's time to break Erhart's heart."

22

NORBERT

I am a nervous wreck.

I can't stop fidgeting, and apparently, that's a dead giveaway that I'm up to something, so I really need to quit it. The problem is I can't. Not only am I more than a little anxious about what is moments away from going down but I'm also concerned that I'll gourd out before anything can happen.

Not good.

Actually, pretty fucking bad. Not only for me but for Vera and all of FUC and the Cryptozoian Council.

After goading Erhart Knope for a good ten minutes, Director Cooper explained to him that he might have a mole in his organization. We decided that if Lisbeth was involved, it had to mean she somehow got to Val Downer.

For a whopping fifteen minutes, Erhart Knope refused to believe that one of the council members was responsible, but the more Director Cooper explained things to him, the quieter he got.

He helped us set this whole sting operation.

Erhart Knope is helping us catch Val Downer.

To say that the hyena shifter is angry is a bit of an understatement. Sort of like stating blood doesn't agree with Vera.

Vera and I are standing by an armored car in a community park parking lot, patiently waiting for Downer. The trap is set, and all we have to do is wait and see what happens.

"Are you okay?" Vera asks.

"Yes," I lie. "You?"

"Yes," she lies right back to me. "Not in the least bit nervous."

I know that T-Bone is close by with a whole team of agents. Mila wanted to come, but we had to put our foot down. We couldn't bring a very pregnant woman who can't shift to a dangerous setup. She was pissed. She feels as responsible as me because this was all linked to her mother's research.

I brought it all back to her doorstep days before she gives birth to her first child. That doesn't make me feel too great. I'll babysit their bundle of joy as much as they allow me. A small apology token.

Who knows, maybe Vera will be with me. Good practice for when we have our own batty pumpkin.

Really, Jack. So not the time.

A black car pulls in beside ours about three minutes later than scheduled.

My gut tightens, and I clench my jaw down to keep from shouting and raging at the agent who put lives in danger. And for what? I don't know her motivation yet, and I'm not too sure it matters.

Immortality is a dumb thing to chase. This coming from the guy who brought Lisbeth Bannon and her cronies *that* much closer.

"You had me worried, Norbert." Val slams her car door. "I've been trying to call the satellite phone nonstop. I was scared something happened."

"Something did happen," I shoot back.

Here it is. The moment of truth.

Or not. Rather, the moment that decides how good of a liar I am.

"I was going over the files you asked me to double-check. I found something. Another file. One that's..." I swallow and look over to Vera. Her face is an unreadable mask. She is a force. So damn strong. I let her strength and resolve sink into me. "The file I have on this changes everything." I hold up a memory stick. It's shaped like a bone because it belongs to Mila.

Val's eyes light up, and she steps forward, her hand held out expectantly. "That's wonderful. It'll bet it's what we need."

She leaves her statement open-ended because she thinks I'm thinking about the trial.

She has no idea I know exactly what she's talking about.

The key to immortality.

At least, that's the hope. Before we get the rest of the agents to move in on her, Vera and I have to try to get her to talk.

"You should call Erhart Knope right away to let him know," Vera says, holding out a phone.

Downer's face falls. "No. I'd rather deliver this news in person."

"I insist," Vera presses, wagging the phone.

The other woman rolls her eyes. "And why should I take my cues from you? You haven't even fully graduated yet."

Vera grins. "Matter of time. I can call him myself."

"Fine."

Downer pulls her own device from her pant pockets and puts on a great big show of calling her boss.

"Hey, Knope. For whatever reason, FUC pseudo-agent Vera insisted on calling you to let you know we might have the evidence we need to charge VH with a lot more than toxic waste dumping." She pauses and gives us the thumbs-up as if she is listening intently to Erhart.

We know she can't be talking to him. It's simply not possible.

She continues her fake conversation for some of the most awkward seconds of my life.

It's one thing to watch someone lie, but to witness them lying so badly and with such conviction? It makes my skin crawl. I'm embarrassed for her and for what is about to happen.

"Not sure why you absolutely needed me to do that, but there. It's done. Happy?" Her anger is barely contained.

"You could do with some acting classes." Vera holds up the phone.

Only, it's not hers. The device belongs to Erhart Knope. The man Val Downer *supposedly* called.

That was the beauty of the trap.

Had the phone rang in Vera's hand, we would have explained everything to her and apologized for not trusting her.

Now, we had her dead to rights.

"I don't understand." Downer keeps cool, but there is a hint of fear in her voice.

"This is Erhart's phone. You know, the guy my boss reports to, who in turn reports our movements to *your* boss. Or your *Cryptozoian Council* boss, I should say, not whoever you're working for on the side. You know, the people to whom you've been feeding classified FUC and Cryptozoian Council info." Vera blinks those beautiful long lashes of hers, daring Downer to contradict her.

"I don't know what you're playing, but this isn't funny." She takes a step back, edging toward her car.

"You should know..." Vera points toward the play structure and the group of people playing baseball on the field. "Everyone you see there? They're agents. Erhart is over there with Director Cooper and more agents. You're caught, Val."

The koala shifter's eyes go wide, her jaw slack. "You're lying."

"No," Vera assures her. "You're in a lot of trouble. The only way you can lessen the hurt that's coming your way is to tell us who you're working for."

"You've lost your mind. I can't tell you *anything*. They'll kill me. They said if I didn't help, they would kill me. They injected me with some kind of serum. If I don't get an antidote every day, I die. They send it every evening to make sure I've cooperated throughout the day."

Vera and I exchange a glance. This turn of events is definitely probable. It sure sounds like something Lisbeth would do, but it's also the perfect cover.

I need the bad guys because only they can save me.

We need to push a bit more.

"You could've told your superiors," Vera points out.

Downer scoffs. "Would you? You've been on *one* mission. I bet you've already broken a rule or two. It's not that cut and dry. I can't *die*. I've got a family."

Vera considers a moment. "Well, lucky for you, you've got the best at FUC. You know that. I'm sure they'll do what they can to help you if you're honest with us. Who are you working for?"

"Zeus and Hera."

I snort. "Come off it."

Downer throws her phone at me. Momentarily distracted, I grab for the device while she makes a run for her car. Vera, quick on her feet, and one hell of an agent, is ready for her. She leaps forward, pins Downer to the car, and holds her in place.

"Get off. Let me go." Downer squirms and tries to wiggle out of the hold.

Vera sighs. "Not a chance. We were having a really nice chat. You were telling us about Zeus and Hera. Go on."

"They'll kill me."

"Yeah, you said that. Your boss and peers just saw you trying to evade, so maybe you should be more concerned that now the good guys won't want to help you. Beware the hand that feeds you lies or something like that."

"That's not even the saying. You're a dumb newbie who doesn't have a badge. You don't have the authority to do this."

"No," Vera agrees. "But they do."

Downer raises her head, and off in the distance, Erhart Knope, Director Cooper, and T-Bone, accompanied by a small army of agents, stalk forward. Downer's legs buckle, and the only thing keeping her up is Vera. The agent weeps, pleading in a nonsensical way. I can't tell if she wants our help or wants to be released to her homicidal blackmailers.

"I'm done for," she whispers finally. "Please don't let me die."

"Then help us," I say with my best stern voice.

It takes her a few seconds, but when she sees the look of complete disappointment on Erhart's face, she turns toward me.

"Password for my phone is 8888. You'll see. Zeus and Hera call the shots. I've never seen them in person."

"Then how did they manage to stick you with that nasty formula?" Vera loosens her hold on Downer as T-Bone cuffs the mole.

"They sent someone who gave me that phone," was the reply. "The guy injected me with the stuff, and then I had a call from both of them."

"Zeus and Hera?" I type in the passcode and immediately spot text conversations giving Downer all kinds of instructions, all having to do with me and the Bloody Doctor research.

"Yeah. I don't know who they are."

Vera and I hook gazes. "Lisbeth Bannon," she mouths.

I shrug. I've got no idea. Either Lisbeth has the exact same phone with the exact same deal with Zeus and Hera, or she *is* Hera.

"This is the first big lead we've got to find out who is behind VH," Vera whispers to me as we watch Downer being hauled away. "We need to get this phone to Jessie right away."

"This isn't over," I sigh, dejected and disappointed.

"No," Vera responds honestly as she takes my hand in hers. "But we're one step closer."

"Vera," Director Cooper shouts.

She gives me a sad smile and goes off with her boss. Being the badass agent I know she will be.

Hell, that she already *is*.

23

VERA

ONE WEEK LATER

This is it.

This is my big moment.

And this time, there will be no paper cut and no passing out.

Nope.

This time, when I walk out of here, I will be a full FUC agent with a badge and everything.

"I've got to admit"—Director Cooper drums her fingers on her desk—"I'm impressed. I sent you out to keep an eye on Jack because I thought it would be easy and maybe it would rekindle your love for the law. I made a grave mistake in judgment. You were never a lawyer. You were born to be an agent. That was some good work, *Agent* Slaski."

"Thank you, Director Cooper. I just wish we had more information. Actual closure on the case."

"Me too, but we have a solid lead with this whole Zeus and Hera business. We'll find out who Lisbeth Bannon is working for. We'll uncover everyone behind Vitality Holdings. It's only a matter of time."

"I really hope so."

"That brings me to your next assignment."

My ears perk up, and I sit straight and at the ready. Director Cooper notices and gives a sly smirk.

"I enjoy your eagerness, Vera. It's commendable. Erhart Knope and I have agreed on something. Probably the first and last time that's ever gonna happen. We're starting an immortality chasers task force. A few of our senior agents will head it up, namely T-Bone. He's got good contacts with human police forces, and he also understands the desperation some of these lunatics go to, given that his mother-in-law is the Bloody Doctor. He'll do it all on base here, of course. I wouldn't take that man away from his newborn for too long."

I grin because ever since Bettina was born three days ago, T-Bone has barely set her down. He coos over his little girl, and it's quite possibly the cutest thing I've ever seen.

"I think that Mila will be happy about that, too," I comment. Delivery wasn't exactly easy, and she needs some rest.

"You're not wrong. You'll be part of this task force, but given that you're still a new agent, we're giving you something right in your wheelhouse. You'll be tailing Lisbeth Bannon. Your bat is tiny, perfect for some recon. You up for it?"

Am I up to get some dirt on the woman who used my boyfriend?

"Yes," I respond. "Absolutely."

"Great. That's what I like to hear. Now, here's what you've been waiting for." Director Cooper slides a badge over the desk and taps it. "I know you'll do me proud, Agent Slaski. And just think. You didn't even have to drink blood to get to where you are. Now get out of here. I've got a mountain of paperwork, and there's an army of people out there who want to congratulate you."

"The blindfold is hardly necessary," I grumble to Jack. "I'm a bat. I can echolocate with the best of 'em."

"Don't cheat!"

"You know I can *hear* the elevator dings, right? I know we're going to the subbasement."

"Hush now. Don't ruin the surprise," he whispers in my ear.

We exit the elevator, Jack holding on to my hand to guide me through the labyrinth that leads to Mila's office. She's on maternity leave, so I don't know why we're going to her lab or why I need to be deprived of my sight.

Jack is now a freelance scientist working in conjunction with FUC and the Cryptozoian Council, and I'm not sure how he got his hands on the key cards that access the bowels of FUCN'A.

Must be special permission or something.

A door opens and closes behind us. The whispered sounds of *sh* tickle my ears. Jack pulls at my blindfold. It falls and reveals my parents, sister, Mila, and T-Bone holding Bettina.

"Surprise," they shouted in unison, using a lower decibel as to not wake the baby.

I half expected Bettina to be born with firetruck-red hair like Mila, but that's not possible. No one—not even Mila—knows what Mila's real hair color is anymore. Bettina is blonde, probably like T. She is the cutest little pink squirming baby I've ever seen. I'll definitely be getting a whiff of her baby scent when I steal her away for a snuggle later.

"What's all this?" I ask.

"We wanted to congratulate you," Mom answers. "An agent! You did it, Vera. We're so proud of you."

"And you basically got Alyce and Erhart to start a task force. That's amazing, Vera," Mila gushes. "I'm damn proud to be your family *and* a bat."

"So damn proud," Raya says, one brow arched. "Of course you had to be a superstar here."

"Aw, thanks. You'll be one, too. I *know* it."

Raya waves me off as Dad gives me a hug. "Nice going, sweetie."

"There's cake," T-Bone announces. "Miranda made it special, just for you."

"That's sweet of her." My eyes prickle with happy tears. "You know that none of this would have been possible without Jack, right?"

The man in question drapes his arm across my shoulders and kisses my cheek. "I refuse to take any credit. You got my pumpkin butt out of the forest. In more ways than one."

Jack is keeping the cabin in the forest, but he's moving closer to FUCN'A. He still insists on being a subsistence farmer, and he's about to close on a tiny hobby farm, but he is rejoining the world in a very big way. He's still pretty shaken that his work is in the wrong hands, but he's working hard to fix that.

He even managed to perfect my blood substitute *and* create a serum that is keeping Val Downer alive.

The agent turned prisoner hasn't said much, but she doesn't *know* much. She's every bit the puppet Jack was. It's scary to think that these mysterious Zeus and Hera figures could have many people on their roster of minions.

I won't worry about that today. FUC is on the case, and that means it *will* be solved.

The silver lining is that I am an agent, I have my next assignment, and now that Jack will live closer, we can actually date.

We also never broke any rules. That makes me very happy.

We're free and clear to date.

And date we do.

Jack slept over every night this week. Maybe some relationship gurus would advise against it, insist that it isn't a good idea, but I don't care. We got to know each other while cohabiting in the smallest cabin known to man. We're used to sharing our space now.

Besides, I dare any woman to share a bed with a man like Jack and not want him there forever.

Impossible.

"You look really happy, V," he whispers in my ear, wrapping his arms around my waist.

"I am. I really am. This is one of those instances in life where you can *feel* just how right everything is. It's a happily-until-next-time sort of moments."

"Happily-until-next-time?"

"Well, yeah. We're really young and only beginning our lives together. We'll have loads of other moments like this. Soak it in, Pumpkin King. This is how *humans* grow in the pumpkin patch of life."

"I'll be there every step of the way, V. As long as you'll have me with my exploding gourd and straw and all."

"Wouldn't have it any other way, Jack."

He kisses me softly and holds me close before my family joins us by the cake.

The big bad might still be out there, but so long as we're together, lean on each other, and lead with kindness, we're winning.

EPILOGUE
RAYA

They say that comparison is a real joy killer.

I don't agree. I'd say that it doesn't so much kill joy as much as it destroys relationships.

Do I love my big sister? Yes, of course I do.

Vera helped me learn how to read. She gave me the best tricks to do hard math. She never complained when I stole her makeup or clothes. She didn't rat me out *once* when we were teens and I snuck out of the house.

Vera is loyal, kind, sweet, and so damn intelligent.

She's got it all. The whole package.

Being her little sister is *way* hard.

Vera excels at absolutely *everything* she does. She is always the smartest, the fastest. She is more clever than Rumpelstiltskin, more cunning than the Evil Queen, craftier than a genie.

The evidence?

Vera wasn't even a full agent. She'd been sent on a guardian duty, and my perfect sister managed to unearth a huge conspiracy.

Because *of* course Perfect Vera was able to sniff out a major plot in the middle of the wilderness in a small cabin with no running electricity and limited internet access.

Her discovery prompted Director Cooper to start a task force to root out all the big players out there who are questing for immortality.

Not even a FUC agent yet and Vera is already setting the bar way too high for me—and that's saying something, seeing as I'm a bat shifter. I should be able to fly right over any goal post.

Now, I have to adjust my objectives and try to live up to the impossible standards Vera set.

The chances that I also manage to suss out a big scheme?

None.

Because not only has my big sister inspired the creation of a FUC task force but *I'm on it*

That's right.

My first assignment as a FUC agent is in the immortality chasers task force.

I can't mess it up.

I'd like to say it'll be as easy as pie to succeed, but that will be a tall order.

My mission doesn't just involve the rich and powerful shifters of the world hunting for immortality.

Nope. That would be too easy.

My assignment involves Santa Claus and a reindeer.

Sweet suffering mammal, but am I ever in for it.

The End.

BAT AND THE BLITZ

RAGTAG BATS BOOK 3

For my husband,

1

RAYA

Deep breath in. Deep breath out.

I force a few more gulps of air into my lungs, but I'm not calmer.

If anything, with every puff, I'm more agitated.

It's got nothing to do with the air quality in the house and everything to do with my sister's stifling presence. Poor Vera doesn't even *know* she drives me nutso bananas. But she does.

I suppose it's a typical way for little sisters to feel about their *perfect* big sisters.

This is way more intense, though.

We passed good old sibling rivalry a decade ago. Maybe even two.

Not that the competition between us is fair *or* right.

There's no contest. I've never had a chance of winning. Not against Perfect Vera. My sister's only flaw is that she cannot stand the sight of blood. It was the one thing I could do better: be a vampire bat. I leaned on it *hard* growing up.

When I got a bad grade—rather, when I got a *lower* grade than the standard Little Miss Perfect set up—it was much easier for me to cope with my parents' disappointment if they were *also* let down by Vera's inability to drink blood.

Is that nice? No.

It's petty as hell, but a bat's *gotta* do what a bat's *gotta* do.

It's basically the only way I survived in my high-achieving family. It's not my fault I don't have the kind of brain that *wants* to sit around and read a whole bunch of theories and write long briefs or do long math equations.

Yuck.

Sitting still is not my jam. I much prefer action.

That's why I applied to the Furry United Coalition Newbie Academy. I was basically killing my soul, trying to complete a university degree in criminology.

It was interesting enough, but a three-hour-long lecture?

No, fucking *thank* you.

I didn't know how to be motionless for that long. I went on so many panic flights halfway through those interminable classes I had to drop it from my schedule.

After discussing this with my older and *very* wise cousin Mila, she suggested that I apply to FUCN'A. As a forensic anthropologist and sometimes teacher at the Academy, Mila was in a great position to tell me what to expect. She helped me along the application process in secret. I figured I'd only break the news to my parents once I was accepted. It was the responsible thing to do, but it was also self-preservation.

If they didn't know I applied, *if* I failed, they wouldn't need to know.

Of course, it wasn't that easy.

Before I even got into the Academy—before I could tell my family I had applied—Vera announced that she was leaving her job as a fancy lawyer to join FUCN'A.

That's right.

Read that three times over, and don't you dare judge me for going a little nutso bananas. I got a cool Bela Lugosi tattoo out of *that* major freak-out, so I suppose it could've been much worse.

Without telling anyone, least of all me, Vera got into the Academy.

I *almost* withdrew my application when I found out, but Mila convinced me to give it a shot anyway.

"Who cares if it *might* look like you were merely following behind Vera? You made the decision *long* before she announced she had been accepted. *You* know, and that's all that matters." Mila's words were comforting enough in the moment, but they're little comfort right now.

Vera graduated from FUCN'A ahead of me after one hell of a first mission. Not to say that the competition between us is more aggressive than ever, but it sort of is. How can I prove myself better than her now?

Simple.

I can't.

I can't even lord Vera's aversion to blood over her anymore.

All because of that silly pumpkin head scientist boyfriend of hers. Vera doesn't even *need* to drink blood to survive anymore. Jack made her some kind of plant-based supplement.

I would be pissed off if it wasn't so damn sweet.

I love my sister. I do. I don't want to see her fail, nor do I wish her a miserable life. I like her fine, but she'd be a hell of a lot more likable if she wasn't so damn good at Every. Little. Fucking. Thing.

Even the dish she brought over to Mila and T-Bone's place for our potluck dinner is better than the store-bought dessert I grabbed. Did I spend hours making something? No. Instead, I hit the gym. I don't regret my choice, but my brain can't help but compare Vera and me.

It's basically how my brain is wired.

In fact, I'm so caught up in my own damn thoughts I lose track of the conversation.

Tuning back in, it takes me a few moments to realize Mila is trying to pry information out of Vera about her latest assignment, namely tracking a woman who was either the mastermind in Vitality Holdings' whole immortality quest or a victim of the shadowy and unknown leaders, Hera and Zeus.

"You're on my husband's task force," our cousin Mila grunts, wrangling her squirming baby into her arms. "You can tell me *everything*. I'll claim that T-Bone told me during pillow talk."

Vera blushes deep. "Oh, no. You know I can't. I'm not at liberty to divulge anything I've learned during my stakeouts of Lisbeth Bannon." She sighs dramatically like she doesn't absolutely *adore* having sensitive information.

Mila clicks her tongue. "I'm on maternity leave. Bored out of my skull. Give me something. An exciting tidbit. I beg of you."

Tiny little Bettina coos up at her mother, and immediately, Mila, the badass, melts away. Her gaze brims with love as she grins down at her offspring. "You're the cutest baby bat *ever*, Bettina Thrussel. Yes. You are."

My sister smirks at me. It's the kind of conspiratorial look siblings give each other, and I *almost* don't return it. I do, though. Because if there is one amusing thing in life, it's that Mila Starling, the daughter of the infamous prolific serial killer known as the Bloody Doctor, has a daughter of her own.

Before Bettina was born, I never would've guessed that Mila would settle down and have kids. But, seeing her holding her kid, big moon eyes shining with happiness, it's clear that my cousin is batshit in love with her child.

Oh, Mila still rocks really funny, albeit borderline-inappropriate shirts and her firetruck red hair. She's also one of the best moms out there. She literally knows *exactly* what *not* to do.

Like don't kill hundreds of people to learn the secret of immortality.

That's hardly a good way to do some mother-daughter bonding.

"Did you hear that? I think Jack is calling me." Vera hastens to the kitchen, undoubtedly uncomfortable with the thought that she couldn't fulfill Mila's desire for information.

As soon as my sister disappears into the kitchen, Mila switches seats and comes to sit beside me. "Okay, sour bat. Tell me what's wrong," she commands, bouncing a gurgling Bettina.

"I'm fine." I'm not, but I'm not going to unload on Mila. She's got a screaming bundle of joy to tend to. I'm not going to pile on my drama. It wouldn't be right.

"You're not *fine*. I can see that vein in your temple about ready to explode." Mila holds Bettina with one arm to poke at the vein that is indeed popping out of my temple.

I *hate* that it does that. It's one of the reasons why I always leave my hair down and wavy. It hides The Vein. It's no fun having a clear physiological sign that tells people *exactly* how you're feeling. It gives them an unfair advantage.

Knocking Mila's hand out of the way, I tug at the lapels of my leather jacket. "I'm just waiting for my first mission right now. I'm antsy."

Mila gives me a knowing look. "This is about the task force."

"Shh." I crane my neck to look toward the kitchen, but Vera is out of earshot, talking with T-Bone and Jack.

"Oh, come on, Raya. It's not so bad. I'm sure you'll find a way to leave your mark on the Academy."

I snort hard. "Sure. Because lightning strikes twice in the same family."

She shrugs. "It does in ours. Think about it. When my mom escaped from prison, I was pulled into the mission to bring her in. We all thought that would be the end of the Bloody Doctor and her super-nasty research. Then? Your sister is sent to be Jack's bodyguard. *Boom.* He's involved in a whole thing with sketchy people who want the key to immortality, too. There's a whole task force dedicated to finding anything and everything we can about any and all immortality chasers out there. If you want, I can ask T to pull you into one of the teams."

I shake my head. "Not a chance."

"Stop being like that. You could do some good out there. You know all about the Bloody Doctor *and* this whole Vitality Holdings, Lisbeth Bannon, Hera and Zeus thing your sister uncovered."

"Well, sure. Because of *course* my sister would discover this huge plot to take over the world during her first mission."

Mila waves me off. "Point is that *you* have a chance to be part of the task force, too. You could even uncover the real identity of Hera and Zeus while your sister is tailing Lisbeth Bannon."

Her words don't sit well with me. In fact, I get the distinct impression that she is keeping something from me. I narrow my eyes at her, pursing my lips as I read her face. Her brows are puckered together with a tiny bit of stress. There's a slight edge of panic wafting off of her that has nothing to do with the baby in her lap.

I gasp and hit a hand to my knee. "No fucking way."

"Don't yell," she chides. "You'll scare Bettina."

The child hasn't budged. She's still sitting there, looking as pleased as the queen of everything, as cute as a button.

"Why do I get the feeling you're trying to warn me about something? If you tell me T-Bone asked Director Cooper to put me on the immortality chasers task force, I'm gonna make ground beef out of your husband."

Mila laughs. "Sweet mother of echoes. T didn't *request* you. Alyce gave him a list of agents to assign to the task force. Your name was on it with an asterisk. The boss lady wants you on this. That's a huge compliment."

The bottom falls out of my stomach, and the blood I had for lunch races back up to burn the back of my throat. "No."

Her apologetic smile twinges. "This is good. It's a good assignment for you."

I inhale long and deep, my hands fisting at my sides.

I should've known that I would be in Vera's shadow in FUC, too.

How in the hell can I make a name for myself now?

2

KLAUS

You've got to be fucking joking.

I try to keep my body still, but my legs are itching, developing a mind of their own. Hell, even my fingers are twitching. Every single particle of my body is vibrating with barely contained annoyance, right down to the hair in my beard. With all of the professionalism I can muster, I clear my throat and run a hand back through my shoulder-length hair. I pull hard when my fingers hit a tangle, but the pain offers no relief from T-Bone's words.

"I'm not sure I understand," I say through *almost* unclenched teeth, leaning back against the chair.

Agent T-Bone Thrussel, a Highland cattle shifter a few years older than me, leans back in his own seat with a sigh. He's almost as tall and built as me.

Even his beard wants to rival mine.

Yet, we are as similar as we are different.

Where T-Bone has a beard, clean-cut hair, and a buttoned-up attitude that *screams* Type A anal-retentive, I'm a tatted-up, long-haired motorcycle-owning, rule-breaking agent.

That's probably why T-Bone has something I don't have: a position of authority.

Not that I would *ever* want to be in his shoes. The man left the RCMP to work with the Furry United Coalition a little while ago. He's already heading up his very own—and brand-new—task force. He's quite literally a golden boy. Not only because of his blond hair but because Director Cooper seems to have a soft spot for him.

That means pissing T-Bone off will only get me into a shouting match with the boss lady.

I don't want that. Not again. Not so soon after the little hiccup on my last mission. I'm on thin ice with Director Cooper, but what else is new? She was aware of what she was getting when she hired me. I've never claimed to be a team player, patient, or even law-abiding.

T-Bone shakes his head when I ask for more clarification. "Look, Klaus. I know you've got this whole loner thing going for you. You don't like working with a partner, and I get it. I do. This isn't negotiable, however. What's going on in the world right now is too important to be left up to only *one* person."

I bite down hard on my teeth. T-Bone might *say* he gets it, but he doesn't.

No one does.

I don't merely *hate* working with a partner. I *can't*.

Sitting around to discuss strategies and taking the time to let someone else in on my plans and theories takes way too damn long.

Too much wasted energy sitting around blabbering. Not enough action.

"I'm sure if you tell me what the mission is, I can set your mind at ease that I can do it alone."

Talk, talkety-talk. Just some useless words, wasting precious time.

T-Bone doesn't appear remotely convinced. He huffs out a breath and rubs a hand across his beard. "Not a chance. I chose you specifically for this mission because of your no-nonsense attitude. We need it in this case. I can't send someone who will be roped into the celebrity and magic of it all. Besides, you have an advantage here."

I have no idea what that means, but it doesn't matter. I don't work with a partner. Forget those harried detectives in the movies who don't work well with others because they're the loose cannons. I'm *not* the loose cannon. It's the partners I've been given over my career who are sketchy and inconsistent. Each one is denser than the last.

"T-Bone, let me assure you. Me working with someone else will only make things complicated."

"No, this is too important for one person."

It's my turn to arch a brow, but I don't insist anymore. The man is a second away from calling the director. I can *feel* his impatience down to the marrow of my bones.

"You're going up north to protect Santa Claus." T-Bone delivers the assignment like he's delivering a death sentence. Not a joke. His face is stern and worried, which is the *only* indication that this might not actually *be* a joke.

I chuckle, nervous for the first time in a long time. "I don't get it."

This cannot be real. This isn't *happening.*

"You know what I'm saying, Klaus. Don't make me elaborate."

"You can't be serious."

T-Bone gets to his feet and begins pacing his office. "I don't need to tell you that up in the very north of the country, there is a small village. It's fly-in only unless you have a sleigh. It's Christmas Town. *The* Christmas Town. Santa lives there with his elves. The towns-people all have jobs in the toy industry, too."

He's got to know that I'm all too familiar with this. The only person in the world who knows *who* I am and *where* I come from is Director Alyce Cooper. I'm getting the serious impression that T-Bone knows now, too.

I cross my arms to keep from bouncing out of my chair and quit-ting my job. I've had a good run working for FUC. I can quit. Go do something else where no one knows my history.

That's not exactly right, though.

I'm not qualified for much of anything else.

"I'm sure you're aware of that legend." T-Bone's eyes plead with me to jump in.

I don't. I *really* don't want to have this conversation.

T-Bone winces at my silence but goes on. "A long time ago, an adventurer supposedly found the Holy Grail."

I blink at him before snorting dryly as he continues.

"The Holy Grail. Just like in Indiana Jones and the Arthurian tales. This chalice is a sacred relic that dates back to pre-Christian times. Of course, *they* took the myth and ran with it. This cup is said to be forged in a blessed and hallowed metal that gives the drinker immortality."

I'm not simply frowning. I'm downright glaring at T-Bone. I don't appreciate the joke, but I'm seriously waiting for him to start laughing.

The man needs a better sense of humor, or I need one, full-stop.

"A legend states that the Holy Grail was melted into a gold wreath and kept in Christmas Town. It gives the village and Santa their magic, or so it's believed. The wreath has always been safe up there. It's so cold and so remote the tale barely made it to the general public."

I open my mouth to comment but snap it shut. I literally have no comeback for this. Besides, the more I say, the lower my chances are of talking my way out of this.

"We can't let anyone get their hands on that wreath. Whether the fable is true or not doesn't matter. No one wants Vitality Holdings to find it."

"Still not sure what the hell this has to do with me," I lie.

"Ever since the Bloody Doctor's research was posted online by her maniacal sidekick Oscar Trow, there has been an increase in immortality chasers. First, it was with the Bloody Doctor's blood work. These people thought they could use blood to live forever. Then, a few months ago, they moved on. They tried to prove immortality could be found in shifter and plant genome."

Right. I'd heard about that. One of the newly minted agents was sent to babysit a scientist, and the next thing they knew, the mad botanist turned into a pumpkin. The damn thing grew legs and arms. It was a damn nightmare to witness. The evil plot to use plants to live forever found a way to infiltrate the Cryptozoian Council. One of the agents there was being blackmailed.

A pair of lunatics, calling themselves Hera and Zeus, injected the agent with a toxin that would kill her unless she had an antidote every day. So long as she listened to the instructions given to her by her blackmailers, she would remain alive.

Silence and cooperation for her life.

That was the bargain.

It's hard to believe. I wouldn't have gone for it. At all. You couldn't pay me enough to make me betray FUC.

Even if that payment was my own damn life.

"You're gonna be heading up to Christmas Town with Agent Raya Slaski. Your mission is to guard the wreath and make sure no one steals it."

I burst out laughing.

How could I not? This was a joke. It *had* to be.

"What's so funny?" T-Bone asks, frowning deep.

"You just told me you want me to go back to *Christmas Town* to guard the wreath and to keep Santa safe."

T-Bone shook his head. "You're making it sound really ridiculous."

"'Cause it is."

"No. It's not. We're trying to get ahead of these Hera and Zeus characters. We've got no idea who they are. All we know is what they want. Immortality. Director Cooper decided that the best course of action is to make sure that every single tall tale or legend about immortality be safeguarded from these immortality chasers."

"Wait." Klaus shook his head. "You really think that someone will walk into Christmas Town and steal this gold wreath *during* the holiday season? The Holy Grail legend isn't even *true*."

T-Bone nodded. "Be that as it may, Director Cooper wants to be safe. Besides, the holiday season would be the best time to abscond with the wreath. The town gets flooded with visitors and workers who visit Christmas Town, thinking it's nothing more than a gimmicky tourist destination. It would be the best time to sneak in and blend in with the higher number of unfamiliar faces." He pauses, taking the time to sit back into his chair, crossing his arms and giving me one hell of a stare-down. "Good thing it's your hometown. You'll have an advantage."

And just like that, I have to go back home for the first time since I was eighteen years old.

Fuck.

3

RAYA

Sweet echoing blood bag.

There he is.

Agent Klaus Thorsen.

No other agent in FUC has a reputation quite like him. In fact, Agent Thorsen is kind of legendary. He always refuses to work with a partner. He stomps around in his motorcycle boots like he owns the place. He's a good agent with exceptional statistics, even though he barely speaks to anyone other than Director Cooper.

I hate him.

Not because he's a bad guy or even because he's a good one, albeit unconventional.

Nope. I don't like Klaus Thorsen because he's too hot. Men who are *that* good-looking always know it down to their bone—if you know what I mean. They believe they're a gift to every other human.

From what I've seen of Klaus around the Academy, he's like that. He pretends he doesn't see people fawning over him with his shoulder-length ash-blond hair and his brooding green eyes.

Real talk? The man bun is a *ridiculous* trend.

On Klaus Thorsen? It's not a man bun.

It's a fucking halo. It's a damn crown of sexiness.

Not that I would *ever* admit this out loud to *anyone*.

I'll have to put my lust on serious lockdown and make sure Klaus knows just how much I hate his dumb, sexy, handsome, moody face.

I'm on a mission, yes, but not only for FUC. I'm here to make a name for myself, and I can't do that if Klaus Sex God distracts me every time he flips his hair like a teenage cheerleader.

Maybe I'll attack him with a pair of scissors as soon as he falls asleep. There's a good chance he draws all of his power from his hair like good ol' Samson.

I drop my duffel beside his and give him a cursory head nod. I don't blush—*much*.

"You're the noob they paired me with?" His voice is a deep baritone that rumbles out of him like a motorcycle revving first thing in the morning.

Oh, my flight.

He's so good-looking I *almost* miss the aggression in his tone.

Almost.

His green eyes are narrowed toward me as he takes in my not-so-winter gear. My trusty and favorite leather jacket might not be the warmest or thickest protection against the northern wind, but it's sort of my armor.

I refuse to ride into battle without it and my combat boots.

Klaus spends too long of a second on my legs for his perusal to be professional. Perhaps that's all in my head. I roll my shoulders back and give him my best annoyed glare.

"I'm Agent Slaski." I don't hold out my hand for a shake.

No chance in hell am I allowing any contact between us. I've got no clue how I'll react to that, and the very last thing I need is to blush because a cute guy touches me.

This isn't middle school, and I'm not some fawning little bat.

I'm a newly minted FUC agent and a grown woman in complete control of her libido. Who cares if his hair smells like pine trees and sandalwood? I certainly don't notice that his eyes are the color of incandescent emeralds. Nor do I pay *any* attention to his ass when he turns around to grab his duffel bag off the ground.

Because if I *did* notice his butt, I'd have to write an ode to it.

Good starry sky above.

Who knew men's tushes could come in that shape? I sure didn't. His ass and his hair are locked in a competition for which body part attracts more of my attention.

Right now, it's a tied score.

"I don't care who you are, agent. All I care about is getting the job done as quickly as humanly possible. I don't want to fuck this up. Got it?"

I arch a brow at him and cock my hip. "Are you serious right now?"

"What?"

"Did you really tell a fellow agent not to fuck up a mission? Do you really think it's necessary to warn me that we have a job to do?"

"Sure feels like the newer generations of agents are too soft. Besides, I don't think a first-timer is an agent. *Way* too green."

I grin at him, flashing my incisors. I've never bitten a human, but he's a second away from making me change my mind.

Oh, buddy. Poor, sweet, innocent little reindeer. Welcome to my trap, jerkface.

"Yeah?" My smirk turns saccharine. "You don't find the newer agents equipped to cope with the field?"

Klaus shrugs. "Nope."

"Is that so, Agent Thorsen?" Director Alyce Cooper snaps, coming up behind him.

His jaw clenches, and he shoots me a murderous and accusatory glance. His gaze screams for revenge.

You can try, pretty boy.

And, by Bela Lugosi's fangs, the man sure is a tasty dish.

Klaus flashes his own teeth at me in a threatening promise before facing our boss. "Sorry, Director."

"No, you're not," she shoots back. "Don't try to backtrack now, Klaus. I heard you loud and clear. Maybe if you've got so many opinions about the quality of the agents coming through the program, I should add you to the next roster of teachers."

Klaus blanches visibly, and Director Cooper, the sly lady she is, relishes his momentary panic.

"I think I'll do that," she goes on. "We'll see how things go with this one." She juts her chin toward me. "You ready, Agent Slaski 2.0?"

I try to stifle my reaction to her words, but I'm pretty sure Klaus notices my back stiffening. Agent Slaski 2.0? Is that really how my boss sees me?

Not going to lie. That hurts.

I spent all my school years being told just how awesome my sister is. I don't need it for the rest of my career. Why couldn't Vera stay a lawyer? Damn her and her perfection.

Every time I walked into a new class in high school, the teacher would take one look at my last name and *expect* me to perform at the same level as Vera. Was it my fault I didn't enjoy studying or staying still as much as her? No. It didn't stop *everyone* from comparing us— and for finding me seriously *lacking*.

For once in my life, I would love to be noticed and praised for my own achievement. For being Raya Slaski. For simply being little old me with my nose ring, tattoos, leather jacket addiction, and badass attitude.

"Are you ready to go?" Director Cooper asks me.

"I am, yes."

"Good. I wanted to come and personally see you off. This wreath you have to protect? It's an important artifact. Whether it is the Holy Grail melted down into a wreath or not is irrelevant. Hell, the fact that it isn't actually magical isn't even significant. What matters is that all of Christmas Town depends on the wreath to propagate their economy because people come from far and wide to see the suppos-edly-magical wreath. Not to mention putting a stop to Vitality Hold-ings and uncovering the identities of Hera and Zeus. A lot is riding on this."

"Yes, ma'am. Of course." I give her my best and most reassuring nod. My legs don't shake, nor do I feel the weight of my entire future career looming overhead.

"I'll keep the mission on course," Klaus cuts in, throwing his duffel over his shoulder.

"Make sure that you do, or else I'll be sending you to the *northiest* north to ever north every holiday season. You can kiss your beach Christmases goodbye if you fuck this up."

Klaus's eyes cut to mine. "Sure thing, Director."

"I haven't forgotten your last slip-up, Klaus. I might remand you to a classroom yet." With another long and heavy scrutiny of us, Director Cooper turns on her heels and leaves the hangar.

I watch her leave, taken in by the sheer magnitude her presence commands. She is one impressive woman. I totally want to be her when I grow up.

The flight from FUCN'A, all the way to Christmas Town, is long and quite possibly the most turbulent flight I've ever been on.

I've gone skydiving, so that's saying something.

The airplane isn't exactly big, but it's large enough that Klaus is sitting a few feet away from me. If I didn't know any better, I would assume the big muscle-man is *scared* of flying. I swear, his jaw looks *that* much more clenched.

I could've *sworn* I saw him watching breathing exercises on his tablet during takeoff.

Not that there is anything wrong with that.

It's nice to see that the Klaus *I-only-ever-scowl* Thorsen has a weak spot. It makes him a little more human and a little less *scary-agent-with-more-experience*.

Klaus hasn't spoken a word to me since his warning earlier. I'm so bored part of me wants to poke at his patience. I curb the impulse. The last thing we need on this mission is more animosity.

This has to go perfectly well. I *have* to prove myself a good agent in my own right. Not because I have the Slaski last name but because of my own actions.

I will *not* be Agent Slaski 2.0.

I am Raya, my very own bat. Hear me echolocate!

If Man-Bun Klaus gets in my way?

Well, he'll be playing a whole different kind of reindeer game.

I flip open the file T-Bone gave me and read over the case for the millionth time. It seems pretty straightforward. Go to Christmas Town, guard the gold wreath, and ensure no one gets their hands on it.

It's basically a security guard job.

Or it would be. These Hera and Zeus characters seem to have a whole lot of cash at their disposal. We have to be very careful. They somehow managed to infiltrate and blackmail an agent in the Cryptozoian Council. Klaus and I will have to be aware of our surroundings at all times. For all we know, there is already a mole in Santa's workshop, vying for the wreath.

"Do you think we should interview people as soon as we land?" I ask after a bout of turbulence so bad I'd half-thought we would fall out of the sky. "Way I see it we should ingratiate ourselves to Santa and his staff. Probably the local police force, too. The more we know, the better we can spot a mole if there is one."

Despite his pallor, Klaus rolls his eyes and doesn't look up from his tablet. I don't know what he's doing on there, but it seems to have all of his attention, the big—beautiful—ass.

"Klaus, seriously. I would appreciate a moment of your time to discuss strategy." *Especially since there's nothing else to do and it's doing my head in.*

"There's no strategy to discuss," he snaps, still not looking away from his device. "We land. We guard. Christmas ends. Back to the Academy. Final."

I purse my lips at him in serious displeasure. Of course, I *knew* his reputation before we even got onto the plane, but this surliness is next level.

"If someone pissed in your tinsel, it sure wasn't me. We need to be a team on this. A little commun—"

"Do. Not. Make. Christmas. Jokes." He enunciates every word and every syllable like a threat.

Or what would be a threat if he were talking to anyone else. But he's talking to me. I can out-stubborn the reindeer any day.

"You don't like Christmas?" I add a twinge of humor to my tone. Not quite teasing but not quite understanding. It's made to antagonize, and why not? I can give as good as I get. I've got a whole life of practice.

The man is a reindeer shifter who abhors Christmas. Fascinating, really. Freud and his buddies would have a collective *brain-gasm* if they got to work with him.

Right then and there, I nickname him Blitzen. It sounds sexy but grumpy, very much like the dude himself.

Klaus doesn't answer, but judging by the firm set of his jaw, he is trying *very* hard not to say anything.

Point to me.

So much for being a team.

4

KLAUS

Sweet suffering Rudolph.

Raya Slaski is one annoying—temptingly hot—woman.

It's not her fault that *everything* she does is downright aggravating. Not to mention gratingly sexy.

I should probably try to work with her. Be a team. I sure don't want Director Cooper to make good on her threat and actually put me on the teaching roster. I'd make a horrible teacher. I don't have the patience for it.

Case in point: I don't have the composure to sit so close to Raya on this bumpy-ass flight.

What's this plane made of anyway? Weld-together toy cars? I swear to the good lords of flight, I can *feel* every gust of wind. If we don't land soon, I will pass out and make a total idiot of myself.

Not that it'll take much.

Anytime I look in Raya's direction too long, I get a little bit dizzy. The silver hoop through her right nostril blinks at me every time I glance up. I want to flick it with my finger and trace the delicate line of Raya's nose all the way to that forehead of hers. A vein pops out of it every time I say something she disagrees with, so basically every time I open my mouth.

It's hilarious.

It's also a little hot.

Raya has a hard time containing her emotions, which means that she has every chance of being one hell of a firecracker in bed. I shake my head to loosen the thought. Getting all turned around because my so-called partner has pretty eyes, lush chocolate-brown waves, and a full red mouth won't help my career.

"We'll be landing soon," the pilot indicates with a loud shout over the plane's unnaturally loud din.

Seriously. Soldered tin roofs with wings does not an airplane make.

I give the woman a thankful nod and slide my tablet into my duffel. The flight is turbulent as hell, but at least, it's coming to an end. The rest of the trek to Christmas Town has to be done by sleigh.

Yup.

Sleigh.

Because going to Christmas Town isn't ridiculous enough, our only possible mode of transportation is a sleigh. I don't know if Raya has been briefed about that part yet, but she's spent the entire flight reading the case file.

Like that will help you where we're heading.

Christmas Town is the fakest, most duplicitous place on earth.

Raya will need a lot more than studying the case notes to survive out here for two weeks. She's going to learn the truth about a lot of things. Like how hot chocolate can easily be doctored with a fair amount of salt. How garlands can be used as rope. How ornaments can be used as missiles.

It's not all tinsel and carols.

It's taunting and contempt.

The landing, done on a very narrow strip of land at the very tip of Canada, is horrible. We lurch to the left, to the right, tip forward. Probably do a fairly good impression of the twist.

By the time the front wheels collide with the permafrost ground, I'm greener than a fir tree.

Shit.

I'm not even in town yet, and I'm already dropping Christmas metaphors.

I shake my head and scrub my scalp with my fingers to dislodge any other latent Christmas vocabulary that wants to make its way out. Better I do it in my thoughts than out loud for Raya to hear.

Her pale face is ashen, her knuckles white as she clutches the armrests. I feel bad for her. This is hardly a fun flight, and as someone who hates flying in general, that's saying something.

"It's normal for it to be like this out here." The words leave my mouth before I can think better of it.

Raya looks up and meets my gaze with a grateful nod. It knocks out the tiny gulp of air still holding firm in my lungs. I really need to remember that this trip is about one thing and one thing only.

Securing solo missions for the next little while—and ensuring I don't end up in the classroom.

I can't get preoccupied with my history, no matter how much my family and the town will try to rope me into their drama. *Again.*

And I most definitely *cannot* be distracted by the batty lady with sparkling eyes, cheeky mouth, and no-bullshit attitude.

She, with her nose ring and cranberry lips, needs to stay the hell away from me.

Once we've landed, the pilot leaves the small cabin with a smile. "We made it." Her surprise is shocking, but I try not to let it get to me. "Storm is rolling in, so you better be quick about it."

"Thanks," I grumble.

Raya rolls her shoulders back, and she tries to be tough, but the vein on her forehead is trembling. Part of me wants to give her a hard time for being a chicken. The other part of me wants to wrap her up in my arms and reassure her that it'll be all right.

I've got no clue where that comes from, but I beat it back like a kid who gets a lump of coal on Christmas morning.

For fuck's sake. Enough with the Christmas stuff, Klaus. You're better than that.

"Director Cooper told me you know how to get to the village from here?" The pilot forms it as a question, unsure what to do with the information.

I answer with a vague head nod, but of course, Raya hears the exchange and crosses her arms. "Sorry, are you telling me that you know where this mysterious Santa village is? And what? I'm just supposed to take your word for it that you can bring us there safely and in one piece?"

I keep my face an unreadable mask, but Raya isn't done. She goes on. "Seriously. How can you know where we're going? Do you get a map? I didn't. I'd like to examine it before we head out."

The pilot chuckles. "Do you have *any* idea who Klaus is?" she asks. I give her the most threatening death glare I can muster, but she misses it entirely. How many people know my secret? Alyce sure didn't uphold our whole secrecy deal. "Klaus here is *from* Christmas Town."

Raya's head snaps in my direction. Her big hazel eyes nearly pop right out of her head with pure jubilation. "Is this for real?"

I don't respond.

"Oh, sweet echolocation. The big grumpy badass is actually from *Christmas Town*? You. A reindeer. From Christmas Town." She doesn't even try to contain her giggles. "Why doesn't everyone know about this?"

"Because it's my own personal business, and I don't like to talk about it."

"I don't know that you'll have much choice after this assignment, *Blitzen*."

My vision goes red at the sound of the nickname. "Do. Not. Call. Me. That."

"You know, you're pretty much the king of monosyllabic conversations. You speak in full sentences, technically speaking, but you punctuate each word with a pause. It's the strangest thing."

"It's not strange. It's by design. My link to Christmas Town is strictly on a need-to-know basis. You're sworn to secrecy."

"By who?" she shoots back, relishing this moment way too much. The vein in her forehead pretty much winks at me.

For one insane second, I almost lean over to shut her up with my mouth. I bet her lips taste like cranberries. They sure are red enough for it. I stuff my hands into my pockets to keep from reaching out to Raya and doing something we will both definitely fucking regret.

"You two are gonna have so much fun together," the pilot cackles on the way back into her so-called craft. "Happy tidings and all that good stuff."

Without sparing Raya another look, I lumber over to the small little hangar. The walls are made of sturdy concrete, but even they seem to shake and shimmy in the strong northern wind. Using the sleigh all the way to town is going to suck. It'll be cold and windy.

Raya will be sharing a very narrow seat with me. With any luck, there will be *two* blankets in the sleigh because I sure don't feel like sharing my close personal space with her.

Not now. Not ever.

I'll take my chances with hypothermia.

The sleigh is bright red with a black leather runner covered with a thick plaid blanket. The eight non-shifter reindeer huff and move their hooves through the thick snow as Raya and I pile our things at our feet. I know exactly how the animals and their sleigh got here, but I'm not offering Raya that information. If she has any questions, she can bug one of the locals when we arrive. I'm not going to explain anything or interact with the town any more than I need to.

"Family of yours?" She juts her chin toward the reindeer.

Of course, that's what she asks. That mouth of her is quirked up in a sly smirk, and I don't know if I want to dish the diss right back or kiss her quiet.

Probably shouldn't do either of those.

Instead, I choose to ignore her.

Raya rolls her eyes, clicking her tongue. "You're gonna need some kind of sense of humor if you're going to be a reindeer shifter in Christmas Town this time of year."

It's on the *tip* of my tongue to tell her that I'm all too familiar with the village, but I don't. It would only invite more questions, and I'm not feeling chatty at all. It's colder than a snowman's ball sac. I forgot how damn freezing it gets here during the holidays.

Only *one* of the reasons I left and never returned.

Please, do not *let Mom and Dad know I'm on my way.*

That's the very last thing I need. I don't want Nosy Raya to know anything about me, my family, or the reasons why I left them behind the second I was old enough to head out on my own.

Really, when you tell people you *hate* Christmas, they look at you like you've got horns. Not the antlers of a reindeer. No. Some real satanic ones.

No one *wants* to believe that someone can actually hate a holiday that is all about love, joy, and giving.

These people seem to forget that it's actually not the season of giving but the season of *lies*.

Seriously.

It's the time of year where everyone pretends to like each other just long enough to overeat and overdrink after overspending.

My best Christmas memories are all on a beach somewhere, drunk off my ass. The hotter, the more secluded, the better. If that makes me hateful, then so be it. My family sure thinks it makes me villainous to hate Christmas.

"Are you going to tell me how a reindeer from Christmas Town ended up as a FUC agent?"

"No."

Raya chuckles softly. "How long is the ride into town?"

"Long."

"Right. How long? Long enough for me to needle all of the information I want out of you?"

I ignore her and climb onto the sleigh. The sound of her laughter is soft and musical. Hell, it's almost *pleasing*. I shake the thought right out of my head and focus on checking the reins.

"Your name is Klaus, and you lived in Santa *Claus*' town. Is he your godfather? Are you named for him? You've gotta gimme something. I'm dying to know how any of this happened."

"No."

"Oh, come on. We're partners."

"We are *not* partners, and unless you're willing to lay down all of your family's reactions to the Bloody Doctor, I suggest you drop the whole twenty-questions act."

Raya arches a brow at me, unfazed. "You think I won't talk about my aunt for hours? I will. I studied the hell out of her crimes. The way I see it, the more I know about monsters like her, the more equipped I am to deal with them. Family or not, evil is evil."

"Agreed," I grumble back with no further explanation.

That shuts Raya up, but I can see the wheels in her head spinning with her next question.

This is going to be the longest two weeks of my life.

5

RAYA

Dear candy cane gods.

This is next-level intense.

When I first learned that I would be posted in Christmas Town *during* Christmas, I expected the whole village to be holiday-crazed. How could it be anything else than every Yule-time cliché imaginable?

I anticipated decorations and lights everywhere. Cheery people rushing busily in the streets on the way to the workshops. Maybe even some super fragrant treats scenting the cold, crisp winter air.

In truth, nothing—and I mean absolutely *nothing*—could have prepared me for this.

The big red, green, gold, and silver sign that announces our arrival in town is strung up with lights. They twinkle and shimmy a greeting for us as we pass by. I hold my breath, but I'm not sure why. It's not excitement, exactly. It's not nerves, either.

It's a whole new kind of emotion I can't name. It feels a little bit sacred, like a long-lost part of me is coming back to life.

So fucking weird.

My tummy is full of little explosions that travel up my chest and sit at the base of my throat. If I don't keep my mouth shut, I'm liable to *ooh* and *aah* like a little kid.

Real talk?

I stopped believing in Santa Claus a *very* long time ago. To be riding into his village like it's nothing? That's a little dizzying. I'm half expecting Director Cooper to pop out with a camera, laughing at me for falling for this fake mission.

Then she would kick me out because I'm not as good as my sister.

"You okay?" Klaus asks, giving me a rare—but sexy—worried frown.

"Fine," I respond, trying to bat away the bad and invasive thoughts.

He rolls his eyes, his concern replaced with annoyance. "Don't let any of this faze you. This place isn't all that it's cracked up to be."

I snort. "Who *hurt* you?" I'm trying to be funny, but Klaus' head snaps up, and his features darken. He doesn't find me hilarious. At all. "Touchy," I mumble.

Klaus ignores me and leads the sleigh through the small town. The main street is wide enough to accommodate three or four sleighs. It's lined with shops and businesses that knock at my curiosity with all the chill of a melting snowman.

Every storefront is decked out with lights and tinsel, with garlands and ornaments. It's basically a Christmas feast for all five senses.

Part of me wants to get directly to work, while another wants to jump down from the sleigh and explore this incredible little town.

I challenge *anyone* to be in this magical place and not go full *kid*.

Impossible.

At least, unless your name is Klaus Thorsen and you're basically made of steel. He glares at every person we pass, sending daggers toward most stores.

I don't know what the man has against his hometown, but he really needs to cool his eggnog or heat up his chestnuts.

I open my mouth to share my hilarious Christmas jokes, but his deep-set frown has me curbing my mischievous jabs.

If we're working together as a team, maybe I shouldn't antagonize him simply because it's fun to rile him up. I roll my shoulders back and ignore him, focusing instead on my pleasant surroundings.

It's hard to imagine how someone would infiltrate this place, but if I've learned anything from the world during my time with FUC and the Academy, it's that everyone has a price.

It doesn't matter if it's money or favors or even *things*.

Everyone can be lured into a bad situation.

"We're here," Klaus announces, pulling up in front of a massive bed and breakfast.

It's something out of a fairytale. The log building is covered in snow, looking more like a giant gingerbread house than an inn. There are red and green ornaments shimmering from every cornice and twinkling lights framing every window and door. It casts happy little illuminated dances against the pure white snow.

The Jingle Bell Inn is adorable, but the owners obviously take great pride in every aspect of their business. I hop down from the sleigh, eager to see the inside of the building. It takes me only a moment to swing my duffel over my shoulder. Klaus mutters something to me, but I don't hear him. I'm way too busy scampering up the steps.

Am I a fully grown woman with a penchant for leather and motorcycles getting excited about Christmas? Yes. So what? There are no rules out there stating that I need to be a grouch because I'm an adult.

Klaus can be grinch enough for both of us.

The second the door swings open, a fragrant wall of gingerbread spice and mint hit me. It's warm and comforting. I've got an urge to curl up the huge fireplace to read. Me! The lady who has a hard time sitting still for more than a minute at a time.

This place really does have magical powers.

My guess is that nostalgia is the kicker. It clenches your heart and memories tight until you can't help but give in to the spirit of things.

The short woman behind the enormous log desk waves me forward. Her white hair spills out of her crisp and starched lace bonnet. It matches the apron draped over her bright red dress, patterned over with poinsettias and holly.

"Hello, there." Her voice is warm and welcoming, like a cup of hot cocoa. "How were your travels into town?"

"Fine, thanks. I'm wondering if my room is ready. Reservations under Raya Slaski." As I drop my heavy bag onto the floor, continuing my visual feast of the inn, the woman flips through a big leather-bound book. The thick cream paper makes a loud *whoosh* noise every time she turns the pages. It almost keeps time to the Christmas song wafting from a small record player sitting in a place of honor beside a huge Christmas tree. "Maybe it's under Kl—"

"The reservations are made under your name," Klaus snaps, letting the door slam behind him. "Raya Slaski. Two rooms."

"Oh, yes," the cheery lady chortles. "There you are. First time in town?" She narrows her gaze as she tries to stare directly into Klaus's eye, but he purposefully avoids her.

The jerk.

Doesn't he want to tell this nice person that he's from here? Probably not. He doesn't seem to be too pleased with being back home again.

"I'm Mrs. Jingle. Let me know if you need anything." She slides two thick candy cane keychains onto the desk, each holding a heavy skeleton key made of shiny metal that looks way too much like gold.

"Thanks so much," I gush. The second I'm in my room I'm guzzling hot cocoa like it's going out of style.

"Breakfast is served from six until ten. Lunch is at noon and runs through to one most days. The first dinner set is at six, but there is a late sitting at nine if that's better." She beams at me, and I return the sentiment. "You don't want to miss my waffle tree in the morning."

"Waffle tree?" I ask, my mouth already watering.

"Every morning during the holidays, I make a big stack of waffles in the shape of a Christmas tree. All the fixings you could want decorate it. It's almost too pretty to eat."

"That sounds amazing. I can't wait."

"No, thanks," Klaus grumbles as he grabs his key and disappears down the hall.

I shoot our host an apologetic smile and race after him. "Hey, you might want to ease on the attitude if you want this mission to be successful. In case you've forgotten, we need the townspeople's cooperation for this to work."

Klaus spins on his heels, nearly crashing into me. He has to reach out and steady me before I land flat on my ass. "Don't tell me how to do my job, noob. I know what needs to happen."

"Well, if you don't want them to know who you are, maybe behaving in a completely different way than your usual sunny self would be to your benefit."

His eyes turn cold, but he doesn't respond, choosing instead to let me go. I stumble back but quickly find my balance. He takes the steps two at a time, away from me and toward his room.

If I had the time, I would take a look around and maybe snap a few pictures to show my parents. That's not my main concern right now. Instead, I chase after Klaus, hissing his name under my breath as to not bother the other guests.

He unlocks his door and tries to slam it in my face, but thankfully, I manage to shove my heavy boot to stop its progress. Klaus glares at me. "What are you doing?"

"Well, before you retreat into your room and go full recluse, we need to discuss our strategy. This is why we should have talked about it in the plane or in the sleigh."

"We can discuss it in the morning. I need a nap and some food."

I scowl, sensing the lie. He's got every intention of going off on his own as soon as he gets rid of me. "Do you *not* remember Director Cooper's warning? If you fuck this up, it'll be the classroom for you. We need to work together." I arch a brow at him with my arms crossed, waiting for his response.

Klaus's eyes burn into mine. The dude is *pissed*. "I told you. I work better alone. Now, leave me be. I need a nap," he says through gritted teeth.

Really, his anger shouldn't be an aphrodisiac. I *know* I should

click my tongue at him and ignore his little *mantrum*, but his annoyance is kind of *way* delicious. I swear, the more furious Klaus is, the
sexier he becomes.

That's saying something.

The man already has a lot going for him. Between his long hair,
beard, and thousands of tattoos, he's already dangerous to my sanity.
Make him frown at me with that glare? I want to push *all* of his
buttons.

That's why it takes all of my self-control not to tell him that I'll be
going off without him. If he wants to dick around, that's on him.

I don't need Klaus to do my job.

6

KLAUS

A whole bag of stinking bah, humbug!

The décor of the bed and breakfast is a little much for me.

It's overwhelming outside, but that's nothing to the suffocating avalanche of so-called Christmas cheer in my room. The thick bright red carpet is offset by blinding white walls with enough shimmer in them to give me a headache.

I know for a *fact* that the paint shade is called Freshly Fallen Snow. It definitely lives up to its namesake.

The comforter is a thick green blanket that would be great camouflage in a fir forest. The pillows are all kinds of Christmas themes and colors, while the scent of sugar cookies seems to be pumped through the vents every two minutes.

My stomach rolls from its overwhelming aroma.

I need to get the hell out of here.

I'm claustrophobic and in severe danger of going into over-Christmas shock.

It's like septic shock, only instead of slow, agonizing death, it's a... well, slow and agonizing death without the death part.

With a mumbled string of curses at being back in my hometown, I slide my boots back on and grab my jacket. Walking through town will hardly give me any kind of reprieve, but at least it won't feel like the walls are closing in to strangle me with Christmas cheer.

I. Hate. The. Holidays.

Mrs. Jingle gives me a warm smile from behind the counter as I head out the door. She waves and giggles like an elf putting clothes on a naked doll. "Have a fun walk-around, dear."

I think I grumble something back to her, but I don't know what. I definitely don't want to interact with her too much for fear she'll recognize me.

I need fresh air and distance from all of this stuff that reminds me of my childhood.

As soon as the wintry blast of wind hits my face, pelting me with crisp and almost painful wind, I close my eyes. I let the cold seep into my skin to temper my nerves. After a few deep gulps, I turn toward the center of town. If I'm going to be stuck here, I might as well take a spin around the village core to get my bearings and see what's changed since I was here last.

The hot chocolate shop is still opened right beside the bakery. Every third business is a specialty ornament store, from precious materials to more affordable ones. There are clothing stores, but everything is patterned over with holiday *stuff*. The shopkeepers and the townsfolk rush around like busy little elves they are, bustling from one store to the other.

They're not *actually* elves. That's simply what people from Christmas Town call themselves, just like people from Ontario are Ontarians.

I have a better name for these people than *elves*, but I digress.

What I *really* want to do is grab the first person I see and shake them out of their Christmas stupor.

It won't help.

Christmas Town is literally the most Christmasy place in the world. It makes Whoville look like the Grinch's cave.

It's *that* bad.

I scan the main street, trying to decide who I should interview first.

Back in the day, I would have started with the bakery or the hot chocolate shop. The married couple that owns those two businesses were always up on the current gossip.

That's precisely why I can't start with them. The second Carol and Evergreen Trimmings learn that I'm back in town, the sooner my parents will track me down and force me to join them for dinner.

No. Fucking. Thanks.

I flip the collar of my coat up to shield my face. As if the long hair and beard didn't hide my identity from the people who used to know me. They're unlikely to recognize me. I was eighteen the last time I was here.

I never intended to return, but now that I'm here, I have to do my job as efficiently and quickly as possible. If all this is put to rest before the twenty-fifth, I might actually be able to celebrate Christmas on a warm, sandy beach with a bikini-clad stranger who redefines the naughty list.

"Well, well, well." Raya grins as she walks up to me. A large red and white bag dangles from her left hand while the other is wrapped around a huge cup of hot chocolate. "If I didn't know any better, I'd say that Grumpy Blitzen is out for a walk around his hometown."

A low growl vibrates at the back of my throat. "Don't call me that."

It's a wonder of life that she's picked that name out of all of the possibilities. It's like a part of her *knows* about my past.

Impossible.

Raya's brows disappear under her brand-new bright red tuque with a silver and white pompom. It jiggles as she laughs. "Oh, come on. Don't be such a grinch. This place is actually really cool. I can't get over how beautiful everything is. Every shop is super committed to the theme, and I appreciate the hell out of it. Or..." She giggles. "I appreciate the *tinsel* out of it." She continues to chuckle softly as she takes a sip of her drink. Her eyes roll back, and she moans. "This is legit the *best* thing I've ever had in my mouth. The hot chocolate is hot but not so much so that it burns my mouth. And the smoothness? It's like swallowing silky chocolate before it does a happy dance in my belly."

I don't know why her description of her beverage sounds so sensual, but it is. I swallow hard and resist the urge to dunk my head in one of the snowbanks lining the street to cool myself down.

"I'm out exploring. Doing recon at the same time. Is that what you're doing too? Or are you on your way to your family's place?"

"I needed out of my room."

"It's really stunning out here. I'm wondering where to go for dinner. Literally every place looks like it'll be amazing. Tell me where to eat."

"No."

"Then join me."

"No," I repeat.

"*Klaus?*"

My breath catches, but I don't have to turn around to know who has spoken my name. Raya's eyes grow to the size of massive ornaments, and a smirk plays across those delectable red lips of hers.

"Hey, Dad," I mumble before the man engulfs me in a hug that smells like pine and sugar cookies. It's the smell of home, but it's also the scent of my own personal hell.

I pull away from him and will Raya away. She stands there, looking on with a dopey grin on her ridiculously lovely face.

"And who might you be? Did my son finally bring a lady home to meet the family?"

Raya bursts out laughing. "No. Oh, no. We're here on assignment."

Dad's shoulders deflate. "Well, then you must be his partner." He holds out his hand for Raya to shake. "Welcome to our little slice of paradise."

She beams at him. "It really is something else."

"You two need to come over for dinner," Dad gushes like it's the idea of the century.

Raya glances at me, and I do everything in my power to silently plead with her to refuse.

She doesn't.

"I'd love to," she answers. "If this grinchy grinch-grinch won't come along, it's his loss."

"Absolutely," Dad agrees, but I can see the hope brimming out of his eyes. "Whaddya say, son? Come for dinner."

"Fine," I grumble.

What else can I do? I get my stubborn streak from my father. If I don't agree, he's going to start telling Raya all kinds of embarrassing stories until I fold.

My childhood home is a small two-story log structure in one of the neighborhoods off the main drag. The decorations *never* come down. My parents keep the place decked out all year round, and none of their neighbors complain—because they do the same.

It's always *almost* Christmas when you live in Christmas Town.

No sooner is Santa back in his leather armchair with a spiked hot chocolate than the countdown for the next year begins.

Dad points to a few ornaments hanging from the big lit-up Douglas tree that frames the front of the house. "Klaus made those when he was a little boy."

"I can see he was very talented." Raya's smile makes it pretty damn obvious that she's enjoying this quite a bit.

I open my mouth to unleash some kind of self-preserving quip, but the words die on my lips when the front door swings open. My mother, clad in a bright red dress and a deep green apron, clasps her hand under her trembling chin. Her blonde hair has started going gray, but it makes her look that much more dignified. She's aged quite a bit during my absence. My heart breaks a little bit, but I try to ignore the pain.

"Is that my boy?" she shouts, tearing down the stairs. She hugs me tight, saying all kinds of things that make me feel like the world's biggest jerk for not visiting at least a couple of times.

"Holly, this is Klaus's partner, Raya," Dad announces.

Mom drops me like a hot chestnut and rushes to Raya. She cups the newbie agent's face in her hands and gasps. "My tinsel, but you are beautiful. A shifter, too, no doubt?"

Raya nods. "Vampire bat."

Mom laughs. "Oh, isn't that interesting. Positively Halloweeny! Have no fear. We'll help you feel right at home." She drags Raya into the house and offers her a pair of thick knit slippers.

Raya slips them on and moves her feet around. "These are amazing. How do you get them so soft and thick?"

Mom taps her nose. "That's a secret. It's Christmas Town magic." She adds a wink before leading Raya into the living room.

Of course the Christmas tree is up and so decorated it's a little hard to look straight at it. It's full of lights and ornaments that shimmy by the twinkling bulbs. Even the large, soft, tan leather couch has been Yuled. A reindeer throw is draped over it, showcasing what the Thorsen family is known for in this part of the world.

Reindeer rearing and training.

I plop into the sofa and cross my arms, unsure what to do with my hands. I spoke to my parents two weeks ago when they called to beg me to come home for the holidays. Before that, it had been a few months.

Before that? Probably a year.

My parents aren't bad people. They're actually *good*. It's not their fault I hold a grudge like a mother fucker. If only they had taken my side all those years ago, our relationship wouldn't be so tense.

"So," Mom says, sitting beside me on the couch. She pats my knee and grins. "Tell me why you're in town. I thought you were going back to that beach resort."

"We're here on business, Mom. I don't have time to do much but work."

"Nonsense," Raya interjects. "If your family wants to see more of you while you're here for *Christmas*, I can totally pick up the slack."

"Not a chance. You're a noob. I'm not trusting you alone with this very important mission."

"Oh-oh," Dad chuckles, handing Raya a glass of eggnog so strong it could probably peel paint off the walls. The man loves his spiced rum. "Do I sense some tension in the team?"

Raya giggles as she takes a gulp of the drink. "This is my very first mission away from the Academy. I'm newly badged. Apparently, that means I'm green."

"Green is one of the best colors in the world. It's right there along with red." Mom nudges her elbow into my side. "But we can't ask you to work more because of this one. If he's here, you should be too." She rubs her hands together like a kid about to tear into a mountain of gifts. "I'm sure the local authorities will be enough help for you two to come to some of our holiday traditions."

"I'd love that." Raya means it, too.

That's when it hits me.

Raya didn't choose this mission any more than I did. I don't like Christmas or being in my hometown, but there is every chance that my partner misses her family. Maybe she wanted to spend the holidays with the rest of the Slaski bats and whatever it is nocturnal creatures do at Christmas.

Probably drink hot blood while dancing around a dead tree or something.

"It's settled," Mom announces. "You'll have Christmas dinner here. Oh, and you can't miss the cookie exchange." She continues rattling off all of the things she wants us to do.

I barely pay attention. My focus is a little wonky.

For some weird reason, I can't stop staring at the twinkling light playing across Raya's features. She's glowing and beautiful. Two things I definitely shouldn't notice about my newbie partner.

Or anyone, for that matter.

We're here to work.

Not to celebrate the holidays.

Not to reminisce about the past.

Not to drool over cranberry lips.

7

RAYA

My evening with Klaus and his parents was one of the most illuminating nights of my life.

Not because of the millions of Christmas lights.

Nope.

It had everything to do with how Klaus interacted with his super-sweet parents. I don't have to be a genius to see that though there is a lot of love there, there was a breach of trust at one point. Klaus's parents know what caused it, and they're trying very hard to fix it.

The problem is that Klaus is the most stubborn man alive.

Must be the antlers on his head that make his skull so thick.

For some reason, I am *always* on the receiving end of his ornery streak. On the walk back to the Jingle Bell Inn last night, I gave Klaus a brief glimpse of my strategy. He shot down all of my ideas. He barely let me get in a word before launching into his own plans.

Apparently, all of mine were crap and reeked of my inexperience. He particularly didn't like it when I reminded him that though I might be green to him, it's one of the best colors in the world.

When I repeated his mother's words, the glare he gave me could have reheated a frozen hot chocolate.

Before we each retreated to our bedrooms, we didn't agree on a course of action. Yet, I'm way ahead of him. He might think that I'm nothing but a wet-behind-the-ears whelp, but I'm a good agent. I know the protocols forward and backward. Not to mention my killer instincts.

Our first stop today *has* to be the big man himself.

Klaus disagrees. He thinks we need to go to the local authorities first. Though he isn't wrong, he isn't right. The CTPD might very well need to know we're on their side, but nothing happens in this town without Santa knowing about it. At least, that's what Holly said. Since she's lived here much longer than her son, I'm siding with her on this.

Somehow, I manage to get Klaus to join me at Santa's workshop.

Probably because I threatened to have every meal with his parents while I'm in town. He doesn't need to know I still fully plan on doing this. Holly and Patridge Thorsen are wonderful people.

Santa's workshop doesn't look like any factory I've ever seen before in my life. It's a palace of Christmas proportions. The double-wide doors swing open to let us into a massive entryway. A huge chandelier hangs from above. The glimmering crystal ornaments are candy canes, sleighs, gingerbread cookies, and all kinds of Christmasy things. It's so beautiful and blinding I almost miss the patterned floor. The big red, white, and green tiles make a mosaic that probably looks like a Christmas scene when you climb up and down the huge swirling staircase.

A tiny little woman wrapped in yards and yards of sparkling crimson material prances toward us with a wide smile. The apples of her cheeks are red with joy—and maybe some morning eggnog.

"Do my eyes deceive me, or is that little Blitz Thorsen I see?"

What the tinsel?

Why does *she* get to call him Blitz?

I nudge his side, and he swats my hadn't away with an annoyed growl. "We're *so* talking about *that* later."

Klaus groans. "No. Not up for discussion. Hi, Vanilla."

She beams at him. "Oh, and he remembers me. Imagine that. I suppose you're here to talk to the Big Man about the wreath?" Vanilla takes a dramatic look around the entryway and leans in close to us.

"Between you and me, Santa is *very* concerned about this whole thing. The wreath can't be stolen. It would ruin everything good and pure about Christmas Town."

Klaus shrugs. "I'm not gonna let anything happen to the town."

"*We*," I correct. "*We* won't let anything happen to the town."

Vanilla nods. "That makes me feel better. Why would we trust our whole world to the man who left over a decade ago and never came back?"

Klaus's entire body stiffens. He runs a hand back through his hair. That's his tell. He does that when he's angry. Or pissed. Or annoyed.

Huh.

Seems that the rainbow of emotions that make up Klaus are all firmly in the *negative* column. I have a hard time reconciling who he is as a person and where he comes from. I was only joking when I asked him, *who hurt you?* But now, more than ever, I know there is a story behind his long absence from home—and his permanently surly attitude.

It might not be my mission to get to the bottom of it, but I will. I am, after all, the better agent.

Vanilla, Santa's head elf, business manager, and accountant, leads us down one of the many halls and to an enormous golden elevator. The doors slide open to the tune of "Santa Claus is Coming to Town," and the song continues as we travel down for what seems like miles. When we arrive at our destination, I am speechless.

The room—if it can even be *called* a room—is so big all of Christmas Town could fit in here three times over.

Little cabooses come and go in perpetual motion on a small train track across the busy factory floor.

Elves rush around, singing and laughing, and all-around having a good time while preparing toys... *and electronics.*

No joke. There is a handful of elves toiling over a series of tablets. *Making* the devices as easily as if they were icing a gingerbread man.

It's a little bit dizzying. I want to pause and soak it all up, but this is hardly the time to fangirl over Santa's workshop.

Vanilla waves us forward, but I get the distinct impression that Klaus knows exactly where we're going. After all, the man drove us here in a damn *sleigh* from memory.

The head elf whistles a few bars of "Jingle All the Way," and one of the cabooses stops right in front of us. We hop in, piling into the minuscule car. Klaus's shoulder brushes against mine. I try not to get all gooey from the heat radiating off of him. I *try* not to take a big whiff of him, but the man smells way too damn good for my sanity.

I focus on the elves and the passing factory floor to keep my thoughts away from my leg pressed into his. Who knew man-thighs could be so damn thick and so damn appealing?

"Here we are," Vanilla announces before leaping down from the caboose. She hops toward a set of gold doors taller than Klaus.

The precious metal is patterned over with a forest scene where a reindeer presents a wreath to a young man. I want to take a few moments to look at the artwork, but Vanilla pushes it open.

"Boss, you've got some visitors."

A tall man sporting a full mane of pure white hair and a long silver beard looks up from a stack of papers. His brown eyes narrow, his skin a shade darker than I would have expected from a man who spends all of his time in the north, away from the sun. I'm a nocturnal creature with a sun allergy, but that isn't even a concern up here. Not in the dead of winter.

"Is that Blitz I see?" Santa's voice booms cheerfully across his office.

Okay. Seriously?

Everyone can call him Blitz but me? We're going to have some words, Blitz and I.

Klaus stiffens beside me at the same name that's got me more shaken than a snow globe

"Hey, Nik."

Nik. Nik?

Did Klaus *really* call Santa Nik like it's no big deal?

The older man crosses his arms and leans back into his chair, grinning wide. "Never thought I'd see you back in town, Blitz."

Klaus shrugs. "It's my job to go where they need me."

Santa—Nik?—smirks, amused. "Oh? And does FUC treat you well? I can't imagine you volunteered for this mission in your hometown. I thought you'd rather be dead than come back here."

"Can we not do this?" Klaus grumbles.

I elbow him. "Dude. That's *Santa*. Do you *want* to be on the naughty list?"

Santa bursts out laughing, his head thrown back and his big belly jiggling. It's literally the happiest sight I've ever seen. Not-so-deep in my psyche, little Raya is giggling and clapping, chanting *again, again.*

"And you must be the partner. Raya Slaski." He smiles at me, and I almost curtsy. Why? No idea. This moment feels important, though. Like I'm meeting royalty.

"Yes. Hi. Hello."

Santa grins, but before he can say anything more, Klaus takes a step forward. "We're here for the wreath. Why don't you just show it to us? We need to know how secure it is."

Santa chuckles. "All business? Sure. We can do that, Blitz." He turns on his heels and makes his way to the opposing wall.

Right there, in a simple glass case, lies a gold wreath. It's nothing special, really. I don't really understand what all the fuss is about. I've seen nicer pieces in museums. But that's not why the wreath is important.

Apparently, it has magical powers.

If the legend is true, this thing is the Holy Gail. How nutso bananas is that? Who would melt down a chalice to make a decoration that can only be used once a year?

"It's been right here for a long time," Santa explains. "I don't know why it's an interesting relic all of sudden. It's most definitely *not* the Holy Grail."

"Who started that rumor then?" I ask.

Santa frowns. "I've got no clue. I think it happened around the early 1900s. There was a revival in the chase for the Holy Grail, and for some reason, the chase led them here." He rubs his beard. "Titus something... that was the fellow's name. He was a shifter, of course. He came here looking to buy the wreath. Vanilla's grandmother warned him that it wasn't for sale. That the town needs it for its magic, but the man didn't get it."

"Didn't get what?"

Santa shakes his head. "That magic isn't real. The wreath doesn't have magic in the abracadabra sense. It has the kind of magic that comes from belief and tradition." He takes the gold object in his hands, turning it over, showing it to me from all angles before letting me take it. "If this were to get stolen? Nothing would happen, really. But the repercussions for what it means to the town? What it means to the holiday? *That* is the danger."

I take my time to inspect it, but I'm not sure what I'm even looking for. We could have a fake wreath made and let the baddies steal it, but I can't see Klaus liking that plan. I bite my tongue, knowing I need to do better.

"So there is no magic to this town?"

Santa shrugs before pointing to a map of the world behind his desk. "I basically run a massive factory. I deliver some toys, sure, but there's no magic to it."

"The world's most famous toymaker is nothing more than a tinkerer with a penchant for family tradition and nepotism," Klaus grumbles.

"Guilty." Santa grins. "If people want to believe in magic? Well, that's on them. The real magic, the kind that is transcendent above anything else, is *stories*."

"That's true," I concur, a bit sad that magic isn't real. I should've known, though. I'm a grown woman who can shift into a one-ounce bat. That's not magic, no matter how improbable it is. It's shifter science.

It makes as much sense to me as the myth of the Holy Grail.

"*Santa* is a name. It's a state of mind that is passed down from father to son. My son Niko will take over for me when I'm too old, and so on and so forth."

Klaus mumbles something under his breath. I'm not sure what he says, but it doesn't sound too good. Something about *assholes being in charge of Christmas.*

That can't be right.

Could Klaus' whole issue with Christmas have something to do with the Santa family?

I make a plan to bug him about it later. If he doesn't open up, I can always go hang out with his parents. They'll be more than happy to share with me.

I would *never* admit this, but I miss my family. Even my sister. I've never spent a Christmas without them. I didn't exactly *expect* to miss the competition, but I do. Or maybe I just miss her—full stop.

"I need to secure the wreath, Nik." Klaus uses his authoritarian voice, pulling me from my less-than-pleasant thoughts. "It can stay in your office, but I'll want cameras on it at all times."

"*We'll* also need a list of everyone who has access to your office," I cut in, putting all of the emphasis I can on the *we*. If Klaus is still trying to make me butt out, he's got another think coming. "You'll need to limit the access to this area if you choose to keep the wreath here."

"I like this pairing." Santa's smirk is as mischievous as can be.

In the end, keeping the wreath where it's always been is the better course of action. If someone is in town to steal it or has been tapped by Vitality Holdings' puppet masters, Hera and Zeus, to steal it, they might make a move before we're ready if they know we're thinking about it changing things around. It would also put others in danger.

Santa leaves us in his office, apparently to go do some rounds of the workshop, but I have a feeling he left for Klaus' benefit.

"You know, I read up on reindeer before we left the Academy. I learned that they are very social animals who like to be in big herds. You're basically breaking your own instincts by being a lone reindeer. That tells me there's a story there."

"No," he grunts.

I laugh. "That's another thing I learned. Apparently, reindeer are *very* communicative and use all kinds of sounds to chat with their peers. You've got the grunts and grumbles down, my friend."

"I thought bats couldn't speak. Shouldn't you be super quiet? Only use echolocation or something?"

"Ha!" I nudge him with my elbow, mindful of the security camera I'm holding. "You did bat research. I'm choosing to see that as you reaching out to make a human connection."

He rolls his eyes and fiddles with a second camera.

All told, we are installing six tiny surveillance cameras that we will be able to access remotely from our phones and from a tiny little office in the depths of the workshop.

Are we *maybe* using the non-magical wreath as bait to catch Vitality Holdings' newest puppet? Yes. Absolutely.

"Are you gonna tell me why I can't call you Blitz?" I watch his reaction.

He flinches. "No."

"So there'll be another *no* when I ask why people here call you that?" I wait for ten Christmases to go by. Nothing. "Fine. Are you at least going to tell me why you don't like it here?" I ask, knowing he won't answer.

Klaus clenches his jaw down tight. "No."

"Why not? It would help me understand you better."

"And why do you need to understand me better?"

"We're partners."

"Only for a little while. Once this is all over, I'm not gonna have a partner for a long time. Best we keep things professional."

I click my tongue. "Being civil and holding a decent conversation with your partner *is* professional. Now, get your burly self up that ladder."

Klaus blanches. I don't imagine it, either. Under his beard, his entire face goes shades paler. I flashback to his boorish attitude on the plane, the breathing exercises he was doing on his tablet.

Klaus is afraid of heights.

"I'll do it." I start climbing up the ladder and hold out my hand for the camera and the bracket I'll need to screw to the wall.

"Don't gimme shit," he rumbles.

I scrunch up my face. "What? Why would I give you a hard time about being afraid of heights?"

"I'm not afraid," he snaps. His shoulders immediately deflate, and he runs a hand through his long luscious hair. "Sorry. I'm just…"

"Used to people giving you a hard time for it?"

He nods, avoiding my gaze.

"My big sister has a pretty big aversion to blood," I state. It's much easier to have this conversation with my back to him, focused on the screwdriver and nail. "As a vampire bat, that's not great. I always sort of teased her about it." I shrug. "It's not like there's anything wrong with her. We've all got our thing."

He snorts. "Yeah? And what's your thing?"

I turn and give him a saccharine smile. "Easy now, Blitz. That's *way* too personal." I add a wink because I'm feeling saucy.

What I *don't* anticipate is the heady look in Klaus's eyes. *That* almost makes me fall off the ladder and right into his big, strong, surly arms.

8

KLAUS

Yesterday, while installing the cameras in Santa's office, Raya figured out my biggest fear. She was *this* close to also learning why I hate my hometown so much.

That irks her enough already.

If I told her I also hated Santa? She might have a coronary or something.

I've mostly been able to keep her questions about my childhood at bay. Not easy. She is one curious lady. You'd think that as a nocturnal creature she would be all grumpy, being up and about during the day.

Not a chance.

There is so very little sun here, in Christmas Town. Raya doesn't ever have to cover her face to keep the harmful rays away from her skin. Of course, it helps that it's colder than a snowman's asshole. Stubborn as she is, Raya still insists on wearing her leather jacket instead of the thick parka the Academy provided for her.

I would give her shit for it if she didn't look so damn *hot* in the stupidly uninsulated garment.

There is no way in hell that I *should* be attracted to the woman.

She's as infuriating as she is kind. Those two things don't really go together.

Raya didn't really *push* to learn the reasons why I don't like Christmas Town or heights. Oh, sure. She asks about it enough to make me want to kiss her quiet.

We're going to ignore that I just said I want to kiss Raya and move right along.

We've turned a small room in the bowels of the workshop into our own little security office. It's the first time in history that a security system has to be implemented, which is worrisome.

All morning, Vanilla has brought elves for us to interview. We don't really know what we're looking for. All we have to go on is what the Cryptozoian Council agent, Val Downer, shared. FUC uncovered that she was a mole a few months ago. The shadowy leaders of Vitality Holdings, calling themselves Hera and Zeus, injected a toxin into her bloodstream. If she didn't cooperate daily, they wouldn't send her the serum she needed to stay alive. They were literally blackmailing her with *death*.

It is difficult to interview the hundreds of people who make Christmas Town a possibility. We need to discover if anyone has fallen prey to the same scheme as Agent Downer. Her loyalty to her badge or job didn't waver.

She was put in an impossible situation.

We also have to consider that Hera and Zeus might be going about their machinations in a whole new way this time around. It would make sense to change their MO when it gets discovered.

Vanilla leads in an elf by the name of Magenta. The tiny woman wrings her hands together, her shock of white hair dyed the same color as her name, if her roots are any indication. The wrinkles in her features make it clear that she has been working for the Santa Claus family for a very long time. If I was a better man, I might give her a warm, comforting smile, but I know from experience that if I try to be nice, it only ends up looking like I'm glowering. I blame the beard. Not my lack of practice.

"Magenta," Raya begins with a closed-mouth smirk. "Please, take a seat. We only have a few things to discuss with you."

"Thanks, I guess," the elf squeaks. "Did I do something wrong?"

"We're meeting with all of the workshop's employees and probably everyone in town, Magenta. We have some questions. Nothing to worry about." Raya punctuates her spiel with a grin. "How long have you been working here?"

"About forty years," Magenta answers. "I like the work. It makes me happy to make other people happy."

Raya jots this down. "And have you traveled outside of Christmas Town lately?"

The elf gasps, like leaving is the most ludicrous idea in the world. "I would never leave town." She shoots me an accusatory glare, and I shrug.

"Any visitors hanging around your home?"

And so it goes on for the rest of the day. We interview as many people as we can, all the while keeping a watch over the computer sandwiched between us. Every now and again, Santa waves at one of the cameras to let us know he hasn't forgotten about us.

During our chat with an elf named Frankincense, I glance at the computer, only to see *him*.

My arch-nemesis.

My enemy.

The world's biggest asshole: Santa's son, Niko.

Santa points out the cameras to him, and it's only by the cheesy and sardonic smile on Niko's face that I can tell he knows I'm here.

Fucking great.

The second he runs into Raya he'll tell her everything. I don't know why the idea of her knowing about The Incident bugs me so much, but it does.

I barely pay attention or take notes during the rest of Frankincense's interview. I'm too distracted by the eventuality that Raya and Niko will meet. I've got to wonder if he's as charming as he always was. If he is, he might very well try to seduce Raya to prove a point. To prove that he can.

Not that I would care if Niko *did* put the moves on Raya. She's a grown woman more than capable of making her own decisions. It's not like there is anything between us but a tense, *somewhat* professional relationship.

If she falls for the dickweed, that's on her.

I wouldn't feel a damn thing. No jealousy. No anger. Nothing.

"Are you okay?" Raya pokes my arm as Frankincense closes the door behind him. *Oops.* "You didn't listen to him at all. He was talking about the trip he took to Hawaii last month. He's one of the only elves we've spoken to who has left town lately. Apparently, he needed time away from his wife, Vanilla. Gossip is that they hit a bit of a rough patch. Did you really not hear any of that?"

"Sorry," I grumble. "I got distracted."

"Well? Care to explain why you checked out? Was I not asking the questions in the right order? Did you want to complain about something?" The burning look she sends my way makes it pretty damn clear she believes she was handling it all perfectly.

She's right. She is a pro.

"No," is my shining answer. She won't get more out of me. I don't trust myself in this tense moment.

Raya clicks her tongue and crosses her arms. "Could you use more than one syllable to tell me what's going on? Be a reindeer, Klaus. Use your words." Raya turns in her seat to face me, and she leans in very close. "*Communicate.*"

The red of her lips is shocking against her pale face. The hazel of her eyes is so sharp I swear I can feel their *color* rubbing against my beard. The nose ring through her nostril shines at me like a beacon, pulling me in.

"No," I insist through gritted teeth. I'm not talking to her but to myself. I'm trying to warn myself off of Raya.

She's a noob with way too much energy and something to prove. I'm a salty mother fucker who wants to be left alone.

"Say," Raya inches forward. The peppermint hot chocolate she had earlier makes her breath nearly irresistible. "More." A couple more centimeters closer.

Her mouth is *right* there. I swallow hard as I look down at her delicious lips.

I'm not too sure how it happens.

One second, Raya is sitting a foot away from me. The next, I've pulled her onto my lap and my mouth is fused to hers.

I half expect her to push me off and away, to slap me and rage out. She doesn't.

The batty chick actually runs her tongue along the seam of my mouth with a moan. Her fingers tangle in my hair as she moves her lips against mine. The embrace tastes like candy canes: sweet with a bite.

My heart thunders in my ears as I explore her mouth with my tongue, drawing out the kiss.

I don't want it to ever end.

The second it's over I'll have to explain what the hell happened. For now, I'll sink into it. Sink into Raya.

"Klaus," she whispers against my lips. "I think we need a break from the small room. Maybe get some air before we do something *really* dumb."

"Yeah." I help her to her feet before leaving her alone in the security office.

I don't bother closing the door behind me. I've got a feeling no physical barrier will ever protect me from the way Raya makes me feel.

9

RAYA

The computer blinks to life as I plop into one of the uncomfortable chairs. The screen fills with the footage of Santa's office. The local officers from CTPD who had the night shift assured me that nothing went wrong during their watch.

The wreath is still in its case.

The missing element to this little scene? My partner.

Klaus is nowhere to be found.

I'd bet my echolocation skills that the man is freaking the fuck out after our kiss yesterday.

I haven't seen him since.

Truth be told, I'm pretty confused about the whole thing. Klaus is hot as sin with his long hair, beard, and grumpy attitude. That's not the issue.

The problem is that I am on a mission. I need to be flawless in my agent work.

How can I do that if I'm obsessing over one single kiss?

The simple answer: I can't.

I have to put Klaus Thorsen and his dumb perfect mouth out of my mind and focus on the task at hand.

So what if he's late? That's on him.

I am a professional—unlike his kiss-giving fine ass.

I won't do like Vera and fall for the dude I'm working with. I'll be better than her.

"Morning," Klaus grumbles as he finally walks into the security office. He places a white and red travel cup on the desk and a crinkly brown paper bag patterned over with gingerbread cookies and boughs of holly. "That's a peppermint latte. For you. Cookies, too." He runs a hand through his hair before shrugging out of his parka, avoiding my eyes as if I were a gorgon.

"Thanks," I say, digging into one of the still-warm sugar cookies. "You didn't have to do that, but I appreciate the gesture."

Klaus's only response is a grunt. He drags his chair farther away from me before settling into it, arms crossed and stare fixed anywhere but on me.

With a heavy sigh, I kick his boot with mine. "Is this how it's going to go from now on? You kiss me and then ignore me?"

Finally, he looks up at me, brows knitted into his hairline. His cheeks are red as Santa's suit under his beard, but Klaus remains silent.

"Reindeer caught your tongue?" I tease, nudging him with my boot again. "Maybe we need to clear the air after—"

"No," he grumbles.

"Yes," I insist.

If any other man had kissed me without explicit consent, I'd be nailing his balls to the wall while singing a cheerful Christmas song.

Jingle balls, jingle balls, jingle all the way.

But the thing is I don't mind that Klaus kissed me. I'm not entirely sure if he pulled me into his lap or if I leaped onto him.

He's a little bit distracting, and that is the *only* reason why I want to discuss this whole kiss situation. To make sure it doesn't happen again.

"Look, drink your latte and get ready for another day of interviews, okay? As far as I'm concerned? That kiss never happened."

My jaw drops down onto the table while my back straightens. *Forget it ever happened?* Is he for real?

There isn't a gingerbread cookie's chance in Christmas Town that I will ever forget that kiss.

It was way too damn good for that. His beard left red scratch marks on my cheeks that I can still feel tingling. His lips were soft and firm, moving perfectly to the right rhythm.

If Klaus can sit there and pretend we never kissed, then surely I didn't make enough of an impression on him.

That annoys me more than his monosyllabic conversation skills.

Without thinking too much about what I'm doing and why, I push away from the table and stand, only to straddle Klaus into his chair.

"What are you doing?" he asks. His hands grip my hips tight, keeping me locked in place. He might not know what I'm doing, but he doesn't want me to budge an inch.

"I'm proving a point."

And then, I lock my fingers into the hair at his nape and fuse my mouth to his on a long, searing, snow-melting kiss.

The gentle graze of his beard on my skin.

The firm movements of his lips on mine.

The strong hold of his hands on my ass.

All of it will be *impossible* to forget. I make sure of it, going so far as to grind against his growing erection. If I started this whole make-out session to prove a point, my goal changes pretty quickly.

I don't want to kiss Klaus so that he never forgets how good it is.

I kiss him because I *want* to. Because I *need* to. Because it is the most delicious thing I've ever done in my life.

The man might be monosyllabic, but he *knows* how to use his tongue just fine. He rubs it against mine, exploring my mouth, alternating between smooth sips of my mouth and deep explorations that make my core clench and flutter in anticipation.

"Raya," he groans against my lips. "What on Santa's red sleigh are we doing?"

"Kissing," I respond before diving for his mouth again.

He moans, cupping my face as he nips my lower lip. "I know *that*. We shouldn't."

"You said our kiss never happened. I wanna make you know that not only did it happen but you won't be forgetting about it any time soon."

He leans away from me, his hands traveling down my arms to rest on my hips. The corner of his mouth quirks up with the hint of a smirk. "And why would you want me to remember the kiss?"

"Because," I whisper, leaning into him once more. I'm taking a page out of his book and only responding with one-word answers.

The truth is I don't want to tell Klaus why I wanted to kiss him or why it's important to me that he never forgets it.

If I try to explain my reasoning, I won't like what I find.

Probably a very inconvenient attraction to an emotionally unavailable grouch who hates Christmas, heights, and communication. Three things that are kind of important for a bat shifter.

Okay, maybe not the *Christmas* of it all, but the rest sure is essential to me.

Heights? I am a winged creature who flies for fun.

Communication? I am a gifted echolocator, but those skills don't exactly make it any easier for me to read Klaus's thoughts.

"Because of *what*, Raya?" Klaus insists as his fingers draw patterns along my arms.

"We've got work to do." I push off of him and return to my own seat.

Despite my burning cheeks and overheated body, I take a long gulp from the latte and make a big show of eating the cookies. I need to keep my mouth occupied before I devour Klaus again.

Better to eat my body weight in sugar cookies than blurting out, *Take me to the inn and screw me hard and fast seven ways to Christmas.*

That's not professional.

Definitely not behavior becoming of a FUC agent on a mission to make a name for herself.

Eyes on the prize, Raya. And the prize is most definitely *not Klaus Thorsen.*

10

KLAUS

The last time my balls were this blue I was seventeen and living in this very town as a social pariah.

The reasons were different, of course.

I was a tall, gangly, nervous wreck of a reindeer with a fear of heights and no way to shake my peers' impression of me as shy and awkward Klaus.

Now, I am a grown man.

There is no reason for my condition.

Only, that's not true.

The *reason* is a person.

A saucy, annoying, stubborn, sexy, pain-in-the-ass, hilarious batty lady.

Raya didn't simply *kiss* me in the security office two days ago. She somehow found a way to weasel her way into my thoughts, under my skin. I swear to Frosty, every time I take a breath, I can hear her voice teasing me for my monosyllabic ways. Every time she moves in close to me, parts of my anatomy perk up. It's like her presence is MiracleGro or something.

I don't understand the attraction between us. That powerful, almost *visceral* reaction she elicits in my body, mind, and soul. I've been on the brink of losing my mind over Raya for over forty-eight hours now.

It doesn't help that we spend a lot of our time alone in a tiny room.

Today, we're going over all the interviews, cross-referencing them with personnel files and what we've learned from town gossip. No one has made a move on the wreath. Not one single person, visitor or local alike, has raised any suspicion.

There's only one person I've got any bad vibes for.

Niko.

I'm not an idiot. It's entirely due to our personal history. My feelings have no real foundation in truth. If Christmas Town wants to crown Niko the Psycho as their next Santa, that is *their* business. Not mine.

Raya sighs, pushing away another file before rubbing her eyes. "I'm gonna say something. It'll sound insane and unprofessional, but lemme get it out."

I arch a brow at her, waiting for her to go on.

"Vitality Holdings is run by Lisbeth Bannon, right? And we know that either she *is* Hera or she is being *controlled* by Hera. The Zeus dude, we've got no possible link. These people are after anything that will grant them immortality. They tried to get their hands on the Bloody Doctor's research. When that fucked up, they went for the plant genome. They were caught again, and what? Now they're literally chasing myths like the Holy Grail? Are they also roaming crop circles in the hopes of finding aliens?"

"Are you gonna get to your point?"

Raya shrugs. "That's just it. There is no point. We came here on the off chance that these Hera and Zeus lunatics will come here to find the Holy Grail. Problem is we have no tangible proof that they'll come here."

"That's why T-Bone and Director Cooper have other teams keeping watch on the other stuff. Crop circles included," I add with a grin.

Her jaw drops after a gasp. "Did you make a joke? An actual *funny* joke? Who are you, and what have you done with Klaus?"

"Stop," I plead. "It won't happen again."

"But it should. That was good."

I smirk because there's nothing else to do. When Raya Slaski beams at you like you've got sunshine coming out your ass, you smile. It's basically a law.

"We should pack it in for the day, or we'll be late for dinner with your parents. Not to mention, we need to clean up all of these cookie crumbs before the local PD gets here." She points to the morsels decorating the front of my black tee.

"Too late," Officer Wassail Sugarplum says, coming into the small security office. "I'm already here."

"Hey, Wassail," Raya greets him with a warm grin. "How's it going?"

He raises his cup of hot chocolate to her. "Can't complain. Lots to do, of course, but that's to be expected this time of year. You two have anything to report before you head off?"

"No," I answer. "Did you manage to get us that list of all the vendors?"

Wassail nods and drops a thick file onto the table. "It took some doing, but we managed. What you've got here is a list of every single company or vendor Christmas Town does business with. The only ones missing will be the ones Santa uses."

"I'm getting that list from Santa," Raya reminds him for the millionth time.

Really, Wassail isn't a bad cop. He's just a bit on the complaining side. He's always got something to gripe about. It's as annoying as it is endearing for a man who should've retired a decade ago. Thing is, it's excessively difficult to find people who want to live in Christmas Town. Unless someone is born here or marries into a local family, it's almost impossible to get people to move here.

Not because no one wants to.

Rather, the vetting system is intense.

That's why Raya and I have decided that if there is a mole in town, it might be one of the vendors who do business here.

It was actually Raya's idea.

The woman isn't merely sexy as hell. She's way smarter than me. Not that I will *ever* admit this to her.

———————

I don't know what to do with this sight.

Raya Slaski is standing in my parents' kitchen, rolling cookie dough into neat little balls before placing them on a large baking sheet. She sways to the Christmas music playing on the small radio, singing about every third word under her breath.

It's strange to realize that she actually fits in here, making my mother's famed sugar cookie chocolate balls.

She belongs here way more than I do.

"Do you think the furnace is okay?" she asks, grabbing more dough from the huge ceramic bowl. We'll be balling for hours yet.

"I think there's nothing wrong with the furnace," I answer.

Raya frowns, but it only takes her a couple seconds to understand. "They're trying to give us space."

"Something like that."

About fifteen minutes ago, once dinner was all cleared away, Raya and I started helping my parents with the Christmas baking. Dad heard a mysterious sound coming from the furnace room at the back of the house. Moments later, he called my mother over to help.

There's nothing wrong with the heating system.

My folks are definitely not as sly as they think they are.

"So, what?" Raya wiggles her brows. "They want us to get all chummy while making cookies?"

"Something like that," I repeat.

"Have they met you?" She snorts on a giggle. "You're not an easy dude to know."

I don't respond because she's right. Though Raya knows more

about me than anybody else outside of Christmas Town, I don't say that aloud. Not because I'm ashamed.

It's more of a saddening realization.

After what happened with Niko and his band of idiots, once the whole town took his side, it was easier for me to pretend that the town was a bad place full of shitty people.

I brought that pain with me into FUC, and since then, I've had a really hard time trusting people.

In a lot of ways, I see the world in the very same way as Christmas Town. A crappy place full of crap people.

And this cheerful holiday thought is brought to you in part by childhood trauma.

"I'll crack you, you know," Raya announces. She breaks one of her sugar cookie balls in two to demonstrate her intention. She pops one of the halves into her mouth with a devilish, mischievous grin. "I've got the skills it takes."

Thing is I believe her. Not only because she is a competent agent.

The more time I spend with her, the more I *want* her to know me. That's... *surprising.*

It's actually downright shocking, especially since I know a lot about her life. She's told me all about her parents and her perfect sister. Her failed university career and her obsession with leather jackets.

I'm developing my own obsession with her coats.

"You can try to crack me all you want, Raya. Doesn't mean it'll happen."

"Oh, I've got my ways." She winks at me, and I nearly swallow my tongue.

Raya takes a few steps toward me, wiping her hands on her reindeer apron. Her hand, that small, warm weight, falls onto my shoulder. "I'll get to the gooey center of you, Klaus Blitz Thorsen."

And at that moment? I want her to do just that.

11

RAYA

My hand is on Klaus's shoulder. Brimming blood bag. What a shoulder it is.

I knew he was muscular, but this is next level. I pat him for good measure, and not at all because I don't want to stop touching him. Klaus grins, the smile barely making it through his beard. It shines in his eyes, pulling a shiver out of me. He really is a good-looking man.

No, that's too simple.

He's his own category of hot. He's not simply tall and muscular with tattoos and long hair like he waltzed out of those rock music magazines I used to read from cover to cover three thousand times every day as a kid.

He's got this whole other quality about him. It lies under the surface, only appearing in little flashes. Like when his mom handed him a frilly green and red apron and he didn't even hesitate to put it on. Like when she asked him for a hug, and he complied. Like when it became clear to me that, though Klaus hasn't seen his parents in years, he hasn't forgotten the sugar cookie recipe his mother is famous for.

He knows it by heart.

"You might think you're an international, supernatural man of mystery, but I'll figure you out." My voice comes out all breathy.

Klaus takes a step forward, one of his hands going to my hip. His long, strong fingers caress the curve. I forget my name, where we are, and what we're doing. I don't know why he's decided to put his hands on me, but I don't ever want him to stop. I want to stay right here for the next eternity or so.

"Raya." My name is a raspy whisper made of naughty things. "You're in danger of doing something we're both going to regret."

Either I've lost the plot or Klaus is looking at my lips like they're the most delicious thing in existence.

"Oh, yeah? And what am I in danger of?"

"You don't want to know."

"Pretty sure I do."

His breath stutters out of him, and he takes another step forward. I have to crane my head to catch his gaze, and of course, the movement puts me that much closer to him. I lick my lips because the more he stares at them, the more my mouth wants him to do something about it already.

"You don't want this," he murmurs.

"I really do."

My hand is still on his shoulder, relishing the flex of his muscle. My body thrums with anticipation.

This moment is leading to a kiss.

It has to.

Klaus cups my cheek with one large hand, his thumb drawing a line across my lower lip. "Did you know that your lips are red like cranberries?" If he was expecting a response, he won't get one. I'm too stunned to speak. "It's the strangest, most mesmerizing thing in the world. You don't even have lipstick on. It's natural. It's impossible to resist doing this..."

He steps forward, his body towering over me. With my cheek in his hand, he tilts my face up to him. His eyes are burning with a desire I recognize.

He is going to kiss me.

And he does.

His lips brush against mine gently. The coarse hair of his beard is in direct opposition to the softness of his lips. He places another kiss on my mouth before letting his tongue run the seam, teasing, tasting, almost testing my reaction.

I won't back down.

I can't. I don't want to. The only thing I want at that moment is to devour Klaus or, at the very least, let him devour me right back. I wrap my arms around his neck, using his height to hoist myself up an inch or two off the ground. I crush my breasts against his chest as I delve my tongue into his mouth, exploring him. He moans, his fingers tightening on my cheek while his other hand cups my ass. He brings me into him, leaving little to the imagination.

His erection presses into my side, and I groan because we're in his parents' kitchen, on a mission. We don't have time to kiss like this, to make our way to the first available surface to chase that blissful oblivion.

Yet, a big part of me wants to throw caution to the wind and do just that.

"Raya," he moans against my lips. "You're the noob who has more sense than a loose-cannon loner like me. You should push me away right now. Give me shit for even deigning to put my hands on you."

"I want your hands on me. I also want *my* hands on *you*."

"You're supposed to be the one with good sense."

"Exactly," I quip before kissing him again.

"Oh!" Holly's gasp pulls me right out of the moment.

I leap out of Klaus's arms, and he turns toward the counter to adjust his situation below the belt. His mother is frozen in place.

"I'm so sorry," Holly stammers. "I didn't mean to interrupt, dearies. I didn't think you two were... That's to say... Patridge, get in here."

Klaus frowns. "Let's not make a big deal out of this."

Holly raises a brow at him. "Oh, we're not going to make any sort of fuss about our son kissing his partner in our kitchen. None at all. We're going to continue making cookies like nothing happened."

And that's exactly what we do.

Holly shoots me sideway glances the entire time we continue our baking tasks. It continues as we clean up and put our work away. When Holly hugs me goodbye, asking me to come back again soon, she whispers in my ear, "He's a good man. He's been hurt. Be patient, Raya."

It stuns me into silence. I don't know what to do with the information. The only thing I *do* know is that I like kissing Klaus, and I definitely don't know how I'll make it another few days without kissing him again and again and again.

The walk back to the Jingle Bell Inn is quiet. In fact, Klaus has barely said a word to me since his mother found us dry humping and kissing each other like horny teenagers.

I can't tell if he's embarrassed we were caught or if he regrets it. If we weren't on assignment in his hometown, I would let it go. I would wait and see what happens.

I can't.

"So it seems that we can't be left alone anywhere we go."

Klaus chuckles softly but doesn't respond. I am seriously starting to doubt the zoologists who claim reindeer are sociable and chatty animals.

"It really does look to me like you can't get enough of my cranberry kisses." I purse my lips at him as a joke, grabbing his arm to stop him from walking away.

The hint of a smirk melts his glower.

I continue pouting at him as I step toward him. It's cold out here, but I'm sure we can find an activity to keep each other warm. I raise myself up to the tips of my toes and press my lips to his furry cheek.

His hands grab my hips, but he doesn't make another move. "Raya," he warns. "What the hell are you doing?"

"I'm tempting you with my cranberry lips. I should think it was obvious. Maybe I need to be more straightforward." Without further ado, I kiss him square on the mouth, my tongue dipping between his lips like a shy little turtle.

It takes him only a second to react. He holds me closer, his lips moving in time with mine. I was right, of course. I don't feel the cold at all anymore. All I can feel is Klaus's arms around me, his feverish kisses, and his hands traveling everywhere he can reach. I want to curse my leather jacket for the first time in my life. Usually, I love it. I use it like armor, but right now, my favorite garment is in the way.

"We really need to figure out what's going on here." He sighs without letting me go.

"We're on the mission, Klaus. First, we'll figure out if someone really is after the wreath."

He shakes his head. "Not what I was referring to. I meant between us. We need to figure out what the hell is happening between us. We can't keep kissing whenever we find a free second."

I roll my eyes. "I know that. Do you think I *want* to want you? Hell, no. My sister met her boyfriend on her first assignment. I don't want to follow in those footsteps. Everyone will think I'm copying her *again*."

Klaus arches a brow. "You really think that's the biggest concern right now? What your family will think?"

"Sort of?" I blush all the way to my toes.

"You really take sibling rivalry to a whole other level, Raya. You should be concerned that it will distract us from our work. That Alyce will be pissed."

"Director Cooper won't say a thing about it. It's not like she would believe it, anyway. Her loner-est loner to ever loner? Kissing his partner? She'll laugh herself silly."

"Loner-est isn't a word."

"It is when it comes to you, Blitz." I wink because I'm joking and totally trying to rile him up. If he's mad, he doesn't even show it. In fact, the dude is still holding me.

In the end, I get what I want.

A kiss.

12

KLAUS

Why I'm still holding on to Raya is a damn mystery.

I command my arms to drop, but the stupid things don't listen. It's not like I really want to let her go, anyway. If I had it my way, we wouldn't have been caught in my parents' kitchen. We would have been in one of our rooms, naked and panting. Instead, we had to go through the awkwardness of cleaning up the kitchen with my mom giving me all kinds of looks.

She was already planning my wedding to Raya.

That wasn't where this—whatever was happening between Raya and me—was going.

Neither one of us wants a relationship. At least, not that I know. Raya is new to the FUC, and she's also very well aware that I don't play well with others.

That I can't seem to keep my hands—and lips—to myself is a whole other issue.

"Maybe we need to establish some rules to make the rest of this mission run smoother."

"By smoother," she quickly replied, "we need to stop tearing at each other like a pair of hormonal teenagers?"

I chuckle. "Yeah. Something like that."

"I've never really been a fan of rules."

I grin, because what else am I going to do? Call her out on it? Unlikely. Besides, from what I know of Raya, she's right. She strikes me as the rule-breaking type. Not that there is any sort of precedent about agents bumping uglies.

Not that I think for two seconds that Raya's bits are uglies.

I bet my left nut they're lovely.

Wait a damn minute.

Did I just really think that? What the hell is wrong with me? I shake my head, still reluctant to drop my hands from Raya's curvy hips. I need to step away from her and make better decisions. As the senior agent, it should be my duty to put an end to this. We need to focus on Vitality Holdings and the possibility that they've infiltrated the town to get their hands on the wreath.

We can't focus on what we could do to each other naked.

There I go again.

"Let's go skating," I blurt out.

Raya laughs. "Why? What does skating have to do with anything?"

"Not a fucking thing, but it's a public activity that still gives us the freedom to talk. We need to strategize, but if we go to the inn right now, I make no guarantees that I won't try something."

Shut your mouth, Klaus.

Raya's eyes spark with interest. "Oh?"

"Keep it in your pants, Slaski. We can't go there. The whole purpose of going to the skating rink is so we'll keep our hands off each other."

She smirks like she has other plans, the saucy bat. "Sure. We can do that."

The Christmas Town skating rink is near the center of town and the majority of stores. Our walk over takes less than ten minutes. The rink is owned and operated by a local family. The Partridges. You cannot make this shit up. That's their name.

We grab skates and settle on the red-and-white-striped benches to lace up. Christmas songs play from the loudspeakers, and massive candy canes line the wooden boards painted to look like a ginger-bread house. Just like everything else in Christmas Town, the holiday exploded on the decor.

"I can't remember the last time I skated," Raya says as she makes her way to the ice, wobbling on her blades. "I remember it being easier. I guess I had less fear as a kid. You know how children are. Those wee fuckers can get away with doing a bunch of stuff that seems to get scarier as your self-preservation skills develop as an adult."

I make a noncommittal sound because I was never one of those fearless kids. That's one of the main reasons why I can't stand to be in Christmas Town. It brings up too many bad memories of all the teasing.

"I like to skate," is what I choose to respond.

Raya giggled. "Of course you do. You gonna tell me why you hate it here now?"

"Nope."

The second my skates hit the ice I bolt. I put all of my speed into my movements, skating with ease around the rink before coming back around, stopping beside Raya.

"Showoff," she grumbles, still trying to move a few feet without pausing.

She almost falls in a dramatic hand-flailing gesture that has me bursting out laughing.

I don't remember the last time I did that. *Laughed.* A real, honest laugh.

"Don't mock me, Blitz," she warns, pointing her mitten at me. "It's not nice."

"I wouldn't dare. Come on. I'll help you." I take her hands in mine and turn to skate backward, dragging her along with me. I give her a few tips on how to move, but she's too stiff to listen.

She's scared of falling, and I've got to say I can't blame her.

"We're supposed to be discussing our assignment, but I can't focus like this. I'm gonna break my face."

"We can't have that." I chuckle. *Because then how would I kiss you?* I try to push the thought away, but it doesn't budge from my mind. In fact, the more I try to *not* think about kissing Raya, the more my brain demands just that.

I ease us to a stop, placing my hands on Raya's hips to steady her. Is it a lame-ass excuse to touch her? Yes. Most definitely. I lean down and rub my lips against hers in the barest hint of a kiss.

"I'm pretty sure that's counter-intuitive to what we're trying to do here."

"I know."

"We don't even like each other," she grumbles.

I guffaw. "I like you fine. In fact, I like you more than most people I meet."

"Then maybe what I should have said is, I don't like *you*." Her gaze is bright, her cheeks crimson, and though she tries *not* to smile, she's failing. I can *sense* her teasing.

"You don't like me?"

"Nope. Not even a bit."

"Hmm." Well, that won't do. I know she's kidding, but I don't like it. I want Raya to have nothing but good - if not *naughty* - feelings for me. If only I knew why that urge is all-encompassing. "What is it you take issue with, Agent Slaski?"

She narrows her eyes, that smirk still tugging at her delicious lips. "For one, your jackass reputation. Then there's your fear of heights. And, of course, the whole story behind why you left home and why you haven't come back. Oh, and why you hate Christmas, of all damn holidays to hate."

"Is that all?"

She takes a moment to consider this. "No. I don't like that you do sweet things out of nowhere. Like bring me lattes and hot chocolates. I don't like that you remembered your mother's cookie recipe by heart. It makes it very hard to keep hating you."

I chew on the inside of my cheek, trying to keep the admission to myself, but it's too late. It's the only thing my mouth wants to say.

"I make those cookies every year at Christmas. I typically bribe the kitchen staff at whatever hotel I'm staying to let me use their tools and oven."

Raya gasps. "What? Why?"

I shrug. "I miss home too, sometimes. Or I miss my parents."

"Then why not visit?"

"Because there's a lot of history here. Not all of it is good. I've offered to pay for my parents' trip to wherever I was, but their answer was always no. If it's not Christmas in Christmas Town, they want nothing to do with it."

"I guess I understand how that would disappoint you a bit."

I run a hand back through my hair. "Their jobs here are more important."

She frowns and wraps her arms around my waist. "That's bullshit, Klaus. Your parents adore you. Whatever it is that has come between you all, you need to fix it. Clear the air. I bet then it won't seem like a slight to you that they don't want to leave town for the holidays."

Whatever I want to respond gets stuck in my throat.

"There's one more thing I really don't like," Raya whispers after a too-long silence.

"Oh?"

"How damn irresistible you are." She smirks, and I could kiss her for changing the subject right when I needed it.

"Let's get back to the inn. We'll do hot cocoa and mission planning."

And at that moment, I really meant it.

Other parts of my anatomy had different plans.

13

RAYA

I pace the length of my room for the millionth time since we got back ten minutes ago. Klaus went to his own room to change, and the plan is to meet back here in a few minutes to *actually* go over our assignment.

Or more to the point: how the hell we're going to *stop* kissing.

I'll be the first to admit that going to the skating rink was a bad idea. Not because I am a terrible skater, though that's still true.

It was a mistake because it was very much a date activity. Everything about it felt like a date.

I can't date Klaus.

He's a notorious lone reindeer who typically communicates in monosyllabic sentences. It's common knowledge that he usually spends his holidays on a beach with a half-naked hottie.

That doesn't exactly scream *well-adjusted adult who is ready for a relationship with a fellow agent*.

To be fair, Vera started dating her jack-o-lantern-shifter boyfriend when he was under her protection. At least Klaus would be a step up from Jack. But he's a botanist who did a cute thing by creating a blood supplement for Vera. The man knows she can't bear to ingest blood, so he fixed up something for her. That's romantic, in its own creepy shifter way.

Klaus doesn't strike me as the cute type.

Even if he did admit to making his mother's cookies every year because he missed her.

Must not find the hunking hunky hunk sweet. There lies danger, Raya.

A soft knock on the door makes me jump right out of my thoughts.

I open the door to let Klaus in, confused by the tray he's holding. It's loaded down with two cups of hot cocoa and a mound of cookies.

"This town is really into its sweets."

He chuckles. "Yeah. I don't know how much flour they have to import, but I'd bet it's one of the busiest vendors."

I nod. "Then I should definitely look into them. You know. For the mission."

"The mission. Right. That thing."

Klaus sets the tray down on the little coffee table. The room is small, and he seems to fill it up completely with his tall and muscular form. The only place to sit is my bed because *of course* it is. He eyes it nervously, but I click my tongue in annoyance.

"Relax already. You're making me nervous."

He fidgets into place before running his hand back through his hair. "I guess coming to the rooms was a bad idea."

"I'd say so, yes."

"Raya, what the hell are we doing? What's going on? Because I'll be real honest with you here. I am really confused. One second I wanna strangle you for being so... *you*. Then next, I want to throw you over my shoulder and have my way wicked way with you because you're so..."

"Me?" I offer.

His throat works on a swallow. "Yeah. Exactly. Explain that to me, will you?"

"Would that I could, Blitz."

"We couldn't stand each other a few days ago. What the hell changed?"

I sit beside him because, really, as baffled as he is, I'm right there with him. "I don't really know. We got to know each other. Interacted."

"Right. Before that, all I knew about you is that you're a new agent who is related to Mila, the Bloody Doctor, and the agent who put me on that plane."

I have to work hard to stifle my laugh. The man really doesn't like heights.

"All I know about *you* is that stellar reputation of yours. I was scared that you'd fuck this up for me. I need to do a good job to prove myself."

"So we both had some pretty shitty information on the other. We didn't *actually* hate each other."

"We didn't know each other," I concur.

"Interesting."

"Isn't it, though?"

"Now that I know more about you..." He lets the rest of his thought drop off. "I wanna know more. Every detail you share brings up twenty more things I wanna know about you."

I roll my lips into my mouth, trying to kill my smile. That's a flattering thing to hear. "I get that. I feel the same. Though you've been a little more tight-lipped."

"I told you. I'm not great at letting people in."

"Then tell me one thing. One thing that you don't want to share because you're scared of how I'll react."

Klaus's jaw clenches as he thinks about it for a moment. He takes so long I start to think he'll keep quiet and leave. He surprises the hell out of me when he places his hand on my thigh.

"Something I'm scared to say because of your reaction," he repeats. "How about this. I want you, Raya."

My jaw drops, and my eyes nearly pop right out of my head. "You what now?"

I never did get to hear his answer. The next thing I know, Klaus was kissing me like his life depended on it. He eases me down onto my back, pushing me into the fluffy mattress. One of his hands cups my face while the other goes down to grip my hip to tilt me into his pelvis. His erection digs into my side, and I moan because *sweet hard candy canes.* The man's got a serious package.

"Raya, is this okay?" he asks, peppering kisses on my cheeks, down my neck.

I arch off the bed and wrap my legs around his waist, lining us up in the most delicious way. "What do you think?"

He sighs in relief. "Thank fuck." His hands slide down the length of my body to grip the hem of my shirt. He pulls it off my head and groans when he sees my bra. It's a lacy black number with tiny red cherries on it. "I'm gonna pretend those are cranberries," he whispers, sliding one strap down my shoulder.

"What's with you and the least sexy fruit in the world?"

"It's not. It's the sexiest because it reminds me of you."

Wow. If he's dropping that line to get into my pants, it is definitely going to work. It's equal parts sweet and equal parts arousing.

Klaus reaches behind me and unhooks the claps before slowly easing the garment down my arms. His eyes are glued to my breasts, his breathing erratic. He flicks my hardened nipples with his thumbs, looking about as pleased as can be. I want to make a snarky comment before I combust, but nothing comes to mind.

The monosyllabic reindeer has rendered *me* speechless.

When his mouth closes on one of my sensitive nubs, I find my voice again, moaning his name loud. My fingers tangle in his hair to keep him close to me. I never want him to stop, but I want so much more.

Klaus senses my desire and begins to kiss across my chest, nipping at the tender skin of my breasts. He spends some time exploring the massive bat tattoo wrapped around my ribcage. He continues to kiss his way down my body until he hits my waistband. With agile fingers, he flicks the button open and unfastens the zipper.

I stop his progress, nearly making my lady parts cry out in protest. I fumble with his shirt, and it takes me a few tries to get it off of him. Klaus's entire upper body is covered in tattoos. He is a colorful canvas, and I want to take a moment to inspect each tattoo.

Later.

When I'm not so keyed up I'm seconds from losing my mind.

Both of his nipples are pierced, the barbells twinkling in the dim glow of the lamp. I flick them, and he groans. I smile because it's hot as hell to make a man like Klaus react so powerfully with the barest of touches. We continue stripping out of our clothes until we're nakedly exploring each other with fingers and lips.

"We don't have to go any further," Klaus whispers against my ear.

"Are you kidding me?"

He chuckles. "I'm trying to be a gentleman here, Raya."

I scoff. "A gentleman would give me an orgasm or two before suggesting we stop."

He grins, one brow dramatically arched.

I point toward his impressive erection. "Besides, I'm pretty sure he's gonna have a temper tantrum if we don't get to the good stuff soon."

Klaus laughs, his head thrown back. His hair, free from its tie, is a curtain around us. He looks so carefree, so unencumbered by whatever keeps him sad and locked in a perpetual bad mood. I like seeing this side of him. I also *really* like thinking that I'm the only person who has seen this side of Klaus. A silly notion to have, given that we've only recently met—and at work, no less. But the thought melts my insides like ooey-gooey chocolate chips in a cookie fresh from the oven.

"Did you just claim that my dick will throw a temper tantrum?"

"I sure did. Whatcha gonna do about it?"

His smirk turns devilish, and the man does the very last thing I expect him to do. He leaps to the end of the bed, pins my knees to the bed, and takes a slow, teasing lick up my heated core. I arch off the bed with a surprised—and pleased—gasp of pleasure. The wicked man chuckles against me.

"Figured that would shut you up for a second."

"Well, don't stop, then."

He wouldn't be told twice. Klaus returns his talented tongue to the tight bundle of nerves. Swoops and licks, tugs and bites. Every single touch is perfect, driving me closer and closer to the edge. My fingers dig into the bed as I arch my hips up to meet him. He doesn't seem to mind. In fact, it only spurs him on.

When my legs begin to shake, announcing one hell of a powerful release, Klaus dips a finger into my core, curling it up to press *right* where I need him to.

It's all it takes.

I cry out his name. Maybe a few deities, too. I don't know. I lose all sense of time and space. The only thing that exists is Klaus and his tongue, driving me wild. He continues to kiss and lick me as my orgasm ebbs away.

"Remind me. A gentleman would give you *two* orgasms before suggesting to stop?"

"That's correct," he deadpans, settling his body over mine. He produces a condom from somewhere and makes quick work of rolling it onto his impressive equipment.

This is hardly how I thought my first assignment for FUC would go, but right this second, I don't really care.

I can totally panic about it later.

Right now, all I want is to soak up Klaus and the way he makes me feel.

His intense gaze hooks on mine, locking me in a haze of lust and need. His long hair is an untamed mane around us. His pine scent surrounds me.

"Raya," he whispers, his ear brushing against my ear. "I want you."

"Ditto."

"Is that all you're gonna say?"

"Is Mr. Monosyllabic really asking me to *talk* when he's about to be balls deep?"

"Guess not," he answers before kissing me deeply.

"Stop stalling. Gimme what we both want. That enough words for you?"

He chuckles as he lines himself up with my entrance. He slowly pushes into me, his eyes rolling back with a groan. My breath catches as I hold on to his shoulders. My hips move to the rhythm he sets for us. It's exactly what I need. The man knows how to move. With every thrust, he pushes me closer and closer to that blissful edge.

I clench my core around him as my release takes hold of me. I grip his shoulders and let go into that perfect oblivion of pleasure. Klaus increases his speed, his grip on my hips tightening impossibly. His lips find my neck, where he lays open-mouthed kisses feverishly before groaning my name through his climax.

Laying his forehead against mine, he gulps for breath. "One sec." He rushes off to the bathroom but quickly returns, taking me into his arms. "Whoa."

"Whoa, indeed." I giggle.

I fully expect him to grab his clothes and leave. He doesn't. He surprises the hell out of me by tucking my back into his front. "Sweet dreams, Raya," he whispers in my ear.

And surprisingly, I have the best night's sleep in a grumpy reindeer's arms.

14

KLAUS

I've never woken up like this before. Ever.

Raya is sprawled on my chest, our legs intertwined and my arm around her waist, keeping her tucked close into my side. I swallow hard, waiting for the panic to set. Usually, my skin is itchy until I'm on my own again.

That moment of alarm doesn't come.

In fact, having Raya pressed into me after a decent night's sleep feels... *normal*. I'm at peace in an all-new way. I don't want to contemplate it too much. It's downright terrifying to think that not only did I have sex with my temporary partner but I don't want her to leave.

What I *do* want?

I want to hold her a little tighter. Maybe go for another round before we start off the day.

Raya stretches out in my arms with a cute morning moan. She stills and sits up, her eyes wide and her mouth agape. "Sweet echolocation. We shared a bed."

"We did," I respond, bringing her back to my side. She comes willingly, but not as quickly as I would have liked. "Is that a problem?"

"Not exactly. It was hardly the best idea for our careers."

I shrug. "Shh. Don't ruin the moment with sense."

Raya snorts and pinches my side. "Sense is kinda necessary for our line of work. I think we need to address what happened last night."

With a sigh, I take a second to consider this. What *did* happen? I'm not too sure. "We make a better team than either one of us expected."

"That's an understatement if I've ever heard of one," she mumbles under her breath.

"Is this about your reputation with FUC?"

She doesn't answer, but that's the only response I need. I sit up, bringing Raya along with me until we're reclining against the headboard.

"This morning, we're going to eat breakfast, get ready for work, and hunker down in the security office while we pour over all the vendors that do business with Christmas Town. Once that's done, we will either have a lead or we'll need to find another avenue of investigating."

"What are you doing?" Raya asks.

"I'm telling you what the day is gonna look like."

"I know that. Why?"

"Because that's what we need to focus on right now. We can sit around and dissect what last night meant later when this mission is over."

That might not be the right thing to say, but it's all I've got.

My track record with people isn't great, and though I do trust Raya, there's a new sensation coursing through my veins. I don't know what to call it, but it starts in my chest and radiates out like a hot wave.

The most awkward thing about all this? It's not even *awkward*.

Usually, after waking up next to someone after a night of sex, I can't wait to tow them to the door or make a quick exit.

Despite my puzzled feelings, I know we need to get to work— even if I want to spend the day in bed with Raya.

"So we're putting a pin in this?" Her voice is full of questions, but she settles on the easiest one. "That makes sense," she answers for me. Without another word, she hops off the bed and goes to the bathroom, locking the door behind her.

So much for not being awkward.

The silence is so heavy it's damn well near a presence of its own in the small security office. Raya has typed away at the computer for the past three hours, making calls and digging into each vendor that sells its wares in Christmas Town.

For my part, I've been looking into every single person that has married into this loony burg. Thankfully, all of the hotels in town have a guestbook. It makes looking up every visitor that much easier. One by one, I have to remove each patron from the possible suspect list. No simple task, given that we have no real idea as to what we're looking for.

A shifter? A human? Someone who is being manipulated by Hera and Zeus? Maybe one of the shady, shadowy leaders themselves?

Who the fuck knows?

No one, that's who.

I take a gulp of my now-cold latte and wince when the frigid drink hits the back of my throat. A quick glance at the clock tells me that it's nearly lunchtime, but Raya doesn't seem to be least inclined to take a break.

"We should step away from here for a little while. Share what we've found."

Yup. Me. Talking sharing. Christmas Town might as well host a Halloween party.

She arches a brow at me, seemingly surprised that I'm still sitting beside her. It's a jest. All morning, Raya has sent furtive glances my way. Her body keeps leaning into mine, but she always catches herself and overcorrects by drifting so off to the other side that her elbow falls.

"No, thank you. We should keep working. Besides, I think I found something. The flour company? Guess what they're called." Raya can barely sit still in her seat. She's a vibrating bat, drumming her fingers on the desk.

"No idea."

"Olympus Flour."

I frown, but my gut clenches. "Olympus," I repeat.

Raya nods. "It's a little bit too obvious for my taste. It couldn't be Zeus and Hera, could it?"

I lean back in my chair and cross my arms to ponder for a moment. "I don't know. That's a very good question. It's not like these people expected to be found out when Val Downer's blackmail situation was exposed."

"Right. So this could very well be a lead on Vitality Holdings."

"We need to check it out, that's for sure."

With a roll of her shoulders, Raya starts typing furiously on the computer. "I'll get Jessie to look into Olympus Flour's finances."

"Good idea."

Truth is, were this any other case, we would have been the ones to do the digging. This *isn't* a run-of-the-mill case. Not even by FUC standards.

We already know that Vitality Holdings uses some pretty shady techniques to do their dirty work *and* stay under every single radar out there, human and shifter alike. Last time I spoke to Director Cooper, the identity of Vitality Holdings' owner was still murky. Raya's sister, Vera, and her gourd of a boyfriend learned that the top of the pyramid was *possibly* Jack's ex, Lisbeth Bannon.

Not a conversation I would ever want to have.

Sorry, honey. Didn't know I was fucking an absolute psycho prone to rule over the world.

No, thank you.

That's the danger of letting people in. Once you trust them, they can do all kinds of damage. Not that I'm saying I've let Raya in.

So we've had sex.

Kissed a few times.

So she's met my parents.

The fact that I can't help but think about her, even when she is sitting right beside me—after a naked night in the same bed—means nothing.

She still doesn't know why I left home. That's a good barometer for how I feel about this woman. So long as I don't share too much, then I know I'm safe.

From her.

From falling for her.

From the inescapable possibility of heartache and betrayal.

"Well, Jessie is on it. She's gonna get back to us as soon as she finds something."

"She usually—"

"If it isn't my two favorite agents," Santa bellows cheerfully, walking into the security office, effectively cutting off my reply to Raya.

I try to give her a sly look to warn her that she shouldn't divulge our newest possible lead, but Raya isn't even paying attention to me. Her eyes are big and bright, and I swear she hasn't been this excited since she was a little girl who got to sit on a mall Santa's lap.

It's endearing because Raya is adorable.

It's also annoying as fuck because I want to warn her.

"Hey, sir," she gushes. "I mean hi, Mister Santa." Raya might continue to blubber if I don't intervene.

"Nik." I give him a curt head nod, and Raya shoots me a grateful smirk. "Hope you're all ready for the big day. It's coming in fast."

Small talk? Really? Who in the fuck have I become?

"The missus and I got to talking last night, and she's dead set on having you over for dinner tonight. I won't take no for an answer."

"We'd love to," Rays squeals excitedly just as I grumble, "No, thanks."

The glare she aims at me is downright glacial. She turns to beam at the big man, smiling brightly. Figures that Raya the Badass would turn into a polite guest because Santa invites her over for dinner.

I want to tell her that she wouldn't be missing much, but really, that would make me a massive dick.

Raya doesn't have to be wary of these people. Not like me. It's not like they'll hurt her like they hurt me. They don't have the right ammunition for that.

At worse, I can find a reason to back out before tonight comes.

There's not a hot chocolate's chance in Santa's workshop that I'm going to dinner. With my luck, they'll invite Niko, too.

As far as I know, murder isn't allowed anywhere.

Least of all Christmas Town.

15

RAYA

Klaus tried to bail on dinner, the big jerk.

I'm not sure what happened to make Klaus hate this town and its people so much, but whatever *did* happen also involved Santa.

Santa.

Of all people to hate.

It's so on-brand for Klaus. It's not like I was going to let him get away with it. If I got the man to eat a few dinners with his parents, I *knew* I could convince him to break bread with Santa.

I managed it.

I'm not *proud* of what I did—the bribe I used to get Klaus to come with me. I'll deal with it later. For now, all I want to do is stare at Santa's house because...

Well.

It's Santa's house.

The place is massive. I'm talking Christmas-castle kind of big. If the four-story log and stone home has under twenty bedrooms, I'll eat my tuque. Every single window and door is decked out in all of Christmas's best friends. Twinkling lights, decorated boughs, wreaths with huge red bows. The house—if I can ever *call* that—is straight out of a kids' Christmas movie. I'm half expecting a talking reindeer to come out of the woodwork with a sassy line.

"I might *sleigh* you for this," Klaus grumbles under his breath, making me snort in the *most* attractive way ever.

Talk about a sassy line from a talking reindeer.

"You'll be fine. Do you need a safe word? How about you say *tinsel tits* the second you want to leave?" I giggle because there is no way either one of us is actually going to *say* tinsel tits in Santa's house.

"I might do it to embarrass you," Klaus warns as he taps my butt.

I don't know if the gesture is loving or teasing. Perhaps both? Regardless of his intent, I'm here for it. Klaus can touch my ass any time he wants.

"Let's get his over with already," he grumbles, ringing the doorbell.

An instrumental and jingly version of "Santa Claus is Coming to Town" echoes through the night, and I burst into laughter. Klaus rolls his eyes, but I jab a warning finger into his side.

"You behave."

"I didn't want to come," he reminds me.

"Well, now you're here. You will be civil because you represent FUC. If you don't try to be nice, then you can forget that *thing*." I wiggle my brows at him, grinning like I mean it. I don't. The chances that I can resist Klaus now that I know what he's packing—and how he uses it—are slim to none.

He balks. "But you promised."

"Be"—I poke his chest—"Have." I jab again for good measure.

The door swings open, revealing a tall, svelte woman with a perfect shock of white hair expertly braided into a crown. Little poinsettias are artistically arranged into the hairstyle.

"Oh, if it isn't Klaus. By Rudolph, you have grown." She hugs him tight before pinching his cheeks. "You're so handsome. I always knew you'd be back. I told everyone for years now that you couldn't stay away forever." She waves us in before taking our coats and gently placing them on a coatrack in the shape of reindeer antlers. She introduces herself and insists that I call her Doris. *Not* Mrs. Claus.

"Let's go straight through to the living room. Everyone is waiting for us."

Beside me, Klaus stills. His jaw clenches so hard I nearly hear his dentist snickering over the money he'll make to repair the damage. If we weren't on the job, I would reach out and take his hand in mine.

I'm not Vera.

I might have boned down with my coworker, but I'm not going to *fall* for Klaus. He's a surly uncommunicative reindeer with a grudge against Santa, who prefers to spend all of his time alone.

Doris leads us into an enormous room, complete with a ginormous fireplace and an even bigger tree. An intricate wooden coffee table sits in the very center of the room, around which two sofas and two plush armchairs are arranged expertly to promote conversation. Doris and Santa must do loads of entertaining in this room.

Santa—or *Nik*, as Klaus would call him—raises his glass to us by way of greeting. A young couple is nestled on one of the sofas, while the other is taken by a man, glaring at the whole room. Most of his ire is cast to the other dude, cooing over his girlfriend. The two *have* to be brothers; they look so much alike. In fact, I *know* they're brothers. I recognize that glow of half-hatred in the younger guy's glower.

Sibling rivalry.

"You remember Nils."

The angry brother barely registers our arrival, too angry to care.

I wonder if that's what I look like when I'm around Vera.

Good gingerbread, I hope not.

It's a little intense and a lot uncomfortable.

"And Niko, of course." Doris gestures to one-half of the couple. "That lovely young lady is Cassie Michaels, Niko's fiancée. They're getting married the day after Christmas if you can believe it."

Cassie gives a timid smile that is so sickly sweet I want to barf. "I've always wanted a Christmas wedding," she explains. "Can you imagine having it here, of all places?" Her earrings, kitschy little red ornaments, jiggle as she giggles. Her whole persona is big on artificial shyness. I'm pretty sure she is *pretending* to blush. Who even *does* that?

"I don't know if I'd want to get married the day after Christmas. Here of all places. Hasn't it made everything more hectic? Not only is it Christmas, but a wedding, too?" I shrug. "I've always wanted to get married on a beach somewhere. My toes in the sand and my wedding dress blowing in the wind."

Cassie's veneer slips a little bit, and though I can't quite put my finger on *why*, I actually like the idea that I've annoyed her. It's a very familiar feeling. It's the same feeling I get when Vera does something perfect that makes me look like the world's dumbest tool.

Maybe I understand Nils a bit more now.

"Klaus!" Niko's exclamation is as fake as his fiancée's joy.

"Niko," Klaus growls.

Actually *growls*. I have to do a double take because I can't believe the man, a reindeer, no less, *growled*. If I was physically close to him, I'd elbow him in the side. Yet one look at his pinched forehead, and the urge is curved. Klaus is *not* happy.

"Good to see you back in town," Niko lies.

"Is it?" Klaus claps back with so much ire it makes the fire crackle.

"Boys," Santa warns.

"No, Dad. It's okay. Klaus was never good at *letting* go." Niko laughs like he's hilarious, but I don't get the joke.

Klaus's reaction makes it pretty damn clear that Niko made a jab. Possibly about Klaus and whatever made him leave town for good.

"Why don't you repeat that?" Klaus's intensity is palpable.

A nervous Doris claps her hands together, her eyes brimming with unshed tears. "You two used to be such friends." She sniffles. "Can't we let the past go? It was a reindeer game. Nothing more."

A nerve in Klaus' neck jumps and twitches. He's about to implode. He forces a smile but gets to his feet. "If you'll excuse me." He vanishes down the hall without another word.

All of the tinsel tits.

"I'm gonna go see if he's okay." I mumble a series of apologies as I chase off after Klaus.

He puts on his boots and yanks his jacket off the coat rack, not even bothering to put it on before braving the literal North Pole. I'm not that insane. I take the time to zip my leather coat before running down the long and snowy laneway.

"Klaus, you great big brute. Would you please stop making me run after you?"

He barely turns to look at me. "Go back, Raya. It's not often outsiders get invited to that house. Go bask in it."

"No. You're my partner, and you're upset. I know you won't tell me why because you've got this whole cone of silence about everything. Fine. Don't tell me what happened. But that doesn't mean I'm not gonna have your back."

His steps falter, and he finally stops to look at me. His cheeks are red under his beard, the tendrils of his breath curling around a month. "You're not gonna get me to spill."

"I know." I mean it, too. "I don't need to know what happened *unless* it becomes directly linked to our investigation."

"It's got nothing to do with that and everything to do with Niko being a grade-A douchebucket."

"Let's go. Pretty sure I saw a bar called the Drunken Elf, and I need to check it out."

I don't turn back to see if Klaus is following me. I know he will.

Just like I know that after a few White Christmases—one hell of a strong alcoholic drink—he'll spill all of his secrets.

16

KLAUS

"Good *morning*, partner," Raya shouts, chipper as a turtledove in a pear tree.

I grunt out my greeting without looking away from the computer. The screen's glare isn't helping my hangover, but I still have to do my job.

Getting drunker than Rudolph after a failed test flight was hardly my best idea.

I'm honestly embarrassed that merely *seeing* Niko made me angry enough to find solace at the bottom of a bottle. Or three.

I'd be a little less disappointed in myself if I actually *remembered* what happened after Raya and I had a few drinks at the Drunken Elf last night. I don't know how much I drank or what I might've said to her.

One thing is for damn sure; we didn't get to that *thing*. Not because I was drunk. Rather, I didn't actually stay for dinner at Santa's place. I lost my chance at another night in bed with Raya Slaski because I can't let go of the past.

"How you feeling?" She puts a peppermint brownie the size of my head and coffee on the desk. "That's for you. Should help with the hangover."

"I appreciate it. If I could make one request, please don't be so loud."

She grins at me, shrugging out of her coat. I shove my sunglasses into my hair to get a better view of her. Not that it's professional behavior or anything. I can't help myself. Her nose ring twinkles under the office lights, while her hair is wavy and framing her face like it always does. Her curvy legs are draped in a pair of skintight black jeans tucked into a pair of boots that look good but surely can't be warm enough for the Christmas Town climate.

I'm a jackass for not telling her she needs better outerwear. All because I want to keep ogling her like she's the last piece of sticky pudding at a family potluck.

"Less loud?" Raya shouts before giggling. "Sorry. Last time I do that. I just want to get *some* payback for last night."

I groan. "Shit. What did I do?"

"Oh, you know." She blushed. "You danced on the bar and did a striptease to 'Santa Baby.' It was hilarious."

"I did not."

"Okay, you didn't, but the look on your face is priceless. You didn't do anything bad, exactly. But you're quite a big man. Getting you back to the Jingle Bell Inn all by my lonesome would've been... *interesting*."

"Sorry."

"Don't be. Nils ended up helping me."

Cold fills my gut as the booze from the night before makes its way back up my throat. "Repeat."

"Back to monosyllabic? Uncool."

"*Repeat.*"

Raya rolls her eyes. "Nils came into the bar. It's not like he followed or anything. He was there for a nightcap. Away from his brother. We chatted about good old sibling rivalry while you downed nearly all of the town's alcohol."

The more I learn, the angrier I am. I don't like the idea of Raya getting all close and chummy with Nils. Sure, he isn't Niko, but the man is still a Claus. I can't trust him any more than I can trust Rudolph to be invisible in the dark.

That mother fucker *shines*. At least, he would if he was real.

"Once you were done with your impression of a fish, Nils helped me bring you back to your room."

If Raya notices that I'm upset, she doesn't let on.

"I'm actually really surprised to see you awake so early. What are you working on?" She takes her seat beside me, her shoulder pressing into mine.

Take that, *Nils.*

"I'm looking into Niko's comings and goings into town."

Raya gasps before decking me in the shoulder. "Are you insane? You can't think that Niko is the mole."

"Sure I can. Maybe he wants to take over Christmas Town before Daddy Dearest retires. Maybe he wants to sell off the town to the highest bidder so he can retire with that fiancée of his."

She narrows her eyes. "What makes you suspect him?"

"Niko is an ass."

"Well, sure. The whole world knows that the next man in line to be Santa is a jerk."

"He is, though." I ignore her sarcasm. "You don't know him."

"Neither do you," she points out like an infuriatingly sexy vixen. "You *knew* him. Before. A long time ago. People grow up. Change. Make better decisions."

"I don't trust him. If Vitality Holdings has a foothold in Christmas Town, it'll be with him."

"You're wrong. I mean that with all of the love and respect in my heart, but really, you're way off base. You're letting the past cloud your judgment on this."

"I'm telling you. Niko is behind this."

"If anyone in that house was fake and in with Vitality Holdings, my money would be on the fiancée. Cassie. Is that even her *real* name? Think about it. Cassie could be a nickname for a whole bunch of names from Greek mythology. You've got Cassandra. Cassiopeia."

I cross my arms and arch a brow at her. "A bunch? Sounds like only two to me."

She waves me off." You know what I mean. It's *not* Niko. I had a

long chat with Nils last night. He told me all about Niko's vision for
the town and how he wants to streamline some stuff. Nils is against it.
Much more of a traditionalist, the baby bro is. I think he'd much
rather be the next in line for the big red suit."

She continues rattling off all kinds of things Nils told her, but I
don't listen. I am too hungover to argue. Besides, I feel it down to my
bones that something is off with Niko.

"We don't even know if anyone is actually *after* the wreath. We've
got *two* solid leads with Olympus Flour and Frankincense."

"The spice?"

"The *elf*," Raya answers with a giggle. "Remember? We inter-
viewed him. He's the elf who went on a holiday to Hawaii. If you want
to grasp at straws, look into Cassie. Don't people have to go through
very intense vetting before marrying into town?"

"Yeah."

"Good. So you dig into Cassie's past. I'll look into Frankincense
while we wait to hear back from Jessie about Olympus Flour."

"I think I should interview Nils and Niko. Separately. Preferably in
a torture chamber."

"Seriously, dude. Who hurt you?"

They did.

I don't say that. I can't. It would mean admitting a whole bunch of
stuff I really don't want to get into. Especially not with Raya.

"You leave those two alone. Until we have solid proof that one of
them is doing something nefarious, they're in the clear."

"I'm the senior agent." The second the words are out of my
mouth, I regret them. "Raya."

"No. I see how it is. I'm good enough to fuck and to bring you
home from the bar. Not good enough to trust with your past or *our*
mission." She grabs her coat and slings it on.

A bunch of interjections create a blizzard of white noise in my
head. I want to tell her to stay. I want to find the words to explain, but
I'm out of practice. I haven't had any sort of relationship in too long.

Anything that comes out of my mouth will be wrong and flawed.

I let her go, knowing this time I'm the one who did the hurting.

17

RAYA

What an absolute jerk.

I really don't know why I'm so angry with Klaus as I make my way out of the security office and down the hall. I'm hurt because I took care of him when he needed me, but there's a whole other mess of stuff going on in my heart.

Yup. My *heart*.

I don't like it.

So we slept together once. Kissed a couple of times.

It's not like he's the best I've ever had.

Only, that's a lie because Klaus Thorsen is *definitely* the best I've ever had. More than that, I can't help but feel that if he let me in, we could be really great together.

As a team.

Partners.

Not a *couple*.

Okay. So *maybe* a couple.

I bet Vera will *love* to hear all about how I went on a mission and caught feelings. Then her falling in love with Jack won't be such a big deal because I did it too.

Livid and more confused than an elf trying to untangle strings of lights, I blaze down the long workshop corridors. I'm so caught up in my anger I don't even notice Nils coming toward me.

"Raya." He smiles shyly. "Think we can talk?"

I blink at him as I try to clear my thoughts. "Nils, hi. What's up?"

His pale cheeks redden, the brown of his eyes darkening. "Not much. I wanted to thank you for last night."

"Walk and talk, Nils. I need to be somewhere."

"Oh. Sure. Can I interest you in hot cocoa? Maybe something to eat? Soak up all the booze?"

"Maybe some other time. I'm actually on the clock right now."

He winces, apologetic. "Right. Well. I'll make it fast. Thanks for letting me vent about my family yesterday. It's not often that I get to talk to someone without fear of reprisals."

"Reprisals?"

"No one wants to be the asshole who hates his family. Especially not when said family is literally the future of Christmas."

"It's okay, Nils. Really. I'm no stranger to sibling rivalry. I still think that you could convince your dad to make you and Niko co-Santas."

We make our way onto one of the cabooses. It's the easiest way out of the workshop, and I have to see an elf about a toy.

"I don't know that I want to put myself out on a limb like that."

"For what it's worth, I believe in you." I smile, hoping that it's as friendly as I mean it to be. Given my mood, I'm not sure the execution is all that great.

"Thanks. Niko has something going for him, though."

"He's firstborn?"

"No. Cassie. His fiancée. The role of Santa isn't given to the first-born but the first to have an heir."

I snort in disbelief. "You're fucking with me."

Nils shakes his head. "No. It's true. My ancestors saw what succession did to kingdoms and tried something different to stave off some in-fighting."

I laugh because, really, it's hilarious. "Did these people not have families? In-fighting and families go together like..."

"Hot chocolate and whipped cream?" Nils offers.

"Something like that, yeah."

"Cassie and Niko haven't been together all that long. Only a few months. I had a girlfriend. Cookie. We broke up a few months ago. Right before Niko met Cassie, actually. Up until then, everyone thought I would be the next Santa in line."

Completely bypassing the fact that his ex's name is *Cookie*, I tap his shoulder. "I'm sorry. That's a lot of loss. Your lady and your dream job. All at once."

He tries to shrug like it's nothing, but his pain is palpable. "I really don't like Cassie. Probably because I can't stop comparing her to Cookie. Cookie would be such a better Mrs. Claus. Her family even owns one of the bakeries in town. She's *from* here. She gets it. Not like Cassie."

I nod. "Planning the wedding the day after Christmas does seem a little…"

"Like my brother is trying to solidify his claim to the Santa suit?"

"That."

"My parents and all of Christmas Town don't see it that way. They think this wedding is saving us or whatever. You said something last night. It stuck with me. I wanted to know if you really mean it."

I gulp. As much as Klaus was drunk and doesn't recall much of the night, I was pretty shit-faced. I wasn't in shape to give any advice. "Look, Nils. I'm not sure you should give any credence to anything I might have spewed with so much booze in my system."

"No way. You were right. You told me that I have to stop comparing myself to Niko. Live my life for me. Do what makes me happy and stop making all my moves like my life is nothing more than a chess game against my sibling. It's bringing me nothing but pain, and that's no way to live."

I'd be more shocked if Nils told me Klaus took flight like a reindeer in an old-school Christmas story.

"I said that?" Damn. Maybe I need to listen to my own advice.

"You're very wise."

"Well, sure." The caboose comes to a stop, and we leap down. "I struggle with that, too."

"You mentioned that. Yeah. That's why I wanted to thank you. The call you made to your sister last night? It helped me realize I need to make amends with my brother. Stop being such a grinch."

"I called my sister?" I stop in my tracks, grabbing hold of Nils' arm. "Are you sure I called Vera?" I have no recollection of that. What the hell was in those White Christmases, anyway?

Nils answers my questions, but I don't hear him. Frankincense, the traveling elf, hops off the caboose, looking about as chill as a raw gingerbread man in the oven. He pretends he doesn't see me, but the crimson tint of his cheeks makes one thing obvious.

He is guilty as hell. Of what, I don't know yet. Given that he's at the top of my possible suspect list, I need to find out.

"Duty calls, Nils. Let's catch up soon." Without waiting for his reply, I duck behind one of the massive pillars and sneak a peek around it. Frankincense swings a huge red bag over his shoulder, nearly toppling down from the sheer weight of it.

What in Santa's beard is he doing?

I'm about to find out if one of Santa's elves is in league with Vitality Holdings.

Rudolph, help me.

If Frankincense is a bad guy, he is by far the *worst* bad guy ever. He can't sneak around to save his life. He greets everyone he passes by with cheerful holiday greetings. It doesn't seem to faze him that he's literally hauling a bag that could crush him to death.

He slowly makes his way down the main street and tries to throw the bag into a small green sleigh. He fails and tries again. This time, when the bag falls, a few townsfolk spot his distress. With big smiles and bright, cheery cheeks, they help Frankincense place his loot in the sleigh.

They've got no idea what's in the bag.

Neither do I, for that matter. All I've got are some instincts that he's up to something shadier than the Grinch in Whoville.

Frankincense hops into his sleigh and drives the damn thing around the corner. It takes some effort to discreetly chase after him. Running stealthily in calf-high snow as dense as a booze-soaked fruit-cake isn't easy.

I'm covered in sweat despite the frigid temperature and a little more than out of breath by the time Frankincense pulls up to a tiny house on the outskirts of town. The elf struggles to bring the bag inside. It takes him about ten minutes to go ten feet.

"What the hell are you doing?" a voice hisses out of nowhere, invading my hiding spot behind a happy spruce.

I strike the newcomer, only to realize a little too late that it's Klaus. He stumbles back, gripping his throat.

Tip: do no throat-punch the guy you're into. Hardly good foreplay. Even when you're furious with him.

"The fuck, Raya," he pants.

"Don't sneak up on an agent. What were you thinking?"

"Umm, that we're partners. I saw you sneaking off with Nils. Then I spotted you sulking and following Frankincense."

"I told you I suspected him," I argue. I'm going to let the whole *but we're partners* thing slide. For now. No point in reminding him that he hardly behaved like a good partner back in the security office. "Hey! Why are you here? Who's watching the wreath?"

"Office Wassail Sugarplum," Klaus responds. "He came in to let me know that Santa removed the wreath from the case last night. He obviously put it back this morning since it was there. But..."

"Why did Santa remove the wreath from its secure spot?" I finish the uncomfortable question for him.

Klaus nods. "That's what I'd like to know."

"You can't seriously suspect Santa Claus of being in league with Vitality Holdings." I can barely get the words out.

"I don't know what to think. The man knows it's under

surveillance, but he waits for one of his oldest buddies to be on shift to move it."

"We obviously need to talk to him as soon as we figure out what the damn hell this guy is doing."

"Frankincense? He's harmless."

I snort. "He's up to some really shady shit." I give Klaus a brief rundown of what I witnessed, and the more I divulge, the darker his features become.

"Shit." He runs a hand over his mouth. "I'm so sorry, Raya. I really let my past get the better of me. I thought Niko *had* to be up to something."

"We don't know what Frankincense is up to yet. All we've got is some stolen presents or whatever else is in those bags. Besides, I'm getting the impression that there is a lot of bad stuff happening in Christmas Town."

"What do you mean?" he asks.

Before I can respond, the cabin door swings open, and Frankincense returns to his sleigh. His movements are quicker. That, plus the reduced size of the red bag, tells me one thing. He dropped stuff off in the cabin.

I think the elf is playing Santa. The why of it is still a mystery.

"Follow my lead." I leave our hiding spot and stride over to Frankincense. "What are you doing?"

The elf squeaks out in fright, dropping the big red velvet bag to the ground. The second he spots us he puts his hands up in the air. "Please. Don't shoot."

"Don't shoot?" Klaus grumbles. "We've got no weapons."

The elf heaves a sigh of relief but doesn't lower his arms. "I didn't do anything wrong," he stammers, on the verge of tears.

Klaus grabs hold of the bag and looks inside. He pulls out a round cookie tin, its contents rattling. "What's going on, Frankincense?"

"I'm part of the workshop cookie exchange. You know, the one your parents organize? I'm delivering the goods."

"Damn. Sorry to have scared you, Frankincense. But now that

we've got you here, we've got some more questions about your trip to Hawaii."

The elf answers everything and then some.

He isn't up to anything besides wanting some time alone from Vanilla, his *darling* wife.

That leaves Olympus Flour and, as much as I hate to say it, Santa.

18

KLAUS

Raya and I have been in Christmas Town for nine days now. We're no closer to figuring out which cracks Vitality Holdings could use to weasel their way in.

There are a lot, too.

We might have cleared Frankincense from any possible involvement, but our list of suspects hasn't budged.

Olympus Flour. Santa. *Niko*.

That's my list. Raya refuses to believe that Niko is in on it. She would gladly put Cassie on there for good measure, but from the digging she's done on the soon-to-be-bride, there's nothing there. By all accounts, Cassie is a young woman very much in love.

That alone raises all my hackles but not because Cassie has done anything *wrong*. It's her choice of future husband I question. It's not her fault; rather, it's all me and my past with Niko.

"Klaus," Raya gasps. "Watch what you're doing. You're ruining it." Raya bumps me with her hip, moving me away from the massive gingerbread house laid out on my parents' kitchen counter.

From their vantage point at the dining room table, Mom and Dad exchange a hopeful glance. They really think that Raya and I will be something serious. Probably because they've caught us kissing one too many times.

The way my hands always find their way to Raya's hips or shoulder or toying with her hair doesn't help me, either. How can they believe that we're only partners when every time they turn around I'm mooning over Raya?

Raya is hardly an innocent bystander. The woman keeps smacking my ass every time my back is turned.

Maybe one more roll in the snow would set us to rights. Get each other out of our system. Put this attraction between us to rest.

"I'm not *ruining* it," I argue with her, pocking her nose with icing. Raya squeals and takes a step back, only to slam against the counter.

She arches a brow at me. "So help me, Blitz. If you mess with the structural integrity of my gingerbread house and cost me first place, I'll never forgive you."

"I like her." Mom laughs. "She takes these Christmas Town activities seriously."

The *and that means you'll be around more often* is implied. I hear it in the loud silence that follows and the hopeful look she gives Dad.

Truth is there's a reason why I haven't gone back to bed with Raya.

I'm insanely attracted to her, and despite our tense beginning, she is quickly turning into the one person I don't mind spending time with. She's funny and intelligent. She's a capable agent who doesn't think inside the box. She creates her own box and smashes it when she isn't satisfied with the outcome.

It's what she did with her first gingerbread house earlier tonight.

It's also what she's done with my defenses.

"I like you, too, Holly. If your son doesn't come back here for Christmas next year, I will. I'll dominate all of the Christmas Town competitions. Win it all."

"Our door will always be open for you, Raya." Dad beams.

I swear, they're already imagining grandkids running around. If there was ever a flying reindeer, could the offspring of a vampire bat and reindeer be it?

Probably.

What a terrifying thought.

Having a kid who would be all roped into the Christmas Town drama—one who could *fly*—that would be too much for me to bear.

Weird that it's not the idea of a kid with Raya that freaks me out. It's my hypothetical child being bullied that has me all up in a fret.

"Blitzy-boo," Raya coos teasingly because she *knows* I hate it when she calls me that. "Do me a favor and plop a peppermint on each dollop of icing I put on the roof?" She bats her long lashes at me, already knowing that my answer will be a resounding yes.

There isn't much I would deny Raya Slaski. I simply have to make sure she doesn't clue into that.

"Sure thing."

To complete the decorations of the gingerbread roof, we have to stand *real* close together. Her toes are pressed into mine. For whatever reason, I think it's a great idea to help her balance by placing a hand on her hip.

Yup.

Me. My hand on her hip. For balance. Never mind that she can *actually* fly.

To avoid thinking too much about how much I love touching Raya, what it means, and what will happen when this mission ends and we have to make our way back to FUC, I pop a mint into my mouth.

"Hey!" Raya shouts. "Don't eat my construction material."

"Sorry."

She hip-checks me again. "It's okay. I forgive you this time because you're so darn cute. Don't let it happen again."

"I make no such promise. Mint is my favorite thing."

"Right after cranberries," the saucy little bat whispers under her breath.

There's no chance that my parents heard her, but I sure did. Her words spark interest in a southern part of my anatomy. I clear my throat while my eyes flick toward her lips.

They're *right* there, looking more delectable than ever. Forget gingerbread cookies. Keep your peppermint lattes. Shove your nasty-ass fruitcakes where the sun don't shine.

But those lips?

Leave me those lips to savor all night long.

Without even realizing it, I lean over her and brush my mouth along hers. I swallow her gasp before kissing her softly again. Raya drops the bag of cementing icing to the countertop to palm my chest. My hand goes to her cheek, tipping her head up to gain better access to her delicious mouth.

"Klaus," she whispers against my mouth. "I think we need to stop."

"Huh?" I blink, my thoughts clearing.

My parents are no longer at the dining room table. I don't actually *know* where they went.

"Fuck. I shouldn't have done that."

Raya's eyes sparkle as she shrugs. "I don't mind. I enjoyed it. Though, maybe next time you wanna go all hormonal teen on me, maybe wait for us to be in our hotel room instead of in your parents' kitchen."

"Yup." I step away from Raya and out of the kitchen. My fingers tear at my hair with so much gusto I have to pull off my hair elastic to retie my mane into its bun. "I'm gonna go for a walk."

Raya blinks at me as if she were expecting just that. "You do what you need to do to figure your shit out, Klaus. I'm gonna be right here. At least until Christmas." She takes a few steps toward me and taps my shoulder. "I get that it's hard for a lone reindeer like you to let someone in. I feel for you, but there comes a time when you need to decide if you're okay with being alone or if you wanna make a change." Lifting herself up to the tips of her toes, she places a kiss on my cheek.

She might be a vampire bat with an obsession with leather and combat boots, but Raya Slaski fits into Christmas Town more than I ever did.

That says something important, but I don't know what.

"I need to get out of here for a bit." Without waiting for Raya's response, I rush away, barely remembering to grab a jacket on my way out the door.

My feet have a mind of their own. They lead me straight to Tiny Tim's Tavern off the main drag. I grab a stool at the very back of the bar, away from the door and from the revel-makers. It's hardly a dive bar. Those don't exactly exist in Christmas Town, but it does draw a seedier crowd.

By that, I mean the laborers who work in the greenhouses. They literally plant seeds for a living. I order myself a pint of Prancer's Pilsner. The hoppy, bitter taste is perfect for my mood.

"You look like you could use a chat," a deep, jolly voice booms as a large man plops into the seat beside me.

"Nik," I grumble. "Pretty sure I picked this seat to be left alone."

Santa shrugs. "Pretty sure I don't care too much what you want right now, Blitzen."

I wince, and he doesn't miss it. "You never did. No one in this town did. You gonna tell me why you took the wreath out of its case?"

"I wanted to get a good look at it. See what all the fuss is about."

"It put you on the suspect list. Right at the top."

"Wouldn't expect any less. You're thorough. I gotta respect that."

"That's it? That's all the explanation you've got?" I almost wanted him to admit he was behind everything.

"The lore around the wreath is a mystery, kid. It's been in the family for so long even if it *was* the Holy Grail, melted down into a wreath, I wouldn't know. That lore is lost to time. It's not like it matters. If it had the power to grant immortality, the world would look a lot different."

"What happened to the power of stories?"

Santa scoffs. "Stories have power whether they're true or not. If these Vitality Holdings people think they will be immortal if they get the wreath? They'll stop at nothing to get their hands on it. Imagine what they could do with the *power* behind that story. It could change everything."

"It's a lot to put on faith."

"That's what life is. I'm an old man who has the same job as my father and my great-grandfather and so on. Having faith in something? That's kind of the point of life. I believe in what we do in this town. The hope we give people. What do you believe in, Klaus?"

"Not this town, that's for darn sure."

He claps a hand to my back. "You ever gonna forgive this town for what happened?"

"Nope." I gulp down a mouthful of my drink.

"That's too bad. Your parents miss you. The reindeer training team sure could use a Thorsen. You're from good people, Klaus. Good, strong, hardworking people. Your kin always could train my reindeer like nobody's business. You know how to make 'em docile *and* real performers when they drive sleighs through town. It makes the tourists so happy. A real essential part of this place."

"It's not hard work. We literally shift to train them. Nothing to it."

Nik laughs. "Well, sure. Because anyone off the street can just decide to shift into a reindeer one day."

I don't respond but focus on my beer. The old man isn't done.

"I never should have sided with Niko. What he did was wrong. The whole town knew, too. That's why there was a lot of whispering about town when Nils got together with Cookie Trimmings. Everyone and their grandma wanted Nils to take over the mantle after what happened that night. Now? With Niko getting married to an outsider? Things are tense. It's got nothing to do with the wreath. Your bad guys aren't in this town, Blitz. But your past is. Maybe you can try to fix it while you're here. That might have to start with me, so let me say this. I'm terribly sorry for what Niko did. For what his merry little band of naughty boys did. They got coal in their stockings for a straight decade, but I should've stepped in and been a better Santa."

"That's it? You apologize, and it's done? I forget all about it? No matter the scars and fears I still have?"

He has the decency to wince. "If I could find another way to fix it, I would."

"Fix it? Make Nils the next Santa. Forget the old rules. You'll ruin this town if you let Niko and Cassie take over when you retire. He might be your son, but if he can throw another kid off a mountain as a seventeen-year-old with no real power? What the hell is he gonna do when he has a whole town at his beck and call?"

And with that, I drop a twenty on the bartop and leave Santa Claus to think about his son.

The one who almost killed me.

.

19

RAYA

Note to self: when spending the holiday season in Christmas Town, be prepared for Christmas celebrations to begin on December twenty-second.

Actually, the entire village has been abuzz for two nights now, when the annual gingerbread house competition was held.

My creation won second place.

First place? Well, that went to Cassie.

The future Mrs. Claus took the top prize with tears in her eyes and a wobble to her slender, pointy chin. I swear, I heard some of the elves accuse her of cheating. Was there any credence to their claims? I've got no idea, but if anyone would be able to cheat and get away with it? It would be her.

Despite my annoyance that I lost, I kind of feel bad for Cassie. The entire town has forgotten that there will be a wedding in four days.

There is a flour shortage, and none is left to make her wedding cake. Cassie found out the night of the competition, and if Vanilla has the right of it, Cassie cried herself to sleep. I don't know when I started listening to all of the local gossip.

Probably right around the time I realized that I *like* it here.

There's no Vera. No overreaching and perfect shadow. I'm the only Slaski around. I can be my snarky, snappy self and people *love* it. I don't get any *"why can't you be nicer, like your sister"* comments every time I open my mouth.

It's awesome.

The only major downer is the serious lack of intel we've gathered. Even with their flour shortage keeping them busy, Olympus Flour is *not* tied to Vitality Holdings.

"Are you sure?" I ask Jessie for the twentieth time in our two-second conversation on the morning of December twenty-third.

"Yep," she answers, the clickety-clack of her keyboard coming through the line. "They're a family-owned company. They only called themselves Olympus because of an incident at the old flour mill a hundred years ago. There was a huge mountain of flour. They called it Olympus as a joke. It stuck."

"Huh, that's disappointing in a very non-disappointing way."

"Don't feel bad, Raya." A voice comes through the line, and I grit my teeth. "Jack heard from T-Bone that loads of potential leads haven't gone anywhere. The task force exists in an overabundance of caution. There's every chance you won't uncover anything."

"Thanks for that, Vera," I snap through my clenched jaw.

I've been avoiding my sister since I called her drunk off my ass a few nights ago. I have *no* idea what we talked about, nor do I want to know. It's probably not great. Obviously, my brain is a cocktail of embarrassment and shame.

"Oh, sorry about that, Raya," Jessie says. "Forgot to mention your sister is in my office. We're going over some footage that she got of Lisbeth Bannon."

"And did *you uncover anything?*" I'm not asking because I'm rooting for her to fail.

If Vera discovered that Lisbeth Bannon is Hera, Klaus and I would have to leave Christmas Town. I'm not ready for that. I want to stay here a little longer while we figure out what we are to each other. I'm enjoying the protective bubble this strange little village has given me.

"I haven't found a damn thing," she complains dramatically. "Lisbeth went on a holiday last month to Waikiki Beach. Since then? She leads a very boring life. She isn't in contact with anyone shady. She's been focusing on the legitimate side of the business. Vitality. You know, the beauty product line?"

I roll my eyes and mimic her yapping to Klaus, who has been observing our conversation with a grin.

"We're not any closer to figuring out who the hell Hera and Zeus are, then."

"Afraid not," Vera sighs. "But listen. Now that I've got you on the phone…"

"Oh, would you look at that. Klaus is waving me down. Bye. Thanks, Jessie." I hang up and push away from the desk. "Don't you dare say a word."

Klaus can't suppress his smirk. "I've never been so happy that I don't have siblings."

"Be quiet." I flip him off. "I didn't want to have a personal conversation with Vera right there. It wouldn't have been right."

"Sure. That's all."

I want to point out that we've also been avoiding a pretty big topic. *Us.* He doesn't have a leg to stand on.

"What's going to happen to the wreath once we leave? Christmas Town can't have FUC guarding it till the end of time. Eventually, a better solution will have to be found."

"You don't want to be stuck here with me forever?" Klaus jests.

I arch a brow at him. It's a joke, but does he really not understand the implication in his words? "Do *you*?" I test.

"No. Absolutely not."

My shoulders fall despite myself, and he notices. He frowns and comes to stand before me.

"Raya, it's not because of you. I just don't like this town. There's too much pain here. Too many bad memories. We've made some good ones together during our time here, yes. You make Christmas Town better, but we can't stay here forever. We have to go back to reality."

"Right."

Klaus takes my hand in his and pulls me back toward the desk. He motions for me to sit, still holding my hand. "I'm kinda hoping that when we *do* back to FUC, we can keep seeing each other."

I don't move a muscle. I don't blink. I don't even breathe. It's not like I gave him an ultimatum the night we built gingerbread houses at his parents' place, but I hoped he did some thinking about what our connection meant to him. Klaus hasn't brought it up, so I was half expecting it to be a wham-bam-thank-you-ma'am sort of situation.

It would have broken my heart.

"You want to keep seeing me," I repeat for confirmation.

He nods.

"Good. You've come to the right conclusion. I really wouldn't have liked knocking some sense into you."

Klaus laughs softly. "Oh, yeah? And how were you going to do that, exactly?"

"I was going to throw my cranberry lips at you every chance I got. Maybe shimmy out of my leather jacket in tantalizing ways." One of his brows hooks up. "Don't even deny it. I've seen you watch me take it off."

"Guilty. What can I say? You do it for me, Raya."

"Ditto, Blitzy-boo. Super ditto."

He leans over and gives me a sweet kiss. "You're gonna need to come up with a better nickname for me if this is gonna work."

"Not a chance. I like calling you Blitz. It fits."

"Did you know I went by that as a kid?"

I shake my head. *This is it! I will finally get the tale of the Blitz.* Easy. Must remain absolutely calm. "No. I literally just shortened the sexiest reindeer name out of the bunch."

"Sexiest?"

I roll my eyes. "Don't even pretend to be a dingus. You *know* I'm into your whole vibe."

"Sorry I didn't catch on right away. I was too mad about having a partner on this mission. Turns out, you're not so bad." Klaus tucks a strand of hair behind my ear. "I don't like it when you call me Blitz because that's what the other kids called me."

I scrunch up my face. "Oh. I apologize, Klaus."

"No. Don't be sorry. You didn't know."

"Why did they call you that?"

Klaus tenses, but as he takes a deep breath, he sits back on the desk. "I was a bit of an odd kid. I didn't like playing with the other children. I preferred spending all of my time with the reindeer. As a Thorsen, I was meant to take over their training one day. It's just what's done for the people in my family."

"I guess training reindeer when you can shift into one makes things a lot easier."

"It sure does. The second I was able to shift I barely ever left them. I don't know why, really. I belonged with them more than with my classmates. They wanted to play workshop and Santa and his deer. I could play with *actual* reindeer."

"Not cops and robbers?"

He chuckles. "No. Niko always played Santa because everyone *knew* he would be Santa one day. It caused a lot of fights between him and Nils. Because I was the only Thorsen and reindeer shifter..." He stops.

"You always had to play the reindeer?"

"Yeah. When I was around eight, a bunch of us kids went up to this small slope near town. We used to slide down on our toboggans there. This one day, Niko decided to push me off the hill."

"What? Why?"

"To see if reindeer shifters could fly. I *obviously* don't. I tumbled down, barreled into a spruce, and flattened it on my fall. I broke my arm."

"Echoing blood bag. That's horrible."

"The other kids banded together and told the adults it was an accident. They were too scared of what Niko would do to *them*. I tried to tell the truth, but no one believed me. No one wanted to hear that their future Santa was a bully."

"That's horrible. Is that why you're scared of heights?"

"No. That came later. After the whole arm incident, *that's* when the kids started calling me Blitz. Because my fall was a swift way to demolish trees. And Niko thought it was very clever because of Blitzen."

"What a little dick."

Klaus shrugs.

"I had no idea. I won't call you that anymore."

"You know what? Don't stop calling me Blitz. I like that you're rewriting what it means. Just like you're changing what it feels like to be in this town."

"It can mean that you demolish my underwear," I add with a wink.

He laughs softly. "Sure. I like that."

"I'm really sorry you went through such a rough time."

"It wasn't the end."

I winced. "Figured."

"Our senior year in high school, I went through a growth spurt. All of a sudden, I was taller and bigger than Niko. I made it pretty damn obvious that I wouldn't stand for his bullshit anymore. He didn't like that."

"Of course he didn't. I really don't think this douchebucket should be Santa."

"You and me both. It should be Nils."

"It should be, yeah. What happened with Niko?"

"We hiked up a mountain a few miles out of town. It was supposed to be a toboggan race challenge."

"Clearly the only way to resolve anything in Christmas Town."

"Exactly. We got to the top, and obviously, being two dumb seventeen-year-olds, we started talking smack. I told Niko that Nils was a better Santa. Some other really shitty stuff too. He got mad and threw me off the mountain."

I gasp and reach out for his hand.

"This time, it wasn't a little hill. It was a *mountain*. I broke a few limbs. Had a concussion, too. Probably would've died if I wasn't a shifter."

"If you tell me it was deemed an accident, I'm gonna…"

Klaus gives me a small smile. It's so sad and heavy my heart nearly breaks for him. "He claimed it was an accident. There were no witnesses, and though Nils tried to speak out for me, once again, no one believed me. As soon as I graduated high school, I left."

I am speechless. I am a lot of things. "No one thought it was weird?"

"I wasn't exactly liked in town. I was the weird reindeer kid. They all wanted to believe Niko wasn't... *isn't*... a piece of shit."

"They literally made you Rudolph. Do they not see that?"

"I don't think so."

"You know what, Klaus? We are going to save this town, and then? I'm gonna give 'em a piece of my mind." I seal my words with a kiss because I *mean* it.

I might be a vampire bat with a serial killer aunt, but I'm going to teach the land of joy and giving a thing or two about kindness.

20

KLAUS

It's the blizzard of the century.

Or so everyone in town is claiming.

Let's forget for a second that Christmas Town is in the north. It snows here. A lot. Yet somehow, every time there's going to be a good dumping of snow, everyone panics. Especially when it's the day before Christmas Eve *and* there's a wedding in three days.

Every elf is bustling around town like their lives depend on it. There's baking, last-minute toy-making, frantic gift wrapping. Tape is running low, but the real tragedy is that there is an actual flour shortage.

The Olympus Flour truck meant to deliver the last of the flour for belated Christmas baking, *and* the wedding cake, is nowhere to be seen. Apparently, it's been delayed due to inclement weather.

Because their truck isn't basically a tank.

Cassie is a mess. Niko is trying to convince everyone in town to pool their flour to make the wedding cake. Doris is trying to keep the peace while Santa is doing what he does: getting the deliveries ready. My parents are with the reindeer, making sure they're ready for the Christmas rush.

That leaves Raya and me alone in the security office, watching the now locked glass case. After we spotted Santa picking the wreath out of its secure spot, we upped security. The glass is bulletproof, and Raya has the only key hidden in her sexy-as-fuck combat boot.

Santa can try to pull the wool over my eyes with all of his faith bullshit.

I don't buy it.

He's still letting his almost-murderous psycho son take up the Santa mantle once he retires. If Nils decided to enlist Vitality Holdings to help him get rid of his brother, I don't even know if I would blame him. The thought makes me uncomfortable as hell.

"Officer Wassail Sugarplum will be here shortly to take over the afternoon shift. He'll do a couple of hours for us while we get an early dinner. I figured he'd want to be with his wife and kids later on."

I grin at Raya's thoughtfulness. Funny how it's an outsider that brings the joy and kindness Christmas Town is supposed to naturally have.

"That was really sweet of you."

"Don't thank me yet. We're making it up to your parents by having dinner with them on the twenty-sixth. We'll celebrate Christmas on our terms, on our schedule this year. So what if it's a little later."

"Good idea."

Raya's jaw drops. "Are you kidding? That's it? I thought this would be a big blowout fight."

"Nope. It's nice. I'm sure you made my parents very happy."

"Stop. Hardly."

You've made me the happiest I've ever been.

But I don't say that. It's too much, too soon. Maybe one day, I'll tell Raya what she means to me. One thing is clear. I do care for her. She is the only person who knows the truth of my history here.

I trust her *that* much.

———

Officer Wassail Sugarplum relieves us of our guard duties for a little while, which is just as well. I'm *starving* and totally jonesing for a massive slice of tourtière slathered in ketchup. We stop in at one of the small restaurants, Scrumptious Joy.

The whole town is in a state of pure panic because of the storm. We eat from our seats at the massive window and watch as large, fluffy flakes fall from the sky.

It's too beautiful to make me dread the steady fall. Sure, if this pace kept up, soon the entire town will be covered in a foot of heavy snow. We are ready for it. It's not like it's an unusual occurrence.

"This is so beautiful," Raya whispers, mesmerized by the snow.

I'm captivated by *her*. "Did you get much snow where you grew up?"

"Some. Nothing like this. This one year, when we were little, Vera and I built this huge fort. It wasn't *that* big, but it felt ginormous for us. We spent hours in there, playing make-believe. It was so fun. I remember begging my parents to let us play some more, even though we were turning into tiny ice cubes."

"That's a nice memory."

She smiles. "Yeah. It is. I honestly forgot about it until just now."

"You used to get along with Vera, then."

Raya sighs with a heavy shrug. "We did, yeah. Actually, we were *really* close when we were itty-bitty bats. It's once she started school that things took a turn. She was a natural student, and I was most assuredly *not*. I don't know who made the comparison first, but it doesn't matter. What matters is that it stuck. It got roped into the whole family dynamic."

"I'm really sorry about that."

She waves me off. "It's nothing. Sibling rivalry isn't that interesting."

I lean over the table to brush my fingers against her cheek. "I don't know about that. We're in a town where sibling rivalry is pretty damn important. It dictates the whole future of this place."

"I guess that's true."

"Do you think you'll ever be close to Vera again?"

She scrunches up her face. "I don't know. I called her when we got drunk. I've got no clue what I said to her."

"Really? I think, deep down, you know."

She points her fork at me before stealing a bite of my tourtière. "Don't you try to analyze me, mister."

"Fair enough." The silence stretches on between us as I wait to see if she'll get it off her chest.

Raya clicks her tongue and rolls her eyes. "I *might* have apologized for being so competitive. And *maybe* I took ownership for my own actions. But I don't want to talk about it anymore. I get all cringy when I think about it too hard. Let's drop it?"

"Yup. Dropping it." I peek at my watch, and a plan takes hold of my mind. "Hey, I wanna show you something." I drop a few bills on the table to pay for our meal and tow Raya across the street and all the way to the reindeer training center.

It's the place where my father and all of my ancestors have worked for generations now. It's where I would work if things had turned out differently for me.

I show Raya around, introducing her to the reindeer. I don't know them by name anymore, but being a reindeer myself, the beautiful animals take to me quite easily.

I show Raya how to saddle them to the sleigh. She's especially taken by a reindeer named Stockings. He's a silly one, barely able to contain his excitement at going for a ride.

"I've missed this. Being around the reindeer like this. Forgot how peaceful it is to just be here, in the barn."

"Probably why you prefer working alone."

I chuckle softly. "You're right."

"You liked it, didn't you? Working here? If things had been different, had things not gone sideways with Niko?"

I sigh as the validity of her words settles into me. "Yeah. I think so."

"It's not too late," she whispers.

"Sure it is. Niko is about to get married. He'll take over the town. I'm not living under his thumb, training *his* reindeer. Not a Grinch's chance in Whoville is that happening."

Now, if Nils *were to be in charge...* I shake my head, hoping to chase away the thought.

Sensing the shift in my mood, Raya changes the subject. "What exactly are we doing? We need to take over for Officer Sugarplum in two hours."

"We'll be back in time." I help her up into the sleigh and tuck a thick red plaid blanket across her knees. "We really need to get you better winter clothes next time we come here."

"Next time, huh?"

"Don't bust my balls about this, Raya."

"Oh, fine. Be that way." She smirks at me, pleased at my slip-up.

In truth, I think I'm planning a whole lifetime of Christmases with Raya. After only a couple of weeks as her partner, that should be *insane*.

It's not.

My parents were engaged after a month, married after two, and I was already on the way somewhere in between.

I've got a feeling deep in my heart that it'll be similar for us.

"It's Christmas Eve-Eve. This town gets a little nutso this time of the holiday season."

Raya throws her head back with a giggle. "A little nutso? We've officially been spending a lot of time together."

A small smile tugs at my lips. "Maybe." I place a soft kiss on her lips.

Two weeks ago, if someone would have told me that I'd be in my hometown with a batty lady I was *definitely* falling for during Christmas time? I would have laughed myself silly.

Yet here it is.

"Are you going to tell me where we're going?"

"I'm taking you to the very edge of town."

"Sweet suffering mammal. Are you bringing me to *the* mountain?"

"Sure am."

"But why?"

"I wanna make a new memory there. One that's all roped up in you."

"Wow. That's a good line, Blitzy-boo."

"Not a line if I mean it."

Raya folds her arm under mine, laying her head on my shoulder as we slide over the thick snow with more of it steadily falling over us. The ride takes only about fifteen minutes on a good day, but after twenty minutes, the mountaintop comes into view over a bushy line of spruce trees. I pull the sleigh to a stop and lean back into my seat to let the peace settle into my soul.

"Damn. I've missed this place."

"It actually suits you. You're so much calmer here. I mean don't get me wrong. You're still *way* grumpy, but it's different. You're more..." She chews her lower lip, thinking for the right word. "Settled. You seem more settled."

"Thanks, Raya. That means a lot to me, actually." I kiss her softly, and it's just as I'm pulling away that I spot it.

A huge light blue truck with the words Olympus Flour painted on the side.

That's not what makes my blood run cold.

Nope.

It's the four busted tires.

21

RAYA

Craptastic tinsel bombs!

"No fucking way," I gasp. "Is that the missing flour shipment?"

"We need to get back to town. *Now*," Klaus roars. "I'm not gonna make the reindeer haul our asses back to town. I'll get them to make their way back safely without us. We need to shift."

"On it," I blurt out, preparing myself for the change. "I'll have to stay close to you. Can't freeze to death before we even get to the good stuff."

He nods. "Destination is the wreath."

"You got it, Blitz."

I wish I could watch Klaus turn into the majestic reindeer that he is, but I'm too busy becoming a one-ounce bat. It doesn't hurt, exactly. It doesn't feel good, either. It's sort of like really bad period cramps when my uterus is basically trying to escape my body to get the hell away from the hormones coursing through my veins.

Like that, only a million times worse.

Thankfully, it only lasts a few moments.

Klaus is through his shift. His coat is a thick, shiny chocolate brown on which snowflakes melt. His antlers are a fuzzy crown of badassery. He can do some serious damage with those. His eyes, usually beautiful emerald green, are now dark green. He groans and moves his head, motioning for me to hop on.

I do. I latch onto one of his antlers, perching there like a bird.

I'd fly if it wasn't snowing like the sky was falling. The wind is so strong it's likely to send me twenty feet in the wrong direction. With me settled onto him, Klaus books it and squalls to the reindeer. The animals don't seem overly concerned but begin to follow in our footsteps at a leisurely pace. We soon outrun them.

The sleigh ride took us about twenty minutes, but Klaus manages to get us into town in half that time. The snow-covered streets aren't deserted. A few courageous souls brave the weather to get last-minute errands in. They don't even see us running by through the wall of flakes covering the town.

This is bad.

I don't know *why* the Olympus Flour truck is in the middle of nowhere with busted-out tires, but it's hardly a good sign.

It basically spells disaster if disaster is spelled Hera and Zeus.

Or Vitality Holdings.

Klaus doesn't stop once we've reached Santa's workshop. I sense what he's about to do and take off, flapping my wings in the frigid wind. Klaus rams his antlers into the doors, forcing them open. As soon as there is a crack, I fly through. It takes him a few more tries to make his way in, but when he does, he quickly catches up.

We run by the cabooses, not bothering to hop on. Our shifter bodies are way more convenient. There isn't a single elf in sight. I wish I knew if it was normal. You'd think that there would be a few here and there, making a few things, wrapping a couple of toys for the kids who changed sides of that dreaded list at the last minute.

"Would you just *break* it?" A shrill voice echoes through the long hall.

"No," a second sniffling response comes.

"You're *useless*. I won't let a full life's work go to waste because of *you*."

I fly with everything I have. I move my wings faster than is safe, but I need to know who is in Santa's office.

We finally come within sight of it, and honestly? It's not what I expected.

A young woman with shiny blonde curls and a freckled face is wiping a steady stream of tears while Vanilla shouts at her, her starched lace bonnet flopping precariously on top of her head.

What the damn hell is going on?

Knowing this will need at least *one* agent in human form to communicate, I shift back.

"Stop right there."

The blonde covers her eyes with a squeak, no doubt surprised by my blatant nudity. Vanilla blanches, turning the color of her bonnet.

"Raya, hey there. I thought you were gone." She tries to appear calm but fails. Her entire body is shaking.

"I came back. What's going on here?" I aim my question to the trembling young woman. "Are you okay? Cookie, right? You're Cookie Trimmings?"

She hiccups a sob and nods. "Yes."

I grab one of the thick throws from one of the chairs and wrap it around me. "Better?" I ask her. Seriously. It's only a naked body. What's her deal? Humans are funny about stuff like that.

Cookie takes a step toward me, clearly desperate to get away from Vanilla. "Help," she mouths.

Klaus, now back to his sexy man-self, takes another throw and hides his dangly bits. "Vanilla, please tell me you're not trying to steal the wreath."

The older woman throws her hands up. "For Rudolph's sake. Of course not!"

I am shocked. Truly. Vanilla is barely four feet tall. She is close to a hundred if she's any age at all. She's Santa's head elf *and* her family has worked in the workshop for *generations*. She told me so herself the very first day I met her. It seemed to be such a point of pride.

"Frankincense," she bellows. "Get your figgy pudding in here."

The blubbering elf, the one who went on holiday to Hawaii—the one we *cleared*—sheepishly walks in, holding a gun.

"Where's Officer Sugarplum?" I growl. I stalk toward him, only to realize the weapon is a toy.

Go figure.

"He's fine, the big lug. We slipped a bit too much booze in his White Christmas. He's snoring at the security desk," Vanilla explains. "What gave us away?"

"Honestly?" Klaus answers. "Nothing. I didn't suspect you at all. We just found the flour truck."

Vanilla rolls her eyes. "I told you we needed to do a better job at hiding that damn thing."

"Where's the driver?" Klaus takes the question right out of my mouth.

"Back at our place. Safe and sound, if a little wrapped up," Vanilla grumbles.

"Holy holly balls," I exclaim. "I know what happened."

"Please," Klaus grumbles. "Enlighten me because I'm so confused right now."

"It's actually super simple. I should have figured it out the *second* I learned that Lisbeth Bannon was in Waikiki Beach. That's in Hawaii. She wasn't on holiday. She was meeting Frankincense. Probably to edge her out of Vitality Holdings after she got caught with the whole Val Downer thing."

"Umm, Raya? Still lost here. Lead me to it, would ya, sweets?"

"Vanilla is Hera. Frankincense is Zeus. *They're* behind Vitality Holdings. I'm guessing they put all of Christmas Town's equity in funding their chase for immortality."

"Please tell me she's wrong," Klaus shouts. "You didn't, Vanilla. You love this place."

"Exactly! I love this place. I would do *anything* for this town. Ever since Santa had his two sons, I've known I would have to step up to the plate and save this town. Everyone assumed that Niko would take the throne, so to speak. I know he's a bad egg. I'm one of the only people in town who saw that lunatic for what he is. He's one donkey short of a manger scene. You should know that, Klaus."

"Of course I do. Why didn't you ever say anything?" he asks.

"Oh," she snorts dryly. "I did. I did. Every day, I was in Nik's ear about his oldest. He wouldn't hear of it. The more I pushed, the more he threatened to replace me. Nils would be such a better choice. I was so excited when Nils was with this one." She juts her chin in Cookie's direction. "I thought they would get married. Then the dolt went and broke up with Nils, leaving the Santa role wide open for Niko."

"I didn't have a choice," Cookie interjects between two sobs. "Niko and Cassie made me do it."

"Fuck me." Klaus runs a hand over his face.

"Well, I didn't know *that*," Vanilla screams. "That would've been good information to have."

"They're not even *together*. He hired her to play his fiancée," Cookie continues.

"Of all the devious bullshit," I say in complete disbelief.

"I knew he was bad news, but this takes the cake. Seriously, Vanilla. You tried to use the Bloody Doctor's research to find immortality? You blackmailed a FUC agent with death?"

"Frankincense is great with all that stuff. He's not just a cook and baker but a bit of a scientist, too. We needed the proper leverage. We need our current Santa to live forever. We can't ever get so close to losing Christmas Town to a demonic spawn like Niko."

I want to point out that she and her husband have been pretty demonic themselves, but I refrain. It's hard to do, but I really don't need to add fuel to the fire.

"And when the Bloody Doctor *and* the Vitality people failed, you what? Started to believe in the magic of the wreath?"

"Oh." Vanilla laughs. "We weren't *after* the wreath at all. That thing has no power. We wanted to break into the safe and steal some of the money. A lot of it is missing already. I had to pay goons to do our busy work. It's not like we could leave town. That would've been too suspicious."

"So Klaus and I being here for the wreath was, what? Just a bad coincidence?"

Vanilla snorts. "Yup. We were going to frame Cassie for the

missing cash tonight. Cookie tried to stop us. She wanted us to come clean to you. Said you could help."

"We could've," Klaus insists.

The elf pouts. "I was trying to avoid jail time. I was hoping to pin the whole thing on Cassie. It would've been fine by me, given that we've been trying to sabotage the wedding all week."

"Hence the flour shortage." I nod. "You weren't merely delivering cookies, were you, Frankincense? You were stashing flour."

The elf blushes with shame. "I'm just trying to save something bigger than myself."

"Yeah, well, you went about it all wrong. More secrecy and lies, more hurt and deceit doesn't do shit. That's like trying to fix a sinking ship with modeling clay." I shake my head, still reeling from this strange revelation. And I thought my sister's first case with a pumpkin-shifting botanist was intense.

"You do realize you'll be charged with a whole bunch of crimes, right?" Klaus asks Vanilla and Frankincense.

"So long as you promise not to let Niko take over, I don't care," the elf states, putting out her arms to be handcuffed. "Frankincense, come on. Time to pay the piper."

The elf's eyes are full of sadness. "Tradition is so important, you know? It's not that we didn't want things to change. We just got so scared that Niko would burn it all down. He's a bad man. He doesn't stand for love and community. He's only after himself. That's not what this town was ever about."

Too bad they didn't speak out all those years ago when Klaus was only a little boy.

More than one life could have been saved, then.

Once we get the big man back to the workshop, pulling him away from his pre-delivery nap, it takes Klaus and me a little while to explain everything. He and Doris listen to every word, more and more horrified.

"Nils will have to take over, obviously. As soon as possible, too. It's clear to me now that I am no longer fit to wear the suit. I've got to step down."

Doris sniffs and dabs at her eyes. "How did we go so wrong with him?"

I wish I had the answer for her. I really do. "Nils is a sweet man. I'm sure he'll do a great job at upholding traditions, all the while breathing new life into town."

"I think Nils should be brought here," Klaus adds. "I'm pretty sure this young lady will want to have a nice long chat with him."

Cookie gives him a grateful smile. "I never stopped loving him. I was so scared that Niko would hurt Nils or me. The whole town, really. He said he'd burn my shop down if I spoke a word. Nils warned me about him. About what he was capable of. I thought if I played nice..." She wipes a few stray tears from her cheeks. "I thought it would work out in the end."

"It will," I cut in. "Things can work out if everyone does their part to *make* it a better place."

Hours later, well into the morning of Christmas Eve, Vanilla, Frankincense, Lisbeth Bannon, and a few other goons are arrested. Cassie is revealed for the fraud that she is, while Niko has been permanently banned from his hometown.

That seems too easy a punishment, but he's a slick bastard. He hasn't done anything illegal. Too bad being a major selfish jackass isn't a crime.

Everyone in Christmas Town knows that, tonight, a new Santa will sit in the sleigh.

Nils.

And by his side, his future wife, Cookie.

EPILOGUE

RAYA

One Year Later

Christmas Eve at the Thorsen house is a little bit hectic but in the best way possible. It's the kind of chaos that fills your heart with so much joy and happiness it could burst.

One year ago, if someone would've told me that I'd be married to a reindeer trainer, living in Christmas Town as the posted FUC agent? I would've laughed myself silly.

That's exactly what happened.

Once Niko was exiled, Vanilla, Frankincense, and their accomplices were arrested, and Nils became the new and much improved Santa, the threat to the wreath stopped.

The possibilities of people chasing immortality also very much decreased.

Yet, somehow, Director Cooper decided it would be a good idea to have a permanent FUC agent in Christmas Town, working in conjunction with CTPD.

I took the job in a heartbeat. It helped that Klaus wanted to stay.

That's right. Klaus I'm-angry-at-the-world-and-hate-Christmas Thorsen wanted to move back to his hometown. He's been working with his father, training reindeer. Honestly, I've never seen my man-bun god happier.

This is where he belongs. He got lost there for a while, but he found his place.

As did I.

All I've ever wanted was a place to call my own. A place where I could stand out and be my own person with no one's shadow or reputation making me feel small. I have that here, in Christmas Town.

The small house Klaus and I own on the outskirts of the village is packed today. Not only are Nils and Cookie here for a quick visit before getting ready for the big delivery, but we're hosting a whole lot of people.

My in-laws, Holly and Patridge, are here.

So are my parents and extended family.

Mila, my uncle, T-Bone, Bettina, and baby Courtney Thrussel IV, better known as Baby T, are here. Though I've warned everyone that the poor kid will need a better nickname down the line, he is downright the cutest, pudgiest little boy I've ever seen. Even at barely a month old, he is a heartbreaker.

Vera and her husband, Jack, are here, too. They got married a couple of months before Klaus and me. Not that there was any sort of competition.

I'm *really* working hard on that. I'm better. I think it helps that I'm on my own turf in Christmas Town, while Vera does all kinds of surveillance stuff for FUC.

It's funny, really. Three vampire bats, adverse to the sun and reliant on blood to live, and we found our happily ever after with the Furry United Coalition.

All different, yet all with one common goal: to leave the world better than how we found it.

That's basically my life motto now.

It's also how I plan to raise my kids. I'm about four months away if my due date is accurate. Announcing it to both our families at the same time so close to Christmas is the best gift ever.

The long table, made up of smaller tables pulled together, runs from our living room to the dining room. The din is loud but happy. Sitting to my right, Klaus brings my hand up to his mouth and kisses my knuckles.

"You ready?" he whispers.

"Yup." I give him a wink before standing. I clink a knife to my glass and wait for the conversations to die down. "I'm so happy that everyone I care about is gathered here right now. This is what this time of the year is all about. Family, whether related or found." Cookie beams at me. "We'll need a new place setting next time we all gather." I pat my stomach. "We're expecting a little bundle of screams —er, I mean *joy*—soon enough."

Mom gasps and bursts into tears, and Dad pats her back, repeating over and over that he's so proud of his daughters for building happy lives for themselves. Vera congratulates me with flushed cheeks and a watery smile.

"Vera?" I ask. "Are you okay?"

She waves me off. "Yes, of course. I'm so happy for you both."

I arch a brow. "You wanna share something with the rest of the class?"

"No, no. I couldn't."

I make my way around the table and tug her to her feet. "Seriously, it's okay." I grin at her because I mean it. It's not about competition or comparison. It's about the joy of sharing life's beautiful moments.

"You're sure?"

I nod, and she grips my hand.

"Well," she begins, smirking at Jack, "we're also having a baby."

The room explodes in another round of cheers, but I hold my sister tight. We might have been caught up in rivalry. We might even live a world apart now. That doesn't matter. She's my sister, and though she drives me nutso bananas sometimes, I love her. More than that, I would *choose* her as a sister.

"Bats are gonna take over Christmas Town," Mila roars. "I love this for us. We're FUC's very merry band of bats, spreading the batty message far and wide."

"Sweet suffering mammal." Cookie giggles, borrowing my favorite expression. "What does the future hold?"

"Hope," I answer, my hand going to the barely noticeable bump at my stomach. "The future holds hope."

Klaus winks at me from his seat, and I soak it all up.

Love, hope, family. And I know, down to the core of my soul, that this happily ever after? It's not just mine. It's *ours*. From the bats to the reindeer to Hairy Coo and the exploding pumpkin. We might be a ragtag bunch, but we fit together.

The End.

ALSO BY A. GREGORY

Bat and the Holly

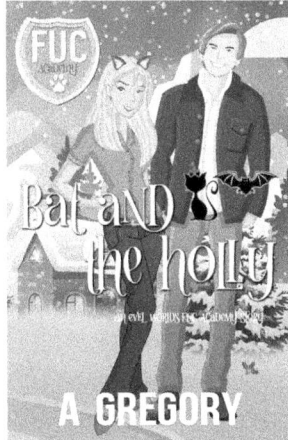

A flying bat won't turn a witch's head, but a ghost might!

For Holly Dickens, getting the Hale family's permission to film a live paranormal investigation in their cabin is a big win. She wants her new show to solve as many cold murder cases as possible—including her mother's.

When Konnor Hale barges into the cabin, accusing her of trespassing, Holly fears her dreams are dashed. But together, they just might set off a chain of events that casts light on old secrets, hidden evidence, and new love...

Buy Now

ABOUT THE AUTHOR

A. Gregory writes magically delicious stories that will transport you to the places where things go bump in the night. Sometimes there's magic, other times there are shifters, but there is always a happily ever after.

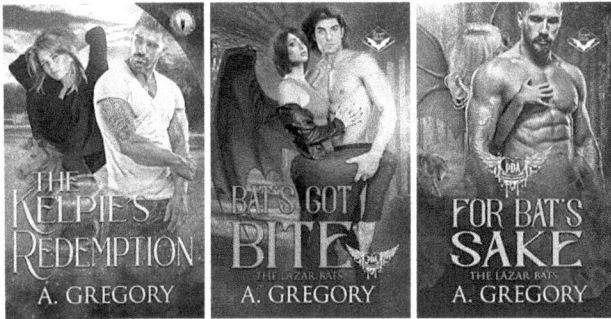

instagram.com/a.gregory.paranormal

Milton Keynes UK
Ingram Content Group UK Ltd.
UKHW022102110624
443988UK00015B/789

9 798224 438860